KAREN SANDLER

rebellion

a tankborn novel

Tu Books
an imprint of Lee & Low Books, Inc.
New York

Copyright © 2014 by Karen Sandler

Jacket photographs copyright © 2014 by Shutterstock—mountains: Zvonimir Atletic/woman: mimagephotography/Thinkstock—sky: denisovd

TU BOOKS, an imprint of LEE & LOW BOOKS Inc.,
95 Madison Avenue, New York, NY 10016
leeandlow.com

Manufactured in the United States of America by
Worzalla Publishing Company, May 2014

Book design by Sammy Yuen
Book production by The Kids at Our House

The text is set in Adobe Caslon Pro

10 9 8 7 6 5 4 3 2 1
First Edition

This book has been manufactured using environmentally friendly materials: the paper is certified as responsibly sourced, the hardcover boards are made from recycled materials, and the inks are vegetable based.

Library of Congress Cataloging-in-Publication Data
Rebellion / Karen Sandler. — First edition.
pages cm
Sequel to: Awakening.
Summary: "In this final installment of the Tankborn series, Kayla has been kidnapped by the group that has been bombing GEN warehouses, and she must pretend to sympathize with them in order to escape" — Provided by publisher.
ISBN 978-1-60060-984-8 (hardcover : alk. paper) —
ISBN 978-1-60060-985-5 (e-book)
[1. Genetic engineering—Fiction. 2. Kidnapping—Fiction. 3. Science fiction.]
I. Title.
PZ7.S2173Reb 2014
[Fic]—dc23
2014002775

To Gary, always there for me, from brainstorm to denouement.

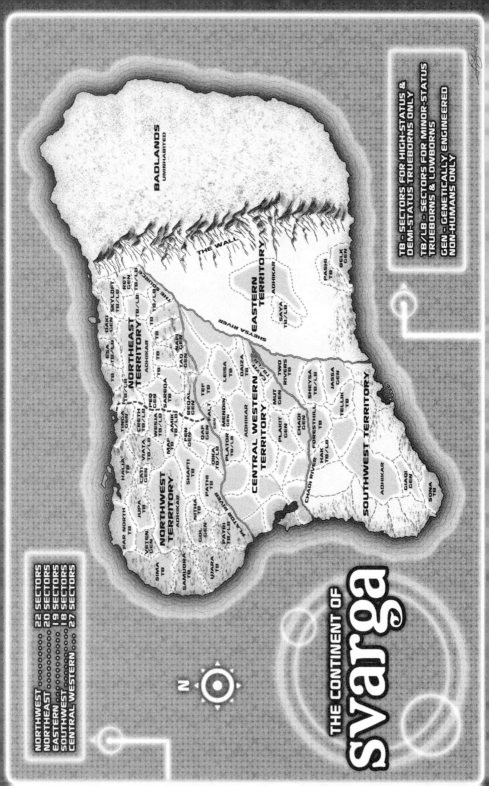

1

Devak Manel floated in nothingness, without sight, without speech, without sensation. If he breathed, he couldn't feel the rise and fall of his chest. If his heart beat, he couldn't hear its thrum in his ears.

Invading the darkness, endless looping nightmare images spun through his mind. Him running along the rocky, uneven ground near his great-grandfather's house in Two Rivers sector. The stench of the Chadi River drifting to him from the left, the warehouses looming on the right. Him calling after Kayla as she ducked into the alley between two warehouses. Him stumbling as the ground suddenly tipped and rolled under his feet, his body torn apart as he fell into darkness.

The nightmare rewound. Kayla hadn't stepped into the alley yet. Devak still had time to save her. As he ran, a lev-car pulled up and a trueborn woman and man climbed from it. The woman dashed toward Kayla and screamed out her name as the man tried to drag the woman back toward the lev-car. Kayla took one last look at Devak, then she vanished down the alley. The world exploded as before.

Another rewind. Now when the trueborn woman climbed from the lev-car, Devak saw she was Kayla, her GEN tattoo wiped from her right cheek. Kayla screamed her own name, warning herself not to enter that alley. But it made no difference. The blast obliterated Kayla and sent Devak into darkness.

He must be dead. The nothingness and the nightmares must be Patala—hell. He didn't know what he'd done in life that was bad enough to send him to this evil place. Maybe it was that he, a high-status trueborn, had fallen in love with Kayla, a GEN girl. Or maybe the sin wasn't his love for her, but that he'd hidden his feelings from trueborn society out of fear of their judgment. If he regretted anything, it was that. He should have held Kayla up to the whole world and declared to all her courage and humanity.

He could feel the nightmares about to start again, the images fluttering out of the nothingness to engulf him. *No*, he sobbed into the silence.

The images retreated. At first he thought his noiseless voice had some power to drive them away. But then he saw light faintly glowing in the darkness. And for the first time, he heard voices, real voices, not just nightmare screams.

The voices were muffled, not so much by distance as by something blanketing his ears. He remembered once his family visiting one of the trueborn preserves, and he'd gone swimming without permission in a man-made lake there. As he was floating just under the surface, his mother had shouted at him to get out of the water, that it was dirty from the GEN maintenance workers walking through it. These voices sounded just like those underwater voices.

But he didn't know who was speaking. The few words he

caught—*options limited, expense quota exceeded*—sounded like just so much nonsense.

Then he heard Pitamah and would have gasped in a breath of relief if his lungs still worked. From the tone of his great-grandfather's voice, Zul Manel was arguing with someone. Devak could only make out Pitamah saying *After all the Manels have done* before the argument faded.

Another long silence with nightmares nibbling at him, then he heard the familiar voice of his friend, Junjie Tsai, calling out, *Devak!* Devak fought to open his eyes, an impossible task. Junjie rattled on and on, his words incomprehensible but comforting nonetheless.

Nothingness pulled Devak down again, sometimes woven with nightmares, sometimes endless blankness. He'd thought hearing the voices meant he was alive, but maybe that was part of his torment, having those he loved just out of reach. He longed for one of those voices to be Kayla's, even if what he heard was an illusion.

Then he felt a tugging and pinching all over his body, a burning as if long needles had been seated under his skin and were now pulled free. The light grew brighter and the liquid he'd been floating in receded. Then there was a horrifying moment when he truly couldn't breathe, as something was dragged clear of his throat, its passage scraping sensitive tissue.

Someone pried something from his ears, and the noise level swelled to a deafening roar. Sound battered his eardrums. Voices, footsteps, the clatter of what he could only guess were tools or instruments being handled. His sense of touch seemed as sensitive as his hearing, the light blanket tucked around his naked body scraping his skin.

Then efficient fingers swiped something from his eyes and

a woman's voice ordered him to open them. It took an effort, and he had to squint against the brilliant light. Keeping them half-lidded, Devak looked around him.

Not hell. A gen-lab. And he was shivering in the last millimeter of gen-fluid draining from a gen-tank.

Through the green-slimed glass walls of his tank, he could make out more tanks surrounding him. Gen-fluid still filled the ones adjacent to him and bodies floated within. Tubes and wires were attached to the bodies as they had been to Devak. The connections ran out to an array of machines positioned around the tanks. The machines beeped and squawked, their lights and displays flickering. Considering the noise level, the room must be packed with gen-tanks.

It made sense he'd been placed in a tank. He'd been injured in the explosion. He'd needed help to heal, so Pitamah had brought him to a gen-lab so the medics and gen-techs could work on him.

But what about Kayla?

He swallowed a few times to get enough moisture in his mouth to speak, finally croaking, "Kayla?"

It came out as a bare whisper. A moment later, a minor-status trueborn tech loomed over him, a small illuminator in her gloved hands. She shone the light source in one of his eyes, then the other. The intensity was uncomfortable, but Devak found he could keep both eyes open after her scrutiny.

"I'm Freda," the woman said, too loudly. "We have to flush the gen-fluid from the tank and from your body before we can pull you out."

Devak knew enough about the science of gen-tanks to know that the green fluid coating the tank and his skin was uniquely designed for his genetics. If someone else happened to absorb the fluid from Devak's treatment, the result would be unpredictable. Growths, scarring, even disease.

Still, why did a high-status trueborn like him have a minor-status tech attending to him, rather than a high-status medic? And it was especially awkward that the tech was a woman. Surely Pitamah would have requested at least a demi-status man.

What did it matter? He should be focusing on getting out of here as quickly as possible, to find Kayla.

The fair-skinned minor-status woman picked up a hose, aiming the nozzle toward his face. "Close your eyes and mouth."

He did, and she sprayed a fine, warm mist across his face. The cleansing solution from the hose would bond with the green gen-fluid, deactivating it.

While Freda focused on rinsing his hair, Devak managed to lift his hand to feel for his bali in his right earlobe. The diamond earring felt peculiar. A little larger than he remembered, but oddly shaped, more oval than round. Was he imagining the difference, or had someone changed his bali while he was in the tank? And did Pitamah know?

"Feeling strong enough to sit up?" Freda asked.

He felt as weak as a newborn seycat, but he let her pull him to a sitting position. The blanket pooled in his lap, but he didn't have the strength to twitch it around to cover his backside.

She sprayed him from neck to waist, front and back. "Hands up," Freda ordered, and she directed the mist to his arms, from shoulders to fingertips. As she finished each arm, she placed his hands on wads of drom wool that cushioned the top edges of the gen-tank wall.

Then she shoved the blanket up to his upper thighs and cleansed his legs too. Devak's stomach knotted in anticipation of her snatching away his last shred of modesty, but once Freda had finished with his legs, she redirected the nozzle to the walls of the gen-tank. The waste solution ran along either side of him toward a drain at his feet.

His head clearer, he asked again, "Is Kayla here too?"

Freda gave him a peculiar look, no doubt recognizing Kayla as a GEN name. This facility might only be for trueborns. Maybe they took Kayla to another clinic.

Freda must have figured his brain was scrambled by his gen-tank session, because she ignored his question about Kayla. "Your great-grandfather is in the waiting room. He'll be allowed in once we clean you up and dress you."

The tech put the sprayer in his trembling hand, then draped two towels over the side of the tank. When she tugged at the blanket, he clutched it as tightly as he could. "Don't."

"I won't look, young Mar," Freda said. There was just the slightest sneer in her tone as she said the honorific *Mar.*

Still, she kept her eyes averted as she took the soiled blanket from him with gloved hands. As she walked away toward the recyc bin, Devak quickly washed the last of the gen-fluid from his body, his teeth chattering despite the warmth of the cleansing liquid.

Just as Freda started back toward him, he grabbed one of the towels and wrapped it around his waist. He used the other to rub his arms, chest, and back dry. Freda stood over him, glancing at the time on her wristlink, sighing with clear impatience as he struggled to reach his wet feet.

His body didn't seem to want to function properly. He couldn't bend farther at the waist than his sitting position. Something in his back seemed to block his motion.

"Bend your knees," Freda snapped. "Your spine has been fused. You'll need more tank work to get it right."

He reached around himself and found the ridges of scars on either side of his spine in the middle of his back. "Why did they leave the scars?" he asked.

Freda just smirked. She dropped a set of clothes on a nearby float table, a rough korta shirt and chera pants made of cheap spun plasscine. No skivs, which seemed shameful.

Freda pressed a control, and the side of the tank slid down out of the way. Then she walked off, disappearing through a door in the far back corner.

Leaving him to dress himself. Except how could he pull on the chera pants if he couldn't bend at the waist? Shaking, he tugged on the korta, flinching at the coarse fabric against the still-tender skin of his arms. He pivoted slowly in the tank, dropping his legs out through the open side, then slid to the floor. He yanked down the shirt's hem and sent thanks up to the Lord Creator when the garment proved long enough to cover his privates.

Clutching the chera pants, he looked around him at the gen-lab. It was even bigger than he'd been able to make out at first, with at least twenty rows of gen-tanks, ten per row. All but a few seemed occupied, if the green gen-fluid and squawking machines surrounding them were any indication. Counting from the row closest to the door Freda had gone through, Devak's tank was in the sixth row, three tanks over from the end.

He was a high-status trueborn. His gen-tank should have been in a private room by itself, or maybe sharing with one or two. If he'd been thrown into a tank farm like this, then what might Kayla's treatment have been like?

If she was still alive.

He couldn't think about that now. It was difficult enough

contemplating his feet, how far away they seemed.

Overcome by his helplessness, by the impossibility of doing something as simple as lifting his feet high enough to finish dressing, tears gathered in his eyes. Mortification at his weakness, both physical and emotional, added a tighter twist to his gut.

A door latch clattered, opposite the side of the gen-lab Freda had left through. Devak quickly draped the chera pants in front of his naked legs. When his great-grandfather stepped inside, followed by Junjie, relief nearly pushed a sob from Devak's throat.

Pitamah zigzagged through the gen-tanks, his expression stormy. "Damn them, they couldn't help you dress?" He scanned the room. "Where the denking hell is the tech?"

"It was a woman," Devak said, leaning against the gen-tank when his wobbly legs threatened to give way. "I was just as glad she didn't help." He gestured with the chera pants. "No skivs."

Pitamah cursed under his breath. "See what you can find, Junjie."

As Junjie detoured toward the storage cupboards ringing the room, he glanced over his shoulder and gave Devak a long searching look, guilt written large on Junjie's round face. Devak's friend looked even skinnier than before, his straight dark hair hanging messily past his collar and ears.

Pitamah also looked unkempt, his clothes rumpled, the diamond bali in his right ear nearly black with dirt. The old man hadn't even used a concealer over the tattoo on his left cheek, the one that looked so much like a GEN's. And Pitamah looked a good decade older than his hundred-and-three years. Devak worried about what that might mean.

A shudder ran up his spine. "Where's Kayla?"

Pitamah glanced around him. "We can't talk about that here."

"Is she . . ." He couldn't make himself say the word *dead*. "Is she okay?"

Pitamah didn't answer. But the bleak look in his dark eyes nearly brought Devak to his knees.

Pitamah gripped Devak's arm. "We'll talk about it later. On our way home."

Devak heard a strange hesitation when his great-grandfather spoke the word *home*, and it ratcheted up Devak's anxiety. "What's the date? How long have I been healing?"

"The explosion happened Deichiu 32nd," Pitamah told him. "It's Triu 3rd."

For a moment, Devak couldn't breathe. "Two months."

"Total time in the tank, although you were moved twice." Pitamah's lips pinched tight. "Kept in a coma both times. You don't remember the moves?"

Devak shook his head. "Plenty of nightmares. But not that. Why aren't you wearing a concealer over your tattoo?"

"No real point to that now," Pitamah muttered.

Junjie returned with a pair of skivs as rough as the shirt and pants. Without hesitation, Junjie knelt, holding the skivs so Devak could put his feet into the leg holes. Pitamah kept a grip on Devak's arm as Junjie pulled up the skivs high enough so Devak could settle them at his waist. They repeated the same ritual for the chera pants.

Junjie had also pilfered a pair of stiff plasscine slippers and helped Devak with those. Then, with Junjie on one side and Pitamah on the other, they made their way slowly out of the lab, dodging pathways too crowded with equipment for the three of them to squeeze through.

In the lobby, a minor-status attendant produced a sekai, and Pitamah paged through the document on the electronic reader, pressing his thumb to the screen in acknowledgement in several places. Devak tried to read the sekai's display, but Pitamah turned to block Devak's view.

Finally his great-grandfather handed back the sekai. The three of them continued outside into cool spring sunshine, the sky a green so pale it was nearly white. Iyenku, the first of Loka's two suns, had barely cleared the horizon and at the opposite edge of the sky, one of the trinity moons—Avish?—lingered.

"I'll get the lev-car," Pitamah said, leaving Devak to lean on Junjie.

Devak looked around at the unfamiliar surroundings. Shops lined the road across from the gen-lab, a storefront for sekai repair, another advertising clothing clearly meant for lowborns. Far off to his right, Devak could make out what looked like a central green.

"Are we in a mixed sector, Junjie?"

A brief hesitation, then Junjie said, "Yeah. We're in Ekat."

"Why?"

Pitamah pulled up then, but not in the AirCloud Devak had expected. It was a WindSpear. "Is that Jemali's lev-car?"

Jemali was a long-time friend of Pitamah, a high-status trueborn medic. Devak had seen the old medic's dark blue WindSpear plenty of times and knew it by sight.

"Yeah, it's Jemali's," Junjie said. "He lent it to Zul."

"Where's the AirCloud?"

Junjie didn't answer. He just helped Devak into the back seat of the WindSpear, all the while avoiding Devak's gaze.

When Junjie would have pulled away, Devak grasped his

arm. Weak as Devak was, Junjie could have freed himself, but he let Devak hold on.

"What's going on?" Devak asked, looking from Pitamah in the driver's seat to Junjie standing over him. "Where's Kayla? And why was I in a mixed sector gen-lab?"

A look passed between Pitamah and Junjie. Pitamah nodded. Then Junjie reached into a pocket for a small, hand-sized mirror. Junjie's prayer mirror, a sign of his new devotion to the Infinite, the GEN god.

Junjie held out the mirror, its reflective surface toward Devak. His belly squirming with rat-snakes, Devak looked at the mirror face on.

At first he saw only the scar stretching along his jaw and cheek from right ear to chin, a tangle of silver-gray across the high-status brown of his skin. Then he registered the real shocker—the color of the bali in his right earlobe.

It was blue, not white. A sapphire, not a diamond.

"Sweet Lord Creator," whispered Devak. "Am I . . . ?"

"Yes," Junjie said. "You're minor-status now."

2

Devak barely noticed Junjie pulling away, shutting the door, and climbing into the front seat of the WindSpear. As Pitamah started up the lev-car and drove off down a street crowded with minor-status trueborns and prosperous lowborn businesspeople, Devak felt so woozy he wanted to lie down and cover his head with his hands.

Instead, he sought out his bali with nerveless fingers. Usually, he could release the clasp and tug the stud from his earlobe with one hand. But his fingers just weren't working right. He had to use both hands, one to pry the backing loose and the other to grip the gemstone and slip it free.

He set the backing and sapphire in his palm. It was bigger than the diamond he'd been wearing most recently. To help buy the house in Two Rivers he and Pitamah had had to sell their larger diamonds and buy smaller, less expensive ones. But sapphires could be produced much more cheaply than diamonds, so the larger blue stone likely didn't cost Pitamah much more than a smaller one.

Then another shock rolled over Devak. He shoved forward

in his seat so he could see Pitamah's right ear. And realized it wasn't a dirty, ill-cared-for diamond bali that Pitamah wore.

It was a sapphire. The marker for a minor-status trueborn.

Pitamah's stone was a shade darker blue than Devak's and about half-again larger. All the years of Devak's life, it had always been a diamond in Pitamah's ear. It seemed impossible that his important, high-status great-grandfather was now minor-status too.

"How?" Devak asked. "Is our adhikar truly all gone? All the droms, the kel-grain fields?"

"Nearly all." Pitamah sighed heavily. "You were badly hurt. Your spine was severed, internal organs damaged. I couldn't let you die, Devak."

Devak sagged back against his seat. "You should have stopped after you sold my adhikar."

Junjie twisted around to face Devak. "He sold his own first, not yours. Zul lost his status way before you did. He was trying to let you keep yours."

Emotions flooded Devak again—love for his great-grandfather, grief for what the old man had lost. Anger at himself that he'd walked into that explosion, that he hadn't somehow sensed the impending disaster, hadn't grabbed Kayla and taken her to safety.

His hand had squeezed tight around the bali, and he felt a stab of pain in his palm. He unfurled his fingers and saw the bead of blood where the tip of the bali's post had pierced his skin. Wiping the post clean on his korta, Devak replaced the sapphire in his ear.

Pitamah went on, "We tried to correct all your injuries. But we didn't have nearly enough dhans to do it all. To restore you completely."

Devak could feel the knots of tissue in his back. "That's why I have scars along my spine. On my face."

"And why your vertebrae are still fused," Pitamah said. "That's supposed to be temporary. You needed more time in the tank to grow new discs. But we'd used everything we had just to keep you alive."

"I wish you'd used it to keep Kayla alive."

Pitamah and Junjie exchanged a quick glance. "We had no choice on that."

Kayla gone. He couldn't think about it. Couldn't bear it. He rubbed the drying blood on his hand on the rough leg of his cheras, wishing that physical pain would distract him from the agony of thinking about Kayla.

"You keep saying we," Devak said. "Who besides you? Has Father been released?" Would Ved Manel have even cared enough about his son to have wanted to help?

"Ved is still in Far North prison," Pitamah said.

"Mother?" In spite of himself, Devak felt a spurt of hope that his mother had had a change of heart, that she regretted abandoning Devak.

"No," Pitamah said, crushing Devak's foolish longing. "Not her."

"By *we*, he means me, for one," Junjie said. "I moved in with Zul so we could consolidate adhikar that way. More dhans to go around."

Devak guessed that his friend hadn't had much to spare. Junjie had already been cast into a financial hole with the death of his mother.

"Jemali too," Junjie said. "He donated his time programming the gen-fluid when we got low on dhans and the other high-status medics wouldn't do it."

All for him, Devak realized. His injuries had taken everything from Pitamah, even his status. Had impoverished Junjie even more.

They'd reached the central green. The neatly mowed scrap grass-covered open space stretched a good hundred meters square to their left. Lining all four sides were lowborn-run restaurants and shops. Ordinarily, the businesses would each occupy a single structure with a flat above it for the proprietor. Here in Ekat sector, six-story buildings faced each of the four sides of the square, with the businesses on the first floor and a multi-story warren above it.

When Pitamah stopped the lev-car, Devak's stomach lurched. Were they living in a flat now? Bad enough to live in a mixed sector, but to share a building with dozens of other minor-status trueborns—or even lowborns—would be too much to bear. Although, what did it matter with Kayla gone?

"Do we live here?" Devak asked.

"No," Pitamah said. "This is just an identity check. Junjie, hand me your chip, please."

Two enforcers approached the WindSpear, one on either side. Both light-skinned, a man and a woman. The red and black bhimkay emblem on their dark shirts added to their menacing look.

Devak leaned forward to watch as Junjie unhooked his wristlink and released a back panel. He slid out a two-centimeter-diameter disk and handed it to Pitamah. Pitamah passed Junjie's and his own to the male enforcer on the driver's side. The enforcer snapped the disks into slots on a sekai reader.

The female enforcer on Junjie's side leaned in to eye the three of them. "Only two IDs. Where's the third?"

"He's just emerged from the gen-tank," Pitamah said,

hooking a thumb back at Devak. "We haven't had the chance to procure his identification."

"Two days," the male enforcer said. He looked at his sekai again. "Chip doesn't say you own a WindSpear."

"It's borrowed," Pitamah said. "From Jemali Dayal. His permission code is on my chip and his call ID is in my wristlink."

The male enforcer narrowed his gaze on the tattoo emblazoned on Pitamah's left cheek. "Zul Manel." He said it as if Pitamah's name tasted very nasty in his mouth. "You're *that* one."

He scrutinized his sekai screen with a scowl, but he couldn't seem to find anything amiss in Pitamah's or Junjie's chips. The enforcer passed them back with a sour look on his face, then waved them on. "Two days!" he called out as a last warning as the WindSpear pulled away.

Devak scrunched back in his seat. "How long have you had to carry identity chips?"

Junjie, snapping his wristlink back into place, twisted around to face Devak. "Not long after that last explosion. Lowborns don't have to carry them. There's too many of them to track down. But all minor-status do. And a minor-status driving a lev-car is guaranteed to get stopped by the Brigade."

He'd woken to a crazy new world. His status gone, his body changed.

Devak scrubbed at his face, feeling the irregular texture of the scarring. With his fingertips, he explored the ridges and lines along his jaw to his chin, then higher on his face. The scarring meandered up as high as his cheekbone, thin as uttama silk thread in places, and as wide as his pinky near his ear.

Had Kayla's face been injured too? Her back broken? Had she been in terrible pain? Devak had been meters away from the bomb, but Kayla had been right at the explosion site.

His heart clutched tight in his chest. "Tell me what happened to Kayla. Please tell me you got there before the enforcers." He couldn't bear the thought of the Brigade carting Kayla off to use her remaining tissue as a source for new GENs.

"Junjie got there right away," Pitamah said. "I heard the explosion, but I hadn't the strength to get out of bed."

Junjie turned so he could face Devak between the seats. "I got there a few minutes before the enforcers. The dust was thick back behind the warehouses, which was why I didn't see you at first. But it was clear enough in the alley to see. Except . . ." Junjie cleared his throat. "There was no body. I only found her . . . uh . . . arm. The left, torn off just above the elbow."

"Oh." The word was barely more than a puff of air from Devak's throat. "But you didn't let the Brigade . . ."

"No, they didn't get her DNA," Junjie said. "I wrapped her arm in my korta and ran home to tell Zul. We burned it. I think . . . I hope the Infinite understood. Took her into his hands."

"Are you sure it was Kayla's?" Even as Devak asked, he knew the answer. Of course Junjie was sure. While the rest of her was a beautiful pale brown, the skin of her arms had been distinctive—patches of every human color, from near-white to her own pale brown to near-black. "You really didn't find anything else?"

"I thought she might be buried under the rubble," Junjie said. "When the Brigade came, I hid. I watched them search. They dug around, but didn't find a body either." Now Junjie got that guilty look again. "The enforcers are the ones who found you. It should have been me. To have left you there as long as I did . . ."

Devak waved away his confession. "Then Kayla was just . . ." He couldn't say it aloud. *Blown apart?*

Pitamah met Devak's gaze in the rear viewer. "Jemali went in later that night with another medic. They tested the debris. There wasn't enough left behind."

"Meaning what?" Devak asked.

"Meaning sometime between the explosion and me getting there," Junjie said, "her body was probably taken away."

"Her body." The weight of that made it hard to breathe. "Then you think she's . . ." Denking hell, he had to force himself to say the word. "You think she's dead."

Silence rang in Devak's ears. Pitamah kept his eyes on the road, Junjie's gaze dropped.

Finally, Pitamah said, "It's most likely."

Devak fought back tears. "Could the Brigade have come back and found her? Taken her to the gene-splicers?"

"It *is* possible," Pitamah said slowly. "But Kinship gentechs have kept an eye on the tissue databases. Kayla's genotype hasn't surfaced."

Nausea rose in Devak's throat. "But some pishacha could have found her and sold her to a black-market gene-splicer. That wouldn't be in the databases."

Pitamah's and Junjie's silence didn't reassure Devak that his guess was wrong—that a body-stealer might have taken Kayla. He leaned back against the seat, shutting his eyes against the growing morning light. He wished he could shut out reality just as easily.

His fingers strayed to his earlobe, to the sapphire, then traced the lines of the scar on his cheek. His mind couldn't encompass the change in status yet. His sense of feeling *less* as a minor- rather than high-status shamed him. But even more disturbing than the demotion was that he was *different*, after nearly seventeen years of identifying himself as high-status.

But that shame and anxiety paled beside the overwhelming grief that Kayla might be gone. The sorrow felt like a crushing hand tight around his heart. Could the great Lord Creator be that cruel to take her?

The rocking of the lev-car through Ekat sector's streets lulled Devak into a half-sleep. Fragments from his nightmares oozed in and out of his mind, the pieces out of order. The woman screaming at Kayla, then time backed up and the woman was climbing out of her lev-car. The lev-car drove away, then time skipped and the woman screamed again.

The slight jolt when the WindSpear's suspension engines shut down woke Devak. Bleary-eyed, Devak stared at the tiny house Pitamah had docked beside. Its white plasscrete walls were pitted and scratched. Overlong scrap grass filled the front yard, marred by clumps of yellow scrub-flowers. A small sticker bush had even pushed its way up in the far corner, its sprinkling of thorns each as long as Devak's index finger.

Junjie opened Devak's door and stood by in case Devak needed help. He got out on his own, but was glad that Junjie stayed close. He wasn't sure how long this small amount of strength would last.

Pitamah backed the lev-car out of the drive again as Devak followed Junjie to the front door. "He has to take the WindSpear back to Jemali in Foresthill. Then Jemali will bring him back."

Devak felt a lurch inside at the mention of Foresthill, the sector just north of Ekat. He'd grown up in Foresthill—it was where he'd lived with his parents. Before Kayla came into his life and everything changed.

Junjie unlocked the door and they stepped inside. The living room took up the front of the house, with a table and three chairs at one end and a sofa and float chair at the other.

The float chair rested on the floor instead of at sitting height. Maybe its suspension mechanism was broken, or it just cost too much to operate.

The living room was open to a food prep area too small to even be called a kitchen. A short hallway led to the back of the house. There were two doors beyond the food prep area, one on either side.

Junjie waved him down the hall. "You and I are sharing the big room."

Devak tried not to notice the grime in the food prep area and the cramped size of the washroom opposite. "Are you still working at the GAMA lab?" Junjie had been doing research on the Scratch virus in the Genetic Augmentation and Manipulation Agency's Plator facility.

"Yeah, but not in Plator anymore. When you got moved that last time, I requested a transfer here to Ekat sector."

Junjie opened the door on the right, revealing a sleeproom about the size of the one Devak had had to himself at the house in Two Rivers. He and Pitamah had lived in that trueborn sector after they'd lost the house in Foresthill.

Two narrow beds and a dresser Devak recognized as the one from Two Rivers nearly filled the tiny space. A small workstation squeezed into one corner held an old-fashioned holographic projector for a computer keyboard and display. The computer box itself was so enormous—a nearly fifteen-centimeter cube—it sat on the floor rather than take up scant workstation space.

A mirror hung over the dresser, its frame exotic Earth-grown wood. Devak remembered it as one of the few items Pitamah had salvaged from the Foresthill house before Devak's mother plundered it.

Devak felt weak and heartsick, and wanted nothing more than to collapse in bed. But the mirror drew him, and he crossed the room for a closer look.

He ran his fingers through his hair, still damp from the cleansing liquid. It was far shorter than he usually wore it, no more than a couple centimeters long.

Junjie came up beside him, then plopped down on the nearest bed. "They shaved it whenever they moved you. Supposedly so they could start the brain reboot process over, but I think it was because it was easier for them."

"It'll grow out."

Devak dropped his gaze to the scar. Against his medium brown skin, the marks of the healed wound stood out as a pale gray, their stretched-tight sheen almost a silver. Where the scarring was fingertip-wide, it bulged slightly above the surface of his skin, although the narrower ones were smooth. He could use a concealer over those smaller marks, but there was no hiding the larger ridged scars.

The pattern of the scarring intrigued him. It looked almost like a GEN tattoo. Nearly the same silver color, its randomness reminiscent of the electronic circuitry implanted in every GEN slave's face. There were no electronics beneath Devak's skin as there had been in Kayla's, but as he stared at the scar, Kayla's familiar mark seemed to superimpose itself over it.

Junjie rose and stood at Devak's shoulder. "Jemali said he would donate tank time at his clinic to take off the scar."

Devak turned away from the mirror. "He shouldn't spend all that time on something so trivial."

Junjie shrugged. "What about your back? Jemali has some injections that can restructure your spine. It's not as good as tank time, but you'll be able to bend over enough to dress yourself."

"Yes to fixing my back," Devak said. "I just don't think Jemali should waste time on the scar on my face."

The lab-issue korta had started to itch. Struggling against his inflexible spine, Devak stripped off the shirt and tossed it aside. Turning his back to the mirror, he could look over his shoulder and catch a glimpse of the scars on either side of his spine. They were fatter and uglier than the ones on his face. The boniness of his spine and the prominence of his ribs told him he'd lost weight in the tank.

He opened the top two dresser drawers and found neatly folded skivs, kortas, and chera pants. Some were familiar, some new to him. All were well-worn and plain.

"Help me?" he asked Junjie.

Junjie scrambled to his feet. Devak dropped the chera pants and skivs and kicked them away with disgust. As he had at the lab, Junjie helped Devak step into fresh skivs and a dark green pair of chera pants, pulling them up high enough for Devak to reach. Devak tugged them up the rest of the way, preserving a speck of his pride. At least he managed the korta himself.

The simple task exhausted him. "Need to lie down," Devak said.

Junjie pulled back the bedclothes—cheap, dull gray sheets and blanket—and Devak eased himself down stiffly. Junjie drew the covers back up, then stood over the bed, the guilty look on his face again.

Junjie wove and unwove his fingers together. "I'm so sorry, Devak."

As much as it sickened him to ask, as exhausted as Devak was, he had to know the truth. "Did you know about the explosion in advance?"

Junjie paled. "Sweet Infinite, do you really believe I would have let you or Kayla go there if I'd known?"

"You were part of them," Devak said. Junjie had been a member of FHE, an insurgent group whose motto was Freedom, Humanity, Equality. FHE had been trying to rouse the GENs into rebellion by bombing their warrens and warehouses. The explosion in Two Rivers had been the first bomb planted in a trueborn sector. And Junjie had been right in the thick of things with them.

"You know I never agreed with the bombings," Junjie said. "And after they tricked me into reprogramming Kayla, I haven't had anything more to do with them."

"Except you *were* trying to program her."

"Not that way!" Flinging his arms as if to reject Devak's insinuation, Junjie paced away in a circle, then back to the bedside. "Yes, I knew FHE was updating some of Kayla's programming, and I could have told her and stopped it. I thought it was for the greater good. Then when Kayla caught me at it, I made a choice. I wasn't going to help them do any more to her. And after the explosion hurt you, killed Kayla . . . You have to know I'm done with them."

Dropping to the edge of the bed, Junjie ducked his head and rubbed at his face. Devak could see the dampness on his friend's cheeks.

"I believe you." Devak gave Junjie's shoulder an awkward pat. "I know Kayla was your friend as much as she was mine." Maybe she felt even closer to Junjie than she did to Devak, with her and Junjie both believing in the Infinite.

"I still didn't do enough," Junjie said. "I should have gone to Zul after I heard about the first bombing."

"Could you have stopped the others from happening?"

Junjie shrugged. "There might have been a way. Maybe I

could have spoken to Neta again. Tried again to talk her out of that plan."

Neta was a shadowy FHE operative Junjie had never met. They'd spoken via wristlink, voice only. Neta wasn't even her name, just what Junjie called her because he thought of her as FHE's leader.

Worn out, Devak shut his eyes. The bed he lay on seemed to spin, and he was glad his stomach was empty. "I have to rest," Devak groaned.

"I'll check on you later," Junjie said, his words seeming to come from a distance.

Junjie jostled the bed when he got up, and it seemed to whirl even faster under Devak. The familiar nightmare images spun out in Devak's mind, faces ripping past him. Kayla's, the mysterious trueborn woman's, Pitamah's, and Junjie's. The Two Rivers warehouse explosion bursting and hiding them all in a cloud of dust. Then everything spun into reverse, sucking itself back into the alley. The woman appeared and disappeared, sometimes with her own face, sometimes with Kayla's. Always screaming.

Then a new image—the lev-car, previously in the background of his nightmares, loomed large as it raced toward the alley. The woman still screamed, but the man with her jumped from the lev-car into the alley. He returned to the lev-car with a burden, then the vehicle vanished back the way it came.

Devak jolted awake. The sleeproom was shadowy, the only light from a small illuminator on the dresser.

"Junjie!" Devak shouted.

Junjie came in a hurry. "Are you okay? Are you hurting?"

Flopping as awkwardly as a headless rat-snake, Devak wrestled himself into a sitting position on the edge of the bed. "I know who took Kayla. I saw her do it."

3

Junjie stared at Devak a good long time, then came over to sit beside him on the bed. "How could you have seen anything? The bomb blast sent you into a coma."

"Yes," Devak said. "You're right, I *didn't* see her take Kayla. Not really. Just in my dreams."

Junjie's eyes widened and Devak could just imagine the calculations going on in his friend's head. *Devak has gone sanaki. All that time in the tank made him crazy.*

"I'm explaining all this really badly. Could you help me to the washroom?" He was desperate to relieve himself.

Devak grabbed both of Junjie's hands and let his friend pull. He winced as he gained his feet. "Back hurts."

"That's good," Junjie said. "Jemali did some vac-seal infusions on you a couple hours ago while you were asleep. A compound that dissolves the fusing between the vertebrae while it forces your body to grow new discs. He said it might pinch a little."

"Was that compound filled with knives? Feels like I've been stabbed." Devak shuffled out into the hall with Junjie leading him, biting his lip to keep from crying out from the pain. "Where's Pitamah?"

"After Jemali finished your treatment, they headed off to a Kinship meeting."

Junjie escorted Devak into the washroom, but left him alone to relieve himself. Devak had to curve his back to wash up, and while he was gratified that it did bend ever so slightly, it was an agony.

Moving slowly from the washroom, he found Junjie in the kitchen. A pot of kel-grain steamed on the radiant stove.

"Are you hungry?" Junjie asked.

"Starving. If I can get something to eat, I know I'll make more sense." Devak eyed the steaming pot without enthusiasm. "Kel-grain would be fine."

"There's nothing to put into it. Not so much as a sliver of synth-protein, or even an old patagobi root." Junjie grabbed the pot from the stove and shoved it into the refrigerator. "If I eat kel-grain for dinner one more night, I'll start grunting like a drom. Could you walk a little ways? There's a curry house up the road owned by Kinship lowborns. I did some work for them and they owe me a meal or two."

"That would be great."

Junjie found a pair of shoes for Devak and helped him slip them on. Devak kept a grip on Junjie's shoulder until they were on the sidewalk outside, then let go. They started down Makti Street, traveling east.

From the position of the trinity moons in the night sky— Avish was long gone, but Abrahm and Ashiv shone their light—Devak guessed it was early evening. Ekat sector was far enough south that the nighttime spring air didn't have as chilly a bite as it might have up in Plator sector, or Far North.

Was his father cold in his Far North prison cell? Doubtful. As former director of the GEN Monitoring Grid for all of Svarga's western territories, Ved Manel had some pull. He likely lived in relative luxury, his cell much nicer than the tiny house that Pitamah's circumstances had forced them into.

The homes on either side of the street were tidy enough. Most about the size of Pitamah's, their front gardens well maintained.

They moved slowly down the walkway, Junjie staying within reach. As they reached the cross street, Devak hesitated before stepping from the curb. Motion from the last house on the block caught his eye as a man emerged.

A lowborn man. Well-dressed and prosperous looking, but a lowborn nonetheless.

The man tapped a lock code into the keypad beside his door. Then the lowborn continued to the sidewalk, giving Devak and Junjie a brisk nod as he passed.

"We live with lowborns," Devak said. "On the same block as them."

"Is that a problem?" Junjie asked.

Yes! Devak kept himself from saying aloud. His mother would be filled with horror that they lived with lowborns. That instinctive reaction was her influence, and the realization that he hadn't left it behind shamed Devak.

Of course, she'd be sickened to learn he was in love with a GEN. So what did it matter if a lowborn lived a few houses down from him and Pitamah? His back stung with pain, and he felt exhausted, hungry, and grimy from the gen-tank. His entire life had changed since he'd awakened that morning. A lowborn neighbor was nothing.

Devak shook his head at Junjie's question, and cast aside

his fast-dwindling pride as he set a hand on Junjie's shoulder. He made it to the curry house two blocks further on, but barely, sagging against Junjie as the last of his energy waned.

Just the scent of cardamom, cinnamon, and sizzling drom meat sent his stomach rumbling. The place was packed, but a lowborn woman with a long, dark braid greeted Junjie cheerfully by name and cleared off a small table for them near the kitchen. It was noisy and busy there, Devak facing the kitchen only a couple meters away, Junjie with a view of the room. The stiff chair tortured Devak's back, but the woman who had seated them almost immediately brought them bowls, two each, one filled with drom curry and a second piled high with spiced kel-grain.

Devak devoured his dinner, mixing his kel-grain into the thick curry and spooning up huge mouthfuls. As the hot curry burned its way down his throat, a realization hit him.

"This is the first food I've had since the explosion."

Junjie nodded. "Unless you count the glop they fed you through the tube in the tank."

Junjie had eaten more slowly and still had half a bowl full. When he caught Devak eyeing his portion, Junjie called out, "Thela!" to the lowborn server. Thela set another fragrant bowl of curry before Devak and whisked away the empty one.

Several more bites wolfed down, and finally Devak's raging hunger was tamed. Setting down his spoon, he turned his chair to get a good look at the curry house. The clientele were about half-and-half lowborns and minor-status trueborns. There were even trueborns and lowborns at the same tables. Their animated and amiable conversations told Devak that the different classes shared their meal out of friendship rather than the convenience of getting fed sooner.

The minor-status trueborns were either pasty white in

complexion or near black. None had Devak's high-status skin color, or his straight black hair. The light faces had pale to medium brown hair. The dark-skinned trueborns had tight curly hair like Kayla's nurture brother, Jal.

The lowborns varied much more widely in complexion— pale, light brown, dark brown, black. Lowborn faces seemed to skip the high-status medium brown, but they represented every other color. He saw tight curls of hair on the pale-skinned, straight black on others, even one redhead.

The greater variety in lowborns was simple genetics— and a different social attitude. The lowborns Devak had met rarely judged a person on skin color the way trueborns did. Lowborns didn't give a sewer toad's wart about status, and they intermarried more.

"How many of the people here are . . ." Devak splayed his right hand on his chest with his pinky tucked in, his thumb and three fingers spread into a crude letter K, for *Kinship*.

Junjie surveyed the room. "I'd wager all the lowborns are. A good number of the trueborns. The ones who aren't would never report the ones who are to the Brigade. Sympathizers, at the least."

The Kinship had been started by Pitamah and his friends Jemali and Hala. Its membership later encompassed not just trueborns but lowborns too and secretly, GENs. Publicly, they were known as promoters of lowborn and GEN rights. Privately, they furthered their goals by freeing GENs from being tracked by the continent-wide Monitoring Grid. Even more significantly, Kinship techs had developed a way to dissolve the circuitry installed in GEN nervous systems. The treatment transformed GENs into lowborns.

Kayla had been at the top of the list of GENs to be converted to be a lowborn. But Kayla had refused the treatment in favor of her best friend, Mishalla. And just before the explosion, Kayla had announced to Devak that she wanted to stay a GEN.

So she'd died as a GEN. Right before his eyes.

Except he hadn't actually seen it happen. He hadn't seen her body fly, seen it torn apart. That was just in his dreams.

Junjie tapped his spoon on his bowl. "What you said about Kayla . . . you're not hoping . . . not expecting to find her alive?"

Devak sucked in a breath. "I . . . no," he lied.

"She can't be, Devak. Kayla's dead. You have to accept that."

"Have you?" Devak asked. "Has Pitamah?"

Junjie looked away. "We're working on accepting it."

Junjie picked at his food while Devak scanned the room again. The clientele had shifted, a few tables clearing and Thela seating those waiting. There was still a crowd by the door.

"Okay," Devak said. "Let's say I accept that she's dead." He didn't though. Couldn't. "Someone took her body. I think I might have an idea who."

Junjie squinted at him dubiously. "You said you saw her in your dreams."

"That sounded crazy, but it wasn't really what I meant. I had nightmares in the tank. I would see the explosion happen over and over. I don't think I actually saw anyone take Kayla. But I do think my brain took what I *did* see and put some facts together into what might have happened. It was those possibilities I dreamt about."

"Or your brain made it all up," Junjie said.

"Either way, it's worth considering, isn't it? To find where she was taken, to bring her body back and . . ." Devak faltered. "We can't do what the Infinite's liturgy says."

"Take her to the gene-splicers? No." Junjie scooped up a

30

last bite. "Most believers favor cremation now. At least converts like me, and enlightened GENs like Kayla do." Enlightened meaning she knew the liturgy had been written by ordinary men to control tankborns.

"How can you worship the Infinite when he was made up by men?" Devak asked.

"How do you know the Lord Creator wasn't?" Junjie shot back. He waved off Devak's defense. "The three so-called prophets borrowed from a true liturgy. From sacred books that were written on Earth. The prophets might have added a bunch of nonsense, but they didn't create the Infinite. But back to the point. Who do you think took Kayla?"

"There were a man and woman there just before the explosion."

"In your dreams?" Junjie asked.

"In my memory. The woman was trying to run toward the alley after Kayla, screaming her name. The man held her back."

"You saw all that?" Junjie asked. "You're sure?"

"Yes. It's the rest of it that I'm guessing at. The man and woman must have taken Kayla's body away."

"And that's helpful, how?" asked Junjie. "When we have no idea who the man and woman were. What did they look like?"

"Minor-status? The woman anyway." Devak thought he'd seen a sapphire in her ear. "The man's face . . . it was a blur. The woman . . . a blur too, except in my dream . . ."

Junjie's attention strayed past Devak toward the door. Devak craned his neck to see what had caught Junjie's notice. Newcomers stood at the entrance, well-dressed lowborns. They were leaning close to some of the waiting customers, passing on some message.

Junjie kept one eye on the door as he focused back on

Devak. "What did she look like in your dream?"

"Like Kayla," Devak said. "As if Kayla was trying to warn herself not to go into that alley."

Devak had lost Junjie again. Devak turned around completely, wincing when his spine scraped against the chair back. The new arrivals and the waiting patrons had fanned out through the room, going table to table. Uneasiness dropped to Devak's belly.

"Not good," Junjie said, pushing to his feet.

He put out a hand to Devak and helped him up. They started for the door, but now a mass of bodies blocked them.

"Denk it," Junjie said.

"What's happening?" Devak asked.

Then he saw the Brigade shove through the door. They wore white riot helmets adorned with the menacing bhimkay emblem, the fangs of the black and red giant spider dripping blood. Devak stared, unbelieving, as the first pair of enforcers slammed their elbows into the patrons nearest them—a lowborn man and a minor-status woman.

Suddenly, Thela was there grabbing Junjie's arm. "This way."

She towed them from the restaurant and through the kitchen. Shouts and cries started up from the other room, and Devak heard the distinctive booming orders from a Brigade enforcer.

"What the denking hell? They can't do this." Devak twisted toward the restaurant, with some crazy idea of stopping the Brigade's invasion. Junjie yanked him nearly off his feet in the other direction.

As he stumbled after Junjie, Devak heard the high-pitched whine of a shockgun followed by a shout of pain. He couldn't be sure, but from the tone of the shockgun, that was at least a medium-power strike, enough to cause serious injury.

Thela and Junjie hustled Devak behind a curtain into a storage room, then Thela fumbled under one of the shelves. A click and the rear wall swiveled open on a center pivot. Darkness lay beyond the ten-centimeter-thick plasscrete door.

The heavy stomping boots of the Brigade grew nearer. Just as the enforcers were at the curtain, Thela dropped a quarter dhan coin into Junjie's hand. "Debt paid," she murmured, then pushed Devak and Junjie beyond the door and shut them into blackness.

They could hear only murmurs, Thela's lighter voice, then the heaviness of one of the enforcers'. Devak tried to feel for the door. "We can't leave her."

"Shh!" Junjie clutched at Devak's arm and dragged him away. "Entrance is here somewhere."

Junjie must have tripped because he let go and Devak heard a thump. "I'm okay," drifted up. "Stumbled on the trapdoor handle."

Junjie nudged Devak backward, then Devak heard the snick of a latch release. A moment later, Junjie gripped Devak's arm. "Sit on the floor. I'll guide your legs inside. Feel for the ladder."

Devak lowered himself, leaning heavily on Junjie, his back screaming in protest. Then Devak dropped his feet into the unseen hole in the floor. He poked around with his toes and found the ladder rungs. Bending his back as far as it would go, he clutched the top rung with his hands.

Devak descended into darkness, listening hard for Junjie. Finally, he heard the trapdoor shut and latch, and his friend's tread on the plassteel ladder.

At the bottom, Devak skimmed the surrounding walls with his fingertips until he found an opening. He stood aside as Junjie dropped beside him.

"Cover your eyes," Junjie said. A moment later, an illuminator flared with light. Junjie gestured with it as he squeezed past Devak. "Thela keeps a few illuminators here. It's about a quarter mile to the next exit."

Devak followed Junjie down the tunnel. "Does this lead to a safe house?" The Kinship had numerous underground safe houses throughout Svarga.

"Used to," Junjie said. "Destroyed months ago. Thela discovered the tunnel when she built her restaurant and cleared it. Figured it would be handy to bring in contraband, black market drom meat, that sort of thing."

"But why'd she help us escape? What about all those other trueborns and lowborns?"

"No way to get them all out," Junjie said. "The Brigade nearly got *us*. Thela was only willing to help me because I arranged a meeting with the gene-splicer who treated her youngest son."

Devak stumbled on the uneven ground, his back wrenching. He bit back the pain. "What was the Brigade doing there anyway?"

"They've never liked how much lowborns and minor-status trueborns intermingle in some of the mixed sectors. Now, with the bombings, they have an excuse. They claim they're rousting dissidents."

Devak, gasping for breath, struggled to keep up with Junjie. "But it was FHE who set the bombs."

"The Brigade knows that. Like I said, an excuse." Junjie turned left at a crossroads. "There haven't even been any bombings since the last one that injured you and killed—"

Junjie stopped abruptly. Devak collided with him, then groaned as the force radiated through his sore back.

Junjie turned toward him, steadied him. "Devak—tell me about your dream again. What the woman looked like."

"When she wasn't a blur, she looked like Kayla. Except I told you, I just think that meant—"

"Did she look exactly like Kayla?" Junjie's voice seemed edged with excitement. "Was it really just Kayla's face on the woman's body?"

"I . . . yes . . . except . . ." Devak groped in his mind for the nightmare image. The trueborn woman with Kayla's face floated in his mind's eye. And then it hit him. "No GEN tattoo on her cheek. Shorter hair. And she seemed older, like maybe a thirtieth-year."

"Older," Junjie said. "But she looked like Kayla."

Devak tried to put the pieces together. "Could she have been genned with the same DNA as Kayla?"

"Kayla wasn't genned," Junjie reminded him. "She started as a trueborn and got changed into a GEN right before she was a fourth-year. Anyway, you said this woman was a trueborn."

A trueborn woman who looked just like Kayla. A minor-status, just like Kayla had once been.

The truth snapped into clarity in Devak's mind. "The woman was Kayla's mother. Her birth mother, Aideen Kalu."

"Yes!" Junjie exclaimed. "My mind was going there, but I wasn't sure. To have you think so too . . ."

Junjie trailed off. As he stared into the darkness beyond the illuminator, Devak could see something calculating in Junjie's eyes.

Devak gave him a poke. "What?"

Junjie glanced at Devak. "After I told Neta I was finished with FHE, she never tried again to contact me."

"Were you so important to them you expected them to?"

Junjie rolled his eyes. "Not at all. It wasn't me they wanted. All they wanted was Kayla."

"And now that she's . . ." Devak swallowed. ". . . dead, they've forgotten you."

"Not exactly," Junjie said. "They've forgotten me because now they've got what they wanted. That woman you saw—she wasn't just Aideen. I think she was also Neta, the woman who was my contact at FHE. And if the woman at the explosion site was Neta, if she really did carry off Kayla like your mind is telling you—"

The final pieces fell into place. "Then FHE has Kayla's body."

Kayla woke sobbing. Grief gouged at her heart, and she thought she'd die from it.

If it wasn't for the dreams, she might have been able to accept Devak's death by now, two months later. But the images visited her most nights—Devak calling her, reaching for her from too far away before being snatched away by a firestorm.

But she hadn't even been there. The explosion that killed Devak had happened days after the FHE rescued her from Akhilesh's GAMA lab.

At the moment Devak had died, Kayla had already been here at FHE headquarters, immersed in a gen-tank. Her super-charged circuitry meant she'd been able to emerge from the tank after only two weeks, but by then, Devak had been dead ten days. And because she was still so physically weak after they'd pulled her from the gen-tank, they didn't even tell her for another two weeks.

Damn Aideen for not telling her right away. Yes, Kayla had had enough to grasp—the changes in her body thanks to FHE's reprogramming of her circuitry. The new efficiency of her GEN healing system. And most significantly, the truth Kayla's birth mother had told her about the FHE bombings— that a rogue member of the group had planted them all, and that they only recently stopped him.

But waiting so long only made the news of Devak's death worse for her. She'd spent much of those two weeks post-tank longing for him, imagining them together and talking, touching, kissing. Even knowing her fantasies were hopeless, they comforted her nonetheless. To then be told about his death, to have her dreams destroyed, had been an unbearable blow.

She took a deep breath to relieve the ache in her chest, then rolled on her side in her narrow cot. The automated illuminators in the ceiling had brightened to morning light level, giving Kayla the illusion that this underground cave room had a window to the outdoors. So she could see that the cot opposite hers was empty and the bed neatly made.

Which meant Lovise, Kayla's GEN roommate, was already up and gone. Just as well. She truly liked Lovise. The seventeenth-year girl was as sweet-tempered as Kayla's lowborn friend, Mishalla. But Kayla hated it when the other GEN girl caught her crying. Lovise would want to sit beside Kayla and pat her back to soothe her. But what Kayla really needed just now was solitude.

Kayla idly scanned the room, one of hundreds within the cave system that comprised Antara, FHE's headquarters. The cream and gray limestone cave walls curved up a good six meters above her, their natural rock striations broken only by a plasscrete door set in the wall just beyond the foot of Kayla's cot. A few stalactites thrust down from above, the fatter ones sheared off so they wouldn't encroach on the living space. A micro-controller above the door, a thumbprint-sized dark spot, housed the electronic controls for the lights and the air circulation system.

This was where they'd moved her the day she'd been told about Devak. It had been their second choice. They'd wanted her to share a room with Aideen Kalu, but Kayla had flatly refused that plan, even as weak as she'd been.

Still, they'd put their foot down on Kayla rooming alone. Likely they were worried about Kayla terminating herself. Not an unreasonable worry—that Infinite-forbidden option had drifted in and out of Kayla's mind more than once after she heard of Devak's death. Just as well she'd been forced to share with cheerful, chatty Lovise.

As Kayla lay there, wishing she could return to the oblivion of sleep, flickers of color and light started up on the periphery of her vision. She squeezed her eyes shut, knowing what would come next, and wishing she could stop it. But the hallucinations formed anyway, images too fragmented to comprehend, but so real she could see them swirling and dancing in the room.

At the first attack of light and color, Kayla was terrified enough to go to Palla, the trueborn medic who'd treated her in the tank. After an examination turned up no physical problems, Palla had determined that the images were just hallucinations, a misfiring of Kayla's brain. Her mind had created the images, using them to fill in blank spaces left behind by her reset.

The splintered images were nothing like the crystal clear recollections of actual memory. She remembered her childhood in Chadi sector with her nurture mother, Tala. Recalled playing with her nurture brother, Jal, in front of the warren where they lived. And she'd never forget whispering secrets with her heart-deep, tank-sister friend, Mishalla.

Nor would she forget her memories of Devak. She clung to those, replayed them over and over again, for fear they might fade. From the first time she met him on the banks of the Chadi River, to the months spent in his home as his family's Assigned GEN, to that last time she'd seen him in Daki sector.

They hadn't parted on the best of terms that night. Devak had feared that if their relationship were discovered, she would be reset. It would be better to give up that hopeless dream of them being together than take that risk. So they'd said goodbye for the last time in Daki.

Then she got reset anyway, by Akhilesh. She should have taken her chances with loving Devak.

She couldn't lie there any longer. She pushed herself off the bed, pulling the thick pile of dromwool blankets with her and huddling inside them. She could use her GEN warming circuitry to ward off the cavern's perennial 12 degree centigrade temperature, the way she used to in the underground Kinship safehouses. But when she'd first emerged from the gen-tank, she'd been so weak, utilizing her warming circuitry would exhaust her. So she'd gotten used to relying on the thick, felted wool blankets. She'd discovered a certain pleasure in ordinary body heat.

Dragging the blankets, Kayla paced the two-meter by three-meter floor space ringed by two cots and a dresser. She should be grateful FHE had freed her from Akhilesh. They'd been too late to stop the gene-splicer from resetting her, but they'd saved her from having a new personality written over her annexed brain, or worse, her body broken down into DNA for creating new GENs.

And it had been a stroke of luck that FHE had already in-stalled a circuit-comm system over her GEN circuitry, despite their having done it without her permission. That had allowed them to covertly download her annexed brain right before the reset. They'd preserved her *self* and were able to later restore it.

Ordinarily, restoring only the contents of her annexed brain before a reset would have left huge holes that only her bare brain could fill in. But before that reset Kayla had been routinely transferring the contents of her bare brain into the annexed part, a trick she'd also learned from FHE. So most of her life experiences had been saved too.

Which included nearly all her memories of Devak.

The several months before FHE rescued her now seemed like a dream. Traveling with the lowborn woman, Risa, Kinship business sending them from one GEN or mixed or trueborn sector to another. Kayla's risky work visiting Kinship safe houses, ferrying secrets and datapods. A few stolen words with Devak, visits that were heartbreaking and far too brief. Devak finally insisting they should cut all ties between them.

And they had. Until the night she and Devak and Junjie drove a sick GEN girl from Ret sector to Daki. With Junjie and the girl asleep in the back, Devak and Kayla had talked. She only recalled bits and pieces of that night, but the most important truth was sharp in her mind.

Devak was so serious as he told her, *I've figured out that trueborn society isn't ready for GENs and trueborns to be together.*

She'd known he was right, no matter how badly it hurt. But couldn't the Infinite have somehow told her she would never see him again after that night? She might have at least shared a final kiss with him.

With nothing to do but rest and heal these last six weeks out of the tank, she'd had plenty of time to think. At first, after she'd been told about Devak, she cursed the Infinite, vowed to tear the great deity from her heart. But with only Him to turn to when she felt so desperately heartsick, she'd let Him back inside.

But she still struggled to understand. *Why didn't you keep Devak safe?*

Impatient with herself, Kayla threw the covers back onto the bed. The room's chill bit her skin through her sleeveless shift. The communal washroom was only two doors down the corridor, fed by an underground hot spring. She twitched one of the blankets from the bed to use as a robe, and hurried down to use the washroom's necessary.

This time of the morning, the washroom was packed with GEN and trueborn women chatting as they lay submerged in the spring's warm water. As tempting as a hot bath was, Kayla couldn't bear the thought of making conversation when her heart was still so heavy with thoughts of Devak.

She quickly used the necessary and returned to her quarters, locking the door behind her. Tugging off her shift and skivs, she tossed them on her cot and grabbed a handful of sani-wipes from the packet on the dresser.

Kayla had lost her small prayer mirror while in Akhilesh's lab, so she sometimes used the half-meter square reflector on the wall to send her prayers to the Infinite. Now she studied her face, using a sani-wipe to clean away any trace of tears.

Faint pink stood out along the edges of the silvery tattoo on her right cheek. Devak would always know if she was embarrassed or angry by that pink along her tattoo. Crying brought it out too. Remembering Devak's fascination with that rosy outline nearly brought the tears again.

She washed her left arm last. Seeing it still distressed her, so she tried not to look at it at all when it wasn't covered. But standing there naked, she couldn't avoid it.

The right arm was the same as it always had been, splotches of every human skin color from shoulder to wrist. But the left had been severed just above the elbow by the gene-splicer Akhilesh Garud. When the FHE techs programmed the arm to re-grow in their gen-tank, they'd genned the skin on the replacement a solid pale brown.

She'd always hated the blotchy skin of her arms. Now that the lower part of her left matched the rest of her body, she should be happy. But it seemed so wrong. She felt a little sick looking at it.

Tossing the used sani-wipes into the room's mini-cin, Kayla pulled on skivs and a band around her breasts. Then she threw on a long-sleeved shirt and leggings and tidied her braid.

The next part of her morning ritual she would only do when she was alone. The cots were too lightweight to bother with, as were the chair and the desk by Lovise's cot. The dresser was heavy enough to test Kayla's strength, but too awkward to handle.

Instead, she'd discovered two handholds in the rock wall high enough that she had to stretch to reach them and deep enough to fit her fingers inside. The wall bowed out just below the handholds, so her body wouldn't scrape against the rock as she pulled herself up. The niche was behind the door when it opened, so Kayla had plenty of time to drop and step back if she heard the latch click.

Fingertips hooked into the wall, she chinned herself up from the floor. She lifted herself as high as she could until her nose brushed the rock wall. She barely weighed fifty kilos, so it wasn't much of a test. But it assured her that the re-genned arm retained its strength. Her skill set—her GEN sket—was still intact.

She lowered herself to the floor slowly, enjoying the feel of her muscles working. Then she lifted herself again, and again, pushing herself to do one more than she had yesterday. It had terrified her that first time when she'd only managed five. Now she was close to counting out ten times that.

Just as her feet hit the floor after fifty-one repetitions, someone knocked at the door. Not Lovise. She would have just entered the unlock code and walked in. Based on the time Kayla read from her internal clock, she could guess who it was. Her birth mother, Aideen Kalu. The woman always turned up around this time. The only question was whether Ohin would be with Aideen so that Kayla could finally meet him. More likely, he'd been called away by "more important" duties as he had been every other morning he'd said he would come.

Until now, Kayla had only seen Ohin, the GEN leader of FHE, from a distance. She'd spied him a few times as he strode through Mahala, the main cavern that housed the kitchen and dining hall. Once she spotted him far ahead of her in the corridors, surrounded by petitioners. As each one approached Ohin, they dipped their head and said something to him, some kind of formula. She was too far away to hear that or Ohin's response.

He'd disappeared by the time she caught up with the crowd. Aideen had told Kayla he'd visited her often when she'd been in the tank. Kayla had dimly-remembered dreams of a man's voice speaking to her. Would she recognize his voice?

What did it matter? He was nothing to her. But even from those distant sightings of him, Kayla had caught the electricity of his personality. Everyone here adored him, revered him.

At another knock on the door, Kayla let go of the rock wall and clapped the limestone dust from her hands. She released the lock and called out, "Come in."

But it was only Aideen who stepped inside. Kayla said, "Ohin's not coming again, I suppose."

Aideen mustered a smile. "He had an unexpected meeting. But he'll be here soon."

Kayla stood aside, giving her birth mother plenty of space. It still sent a chill down Kayla's spine seeing Aideen, the lowborn woman's face nearly a mirror image of Kayla's own. That is, if the mirror had aged Kayla seventeen years.

It was perfectly normal for trueborns to see their own faces in their mother's or father's. But Kayla was a GEN, raised by her GEN nurture mother, Tala. GENs almost never looked like their nurture parents.

Tala's face was a very light brown, her hair smooth and straight. Kayla's skin was shades darker than Tala's and her thick hair was wild and curly. Those contrasts between her and Tala seemed right to her. The sameness between her and Aideen seemed unnatural.

Kayla hated the way the woman's presence always unsettled her. What was she supposed to talk to her about?

Her gaze fell on Aideen's right earlobe, where there was an empty earring hole. "We all know you're trueborn. You can't change who you are by not wearing your bali."

Aideen's fingers brushed her earlobe. "The bali is a symbol of outsider trueborns' dominance over GENs." It sounded like she was quoting from some FHE handbook.

"So's my tattoo." Kayla gestured at her cheek. "Except it's not so easy for me to take off as your bali is."

Aideen never seemed to know what to say when Kayla brought up the bhimkay in the room—that her birth mother's choice nearly twelve years ago had led to the enslavement of her daughter.

Aideen took a step closer, reaching out, but not quite touching Kayla. "How are you feeling today?"

It unnerved Kayla that they were nearly the same height. Kayla could see she made Aideen uncomfortable too, although for different reasons. There was always an edginess in the woman's smile, a stiffness in the set of the trueborn woman's shoulders.

Kayla supposed she couldn't blame her supposed birth mother. Who wouldn't feel awkward around the daughter she'd abandoned? Who wouldn't feel guilty about turning their fourth-year child over to a gene-splicer and allowing her to be converted into a GEN?

"I'm fine," Kayla said. "I want to go home."

Which of the usual responses would she get? *You still need to regain your strength.* Or, *We're worried about your safety.* Or the one that especially enraged Kayla, *This is your home now.*

But Aideen took a new tack. "Devak is gone, Kayla. You have to accept that."

That unexpected strike left Kayla breathless for a moment. Hatred for Aideen spurted up, but Kayla thrust aside the useless emotion.

"Tala isn't gone. And neither is my nurture brother, Jal, or my friend Mishalla. Do you think they mean nothing to me?"

This was another old argument. They'd had it nearly every day since Kayla had recovered enough from the fog of her tank time to start asking about her family.

"Of course they're important to you."

More than you are, Kayla wanted to say to Aideen, but she bit her tongue to keep the childish response inside. "You keep telling me they're fine, but I want to see for myself. If I could be in danger out there, don't you think they could?"

Aideen stared at Kayla, her smile fixed. Then her shoulders sagged with relief at a tap on Kayla's door. "He's here."

Kayla's stomach immediately knotted as the FHE leader stepped inside. He was close to two meters tall, his eyes an intense blue, his skin a pale brown that would have marked him as a minor-status if he'd been a trueborn like Aideen. Kayla gauged he was maybe twice her own nearly sixteen years.

Aideen turned toward Kayla. "This is Ohin."

He nodded at Kayla, his smile gentle. "I apologize for taking so long to meet you officially."

Just seeing him there, Kayla felt drawn to him. Something in his intensity made her glad to be around him. "I've been a long time healing."

"Still, it should have been before now." Ohin squeezed Kayla's shoulder, just long enough to feel the caring in his touch, but not so long as to feel uncomfortable.

Something familiar about him nagged at her that she hadn't noticed in her earlier brief glimpses of him. The set of his wide shoulders, maybe, or the shape of his face. "Could we have met before? On the outside maybe?"

Something like caution flickered in his eyes. He glanced over at Aideen. The trueborn woman shook her head, the movement nearly imperceptible.

He turned back to Kayla. "Your reset has made your memories so unreliable, it's hard to say what's real and what isn't."

He only spoke the truth, but her heart wrenched at what might have been lost. "Devak was real. My nurture mother and brother are."

Ohin's expression was so kind, it squeezed her heart even tighter. "That's true, Kayla. I know you miss them."

47

"How far are we from Chadi sector?" Tala and Jal lived in Chadi, the sector where Kayla had been raised. "If there aren't the dhans to take pub-trans, I'd walk if I had to."

"No need to worry about that."

Meaning what? That they had plenty of dhans to transport her? Or could they be so close to Chadi it would be a short walk?

Ohin's gaze grew distant, the way the other GENs' did when someone contacted them via their circuit-comm. In that same moment, a vibration started up at the base of Kayla's skull. It was odd because her circuitry had never reacted that way when any other GENs used their comms nearby.

"I'm afraid I've got an issue to resolve," Ohin said. He nodded toward Kayla, then left the room.

There was no mistaking the adoration lingering in Aideen's eyes. Kayla was surprised to feel it too, from nothing more than seeing Ohin at close quarters. She found herself reviewing everything he'd said.

Her mind circled back to what he hadn't said. "When I asked him about Chadi, he didn't say how close we were."

"If Ohin decides you should go to Chadi," Aideen said, "or that Tala and Jal should come here, it won't matter how far it is."

Kayla sighed with frustration. No matter how many times or ways she'd asked, Aideen refused to tell her what sector they were in. Either everyone else in the place had been sworn to secrecy, or they didn't know themselves. Not unreasonable since so many GENs had been brought here reset like Kayla had been, then restored after they'd arrived. Kayla couldn't get an answer from any of them, not even Lovise.

She'd made guesses. Back in Doctrine school, in the

geography unit, she'd learned about various limestone cave systems beneath Svarga continent. Far North sector was riddled with them. But Far North was a trueborn sector, known mostly for its prison, so that seemed unlikely. There were caverns in the northernmost point of Nafi and in the eastern edge of Mut, both GEN sectors. But those underground systems were well known, even opened up for trueborn tours sometimes. So FHE's cave system, whichever sector it was in, must be undiscovered.

If only she could get to the surface. Thanks to the Kinship, Kayla had a map of all of Svarga stored in her annexed brain. That, coupled with her locator software, would pinpoint where Antara lay. But Kayla had been restricted to Antara's lowest level. She didn't have access codes for any of the various lifts and she had no idea which of them went all the way to the top.

As she considered how to further press the argument with Aideen, Kayla's left arm itched. She shoved the sleeve up impatiently to scratch it, trying not to look at that alien skin.

"Why did they re-gen it this way?" Kayla asked for the tenth time, or the thirtieth. She wished she'd thought to ask Ohin. "Why didn't they make it like it was?"

"I told you. It would never have been like it was," Aideen said. "We couldn't duplicate the original genetic pattern. Besides, why would you want the same skin that the outsider trueborns gave you?"

When Aideen had turned Kayla over to the Brigade all those years ago, she'd had no arms at all. She'd been born that way. It was the gene-splicer—Akhilesh, as it turned out—who'd programmed those patchy colors when he'd grown arms for her.

As Kayla drew her fingernails across her skin, she had the

sense she was scratching a different arm. Maybe the one that Akhilesh had cut off, eleven years after he'd first created it.

Aideen reached toward Kayla's left arm as if to touch her. The trueborn woman never quite made contact, though, the old superstition about trueborns touching GENs too ingrained.

Kayla yanked her sleeve down again and strode past Aideen. "Let's get to Mahala. I'm starving." With a sigh, Aideen followed Kayla into the corridor.

Once Aideen caught up, she stayed right alongside Kayla. They were so alike, even their legs were the same length, their stride identical. Kayla considered speeding up or slowing down or even pretending to trip just to see what Aideen would do. But she kept her eyes forward so she wouldn't have to look at the woman. Aideen shook loose too many painful emotions inside Kayla.

The Kinship safehouses had been entirely excavated, lase tools used to cut the underground granite. Here, the FHE had utilized a natural cave for Antara, only reshaping it where the spaces were too small to be useful, or trimming off stalactites, stalagmites, or other limestone features that were in the way. The corridor had been smoothed by lase tools, the natural limestone passageway made larger and straighter. They'd also drilled through the rock to install the micro-controllers, the dark dots on either side wired to the lights and air circulation system like the one in Kayla's room.

Like Mahala, the largest cavern in FHE's headquarters, every single space in the cavern large enough to have a use had a designation as well. The overall cave system had been named Antara. Kayla's and Lovise's quarters were called Seycat—apparently the six-legged wild felines fascinated Lovise, so she had chosen the room for herself and Kayla.

The doors to the private spaces on either side tended to be closed, the public rooms open. All had an identifying placard beside the door. If a space was private, like Seycat, the occupants' names were listed below the room name. For a public space, the placard indicated its name and purpose, the way it did for *Vijnana Center 2, Computer Lab*, just coming up on their left.

Next door to Vijnana was the Bhimkay Lounge, an extra-large space where young GENs and trueborns played rough-and-tumble games. Charf, a stout minor-status trueborn woman, roamed the room, barking at rule-breakers, sometimes ejecting the transgressors when they got too wild.

It was mostly boys who used the Bhimkay Lounge, twelfth-years to a few as old as eighteenth-years blowing off steam between their work tour hours. The seventeenth- and eighteenth-year GENs in the group called themselves the Bhimkay Boys, although why only the older GENs got that title and not the trueborns as well, Kayla didn't know.

The only girls Kayla had seen in there clustered along the edges to watch. She'd considered joining the boys, to show them what a GEN girl could do. But as powerful as she was, even without being up to full strength, she could hurt someone. It wasn't worth the risk just to show off.

GENs and trueborns passed them in the corridor, or came up from behind and outpaced them on their way to whatever errand drew them. They nodded in greeting, or smiled and called to Kayla and Aideen by name. A few of them murmured, "Always one with him," which Aideen repeated. Kayla wondered if that was some kind of prayer to the Infinite, one she'd never heard before.

In the four or so weeks that she'd been strong enough to have the run of this lowest level of FHE's headquarters, Kayla had come to recognize the faces, and had their names stored in her annexed brain. But she only nodded in response rather than greet them by name, still not trusting their apparent good will. She certainly didn't repeat the strange prayer.

They'd nearly reached Mahala when the broken images of disconnected memories suddenly sparked at the edges of Kayla's vision. She did stumble then, scraping her elbow against the corridor wall. Aideen nearly grabbed Kayla's arm, but a passing GEN saved the trueborn woman from having to. The GEN man made sure Kayla was secure on her feet before he moved on.

"Are you okay?" Aideen asked.

She waved off Aideen's concern. "Fine."

"Is it the hallucinations?" Aideen asked.

Kayla shook her head. "I don't see them anymore," she lied, then rushed past Aideen to step inside Mahala.

The cacophony in the enormous room drowned out Kayla's thoughts, let alone her fragile memories. A rough half-sphere, nearly two hundred meters around, Mahala's fifty-meter-high ceiling was thick with stalactites and other hanging features. The floor had been smoothed of its stalagmites, and plasscrete dividers sectioned off areas for the kitchen off to the left and meeting and workspaces in the back. There were a hundred times the number of tables and seating as in a Kinship safe house, and three quarters of them were in use.

Sound dampeners had been hung from the ceiling, partitioning off a smaller section of Mahala. Their foamed plasscrete composition was augmented by electronic white sound. It was impossible to find a quiet spot in the main dining area at meal times, but on the other side of the dampeners, the noise level dropped to near silence.

Aideen led the way behind the dampeners. One look from her and the two trueborns sitting at the first table got up and took their bowls of spiced kel-grain elsewhere. Another glance from Aideen and a pair of bowls for her and Kayla appeared like magic, piled high with kel-grain and covered with synth-protein strips.

The relative quiet let the sparking images back into Kayla's mind, the elusive flashes of color dizzying. Kayla had to focus hard not to sway as she took her seat.

Aideen sat on the opposite side of the table. The first time they shared a meal, Aideen had sat beside her, and Kayla got up and put the table between them. The trueborn woman hadn't tried since then.

The kel-grain was skillfully spiced with turmeric and ground chaff seeds, the synth-protein portion generous. Kayla had learned early on in her healing process that food meant strength, so even if she hadn't been hungry, she would have cleaned her bowl.

She downed the white protein strips and half the kel-grain before finally lifting her gaze across the table to Aideen. "The hallucinations haven't gone away," she admitted.

"Are you seeing them now?" Aideen asked.

"Just on my periphery. The more noise there is around me, the less I can see them."

"Could it be," Aideen suggested, "that someone is trying to speak to you on your circuit-comm and it's malfunctioning? It's translating verbal communication into visual? One of the techs could take a look at it."

"I thought no one could tap into my circuit-comm without my passkey." The twenty-digit string was unique to each GEN and identified their DNA structure. "I haven't given it to anyone. Unless you've been passing it around."

Not long after Kayla emerged from the tank at Antara, Aideen had admitted how she'd gotten Kayla's passkey nearly a decade ago. She'd applied to the Judiciary Council and had had Kayla's records released to her, including the passkey. That was how she'd been able to contact Kayla via her circuit-comm when she'd been trapped in Akhilesh's gen-lab.

"I haven't been," Aideen insisted. "I would never give that out. Not without your permission."

Kayla's morning meal churned in her stomach. "How can I trust any promise from you, after you gave me away? After what you let the gene-splicers do to me?" Kayla could see the wounded look in Aideen's eyes, but the woman deserved that pain. "I don't ever want you reaching into my head again."

"I haven't been. I swear. Not since we brought you here."

"I never gave you permission to use my circuit-comm in the first place. Denking hell, I never asked to have FHE's programming installed. I didn't get to choose like you did." Kayla gestured toward Aideen's throat.

The woman brushed the slight bump centered just above her collarbone. It had sickened Kayla when she'd discovered Aideen had had a comm device implanted and connected to her own brain. It was crude compared to Kayla's GEN circuitry, but it allowed her to tap into GENs' circuit-comms without a wristlink.

Kayla narrowed her eyes on Aideen. "You think being a GEN is so wonderful, why not have the rest of the circuitry installed? Maybe put the mark on your face too."

"I'm sorry." The trueborn woman tipped her chin up, and Kayla saw where she'd inherited that defiant look. "I didn't mean to offend you."

Your existence offends me. Kayla kept the thought clamped down.

Aideen looked away, past Kayla. Kayla realized the chattering noise in Mahala had hushed. Those at the other tables behind the dampener privacy wall were turning in their chairs, all of them looking in the same direction as Aideen.

Kayla couldn't help herself—she felt a longing as Ohin approached. Even having just seen him less than an hour ago, her heart lifted at seeing him again. As those he passed murmured, "Always one with you," she understood that what she'd heard in the corridors hadn't been a prayer, but some kind of oath in solidarity with Ohin.

And great Infinite, she felt those same words on her own tongue. She gritted her teeth to keep from speaking them.

He was still out of earshot when Aideen leaned across the table toward Kayla. "If you decide to use the circuit-comm to communicate with me, with anyone, Seycat is always safe. I made sure of it."

Safe? From who?

Then Ohin was there. Aideen murmured the greeting the others had, and Ohin answered, "Until the day." For a moment, Kayla wondered if Aideen's smile was forced, but then seeing the brightness of the trueborn woman's eyes, her gaze as worshipful as any GEN with her prayer mirror, Kayla doubted it.

"Ohin!" Aideen said brightly, "did you work out that problem?"

"I wasn't needed after all," Ohin said. "And I didn't feel right cutting short my first visit with Kayla."

He laid a warm hand on Kayla's shoulder. This time the contact went on long enough that Kayla was about to shift out of his reach when he took his hand away.

Kayla looked up at him sidelong, wondering what it was about him that set off such adoration. His height was unusual, his blue eyes compelling. There was something in that intense gaze that made her feel he could solve any problem she might have.

Despite the GEN tattoo on Ohin's left cheek, the GEN leader reminded Kayla more of a high-status trueborn, like Zul, than any tankborn. Both men had that same imperious bearing and arrogance, despite their pretension that they were just another part of the group.

"On my way here, I gave some thought to your request to see your family," Ohin said. "Going back to Chadi seems impractical, though. We're still concerned about your health. That's why you haven't been given a work tour yet. We don't want you to overdo it until you've recovered."

She wondered if he or Aideen would ever consider her healthy enough to let her leave. "What about bringing my family here? I know people who could transport them secretly." Her lowborn friend, Risa, would bring Tala and Jal in her lorry, Kayla was sure of it.

Ohin's blue, blue gaze fixed on her face. Even having known Zul as long as she had, even seeing how the old man's power could mesmerize others, it was difficult not to feel as persuaded by Ohin's force of will as the crowd around them was. Several from the other side of the privacy wall were massed in the half-meter spaces between the dampening dividers, trying to catch a glimpse of him. Others stood at a greater distance, but all had their eyes on him.

Kayla tipped her chin up at Ohin, then lowered it again when she remembered Aideen using the gesture. "I think it would help having my nurture family close to me."

"It might."

What did that mean? That he would bring Tala and Jal here? Kayla would have asked him to clarify, but he got that distant look again that meant he was using his circuit-comm. She felt a vibration in the base of her skull again.

. . . both here . . .

The words zipped along her circuitry, not like the mishmash of images and sounds of her hallucinations. As clear as if someone nearby had spoken to her.

As if *Ohin* had spoken to her. In the flat tone of a circuit-comm communication that nevertheless had the flavor of Ohin's voice. Not quite emanating from where the circuit-comm had been installed, but as if it had blazed a path of its own.

But had he spoken? And how? Aideen had sworn she hadn't given out Kayla's passkey. But maybe in Aideen's mind, Ohin was an automatic exception.

Except it didn't look as if Ohin had intended to say anything to Kayla. He didn't even look her way. He just gave Aideen a brusque farewell before striding away. He moved along the dampeners, answering the greetings of the crowd knotted in the spaces between. Then he disappeared through one of the meeting room doors set in the back wall of Mahala.

Aideen watched every moment of his departure, as if she wanted her eyes on him for as long as he was in view. Kayla wondered if her birth mother loved Ohin, despite his being a GEN. If Aideen did, if she longed for him that way, what did it mean that it repelled her to touch her own GEN daughter?

Suddenly, Kayla couldn't stand to look at her birth mother another moment. She grabbed her bowl and spoon and carried them to the sterilizer basin. The crowd that had gathered to idolize Ohin had gone back to their tables, so there was no one between Kayla and the exit.

As she reached the quieter corridor, the images flashed around her again, a comfort after Ohin's apparent intrusion on her circuitry—at least these were her own creation. Kayla doubled her pace down the corridor, head down, not caring if those passing her thought she was crazy.

Five meters from the door to her quarters, the hallucinations started making sounds. Not along her circuitry like Ohin's voice had been. Like the images, the sounds came from her bare brain.

Luh. Yew. Lah. Those three fragments whirled around and around like a scattered puzzle of light and sound trying to remake itself.

Luh, yew, lah. Luh, yew, lah. Faster, louder, running together, breaking apart.

Then the image and the sounds came clear.

I love you, Kayla.

It was Devak's face. Devak's voice.

5

Groping for the rough limestone wall for support, Kayla
stumbled blindly the last several feet to Seycat. Her heart
felt ready to explode in her chest. Hope dizzied her, that Devak
was alive, that he was speaking to her via her circuit-comm.

She slipped inside her quarters and shut the door.
Closing her eyes, she listened hard, using the peculiar shift of
consciousness necessary to pick up communication from her
circuit-comm.

Could it really be Devak? He had her passkey, and he and
his friend Junjie were smart enough to have figured out how to
connect with her circuit-comm using a wristlink.

She gasped as she heard him again. *I love you, Kayla.*

She couldn't suppress her joyous smile. Fighting for focus,
she zeroed in on the circuit-comm's transmitter within her.
Devak! Is that you?

Silent seconds ticked away. It was almost painful holding
that intense listening focus.

Then he spoke again. *I love you, Kayla.*

There was something odd about the way he'd repeated

the words. Could he not have heard her? She focused harder, inwardly screamed out at him. *I'm here, Devak! Where are you?*

I love you, Kayla.

And then it hit her. The source of Devak's voice wasn't her circuit-comm. It was from her bare brain, and the intonation, the phrasing of the words, had been identical for all four repetitions.

As if it were a recording played back on a sekai. A recording of a boy long dead.

It wasn't Devak reaching out to her. Which left two possibilities. She'd created that voice herself with wishful thinking.

Or it was a real memory.

Medic Palla had told her the images Kayla had been seeing were nothing but hallucinations. But what if they were fragments of actual memories scattered in her bare brain? Would it be possible for her to put those fragments together and make sense of them? Or was her damaged brain like a defective holographic projection device? If image data in an HP was corrupted, the 3-dimensional hologram was too blurred to make out. It might be the same in her own brain— the memories too foggy to interpret.

Kayla's reset had not only completely wiped away her annexed brain, but it also had corrupted the "data" in her bare brain. Enough to scramble memories of conversations she'd had with Devak so much that she'd put together a phrase he'd never spoken in real life.

Devak had never told her he loved her. That supposed memory was a lie.

Kayla pushed off from the door and paced the room. She wanted dearly to pick up the cots, the dresser, even the mirror, and throw them, break them all if she could. But what good would it do?

Instead, she went to the mirror and took it carefully from the wall. She sat on her cot and rested the mirror in her lap.

Her tattoo glittered on her right cheek as she whispered at her reflection. "Sweet Infinite, please keep your hand over Tala and Jal. Keep them safe. And bless Mishalla, even though she's turned away from you."

She took in a long breath. "And Devak . . ." Her voice quavered. "If there's a way to bring a trueborn soul into your hands, to keep him for eternity with you, I beg that you take Devak's soul."

Her throat was too tight to say any more, so she returned the mirror to the wall. She was just hooking the mirror back over the dresser when Lovise entered.

"Do you need privacy?" Lovise had one hand on the door, ready to leave again to give Kayla a little more time alone.

"Just finished."

Lovise crossed to the desk and started checking the drawers. A head taller than Kayla, the broad-shouldered girl wore a gorgeous red shirt embroidered with black and silver-gray thread paired with tidy red leggings.

"You're not done with your work cycle, are you?" Kayla asked.

Lovise worked in the underground hydroponics lab, nurturing tanks of kel-grain and soy. "Barely started. I came back for my sekai." Her brow furrowed, Lovise moved her search to the dresser top.

Lovise routinely forgot the sekai in the room, and Kayla had more than once taken advantage of the GEN girl's absent-mindedness. A sekai wasn't a wristlink—which Aideen had so far refused Kayla—but a sekai's network function was nearly as good for communication. Unfortunately, Kayla hadn't been able to get a signal beyond the cavern walls.

Kayla spotted the palm-sized device on Lovise's cot, nearly concealed by the covers. "There it is."

As Kayla pulled the sekai out from under the blanket, an idea popped into her mind. The device hadn't been able to get an outside signal on Antara's lowest level. But maybe it would in the hydroponics lab, the next level up.

"Take me with you," Kayla said.

Lovise glanced worriedly at the sekai in Kayla's hands. "Take you where?"

"To the hydro lab. I'm sure there must be something I could help you with there."

"I don't know . . ." Lovise's gaze wandered to the sekai again.

Reluctantly, Kayla handed it over. "I'm going crazy with nothing to do. I've had enough rest. Please."

Lovise tucked the sekai into her breast band. "I should ask Ohin. Or at least Aideen."

"No, please," Kayla begged. "Aideen will just say no. She always does. We'll tell her later, then she'll be glad to hear I'm keeping busy. Ohin won't mind either, because I've got my strength back. Truly."

Lovise shifted foot to foot for a few moments, uncertainty clear on her face. Then she smiled. "Sure. That will be fun."

Lovise led the way from the room, then turned to the keypad to lock the door. Watching her, Kayla rubbed at the ever-present itch on her left arm.

"We hardly have anything in there worth locking up," Kayla pointed out. "And who here would steal from us?"

Lovise blushed, red washing over her pale cheeks. "I was never allowed a room with a locking door when I worked for trueborns." Lovise had a botany sket, and on the outside she'd tended fragile Earth plants in an experimental lab. She'd told Kayla she'd had no real quarters, just slept in a corner of the lab.

They started off down the corridor opposite the direction of Mahala. Most of the doors on either side led to private rooms and dormitories for the under-tens FHE had managed to rescue. There was a mechanical plant on the left that contained the power and air circulation equipment. Most of the cavern's power was generated via concealed aboveground solar panels and wind turbines, and hydro-electric using underground rivers.

Just as they reached the lift, Devak's voice whispered inside Kayla's head again. *I love you, Kayla.*

Knowing it was false, it broke her heart to hear it. She thrust aside the pain. "You were reset and restored, right?" she asked Lovise.

Lovise gave her a sideways glance. "That's what the medics here told me."

"*Told* you. You say that as if you didn't believe them."

"Of course I believed them." Lovise pursed her lips and stared at the lift door.

When the lift arrived a trueborn man exited, and out of habit Kayla guessed his rank. From his perfect skin color and sleek black hair, he was likely high-status, despite the lack of a diamond bali in his right earlobe. He gave Lovise and Kayla a cordial nod as he passed.

Kayla said softly to Lovise, "Don't they mind not wearing their balis?"

Lovise stepped into the lift and gestured Kayla inside. She pulled the outer and inner doors shut. "It makes no sense to wear signs of rank when we're all equal here."

"Then Ohin told them they couldn't wear them?"

Lovise's eyes widened, then she glanced at the ten-centimeter square black glass panel to the left of the door. No, not at the panel, but at the micro-controller embedded above it. Since the micro-controller linked all the powered systems—steam, electric, solar, and hydro—it must feed the lift as well.

Kayla tried to see over the taller girl's shoulder. "Is there something wrong with the lift?"

"The lift is fine," Lovise said, an edginess in her voice.

Too used to ordinary electricity, Kayla didn't quite trust the alternatives, especially steam. But she'd been lectured on the importance of conserving power and using the easier-to-produce alternatives. Where possible they used steam to operate machinery like the lift.

Lovise hunched away from Kayla to face the square of black glass, blocking Kayla's view with her broad shoulders. Kayla ducked a little so she could see past Lovise from her other side.

With a brush of the tall girl's fingers against the glass, a keypad displayed. That at least must be run on electricity. The girl's fingers flew over the keys, typing in an access code so fast Kayla could only read and memorize part of the sequence.

Lovise threw the lever to start the car rising, and Kayla stumbled at the lift's first lurch. It crept slowly upward.

"But if it wasn't," Kayla persisted, "how would we get out?"

"Someone would come for us," Lovise said. "They'd crank the car up or down by hand."

That wasn't particularly comforting. Kayla didn't like the idea of relying on anyone's strength but her own. "What if they didn't know we were stuck in here?"

Lovise huffed with impatience. "There's an escape hatch."

She pointed up. "And a ladder in the shaft. I don't recommend it. Rat-snakes make nests in the ladder rungs."

Kayla glanced up and saw the hinged hatch above them, a simple latch keeping it in place. A release handle hung down from a chain, low enough for most people, but Kayla would have to jump pretty high to grab it.

Lovise gave the micro-controller another glance and for a moment Kayla worried about the lift again. But then it hit her—every time Kayla asked a question, or hinted at criticism of Ohin, Lovise eyed the dark spot that hid the micro-controller.

A chill fingered down Kayla's spine. Did the micro-controllers double as listening devices?

Great Infinite, the controllers were everywhere. All along the corridors, *in her own quarters!* She felt sick that they might be listening to her every move.

And Aideen had just told her that Seycat was safe if she wanted to talk. No . . . she'd said talking via the GEN circuit-comm was safe in Seycat. But did that mean that in the public areas even their circuit-comms were tapped into? How could that be if they only gave out their passkey to a select few? Could it be that the communications could be intercepted as messages traveled between one GEN and another?

Should she ask Lovise straight out? But the girl might lie. Even if Lovise told the truth, that would let Ohin's people know that Kayla knew she was being monitored. It might be better if he didn't know. She would have to guard her words, assume that anything she said would get back to him.

Kayla circled her mind back to her question about being reset. Surely Ohin already knew about Kayla's hallucinations. So talking to Lovise about it wouldn't reveal much more to him. She might as well ask.

"Since you've been restored, Lovise, have you had memories of things that happened before? Or that you think happened? Like something someone might have said to you?"

Lovise waved her hand dismissively. "Nonsense words. Bits and pieces my mind puts together. It doesn't fit with anything else the medics had saved for me and uploaded."

"So you don't think there's anything from before that wasn't in the FHE restoration upload?"

The lift had finally shuddered to a stop. Lovise didn't seem to be in a hurry to open the doors. "Nothing that matters. If it was important enough to remember, I would have moved the memory from my bare brain and stored it in my annexed brain."

Except for what she might have wanted kept private. Because the annexed brain contained circuitry, anything stored in that brain partition could be read by an outsider via a datapod download. Even though FHE-modified GENs could deny permission and block a download, Lovise might not have archived everything to her annexed brain in order to protect its privacy. The risk was losing everything when a reset erased the annexed brain and damaged the bare brain enough to destroy the memories.

"You don't think those hallucinations I've been having mean anything?" Kayla asked. "Like something in my bare brain might have survived the reset?"

"That gene-splicer who reset you knew plenty about how to scramble your bare brain. Enough that whatever was stored in there is gone forever."

Kayla knew that, had witnessed enough resettings to understand the process. "Every GEN I've met here has told me they were reset before they arrived. Why hasn't FHE rescued any GENs before they're reset? It would have been nice to come here with my bare brain intact."

"You got your annexed brain back," Lovise said, pulling open the doors. "You should be happy with that."

Kayla couldn't let it go. "Are you happy?"

Lovise strode from the lift, then turned back toward Kayla. "I have some new supplies. Do you feel up to storing some heavy crates away for me?"

Kayla considered pulling shut the lift doors again, to see if she could reconstruct the access code to activate the steam motor. But it wouldn't do her much good, not when the lift lever only had two settings, up and down. It seemed it only traveled between the lowest level and this one just above it.

Kayla started toward Lovise. "Glad to help."

And she was. Once, Kayla would have been irritated to be asked to tote and carry, as if she were nothing more than a strong pair of arms. But now she relished the chance to use her sket, to have the work help build her back to where she'd been before.

Lovise led the way down unfamiliar corridors. Most of the doors were open here, the well-lit rooms full of computers, light-scopes, and lase tools spread out on tables. The door to one room was just closing as they passed it and the glimpse Kayla caught of what was inside made her shudder—rows of gen-tanks. There were people floating in the ones she'd spied.

Kayla stopped, transfixed by the closed door. "Were we in there?"

Lovise turned to come back for her. "You were. I was in the other Maramata room across the way."

Now Kayla saw the placard—Maramata 2, and across the corridor, Maramata 1. Kayla both felt compelled and repelled by the gen-labs. She wouldn't have the use of two arms without the tank she'd been immersed in, not to mention have the damage to her bare brain repaired. But there was always the question of what else the trueborn medics might have done when she was so vulnerable.

Kayla lowered her voice. "Do you trust them? FHE? Ohin?"

Lovise narrowed her gaze down toward Kayla. "Why wouldn't I?"

"That's no answer."

Lovise's pace slowed, and she spoke so softly, Kayla had to strain to hear. "Can we ever trust trueborns?"

All too aware of the listening controllers, Kayla said just as softly, "The medics and gen-techs might be trueborns, but Ohin's not. Do you trust him?"

"I am always one with him," Lovise said, parroting the greeting Kayla had heard repeated again and again in Antara. "That is enough for me."

Lovise hurried on, stopping at a bend in the corridor, waiting for Kayla to catch up. Lovise opened a door labeled Kheta 3.

As she stepped into the room, Lovise all but bellowed, "Always one with him!" Those working in the room looked up long enough to call out the same greeting. Kayla couldn't help but wonder if they all truly believed that about Ohin or if their declarations were for the benefit of those hidden listening devices.

If they even existed. Sometimes Kayla's own innate distrust of trueborns made her suspicious where she had no need to be. But considering Lovise's quick scan around the low arching ceiling as they entered, the GEN girl must have believed that what she said aloud had a consequence.

The Kheta room was expansive, maybe a quarter the size of Mahala, and twice as long as it was wide. One- by three-meter grow tanks stretched in long rows, their fifty-centimeter depth about half that of a gen-tank. GENs and trueborns worked side-by-side tending the plants.

"You were mainly a city girl, weren't you?" Lovise said, nudging Kayla into the room with a hand on her shoulder. "I bet you've never seen kel-grain or soy growing."

Kayla had seen plenty of it. Her and Risa's Kinship-assigned missions took them past huge agricultural fields in four of Svarga's five territories. The grain and soybeans grew in massive tracts of adhikar land, acres bequeathed to trueborns at birth, the adhikar sized according to their rank in society.

But for Kayla to reveal how often she'd seen those two staple crops growing meant confessing she'd been part of the Kinship. She still wasn't sure just how much FHE knew of that other organization. Because of Devak, if for no other reason, she still felt a loyalty to the Kinship, so she kept what she knew to herself.

"How does this all work?" Kayla asked instead.

Lovise seemed happy enough to give her a tour, pointing out the illuminators hanging from the ceiling that directed heat and brilliant light down on the plants. The clear solution filling the tanks provided the same nutrients as soil would. The plants were supported by a screen that allowed them to send their roots deep into the liquid.

The special solution and the hydroponic method allowed the techs to grow triple the plants that could be grown in soil, Lovise told Kayla. And they grew twice as large, reaching up to the illuminators as if the warm lights were Loka's brother suns. Some plants were so tall, they nearly brushed the ceiling.

Lovise plucked a pod from a soy plant and cracked it open. She offered a couple of the beans to Kayla. The soft round beans tasted creamy and slightly salty, nothing like the synth-protein they were used to make.

Lovise emptied the rest of the beans into her mouth, then tossed the empty shell into a composting box. "Harvesting duty is my favorite part of the job."

"Is this enough to feed everyone in Antara?" As many people as Kayla saw during meals, even this lush growth didn't seem to be nearly enough.

"There are two other Kheta rooms," Lovise said.

"Even so, what's growing in here isn't even all ready for harvest. If it's the same in the other rooms—"

Lovise headed off between long rows of hydroponic soy plants. "Let me show you what I need moved."

Her questions unanswered, Kayla had no choice but to follow. They made their way along the back wall, where techs in float chairs hunched over lase-scopes or tapped away at computer holo-boards. Images of DNA shifted on their holo-screens.

Kayla hung back a little to get a better look at the displays. "Are they regenning the plants for better yield?"

Lovise came back for her, an alarmed expression on her face when she saw Kayla's focus on the techs' displays. "Yes, of course." Lovise clutched Kayla's arm to pull her away from the computer screens.

Before Lovise took her out of view, one word jumped out at Kayla—*fungus*. She remembered something about fungus being an issue if kel-grain got too much rain for several days without any time to dry out in between. Maybe the techs were working on genning kel-grain more resistant to that problem.

In the back corner of the room, a door hung open, shelving

and cabinetry marking it as a storeroom. Crates were stacked just inside the door.

"These are all chemicals for the nutrient solution," Lovise said. "The crates need to be unpacked and stored away on the shelves. Everything is labeled."

"How does FHE get all this in here?" Kayla asked.

"The lifts, I suppose," Lovise said.

"Don't be stupid. I mean how do they get their hands on it? Get it into Antara without anyone seeing." As many people as were housed in Antara, wouldn't someone notice?

Lovise didn't answer, but something in the way her eyes shifted told Kayla that the GEN girl knew quite a lot more than she was willing to say. Kayla wanted even more desperately to get her hands on Lovise's sekai. No one would see her using it in the storage room.

"Could I borrow—"

"Thanks for helping," Lovise said, then turned on her heel and walked away.

Could Lovise have had an inkling of what Kayla had in mind? In any case, her whole purpose of coming up here had been foiled.

She might as well do the work she'd promised. Checking the labels on the crates, she moved them from their stack and set them in front of the shelves where their contents belonged. Then she broke the seals on the crates and unpacked the plasscine bottles.

Those were commercial labels and seals on the crates. From what she could make out of the data coded on the labels, they'd originated in various mixed sectors—Sheysa, Creth, Plator. Maybe they'd been purchased legitimately. Perhaps there was a warehouse aboveground that was used to stage materials for

Antara, disguised as having some other purpose.

Just as she stowed the last bottles, one of the techs came into the storage room. The trueborn woman—a demi-status with thick dark hair to her waist—nodded in greeting, then pulled two boxes of powdered nitrates from a shelf. She turned to go, stopping at the exit to open an access panel.

There was a sekai inside it, one of the larger thirty-by-twenty-centimeter models, installed in the wall. Kayla had seen the access panel, but had assumed it was a door lock mechanism.

The woman studied the box labels, then ran her fingers over the sekai's input plate. She turned to Kayla and gestured at the emptied crates. "Have you entered all this into inventory?"

"I was about to," Kayla lied. "But Lovise didn't give me a password to the sekai."

"Use mine," the woman said, then walked out, leaving the access panel open.

Kayla poked her head out the door. If Lovise was anywhere around, Kayla couldn't see her.

Swinging the door nearly shut, Kayla scanned the sekai screen, praying to the Infinite that it had a network function. It might not if it was used mainly for inventory.

But she found the familiar icon and when she tapped it, a comm interface displayed on the screen. She didn't dare use voice or video, not when she might be heard. She'd have to send a text message.

But who could she reach? Devak's great-grandfather, Zul, made the most sense. She still had his wristlink code stored away in her annexed brain. He would have the power to send someone after her.

But when she entered Zul's code, the sekai responded

with *Invalid entry*. Did that mean the network function wasn't working after all? Or could Zul have changed his code?

For a fleeting moment, she thought to contact Devak, then suffered through the pain of remembering once again that he was lost to her. She redirected her thoughts to who else she could call.

There was only one other person she knew she could trust her life with. Mishalla, her heart-deep best friend. Not long after Mishalla had been converted from a GEN to a lowborn, Zul had given Mishalla a wristlink.

Kayla entered in Mishalla's memorized code. To Kayla's everlasting relief, the sekai's network function responded with *Connecting*.

Her hope that Mishalla would immediately respond was dashed when the sekai displayed the message, *Connection in use*. Mishalla was communicating with someone else. Kayla would have to just send a message and hope her friend got it.

As Kayla dithered over what to say, the familiar pattern of Lovise's footsteps approached. "Kayla?"

With quick, awkward jabs Kayla typed out, *Need help! —K*, then hit send. Lovise called again, "Kayla, are you still in here?"

Lovise would step inside any moment, but the message was still sending. The thick limestone walls must be diminishing the signal.

Even as the *Sending* message still displayed, Kayla pressed the terminate icon for the network function. She returned to the sekai's home screen and shut the access panel just before Lovise came through the door.

The girl narrowed her blue gaze on Kayla, as if she suspected Kayla had been up to something. "Aideen found out you were here, and she wasn't happy."

"I'll go talk to her. Tell her it was my fault."

Kayla started to walk out, but Lovise grabbed a handful of Kayla's shirt and pulled her back. The girl might not have Kayla's sket, but she was strong.

"I know you wanted my sekai, and I know why," Lovise said. "Were you using that one? Did you send someone a message?"

Kayla shook her head, but Lovise opened the access panel and tapped the network icon on the sekai. When the communication interface came up, there was Kayla's message still trying to send.

Lovise halted the send and deleted the message, then powered off the sekai for good measure. She slammed shut the access panel.

"This is your home now," Lovise said. "These are your people. Get used to it."

Lovise gave Kayla a none-too-gentle nudge from the storage room. She shut the door and tapped the keypad to lock it from the outside. Then she prodded Kayla down the long rows of tanks and out into the corridor.

"You don't really believe that, do you?" Kayla asked as they hustled down the corridor toward the lift. "That this is your home?" How could she when they were prisoners here?

Lovise waited until they back at the lift. She glanced up left and right at the micro-controllers set high in the wall. Then her expression got mean, all trace of friendliness gone.

"This is more than my home," Lovise said in a hard-edged voice. "And you'd better start feeling that way too. Because you're part of FHE now, whether you like it or not. You are always one with Ohin, and if he wants you here, he will never let you leave."

By the time Devak and Junjie got clear of the escape tunnel and made their way back to Pitamah's house, Devak was exhausted, every muscle screaming in pain. Pitamah hadn't returned yet, but Devak didn't think he had the energy to tell his great-grandfather what he and Junjie had figured out about Aideen. Devak didn't know yet what the next step should be anyway, so he endured Junjie's help getting him showered, then dressed in a long sleep shirt before he collapsed in his bed.

When Devak woke, Pitamah's medic friend, Jemali, stood over his bed holding what looked like some sort of primitive weapon. It had a tube the length of Devak's hand, about as big around as a half-dhan coin. A long needle protruded from one end.

"What is that?" Devak asked, instinctively cringing away from the tall, gaunt high-status trueborn.

"An old instrument for spinal injections," Jemali said.

Now Devak recognized it. He'd seen an image of it during an Academy network lecture. It was a syringe. And on the heels of that recollection came a realization of how syringes had been used.

"You can't mean to put that in my back." The glinting needle seemed to grow in size. Panic clutched at Devak. "Pitamah! *Pitamah!*"

His great-grandfather hurried into the room, Junjie on his heels. The old man looked haggard and distraught seeing the instrument in Jemali's hands. Junjie looked sick.

"Is there another way, Jemali?" Pitamah asked.

Jemali set the thing aside on the dresser. "You know the choices. It would be best to fix his back in the gen-tank. Barring that, we could infuse the same compound we gave him yesterday via vac-seals."

Pitamah, a taller man than Jemali, seemed to shrink in size. "And you know I haven't the dhans for either one."

"But I do," Jemali said.

A long quiet moment, then Pitamah passed a hand over his face. "I can't keep letting you do that. You'll lose your status too."

"Do you think that matters to me?" Jemali asked.

"One of us has to hold onto it," Pitamah said. "Or the Kinship will crumble even more."

Devak rolled onto his side, laboriously pushing himself up and dropping his legs over the side of the bed. "What do you mean? What's happened to the Kinship?"

Pitamah sat at the foot of the bed. "I think we've been infiltrated by those opposed to the cause. I thought at first it was just the fact that the Manels had lost so much face, so much wealth. But at the meeting last night, it was clear that at least half of those attending—all high-status—had no interest in GEN or lowborn rights. On the contrary, they want even more restrictions."

"So if Jemali's status dropped down," Devak guessed, "that would be one less voice for GENs."

Pitamah nodded. "Our friend Hala was so disgraced by his association with Akhilesh he's barely high-status now. He can't risk being involved in the Kinship. People are watching him." Akhilesh, head of GAMA, had tricked Hala into helping him with an illegal scheme to harvest punarjanma, a rejuvenation fluid, from GENs.

"Jemali needs to keep his status," Devak said. "And I need my back healed. The injections are the best choice." Even as he said it, he cringed inside.

Devak looked up at the old medic. "Will this hurt as much as what you used on me yesterday?" That pain at least had been bearable.

Jemali shook his head. "The syringe will be worse."

Devak struggled to take a breath. He angled his gaze up at Pitamah. "Do you still have my sekai?"

Pitamah's eyes widened ever so slightly, and Devak could see some calculation in them. "It's lost. I haven't been able to find it since we moved here."

Devak hung his head. "There was an image of Kayla on it. I thought if I could look at her during the injections . . ."

Junjie started fumbling with the latch on his wristlink. "We could find an image of her in the GEN database."

Pitamah put out a hand to stop him. "She's been declared destroyed. Her records have been deleted."

"Except . . . did Junjie tell you what we figured out last night about Kayla?"

"He did." Pitamah drew the words out. Was that disapproval in his tone? Doubt?

"Do you think we're wrong? That FHE had nothing to do with taking her body?" Devak asked.

A long hesitation, then Pitamah said, "I think you're

having a hard time accepting her death. That perhaps you're leaping to conclusions that are on unstable ground. Her ashes have already been sent up to the Infinite." Yet another twist of sorrow added to Devak's grief. The agony of the injections would at least tear that sadness away for a short time. "Let's get it over with."

He had to lie face down, which was painful to start with. Pitamah and Junjie sat opposite Jemali, Junjie holding Devak's hand. Jemali washed Devak's back over and over with cold, wet sterilizing cloths, then finally dried him and readied the syringe. Devak shut his eyes as the vile instrument came closer.

With the first insertion of the needle, Devak gripped Junjie's hand so tightly he was sure he would break a bone. Then Jemali injected the fluid and Devak swallowed a scream as the liquid burned into his back.

He barely had a chance to catch his breath before Jemali moved the needle down his spine. It wasn't just the one injection. Jemali said he needed it in every vertebra. Devak thought he might get used to the pain, but the second injection was worse than the first. He wanted to die by the fourth or fifth, which would have been a blessed relief—the pain would be gone, and maybe he could see Kayla again. But Jemali's treatment went on and on until he lost count of the needle stabs.

When it was finally over, his entire spine was on fire, and the agonizing heat radiated throughout his body. He wept, uncaring that Junjie or Pitamah saw his tears. Then when Jemali laid the dressing on, light as uttama-silk, Devak screamed at its weight.

The bed shifted as Pitamah rose. "Is that the end of it? You won't have to do that again, will you?"

"No, not again," Jemali said, and Devak almost wept again.

"I wouldn't be able to get the medication anyway. That was expired and meant to be destroyed."

Devak shifted his eyes enough to look up at Jemali. "But it will work?"

"It should," Jemali said. "With a month of bed rest."

"A week," Devak said.

Jemali sighed. "Two."

"Ten days."

"Ten days." Jemali bent over the bed. "But if you set a toe during that time anywhere besides the sleeproom or the washroom, I'll sedate you."

Devak nodded. Willing his body to heal, he drifted off to a restless sleep.

four weeks later

Flat on his back on the floor, knees bent and toes pressed against the wall of his sleeproom, Devak curled up until his chin touched his knees. "Twenty-three." He slowly lowered himself to the floor again, sweat pouring down his face and the muscles in his back and belly trembling with the effort.

Seven more. An impossible task. Or it would be, if not for Kayla.

His fantasy of her, anyway. In his imagination, Kayla held his feet as he curled up again. She smiled at him, encouraging him, the silver tattoo on her right cheek shimmering against her creamy brown skin in the noon light.

The first three days after the injections had been torture, Devak unable to get out of bed even to use the necessary. Junjie had had to help him with the bedpot, and even though his friend would leave the room, the awkwardness of it filled

Devak with shame. The pain in his back was so great, he would hallucinate, see his scornful mother or his disapproving father standing over the bed.

He would have gone mad if he hadn't forced away the illusions and put Kayla in their place. He would smile at her, imagine touching her, even though he was too weak to even reach out.

On the fourth day after Jemali's treatment, Devak discovered he could bend his back, as long as he didn't mind the excruciating pain it caused. At least he could get up to use the necessary himself, although Junjie or Pitamah had to hold his arm on the way there and wait right outside the door. He would picture Kayla on his other side, lending him her strength as she escorted him, waiting outside the door for him to finish.

On the fifth day, Devak felt almost human, and made his first trip to the washroom alone, although Pitamah scolded him afterward. Despite the throbbing in his back, Devak joined Junjie and Pitamah at the kitchen table for a meal, sitting in a chair well-padded with pillows. It was only kel-grain and gamey ground drom, but after four days of nothing but kel-grain gruel, it tasted delicious. In his mind, he saw Kayla at the empty place at the table, smiling at him, her gray eyes soft.

By the eighth day, Devak felt so good, he decided he must be fully healed. With Junjie gone to work, Devak climbed from bed on his own. He dressed himself, making sure to tuck his identity chip in the hem of his shirt where he'd loosened a few stitches to make a pocket. Longing to be outdoors, he decided to go out on his own when he saw Pitamah was still asleep.

But two blocks later, he realized he'd overestimated his strength. He all but dragged himself back to Pitamah's house, ready to crawl into bed. But Pitamah had woken and gave Devak another scold as he followed Devak into the sleeproom.

That folly had set Devak back another two days, so that Jemali got the two weeks' rest he'd wanted from Devak. When Jemali laid out a two-week schedule of rehabilitation, Devak didn't argue. He performed the exercises exactly as Jemali had stipulated, working through unbearable pain. The Kayla of his imagination would always be there goading him, demanding he work even harder.

"Twenty-nine," he gasped, Kayla counting with him. "Thirty."

Just as Devak touched his chin to his knees that last time, Junjie walked in and spoiled Devak's illusion of Kayla. Devak curled back to the floor and lay on the worn carpet, completely spent.

Junjie flopped onto the bed beside him. "Where's Zul?"

"Lunch with Councilor Mohapatra. Get your shoes off my bed." Devak rolled to his side, then up to a sitting position. "Any more ideas on finding that boy?"

Junjie had been trying to track down the boy who used to be his FHE contact, a boy whose name Junjie never even knew. The boy had always passed Junjie on to Neta, the woman they now suspected was Kayla's mother, Aideen Kalu. So the boy was their only connection to FHE.

Junjie shoved his shoes off onto the floor and turned to face Devak. "You know that old saying about how when your only tool is a datapod, every problem looks like an upload?"

"Yeah."

"Well, my only tool is a wristlink call ID," Junjie went on. "And over the past four weeks, I've called it every day, all different times. He's never answered. The last few days, the call didn't go through at all, just answered to dead air." Junjie sighed. "Then today, someone else answered. A man, some ancient high-status Mar. Insisted he'd had that wristlink ID for a century or something."

Devak heart sank. "Isn't there some other way to find the boy?"

"Believe me, if there was, I'd use it." The emphatic way Junjie made that declaration tickled a suspicion in Devak. Maybe the boy meant more to Junjie than just a connection to FHE.

Devak tucked that away. "Did you ask the old trueborn if his ID matched the one you called?"

Junjie slapped his forehead. "Great Infinite, I never even thought of it. The old sanaki seemed so insulted that I'd called him, I hardly got in a word before he disconnected."

"Your FHE friend, was he clever enough to re-route his ID?" Devak asked.

"Oh, yeah. That's exactly what he'd do. I know I would, to throw off someone I didn't want to talk to." Disappointment flickered in Junjie's eyes. "But he's not my friend."

"We can't keep calling him *that boy*."

Junjie pondered a moment. "Call him Shun."

Shun—*agreeable*. Although how agreeable had the boy been when he wouldn't answer Junjie's calls?

Throwing out a hand for Junjie's help, Devak got to his feet. "I have an idea how we might find Shun," Devak said. "Grab a couple of the kitchen chairs."

While Junjie got them something to sit on, Devak woke up the old computer Pitamah had given him. Devak remembered it as one that had been stuffed away down in the basement of the big Foresthill house and more recently under Pitamah's bed in the smaller Two Rivers house. The computer was slow and the storage chips sometimes put out an alarming whine, but it worked, and the holographic projection screen was touch-responsive. And despite his time in the tank, Devak hadn't lost his skills at hacking into systems and databases he had no business snooping into.

Junjie set the kitchen chairs down in front of the desk holding the computer, and they both settled in. "What's your idea?" Junjie asked.

"Dig into the communications network," Devak said, laying his hands on the holographic keyboard. "See if I can reconstruct the re-routing algorithm Shun used so we can direct a call to his actual ID without the spoofing."

The HP had been knocked around enough that the holo image of the keyboard and display were both blurry. Some of the keyboard characters were almost invisible. That made it more of a challenge to position his fingers correctly as he typed in commands. But he could operate even a primitive computer like this old one in his sleep. His hands seemed to know where to go on the keyboard with only infrequent mistakes.

"Okay," Devak said, typing rapidly. "I'm in the comm network. Read me Shun's call ID." Junjie called out the ten-digit sequence, and Devak entered it.

An intricate three-dimensional map flashed onto the holographic display, nodes represented by a myriad of varying sized circles with lines interconnecting them, overlay upon overlay of complexity. Devak scanned the incomprehensible map. "Your friend doesn't do things halfway, does he?"

"He's not my friend," Junjie protested.

"But you'd like him to be," Devak said.

"How could I?" Junjie blurted out, looking miserable. "He's FHE, and they're the ones who hurt you and killed Kayla."

"As far as you know, did *he* ever set a bomb?" Devak asked.

Junjie scruffed up his already messy hair. "I don't know. He never said. Except . . ."

"Except?"

"I could tell he didn't like it. Sometimes we'd talk a few minutes while waiting for Neta—for Aideen to come on. Once I brought up the bombings, and he said they were a stupid, bad idea. That they'd hurt someone eventually. And right after he and I talked, that little girl was killed."

An ache started up in Devak's chest as he recalled the sixth-year GEN girl lying pale and still after the Nafi sector bombing of her warren. The girl's nurture father had been distraught and angry, as close as a GEN could be to outright rebellion.

"Do you think good ends can justify bad means?" Devak asked. "The FHE wants freedom for GENs, so they forced that programming on Kayla to make her immune to the monitoring Grid, to forced uploads and downloads. They set off explosives in GEN sectors to make the GENs angry enough to revolt. All for the GENs' benefit."

"They killed people," Junjie said. "That wipes away anything good about them."

"But your friend—" At Junjie's scowl, Devak changed his words. "You said yourself, Shun didn't like the bombings."

"But he was still FHE."

"So were you. And I forgave you."

"Maybe you shouldn't have," Junjie said. "Maybe I don't deserve it."

Devak waved off Junjie's misery, feeling time pressing on him. "I need to focus on untangling this comm map. Maybe you could get us something to eat."

As complicated as the map was, the work to decode its structure was rote. A series of algorithms read the nodes, loaded them into a database, deleted any identical records, and sorted the remaining rows into a table. Devak had done this before, except it was GEN IDs he was sorting, living beings instead of comm devices.

After he'd set up the processes and the computer worked on its own, he had his hands free to wolf down a bowl of kelgrain and some kind of dark brown meat that didn't look like drom. If he had to guess, it was probably rat-snake, and likely it was Junjie who'd gone hunting for the vermin. Devak didn't ask. What did it matter? Junjie wouldn't have served it unless it was wholesome. And it was tasty enough, just a little gamier than drom.

While he and Junjie shared a sweet, juicy redfruit, Devak let himself imagine Kayla there. She'd be sitting on the workstation, swinging her legs and bumping his knee with her feet while she enjoyed his offered bites of redfruit. Or she could be standing behind him, looking over his shoulder, her hands on the back of his chair, and he could lean against her fingers.

The computer's series of beeps drew Devak out of his fantasy. The comm network was displayed on the screen again, but now, a bright line delineated a path through the 3D structure, from node to node to node.

Devak traced his finger along the bright line suspended in the holographic display. He gestured at its terminus. "There he is."

"But where is that?" Junjie asked. "It still just looks like a bunch of wristlink IDs."

With a gesture of his fingers across the touch-responsive display, Devak swiped the bright line into a processing algorithm. "Except now I have a path. Now I can use it to track Shun's physical location."

7

"Just like that, you can find him?" Junjie's voice rose with excitement.

"Not exactly." Devak tapped at the keyboard. "That was a snapshot of where he was yesterday. If my algorithms can figure out a pattern in how he re-routed his ID, then I can overlay that pattern on a physical map of the send-receive towers. It might give me enough information to triangulate on his location. Well, where he was yesterday, at least."

Now Junjie hovered over Devak's shoulder, the way Devak had imagined Kayla doing. When the methodical process of teasing out the patterns in the comm path dragged on, Junjie's usual restlessness kicked in, and his pacing started wearing a path in the already thin carpet.

Devak turned in his chair and put out an arm to stop Junjie. "Don't you have to get back to work?"

Junjie checked his wristlink. "Denking hell. Later than I thought. Guru Aboya will have my neck."

"This will take a while. I might find a way to use Shun's spoof pattern to call him before I figure out where he actually is." Devak tipped his head toward the wristlink Junjie wore on his left arm. "I could use that."

Junjie's hand closed over the device. "Don't you think I should be the one to talk to him? I mean, he knows me."

"And he's been avoiding you."

"But if you call him from my wristlink, he still won't answer."

"Don't you think I know how to spoof the source of a wristlink call?" Devak asked.

"Yeah, I guess." With clear reluctance, Junjie handed the device to Devak. "You wouldn't go anywhere without me?"

Devak latched the wristlink to his own arm. "I'll wait for you."

"Shun's code is programmed in there. So's the lab's if you need me."

Junjie dawdled a few more seconds, probably hoping something would happen while he waited, then hurried out. Once he was gone, Devak could recreate his fantasies of Kayla, imagine her talking him through the problem of deciphering the tangle of Shun's spoof.

She would lean over his shoulder, staring at the holo display with those intense gray eyes. She might ask him, *What do all those criss-crossing lines mean?*

He'd explain that it was a state machine, and where the lines intersected, the "state" was a particular routing of one of Shun's calls. The more lines coming into a state point, the more often Shun had used that routing. The more times he used a particular call relay station, the more likely he was physically near it.

Kayla would nod, understanding his explanation, no matter how complex. Partly because her annexed brain had so much information stored that she could tap, but also because she was smart and so good at making mental connections.

Devak's gaze moved across the display from state point to state point. There was no way he could discern the spoof pattern better or faster than the computer could, but sometimes when staring at a problem his human mind could put things together in a way a computer couldn't. Make connections like Kayla did.

Almost as if she was whispering in his ear, a realization popped into Devak's mind. A couple of the most thickly clustered state points were located in GEN sectors. The Brigade had netcams installed in GEN sectors, particularly inside and outside the warrens.

What if Devak tapped into the database of netcam images? What if by some chance an image of Shun had actually been captured? A non-Brigade, minor-status boy would stick out in a GEN warren like a rat-snake in a high-status kitchen.

Devak launched the netcam hacking program he'd gotten from Pitamah. Devak had refined it to not only access live feeds, but the database where the images were stored. He could correlate the time and location info in the netcam database with the state points where the map showed the most intersections in GEN sectors.

It looked like Shun had spent time in Qaf, Fen, and Beqal. Fen had the most intersections, so that was what Devak used to correlate.

Because the computer was still untangling Shun's communication spoof, it took an hour of crunching before images started spitting out. To save space, the database had stored just the faces, in some cases shadowy and out of focus, in others, sharp and bright. GEN adults, GEN over-tens who were not yet old enough to be Assigned but often did work in their own sectors, GEN under-tens, and tiny children in their nurture parents' arms.

His eyes grew bleary scanning them before it crossed his mind to use the computer to scan for the GENs' DNA marks and discard those. That left faces of GENs with their tattooed cheek turned away, the occasional Brigade enforcers, and medics. Devak made quick work of discarding those.

Then an untattooed face enlarged on the display and Devak's hand froze. A boy, maybe a fifteenth-year, staring full-faced up at the netcam as if he knew it was there. No tattoo, and wasn't that a sapphire bali in his right ear?

Devak grinned and suppressed the urge to get up and do a dance. Junjie would be thrilled to see this. He could finally know what Shun looked like—the light brown skin about Kayla's color, straight brown hair to his shoulders, dark eyes.

With a swipe of his fingers, Devak copied the image from the netcam database to the computer. Then he sent a copy of the image to the wristlink as well. He couldn't wait to show it to Junjie.

He imagined Kayla beside him again, giving his shoulder a squeeze at his good work. Lord Creator, he wished he had an image of her too. He could try the netcam database, but the odds were even worse for finding her in an image. By now, months after her death, any images of her would likely have been purged.

He'd stored a holo of her on his sekai, an image he'd filched from her GEN file back when she was caring for Pitamah. That was nearly a year ago now.

He'd had a duplicate on his wristlink, but he'd worn that device the day of the explosion. Pitamah told him it had been damaged beyond use or repair.

So where could the sekai be? Pitamah had said he hadn't seen it since the move. That could mean they'd lost it back at Two Rivers, or maybe it had made its way here but had been misplaced. Considering the chaos of having to move while keeping his tank sessions ongoing, Devak could imagine the sekai being stowed away somewhere, then forgotten.

He set the computer running through yet another automated process and pushed away from the workstation to search for the sekai. Could it be stuffed somewhere in the dresser and he'd never come across it? Doubtful, but he looked there anyway, thumbing through each pile of clothes, both his and Junjie's, and running his hand along the bottoms and sides of the drawers.

He took a look under the beds next, pulling out the heavier winter blankets that had been stuffed there, shaking them out. The little table between the beds had a drawer and a cubby, but the cubby was empty. The drawer contained nothing but the innards and cases of several defunct datapods, plus the mini-holo that displayed an image of Junjie's mother.

In the living room, Devak flipped up sofa cushions, ran a hand along the crevices where a sekai could have fallen. There was nothing in the four kitchen cupboards—two up, two down—but a sparse collection of pots, pans, and cooking tools.

Which left Pitamah's room. Devak had been in and out of his great-grandfather's sleeproom back in Foresthill. But that was when Pitamah was bedridden. When they lived in Two Rivers, Devak waited for an invitation to enter Pitamah's private space, even when he knew the old man needed his help. To enter without permission, then search the room, seemed disrespectful and wrong.

Stalling, Devak checked the computer's progress,

reinitiating the winnowing process when he saw it had finished the previous phase. Then he went down the hall to Pitamah's room, nudging open the partially closed door.

His great-grandfather was as messy here as he'd been in both Foresthill and Two Rivers. Dirty bowls, a glass vase filled with dried chaff flowers, and a paper book cluttered the bedside table. Devak recognized the paper book as Pitamah's old journal from the days when GENs were first created. Clothing draped over the top of the dresser, the arms of kortas tangled with the legs of chera pants. Wind chimes hung from the ceiling, dangling crystals reflecting the afternoon sun through the high window.

Devak didn't see any paper books other than the journal. Pitamah must have sold the rest of the precious things, their value too great for them to be held back. Those books had meant more to Pitamah than anything. Anything except his great-grandson, Devak realized, since Pitamah had sold them for Devak's months in the gen-tank.

When he didn't spot the sekai with a casual scan of the room, Devak checked the drawer of the bedside table and under the clothes on the dresser. When he still didn't see it, he hesitated. Should he look through the dresser drawers?

Where would Kayla look? He pictured her there, standing beside him. Memories of the old days came back, when she was Pitamah's caregiver in Foresthill, before the punarjanma injections restored most of his great-grandfather's strength, and Kayla was re-Assigned to Councilor Mohapatra.

But in Foresthill, the three of them would sit together in Pitamah's room, the old man in bed, and Kayla reading to him from a sekai. Sometimes Pitamah read the sekai himself after Kayla helped prop him up with pillows.

That image of Pitamah reading in bed froze in Devak's mind. He stepped over to the unmade bed and shook out the covers. Nothing. He peeled back the blankets one by one, then the sheet. No sekai.

Discouraged, he glanced back over his shoulder at the dresser. He'd have to check it. Or give up the search, but now that he was in for a half-dhan he was in for a dhan. He had to satisfy himself that the sekai was truly lost.

The clothes in the drawers were folded, and Devak suspected it was Junjie who'd put them away. Devak squeezed the piles to see if the hard-cased sekai lay within, then ran his hands around each drawer's sides and bottom as he'd done in his own room. Nothing but clothes in the upper drawers. The bottom drawer held a surprise—a carrysak with two vac-seals of crysophora and one of jaf buzz, both super-stimulants.

The imprinted dates were long past. So maybe these were leftovers from when Pitamah used the powerful drugs to cope with his body's former debilitation.

Devak shut the drawer, even more sorry he'd invaded Pitamah's privacy. To soothe his guilt, Devak pulled up the covers again. He'd tell Pitamah he'd noticed the bed was unmade and had come in just to tidy it. He wouldn't mention his searching.

Pitamah's bed was up against the wall, and Devak had to lie across it to tuck in the sheets and blanket on the wall side. As he was poking the bedclothes in between the mattress and bed frame, his fingers hit something hard. His heart raced as he tugged at the edge of the thing to pull it free.

Devak got slowly to his feet. It was his sekai. His, not the extra slim device Pitamah used to own. That more expensive sekai must have been sold. This one, Devak's old sekai with its scratched case, wouldn't have brought more than a couple dhans, so Pitamah had saved it.

Had he hidden it between the mattress and frame, then forgotten his hiding place? Was that why he'd told Devak it was lost?

Pitamah might be past his hundredth year, but his mind was just as sharp as Devak's. It seemed unlikely that the old man had forgotten. Which meant he'd lied.

What Pitamah revealed and what he kept secret was always a slippery and shifting thing. For the moment, Devak didn't care. He just wanted to see Kayla's face again on the sekai.

One-handed, he finished neatening the bedclothes. Then as he headed down the hall to his own room, another unsettling thought struck Devak. Pitamah could have wiped the sekai's data storage. Kayla's picture could be gone.

Well, he knew ways to restore deleted data. He seated himself at his workstation again and powered on the sekai. And discovered several unfamiliar icons lined up on the screen.

Which meant Pitamah had used the sekai, and had loaded it with his own programs and reading material. So he had been using it.

Other than dates that stretched over the past few months, none of the icons were identified. Devak tapped the first one in the upper left, and couldn't make heads nor tails of the file that popped up. He thought at first it was in some secret code, then he recognized it as one of the ancient Earth languages. He'd seen samples of it in an Academy class on pre-Lokan history, but couldn't remember what language it was.

It didn't surprise Devak at all that Pitamah knew the language. It was the perfect code since so few could read anything but Bhasha anymore.

Devak went on to the next icon, and the next. They led to more coded files. No images at all.

The arrow at the bottom right pointed to another page of content. Devak tapped it and the last four icons displayed. He tapped the first, and another incomprehensible file came up. He closed it and selected the next icon.

An image of Kayla filled the screen. For an instant, he thought it was the one from the GEN database that he'd stored on the device. Then he realized it was an entirely different image.

Because the sekai couldn't render 3D, the image was slightly out of focus. It didn't help that the light had been poor when the capture was taken. Still, he could see the familiar wariness in her gray eyes, the frank distrust in her face. She'd turned slightly to the right so her tattoo wasn't visible. Anyone else looking at the image might think she was a minor-status trueborn.

She was walking toward the holocam, her arms swinging, the left one forward. Shadows dappled her. He could see the slender arm of someone to Kayla's right, someone taller and pale-skinned.

Was the image taken in one of the Kinship's underground safe houses? The little he could make out didn't look like any safe house he'd ever visited.

Had Kayla always been that thin? And what were those spidery lines across her forehead? A trick of the shadowy light or a flaw in the holocam capture?

Tapping the screen, he zoomed in tighter on Kayla's face. His hand started trembling as he realized those silvery lines weren't caused by a problem with the holocam.

The lines were scars. Scars much like the ones marring his own face. Scars he'd never seen before.

Could this be an image from earlier, maybe even before he'd known her? Her GEN healing might have wiped away the scars before she came to care for Pitamah.

He shifted the zoomed image down lower. Akhilesh, the trueborn gen-tech who had captured and tortured Kayla, had inflicted a deep cut on her left arm, two days before the explosion. Devak remembered the scar ran from a few inches below her shoulder to nearly the crook of her arm.

There it was, fainter than the other scars but still visible, a surgically straight line. Which meant the image was recorded after Devak rescued her from Akhilesh.

Devak stared at the bend in her arm. He zoomed in even closer. And it hit him with the force of a shockgun blast.

The skin on her lower left arm was all one color. From her wrist to just above her elbow, where it should have been a myriad of skin colors, the flesh was a solid pale brown like the rest of her. The dappling of shadow had fooled him into thinking the distinctive coloring was still there.

The change started right where Junjie had told him the left arm had been severed in the explosion. It wasn't an even line, not like the surgical cut Akhilesh had made. It was jagged, as if they'd tried to save as much of her original tissue as they could.

The truth all but slapped him in the face. The image had to have been recorded after the bombing.

Which meant Kayla was healed. Which meant Kayla was alive.

8

And Pitamah knew it. He knew Kayla was alive and hadn't told Devak, even knowing Devak's pain.

So when was the image recorded? Where? Devak flipped back to the icon, but the date had been erased. A small matter since Devak knew how to ferret out that kind of information from the image itself.

Devak put aside the enormity of Pitamah's latest lie. Instead, he focused on what he could find out about the image. First he sent it both to Junjie's wristlink and the computer. Then he checked the other two icons on the sekai. Both were coded files. No more pictures of Kayla, so Pitamah had deleted the original one that Devak had stored on the sekai.

It didn't take him long to discover the date embedded in the image. Recorded just a few days ago.

He went back to the sekai and re-checked every icon, making sure there wasn't another image of Kayla embedded in one of the documents. There wasn't. He checked the sekai's deleted data storage, hoping to find the original image of Kayla. The deletion storage segments had been written over, thoroughly enough that there was no recovering anything that had been on the sekai before.

Other than the old image of Kayla, he hadn't been in the habit of storing much on the device. There had been holocam captures of him and Junjie, images of other girls he'd thought he loved, a blurry vid of a bhimkay spider he'd spotted on a visit to the Manel adhikar when he was a tenth-year.

He turned back to the larger computer display and opened the image of Kayla. Where the sekai did a poor job of rendering in 3D, on a computer, even one as ancient as this one, Kayla's image popped into greater reality. Devak could even turn it slightly, though not enough to see her tattoo, which wasn't captured in the original file. But between the three-dimensionality and the crisper focus, it was as close to having her there before him as a holo image could be.

As good as his imagination was in picturing Kayla, the image shaded in details he hadn't realized he'd forgotten. Like the stubborn set of her chin, or the way her thick, tightly curled light brown hair refused to stay in its braid.

I love you, Kayla. One of the last things he'd said to her. He was glad to have said it.

The computer had finished its processing and was ready for another round with the winnowed data. So he started the sorting procedure again in a separate window on the display, then sat staring at Kayla's image.

He was still there an hour later when Pitamah returned. When the old man called out for him, Devak answered, "In here." He didn't even bother hiding the sekai or swiping Kayla's image off the screen. He turned to watch as his great-grandfather strode into the sleeproom.

Pitamah's pace faltered as he took in the sekai and the

computer display. He puffed up in anger. "What were you doing in my room?"

Devak swept up the sekai. "You never lost it. You hid it under your bed. Yet another lie to add to all the others."

Devak might as well have struck the old man. He took a step back, looking small despite his nearly two-meter height. "I'm only trying to protect you."

"By not telling me Kayla is alive? How long have you known?"

The last of Pitamah's bluster vanished. He crossed the room and sank onto the foot of Devak's bed. "I've only known for certain since I received image. I've been trying for months to find her."

"You should have told me. That you were looking for her. That she's alive." Devak locked his hands together to stop their trembling. "Where is she?"

"I don't know."

"Stop lying!"

"I'm not!" Pitamah fussed with his korta, the white shirt hanging on the old man's bony frame. "I know Kayla's with FHE. Your guess was right there."

"How did you find her?"

"Through a Kinship GEN girl named Essali," Pitamah said. "She's been a double agent for us and FHE. They rescued her after she was reset by the Brigade, and took her to their headquarters. They had no idea Essali was Kinship—neither did she until her memories started coming back. Once her mind put everything together, she got hold of a networked sekai, and she's been sending me coded notes."

"The ones in that old Earth language on the sekai," Devak said.

"They're in Kiswah," Pitamah confirmed. "Essali's GEN Assignment had been to translate old Earth documents into Bhasha, so she had several languages uploaded in her annexed brain. She's been at FHE headquarters for months and whenever she can, she's been passing along what she's learned."

"Then she knows where Kayla is. Tell me and I'll go get her."

"Essali doesn't know," Pitamah said. "When FHE rescued her, they didn't restore her until they'd returned to their headquarters. So she had no memory of the trip. Which means she doesn't know where she is. And she's not been allowed out to discover their location."

"Someone there must know what sector they're in," Devak said. "Why doesn't she just ask?"

"She has to be careful so as not to draw suspicion. All the other GENs she's spoken to are in the same boat as her—reset and restored with no memory of the trip there. Essali only knows it's a natural cavern. It could be in any number of sectors."

"Why did it take so long for her to find Kayla?"

"It took time for Kayla to heal, then she was restricted to the lower levels. Essali finally spotted her and captured that image."

"They changed her arm," Devak said. "It doesn't look right."

"There's a lot not right with FHE," Pitamah said. "I got hints from Essali. She knew something was happening, but couldn't tell me what."

"Knew?" Devak asked.

"I haven't heard from her since she sent the image of Kayla." Pitamah's shoulders sagged. "She's supposed to at least ping me once a day. I only pray she's busy and just hasn't been able to get back to me."

A beep from the computer snagged Devak's attention. The winnowing process had completed. "I've found Shun. Junjie's FHE friend."

"You know where he is?" Pitamah came to look over Devak's shoulder.

"Somewhere in Creth sector. At least he was yesterday." Devak sent the location information to Junjie's wristlink. "With luck and the Lord Creator's grace, he's still there."

So what message should he send? He couldn't mention Kayla or Junjie or FHE. Referring to Neta would be a mistake. It had to be a message Shun couldn't resist replying to—because a reply would confirm his location, and perhaps narrow the coordinates.

Money was always a draw, especially for a minor-status trueborn. *I have some dhans I've been asked to give you.* Devak tapped in the message, then used a spoofing algorithm that he hoped was stronger than the one Shun had used. It was possible Shun would associate the mention of dhans to FHE and would run, but Devak felt he had to take the chance.

Message sent, Devak got up and nudged past his great-grandfather. Before he left the sleeproom, he turned back. "You should have told me. All of it. It would have given me hope."

With Pitamah calling after him, Devak hurried from the house. He headed west on Makti Street, away from the busy central green, with no idea where he was going. He just knew he had to get away from Pitamah.

He didn't usually walk this way, away from Ekat sector's business center and deeper into the neighborhood. At first it was because he hadn't felt safe amongst the lowborns and minor-status. He'd lost that knee-jerk reaction by his second week of living here once he'd discovered how much more welcoming his neighbors were than they'd been in the trueborn-only sectors.

The homes on either side of Makti were simple plasscrete, some of them painted, some the natural pink-beige of plassfiber. The yards of some were filled with vivid green scrap grass, neatly trimmed, edged with native plants like blue chaff head and yellow scrub flowers. Others featured one or two large sticker bushes studded with periwinkle blooms, gravel laid down in lieu of a lawn.

He honestly couldn't tell which were the residences of minor-status trueborns like him and Pitamah and Junjie, and which housed lowborns. A minor-status woman sat idly on the front porch of an ill-kempt home while a lowborn man worked industriously in the garden of a well-maintained cottage.

Everything seemed turned upside down in this new world he'd woken up in four weeks ago. It tied his stomach into knots.

Yes, he felt joy that Kayla was alive, but discouraged that he had no idea how to find her. Pitamah once again keeping something so important from him filled him with disquiet. The old man probably thought it was for Devak's own good, so he could keep his focus on healing. But not knowing had made things worse.

Devak kept walking, the first verdant blur of Southwest Territory's adhikar coming into view. The acres and acres of pastureland and grain fields were only about two kilometers west of Pitamah's house. This was the first time Devak had walked close enough to see it.

The adhikar parcels had been set aside strictly for trueborn ownership. When he was high-status and they lived in Foresthill, Devak had owned hundreds of acres of Southwest Territory land. He'd been awarded the minimum two hundred when he was born, just as every high-status was. Later, his father's wealth bought him hundreds more, some in Southwest, and additional acres in Northwest and Central Western territories.

Then his father, Ved Manel, had gone to prison. Devak's greedy mother, Rasia, had stolen all but Devak's birthright acreage. Rasia had stripped Pitamah of all but his birthright adhikar too. Only donations from Kinship friends had kept Devak and Pitamah barely above water as high-status. With so little to spare, it wasn't surprising they'd been demoted.

Back in Foresthill, when they were still wealthy, Devak's parents had indulged him with a lev-car, a sleek Bullet. It had been one of the first things to go when his mother had wrenched his adhikar from him. The high-speed Bullet was a luxury that he and Pitamah couldn't afford.

But if he had it now, Devak would have charged it up and headed up to Creth sector in Northwest Territory. Although he had promised Junjie to wait for him. It was clear that Junjie wanted to talk to Shun again, to meet him in person. It would be him and Junjie going up to Creth together. Devak felt only the faintest twinge of guilt at leaving Pitamah behind.

The primary sun, Iyenku, had nearly finished its path across the sky and hung a hand's width above the horizon. The details of the adhikar came into view—the high, electrified fence, the close-eaten pasture dotted with droms. The creatures that Devak saw first were the larger, genetically engineered variety. As he got nearer, he spotted a few smaller native droms off in the distance.

All that meat wandering out in the pasture and it fed so few. The choicest cuts from the shaggy six-legged creatures were reserved for high-status trueborns, and the best quality sheared wool warmed that most elite class. The lesser trueborns and lowborns had to make do with the inferior leftovers.

He got as close to the electrified fence as he dared. A few dead rat-snakes rotted close to the plassteel boundary. They'd likely been tempted by the lush scrap grass on the other side and had been zapped by the current. Even the genned droms, less clever than their natural cousins, were smart enough not to graze so close to the fence, which was why the grass along it was so fat with seed heads.

Suddenly, the half dozen or so native droms popped their heads up. The genned variety kept munching, unconcerned. Even when the small herd of natives thundered off deeper into the adhikar, the larger droms continued to graze.

Devak saw it then, thankfully on the other side of the electrified fence—a bhimkay spider, a meter high, creeping toward the drom herd. A young drom, no bigger than the spider, had wandered away from its mother, and the bhimkay had the baby in its sights.

Devak shouted, waved his arms. The droms kept eating. He found a rock alongside the fence, but the fence was twice his height, and the mesh too small to throw a rock through.

The young one screamed as the bhimkay caught it, and finally that spooked the rest of the herd. They ran off, even the mother leaving the baby behind.

Devak turned away as the bhimkay dragged the paralyzed young drom away. As he half-ran from the adhikar fence, the image of the captured drom got overlaid in his head with his gen-tank nightmare—Kayla being dragged away from the scene of the explosion by faceless trueborns.

It wasn't the same. She would be safe with FHE, wouldn't she? She'd been their target, the one GEN they'd wanted above all others, at least to hear Junjie tell it. Surely they wouldn't cause her harm. Still, he couldn't seem to let go of his anxiety.

When Junjie's wristlink beeped, Devak was so wound up, he jumped, gasping. Pitamah calling? Or maybe Junjie from the lab?

It was neither. It was Shun.

It wasn't a voice call, just a text. *How many dhans?*

The source ID didn't match the one Junjie had saved in his wristlink, so Shun was still hiding. But he must be desperate enough for money that he'd responded when he had to have been suspicious.

Devak needed the computer's algorithms to see if he could track the ID back to the same location. But he was certain he'd found the boy, and if Shun triangulated to the same place, he and Junjie could go looking for him.

Devak broke into a full run, his back only complaining a little bit. It felt good to work his muscles, to stretch his stride to its full length.

He spotted Junjie coming toward him from the pub-trans stop in the business center. Devak caught up with him two houses down from Pitamah's. "Kayla is alive!"

Devak looked for any sign in Junjie's face that his friend had kept that secret along with Pitamah. But Junjie only gave him a cautious smile. "How do you know? Are you sure?"

"Positive. I found a holo of her taken after the explosion."

Now Junjie grinned and did a little dance. "Did Shun send it to you? Have you contacted him?"

"Yes and no." Devak turned toward Pitamah's house and

Junjie fell in alongside. "I was able to send Shun a message. He sent one back. No way to be a hundred percent sure it's him, because the ID is spoofed like before. But if the message path correlates with the routing map we have, it raises the probability."

"Good, good!" Junjie seemed ready to burst at the news. "Where did Kayla's image come from?"

"From Pitamah." Devak showed Junjie the image on the wristlink as he explained about his search for the sekai, how he confronted his great-grandfather with what he'd found.

Junjie squinted at the small image as they climbed the front porch steps. "How can you tell this isn't an image from before the explosion?"

"You'll see when I show it to you on the computer. And I have more good news." Devak tapped at the wristlink, then handed it to Junjie. "I have a picture of Shun."

Junjie's dark eyes fixed on the image. "How do you know it's him?"

"A very good guess. Now we have something to show people when we go search for him."

They went inside. As Devak passed his great-grandfather in the living room, he barely looked Pitamah's way.

The image of Kayla was still displayed on the computer. It looked as if it had been zoomed in even more, as if Pitamah had been viewing it. At least it hadn't been deleted, nor had Pitamah taken away the sekai.

Junjie goggled at the larger version of the holo image of Kayla. "What happened to her arm?"

"They re-genned it with regular skin," Devak said, "not the colors it was supposed to be."

He sat at the computer and uploaded the source call ID from Shun. Junjie paced behind him, his anxiety coming out as jitters. "Considering you were offering dhans, someone else could have responded."

Devak shrugged, his focus on his algorithms. Since the input was only one instance rather than the tangled map he'd dealt with before, the processing went quickly.

"Hah!" he shouted in triumph. "There it is."

He pointed at the computer's holo display. "Look here. This path that's glowing brighter is the route that Shun's text took this afternoon. It exactly matches this path from the previous data." Devak swiped the new path aside slightly so Junjie could see how neatly the new one overlaid the older one.

"I thought Shun's spoof was supposed to choose random paths each time," Junjie said.

"No spoofing method can be truly random. Some are better than others. My algorithms happen to be better than Shun's." Devak sat back. "I'm pretty denking sure he's still in Creth."

"Should we answer him? Send him another message?"

"I don't know," Devak said. "I could tell him we have to meet with him to make sure the dhans are his."

Junjie shook his head. "That would make him suspicious."

"Then maybe we just go to him."

"When do we leave?"

"Right away," Devak said. "Now. Tonight. The longer we wait, the more likely he'll be gone when we get there."

"But how do we get to Creth?"

"We borrow Jemali's WindSpear," Devak said. "Drive there tonight and return in the morning."

Suddenly, there was Pitamah in the sleeproom doorway. "You can't do that."

"Why not?" Devak asked. "Because you don't want us to go? Because you don't want us to find Kayla?"

"Because the Brigade will stop you." Pitamah came into the room. "They might give me a pass because I'm still close to a few powerful people like Councilor Mohapatra, but if they catch you with Jemali's WindSpear, they'll impound it and cause Jemali no end of trouble. And even if you weren't stopped, how will you pay for the charging dock? It's a long way to Creth."

Devak squelched the hopelessness that threatened to drown him. "I'm going, Pitamah. I'll walk if I have to."

Pitamah scowled. "That's a sanaki idea."

Of course it was crazy. Even if Devak's still-fragile back could survive the long trip, Shun would be gone before they'd traveled the thousand or so kilometers between Ekat sector and Creth.

"I'll find a way," Devak said stubbornly.

"We have a way," Junjie said. "We can take pub-trans."

Now Devak felt even more stupid. It had never crossed his mind to take the public transportation system, because high-status trueborns never did. Setting foot on one of the lumbering multi-transports would be scandalous for a diamond-wearer.

"Do we have the dhans?" Devak glanced up at Pitamah.

Pitamah hesitated a moment, then he said, "I think we could scrape together enough."

"I have a little bit I've tucked away, just in case. I'm glad to bring it." Junjie went to the dresser and dug in his bottom drawer. He came up with a few coins and some crumpled paper dhans. "Pub-trans isn't so bad. Guru Ling used to ride that way all the time."

Guru Ling was the geneticist that Junjie worked for until she drowned in the Plator River. The Brigade had tried to pass it off as suicide, but Devak and Junjie figured out that the former GAMA head, Akhilesh, had arranged her murder.

"If it will get us a step closer to finding Kayla," Devak said, "I'm all for it."

Pitamah fixed his dark gaze on Devak. He wanted to talk them out of going after Shun, Devak was sure of it. But then Pitamah said, "I'll get the dhans. You two start evening meal." Then he strode out of the room.

The three of them ate in silence. The drom curry Devak had thrown together was bland and watery, the kel-grain they'd poured it over scorched because Junjie was too distracted to keep his eye on it. Pitamah barely touched his.

Seeing how shrunken his great-grandfather seemed, Devak couldn't hold onto his anger. A thread of forgiveness wove its way into Devak's heart as he watched Pitamah's hand trembling as he lifted his spoon.

"Is the punarjanma wearing off?" Devak asked. "Are you getting weaker?" Guilt roiled inside him that he was abandoning Pitamah.

The old man wouldn't meet Devak's gaze, making him feel even more uneasy. "Just tired," Pitamah said.

They cleared the half-eaten evening meal, then went to pack. Neither Devak nor Junjie had more than a few days' worth of kortas or chera pants, so there was more than enough room in a single carrysak. The stack of dhans Pitamah gave Devak was alarmingly small.

"If you need more . . ." Pitamah's voice trailed off. "I'll find it somewhere. Call me on the wristlink."

"We won't need to," Devak said. "We'll find him right away and bring him back here." He stuffed Pitamah's dhans and Junjie's stash into a hidden pocket in the carrysak, then slipped his identity chip in there as well. He pressed the mag-connector closed with his thumbprint, locking it so only he could open it.

Junjie headed out the door, but Pitamah held Devak back. "Do you have the sekai?"

Devak clutched the carrysak tighter. "Yes."

"I realize it's yours, but I could make use of it," Pitamah said. "I haven't finished translating the stories Essali wrote in Kiswah. There might be clues to help you find Kayla."

"I'll bring it back after we find Shun," Devak said. "You can do the translation then."

Pitamah compressed his mouth and the lines on his face seemed to cut deeper. "There may not be enough time."

A foreboding settled in Devak's belly. "I won't be gone forever, Pitamah."

The old man stared at Devak a long time, and foreboding morphed to stark fear. "I should tell you, Devak. There was a problem with the last punarjanma treatment," Pitamah said. "Jemali thinks I might be dying."

Kayla set down three kel-grain-filled crates on a waist-high stack, then turned and threaded her way through Godama 2 toward the freight lift. Thank the Infinite, only the last load left. Her arms tingled with the exhaustion of a six-hour shift in the foodstores cavern, her re-genned left arm slightly more tired than the right.

As she stepped inside the freight lift, Penba, the GEN man who managed Godama 2, kept a sharp eye on her every movement. Penba stretched his mouth into a smile when Kayla nodded his way, but that didn't fool her into thinking he was just being friendly. He was watching her.

Hefting the last crates from the lift, she carried them past tall stacks of synth-protein and soy milk powder, then returned to the section of the enormous cavern where the kel-grain was stored. Although she didn't look back, she knew Penba's gaze was on her, the middle-aged GEN fulfilling his double duty as manager and minder.

Despite the exasperation of having her every move noted by Penba, Kayla did appreciate having the work tour to occupy her time. Five out of the six days of the week, she worked in Godama 2 toting kel-grain, synth-protein, and dried soy milk. Occasionally she carried the foodstuffs to Mahala for the cooks.

What she never was able to do was examine the freight lift, to see if the access code she'd memorized worked for it. Penba's seycat-sharp eyes and unwavering attention every moment Kayla was in the foodstuffs cavern scrapped that notion.

The most she'd been able to ascertain was that the lift went all the way to the surface. Lovise had danced around the truth when Kayla had asked if the Kheta rooms supplied all of FHE's needs. The crates Kayla toted in here confirmed what she'd suspected—that their harvest was insufficient to feed everyone in Antara. Which meant FHE had to bring down additional foodstuffs from aboveground.

Kayla moved the ladder to the kel-grain towers that she'd set her last load on, and put the final crates on top. She was about to lock the crates into place when Shakki, the dark-skinned thirteenth-year GEN girl who was Kayla's new roommate, appeared at the foot of the ladder.

"Finished for the day?" Shakki asked with a cheerful smile. She'd asked the same question in that same friendly tone of voice nearly every day for the four weeks of Kayla's work tour.

Kayla wanted to say no, just to thwart Shakki's mission. The diminutive girl was here to take over "minding" duty from Penba. She would escort Kayla from Godama 2 to Mahala for the evening meal.

The transition from Lovise to Shakki still troubled Kayla. Two days after her visit to the Kheta room, Kayla had returned to Seycat from morning meal to find fresh bedding on Lovise's cot and all her things gone from the dresser. Shakki had showed up later that day.

Had the change been because Lovise hadn't been "minding" Kayla well enough to keep her from sending a message from the hydroponic storage room? Or because the netcams had caught Lovise revealing too much to Kayla? Despite Lovise's fervent commitment to FHE, maybe Ohin hadn't wanted Kayla to know that he would never let her leave Antara. Or was that only Lovise's belief, and Ohin had no intention of keeping Kayla trapped? In any case, since then Kayla had been even more wary of the FHE leader.

The work tour came shortly after Shakki arrived. Ohin and Aideen turned up unannounced one morning at Seycat, and Ohin presented Kayla with her new duties. Aideen seemed to think it was a great honor that Ohin himself had selected her work tour, and that he'd come in person to give her notice of it.

Kayla wasn't the least bit honored, especially when Ohin dodged her question about when her family might come to see her. "We're working on it," he'd said, his intense blue gaze so sincere. With Aideen, it was easy to read a lie in her face. Ohin was more of a mystery. Between his enigmatic ways and Shakki's sudden replacement of Lovise, Kayla was constantly second-guessing herself about Ohin's motives.

Kayla locked the last three crates in place, securing the completed tower to its neighbor. "That's it," she said to Shakki. "I'm done."

Another bright smile from the GEN girl. "Then let's go." She gave Kayla a hand down from the ladder.

As Kayla's toes were searching for the last rung, the hallucinations—memory fragments—suddenly nibbled at the edges of her vision. She faltered and would have toppled if not for Shakki's hand. Kayla swept away the jumble of memories, the action automatic after weeks of practice, and they faded again.

"The hallucinations?" Shakki asked.

Kayla shrugged. She hadn't bothered to propose her theory to Shakki that they were actual memories. Instead, she kept them muted—which worked most of the time—and only allowed them into her conscious mind at night, when she had time to puzzle them out. Not that she'd made much progress understanding them.

As they made their way out of Godama 2, Kayla asked, "Why is it you seem to have nothing to do but be my minder?"

"Medic Palla has all the assistants she needs," Shakki said. "That's what I did in my outsider life, trained with the GEN healer in my home sector. I have other activities to keep me busy when I'm not with you."

Not so busy that she didn't know exactly when Kayla was ready to leave for the midday meal or was at the end of her shift, even when Kayla tried varying her schedule. The GEN girl was more effective than the trueborns' Monitoring Grid. Kayla had thought her days of being constantly tracked were over.

But it was starting to seem that FHE's treatment of her wasn't much different than the outsider trueborns', or Zul's and the Kinship's. They all wanted to control her. She hated it, but it just pushed her all that much harder to find a way out. If only she could shake Shakki.

Aideen had chosen Kayla's constant companion well. The GEN girl was impossible not to like, and she was so tiny—even smaller than Kayla—that Kayla would have felt like a monster turning her anger on the younger GEN girl.

"There's real meat tonight," Shakki said as they walked along the twisting corridor. "Not just synth. I was just in the kitchen and it smelled great."

"It's probably just rat-snake." The vermin were numerous in Godama 2, always sniffing out stray kel-grain, and larger than any Kayla had ever seen. On her delivery trips to the kitchen, she had seen the snaky things cleaned and laid out for cooking.

"It's not rat-snake," Shakki assured her. A mysterious smile played on the girl's face. "Something from aboveground."

That sent Kayla's mind off in a new direction. Could FHE have snatched a drom or two or three from some trueborn's adhikar pasture? Could this underground cavern be beneath one of the five adhikar tracts? She'd never heard of limestone caves beneath trueborn pasture and farmlands, but that would explain how FHE managed to amass so much kel-grain and stores of root vegetables like patagobi and gajara. They could be pilfering from the adhikar.

They reached Mahala, and Shakki took Kayla's hand, towing her through the entrance. The noise level of the crowd rose in volume as they reached the middle of the massive cavern, and Kayla could feel the memory fragments recede enough that it took no effort to keep them muted.

Shakki seemed to have a smile and a greeting for everyone, and everyone seemed to know her. But she waved off every offer to join this table or that, pulling Kayla along between two of the sound dampeners to the quieter area where she and Kayla usually sat.

Aideen was already there at their usual table. When Aideen had first invited Kayla to eat with her, Kayla had flatly refused. But then Kayla remembered that Aideen had let slip that nugget of information about Seycat being safe. Who knew what else she might learn from her birth mother?

Aideen gave every appearance of being firmly committed to Ohin. It was unlikely she'd do anything to oppose him.

But if enduring her birth mother's presence for meals meant gaining some other information that could lead to a way to escape, Kayla would do it.

As always, Kayla let Shakki sit opposite Aideen, while she herself settled on the bench beside Shakki. That gave Kayla some separation between her and her birth mother.

In the relative quiet behind the dampeners, the memory fragments nibbled again in her bare brain. Kayla let them come, grabbing images and words and phrases that she knew were real.

. . . thought we were friends . . . so beautiful . . .

The first words were Devak's, the others spoken by a different boy—Abran, the traitor. Then Devak again.

. . . too heavy for me to carry . . .

He said it that night in Daki sector, but she couldn't remember what it was that was too heavy. Their friendship? That she wanted more from him than he did from her?

And then, his ultimate declaration: *I've figured out that trueborn society isn't ready for GENs and trueborns to be together.*

Her heart seemed to crumble inside as she remembered. She shook off the heavy ache, storing the words and images away. Tonight, after the illuminators switched off, she would sift through it all, looking for more clues that would help her put together her more recent past. Although the only thing her bare brain had offered up that meant anything to her were those four precious words—*I love you, Kayla.* But she had no memory to support Devak saying them, so they were probably not even real.

Kayla returned her attention to the room and realized Aideen was trying to catch her eye. Kayla ignored the trueborn woman, instead focusing on the server approaching from the kitchen with a tray laden with three bowls. The fragrance of curry and meat arrived before the server did.

The bowl of food gave Kayla another excuse not to meet Aideen's gaze. Kayla spooned up the spiced kel-grain and a bite-sized piece of the browned meat. Not rat-snake certainly, but not drom either.

Kayla couldn't avoid her birth-mother's voice. "Penba tells me you're a hard worker," Aideen said.

Kayla would have just shrugged, but she could imagine her nurture mother, Tala, scolding her for such rudeness. "It's easy enough work."

"You'll tell me if there's anything you need." Aideen said that at least once during every meal she shared with her and Shakki.

Now Kayla swung her gaze up at Aideen. "What I need is to get out of this prison."

Before Aideen could make some placating remark, Shakki said, "*This* isn't a prison."

Kayla slanted her a glance, wondering at the emphasis on *this*. Shakki didn't look her way, she just kept fidgeting with the remaining kel-grain in her bowl, marking out a pattern over and over.

The letter K.

Or was she seeing things? Kayla might just want the girl to be Kinship, when she was really just idly spelling out her name. There were two K's in Shakki, after all.

The moment Aideen looked Shakki's way, the GEN girl started spooning up kel-grain. Shakki smiled at Kayla. "Nice to have real meat, isn't it? Nice when we can bring down the real thing."

As in hunting some creature and bringing it down? Or as

in capturing a drom from some unsuspecting trueborn's adhikar and bringing it down into the cavern? The genetically engineered droms were so domesticated, they wouldn't balk at being led into the cavern and even into the freight lift. Kayla would have seen signs of a creature that big coming through Godama 2, but it could have been brought through Godama 1 or 3.

Kayla chewed another bite of the stringy but tasty meat. The flavor really wasn't right for drom, nor the color. It was darker, with just a hint of gaminess. Not as wild-tasting as rat-snake, but not the mellow flavor of drom, either.

Aideen slid closer and laid her hand near Kayla's. "Ohin would like a chance to spend some time with you. He has a few minutes free tonight."

Even though Aideen wasn't touching her, Kayla pulled her hand away. "Why not come here during mealtimes, like that first time? He could see me all he wants." She wasn't particularly keen on the idea, but it was better than meeting somewhere with only him.

"He'd rather see you in private," Aideen said.

Her birth-mother wouldn't quite meet Kayla's gaze. A prickle ran up the back of Kayla's neck. What was Aideen hiding?

Kayla glanced over at Shakki, and the worry on the GEN girl's face alarmed her even more. Then Shakki smiled and gave Kayla a pat on the shoulder. "She can't tonight. We have plans."

That was news to her. But before Kayla could ask Shakki what the girl was talking about, the dainty thirteenth-year scooped up Kayla's empty bowl and stacked it with her own. She headed off toward the kitchen.

"After you're done with Shakki," Aideen said, "drop by Ohin's quarters."

Not for a million dhans. Kayla scrambled to her feet and followed Shakki. Kayla caught up as Shakki dumped the plasscine bowls into the washtub with a clatter.

"Come on," Shakki said, hooking her elbow in Kayla's. The girl's skin matched the darkest patches on Kayla's right arm. Her head barely topped Kayla's shoulder.

They emerged from behind the dampeners, and the noise grew again to a deafening level. Shakki pulled Kayla to a stop a few meters from the nearest table and went up on tiptoes to murmur in Kayla's ear. "Pretend we're telling each other funny stories."

Her curiosity piqued, Kayla played along, smiling and laughing along with Shakki. She bent and whispered back, "What is this all about?"

Shakki grinned as if Kayla had said something terribly funny. She leaned in close again. "Let me link with you."

Kayla shook her head. "I don't want to use the circuit-comm. Not with you. Not with any GEN."

Shakki gave Kayla a poke, scolding loudly, "I thought you liked my jokes."

Kayla laughed on cue, but inside she wanted nothing more than to run away from the GEN girl. She could have easily tugged free, since Shakki's strength didn't nearly match her own. But the way Shakki looked up at her, the pleading look in her dark brown eyes, made Kayla stay put.

Shakki spread her mouth in a fake smile as she whispered urgently. "I can't talk to you any other way. They're listening. Even here, the netcams are watching. We can't hang around here arguing about this or they'll see."

Kayla forced an answering grin as she bent toward Shakki's ear. "How do I know that linking with you wouldn't just be another way for them to spy on me?"

"I'll show you a trick that will block anyone from your circuit-comm, even me," Shakki said. "It's not a coincidence that I became your roommate, Kayla. When I'm not minding you, I put my talents to work in one of the Vijnana Centers."

"Lucky you." Since her brief hack into the sekai in the Kheta lab, Kayla was not allowed anywhere near a computer, never mind her sket wasn't for tech.

Shakki lowered her voice even more. "I hacked into Ohin's system so my name would come up at the top of the list."

"You've never given me so much as a hint. Until today."

"I had problems to solve," Shakki said. "Will you give me your passkey?"

The twenty digit passkey did more than uniquely identify Kayla. It could be used to reset her as well, wipe away her personality. That was how Akhilesh had reset Kayla. If not for Aideen downloading the contents of Kayla's brain from FHE headquarters right before the GAMA gene-splicer's reset, Kayla would be someone else right now.

"Okay," Kayla said finally.

"Not here," Shakki said, towing her along around the edge of the crowd. She nodded and waved as she passed friends seated at the long tables, but she kept her grip on Kayla until they left the room.

"How do you like your work tour in the warehouse?" Shakki asked, casting a friendly smile in Kayla's direction.

As Kayla puzzled over the banal question, she caught Shakki's glance up to her right. They were just passing a micro-controller on that side. When Kayla started to tip her head up to look, Shakki squeezed her arm hard. At first Kayla didn't under-stand—the listening devices wouldn't hear her look at them.

And then it hit her with all the weight of the thousands of

kilos of rock overhead. Horror washed over her, and she leaned close to Shakki's ear. She forced a smile so it would look like she was revealing some innocent secret. "Are they netcams?"

Shakki laughed, as if delighted with what Kayla had related. "Of course."

Kayla felt so stupid that she hadn't realized that before now. Then horror turned to nausea as it hit home that her earlier fear that they were *listening* to her in her private quarters was the least of it. They were *watching* her as well. Great Infinite, did someone watch her dress and bathe?

Kayla felt like ripping the denking devices from the wall, all along the corridor. But she held her temper and answered Shakki's earlier question. "It's good to work."

They continued the mindless conversation until they reached Seycat. Kayla hadn't bothered locking the door since Lovise left. Shakki pushed inside, all but dragging Kayla with her before shutting and locking the latch.

Shakki kept moving until they were both pressed inside the shallow alcove where Kayla had been chinning herself up to strengthen her arms. Shakki hooked a thumb up toward the netcam over the door then shook her head.

The netcam couldn't see them there. That was a relief. When Kayla took a breath to speak, Shakki pressed a finger against Kayla's mouth. Then she held up that finger to get Kayla's attention. Shakki tapped on her palm three times, then put up three fingers. She tapped five times and put up five.

Kayla nodded that she understood, then took Shakki's hand. She tapped four times, waited for Shakki's nod, then tapped twice, another nod, six times, a nod. Kayla continued until she'd relayed all twenty digits of her passkey.

Shakki pointed her thumb to herself, then gave Kayla her

own twenty digits in the same fashion. Kayla nodded with each digit as she stored it in her annexed brain.

She had to think a moment about how to activate the link with Shakki. Aideen had forcibly used Kayla's circuit-comm that night Akhilesh reset her, but Kayla hadn't retained any knowledge of how to operate it.

Finally, Kayla found the part of her annexed brain where the communication system had been programmed. She fed in Shakki's passkey.

Can you hear me?

Kayla started, whacking her hand against the wall. Like that stray word she'd heard from Ohin, Shakki's inner voice sounded flat, with only a trace of the GEN girl's tone in it. But Kayla could recognize the passkey embedded in the communication.

Kayla nodded, then realized she ought to "speak" back to Shakki. *Tell me that trick for blocking people.*

Overwrite the FHE circuit-comm programming with this. Shakki sent a stream of computer code. *Once you've loaded it, block me.*

Kayla shunted the stream of instructions into the part of her annexed brain where FHE had created the virtual comm system. She found the part of the code that toggled a particular comm stream on and off.

Shakki said, *Have you loaded—* and as easily as flicking a switch, Kayla turned off Shakki's communication. Then, as Shakki pulled Kayla toward her bed, she turned it on again.

But they can see us here, Kayla said as she sat beside Shakki.

It doesn't matter, Shakki said. *They can't hear us. Not if we use the circuit-comm.*

That's what Aideen said. That it was safe to use it in Seycat.

I wonder how she found out. She can't have told Ohin or the comm shield wouldn't still be working. That was one of the tricks I had to accomplish before talking to you.

So when we use the circuit-comm outside Seycat, in the corridors, in Mahala—they can hear it?

They can pick up the transmissions from one GEN to another. They can't actively listen to everyone, every minute. That's too much information. But you can bet they record all the comms to sort through later. And I'm sure they have certain people they focus on.

I'm guessing I'm one of those certain people. No wonder Aideen keeps bugging me to use the circuit-comm.

But she told you it would be safe in here, which makes me wonder whose side she's on. Shakki took Kayla's hands. *I'm going to tell you something. You have to promise not to react.*

React to what? Kayla asked, dread blossoming in her stomach.

The truth, Shakki said, holding Kayla's hands so tight, it hurt. *Devak isn't dead.*

10

Impossible hope dug its claws into Kayla, making her careless. "How can that be?"

Kayla didn't even realize she'd spoken aloud until Shakki gave her arm a painful squeeze. Kayla clenched her teeth tightly. *Devak was blown up in an FHE explosion.*

Shakki's grip had loosened, but she kept her fingers wrapped around Kayla's upper arm. *He was injured badly, but not killed. Just like you were.*

Kayla struggled to untangle Shakki's baffling statements. *Akhilesh injured me. Not an explosion.*

That's what they told you, Shakki said. *What Ohin had them tell you.*

And Aideen. Despite Shakki's doubts, Kayla was sure her birth mother was in lockstep with Ohin.

What is the truth? Kayla asked. *What really happened?*

I only know what my source knows, Shakki said. *She only knows what she's been told, which might not be everything. So you have to work it out on your own.*

How? Kayla asked. *Akhilesh reset me.*

Shakki edged closer, as if to whisper, although the communication between them was silent. *Akhilesh never reset you.*

Of course he did, Kayla insisted. *I don't remember anything after being in his lab.*

Shakki leaned her head against Kayla's shoulder, a show of affection to fool the netcam. *That's because the bomb damaged your brain, so they didn't need to reset you. Everything that happened between when Aideen downloaded you and the explosion, got scrambled.*

Except she could remember nothing at all from those few days. Nothing except . . .

And suddenly, as clear as the images on a sekai screen, Kayla saw it. Her, collapsed on the floor, sick with Scratch, after barely escaping Akhilesh's lab. Devak lifting her in his arms to carry her to safety. Those sweet, murmured words that she'd thought were a lie.

I love you, Kayla.

Overwhelmed, she dropped her face in her hands. "He was there at the lab."

She'd said it softly enough, she hoped the netcam hadn't caught the words. Kayla picked up the link with Shakki again. *Is Devak okay? You said he was badly hurt?*

He spent weeks in the gen-tank, Shakki said. *Longer than you because he's not a GEN.*

Kayla leapt to her feet, started to pace, then remembered the netcam. To keep herself still, she crossed her arms, gripping her elbows until her shoulders ached.

The images she'd been seeing on her periphery, the ones Palla had called hallucinations, they really were memories trying to push themselves into her consciousness. *Actual* memories, not the ones they'd been trying to feed her so she'd believe something that had never happened.

Kayla dropped beside Shakki again. *How do I get out of here? How do I get to him?*

There's no way, Shakki said. *No way you or I would be able to manage.*

There has to be. All that kel-grain comes from aboveground. If it can come down, we can go up. Get out of Antara.

It's not nearly that easy.

Where are we, Shakki? What sector? I can find someone to get us out, no matter what territory we're in.

I can't tell you, Shakki said.

Of course you can. They'll never know.

I'm sorry, Shakki said, misery clear in her face. *I can't tell you where we are.*

Can't . . .

And now Kayla remembered the block that the FHE updates had placed on her mind. When Junjie had unintentionally launched the FHE programs in Kayla's annexed brain, activating new abilities like her enhanced healing and ability to block future unwanted uploads, one program prevented her from talking about FHE. The thoughts were there, the words hovering on her tongue, but she couldn't speak them.

So you do know where we are, Kayla said. *But their programming won't let you tell me.*

Shakki nodded. *I'm one of the few GENs who never got reset.*

So I saw.

Maybe it didn't matter. Whatever sector they were in, or if her guess was right and they were in some trueborn's adhikar, Kayla would figure out a way back to Devak.

Kayla circled back to another question that had gnawed at

her. *Why are all the GENs coming in reset? Why not more like you?*

Because the ones the Brigade hadn't reset before they arrived, Ohin almost always stuffs into portable gen-tanks and has the techs here reset them. He says it's because their annexed or bare brains have been damaged, and the reset is best for them. How do you think Aideen had a gen-tank handy when you were hurt? She planned to put you in it either way. If you hadn't been hurt, you would have been reset.

I thought the FHE changes to GEN circuitry let us block a reset.

FHE techs wrote that code, they know how to sidestep it. Some they've even persuaded to voluntarily reset, promising all their old memories will be restored without the glitches. But they upload some additional programming in the tank to make them loyal FHE zealots—himayati. In a select few he plants the compulsion to go out and set the bombs.

Aideen told me the bombings in the GEN sectors were done by a rogue FHE member. Was Kayla really surprised that her birth mother lied?

The bombings were Ohin's plan, start to finish, Shakki said. *And even the himayati who haven't been programmed beg him to let them martyr themselves. I've had to dance a thin line, once I figured out what Ohin expected of me. I took the himayati oath, vowed to support FHE to the death. I say the right words when I see him.*

Always one with you, Kayla parroted. *But he has to know I don't feel the same way.* A thought suddenly struck Kayla. *Do you think that's why he wants so much to see me tonight? Could he be considering resetting me? Reprogramming me to be one of them?*

You're Aideen's daughter, Shakki said. *That has to mean something.*

Kayla wasn't so sure. Her relationship with Aideen would

only mean something if Aideen had some special connection to Ohin. But he so often seemed indifferent to the trueborn woman.

If I could get outside, Kayla said, *use my locator to figure out where I am, I could make plans.*

Knowing where we are won't help you, Shakki said.

Can you at least tell me if the code is the same for all the lifts? Kayla asked. *I memorized it for one of the passenger lifts to the next level.*

Shakki shook her head. *All different. And your GEN tattoo has to be valid for the freight lift.*

Which meant Kayla would never be able to operate it on her own. An idea blossomed in her mind. *Your programming keeps you from speaking. Does it keep you from doing?*

What do you mean? Shakki said cautiously.

Can you take me outside?

Shakki stared at Kayla as if she were crazy. *And what would I say when they come to reset us both?*

You tell them I threatened you. I forced you. Can you do it? Will you *do it?*

Shakki turned away. Her hands flexed, open and closed, as if she struggled for an answer. Then her head whipped back around, and she speared Kayla with her gaze. *I hope you can break a door down, GEN girl. Because I don't have the unlock code to Godama 2.*

Kayla leaped up, snatching up Shakki's hand and making a show of dragging her out of Seycat. Moving as quickly as she dared without pulling the smaller girl off her feet, Kayla plunged down the twists of the corridor. Shakki stumbled once or twice, but she kept up as they raced for the foodstores cavern.

The corridors weren't empty, and the GENs and trueborns

they encountered gave them peculiar looks as they passed. Kayla kept her head down as she dodged them, any moment expecting one of them to stop her. But not one did as they reached the last corridor leading to Godama 2.

Both of them gasping for breath, Kayla tried the handle. "Locked. Should I—"

Shakki put up a hand to stop her from wrenching off the latch. A stout minor-status trueborn woman approached from around the corner. It was Charf, the one who kept the boys in line in the Bhimkay Lounge.

Charf narrowed her gaze on Kayla and Shakki, scowling, her steps slowing. "Always one with him," she all but growled.

"Always one with him," Shakki responded.

When Charf glared at Kayla, she stuttered out, "Always one with him."

With Charf glowering down at them, options raced through Kayla's mind. She could abandon her ill-planned mission. Or with one blow she could eliminate Charf as a threat.

She was about to choose the second option when Charf got that distant look in her eyes. Now Kayla saw the telltale lump of a trueborn circuit-comm at the base of Charf's throat. With one last scowl at Kayla, Charf continued on her way.

As Charf disappeared around a bend, Shakki whispered, "We don't have much time. Even if no one's noticed us yet on the netcams, Charf is sure to tell someone she saw us."

Kayla ripped the latch from the door. When it didn't give way, she made a club of her joined fists and bashed at the door until it crashed open, uncaring of the bruises she'd have later. They slipped inside.

"Once they come," Shakki said, "there's no way to keep them out."

"I have an idea."

Kayla raced to the towers of kel-grain. She unlocked the top four from one tower, the crates wobbling as she pulled them free. Even with her strength, she staggered under the four-hundred kilo weight carrying them to the door. Once those were in place, she went back for stack after stack, building a wall at the door, six high, four across, two deep.

Kayla put a hand on the crates, feeling weak from her effort. "That's thousands of kilos they'll have to shift to get at us."

They ran past the towers of kel-grain toward the freight lift. Shakki gasped out, "We're a couple of cornered rat-snakes if someone thought to call the lift up to another level."

But the lift was still there, doors open. As they pelted toward it, Kayla heard shouts from the warehouse door—Aideen begging them to stop, Charf bellowing out orders for her to come back, other voices she didn't recognize.

Shakki moaned and muttered a prayer to the Infinite, but she jumped into the lift alongside Kayla and helped tug the doors shut. Shakki woke the keypad display with a brush of her fingers against the black glass panel.

"Only two chances to get it right," Shakki said, "then it'll lock out."

Shakki entered the code with deliberate taps. When she hit Enter, the screen flashed red and made a rude noise.

"Denking hell." Shakki shook out her hand. "Fingers slipped."

This time she went even slower. Through the lift door, Kayla heard the scrape of plasscine crates against the rock floor of Godama 2. Her heart in her throat, she sighed with relief when Shakki hit Enter and the panel flashed green.

Shakki pressed her tattoo against the screen. For endless

moments, nothing happened.

Then an ACCEPTED message flashed on the screen. Shakki pushed the lever all the way to the right, past the intervening stops of L2 and L1, all the way to S. S had to be Surface.

The lift shuddered even harder than the smaller ones did as it started up. It began its slow crawl upward.

Kayla!

Kayla was shocked to realize it was Aideen, via the circuit-comm. Another promise broken.

Kayla, you can't go now, Aideen pleaded. *If you do, I don't know if I can keep you safe.*

What the denking hell did that mean? How was the woman keeping her safe now? She would only be safe if she could get away from Antara, and FHE, and Ohin. Kayla blocked Aideen's communications the way Shakki had taught her.

"Does it always go so slow?" Kayla asked as she stared at the glass panel that displayed the level. It lingered forever on LL, then finally L2 faded in to take its place, then L1 replaced L2.

"Surface is next," Shakki said.

Suddenly, the lift lurched to a stop. A moment later, the dim illuminator in the ceiling went out, and the glass panel display shut down. The total darkness seemed palpable.

"How do we get out?" Kayla asked.

"We don't," Shakki said. "They've got us."

There had to be a way. She only needed a few moments on the surface.

Groping in the dark, Kayla found the door handles and yanked them open. She reached out farther, her palms slapping a wall of limestone just centimeters from the doors. She felt around the edges of the doors and couldn't squeeze much more than her hand through. There was no escape that way.

Then she remembered what Lovise had said. "There's a hatch, isn't there?" Kayla asked. "And a ladder in the shaft." Lovise had also mentioned rat-snake nests in the ladder rungs, but Kayla wouldn't think about that.

The lift lurched again. Then the lights flickered on and the car started slowly traveling downward, back to the lower level.

"I can't go back," Kayla said. "I have to see."

The hatch handle dangled from a plasscine chain above her, out of reach. She crouched and jumped as high as she could. Her first try didn't come close, but with her second leap, her fingers brushed the handle. A third clumsy try, then the fourth she hooked her fingers around the plasscine loop. The door fell open and swung above her.

She turned to Shakki. "Help me up."

"You can't go without me," Shakki said.

"I won't. I'll pull you up once I'm through the hatch."

Shakki cupped her hands and Kayla stepped into them. Kayla teetered precariously, using the wall for balance as she reached as far as her arm would stretch. Then she dragged her body up, higher, higher, until she was scrambling onto the top of the elevator.

"Now me," Shakki called. "Pull me up."

Kayla leaned through the opening. "I have to leave you. That way they'll believe that I forced you to take me."

"Kayla, no. You can't go out there without me."

"I only want to know where we are." And try to escape if it was at all possible.

"You won't be able to. And it isn't safe."

Kayla could see real fear in Shakki's eyes. "If I get away, I'll come back for you."

She pulled the hatch door shut, closing off Shakki's terrified face, blocking her circuit-comm at the same time. Luckily, a few dim illuminators lit the shaft, enough light that she spotted the shallow ladder reaching to the top. She jumped from the lift car to the nearest rungs. Climbing the ladder was easier than pulling herself through the hatch, but her muscles were so worn out already. Was it possible she'd done damage to herself by overusing her sket? She'd already worked so much today on her shift before all the hurried lifting and bashing.

She kept moving, her head spinning as she moved higher. She knew the moment they'd figured out she wasn't in the lift by a faint shout and the almost immediate change of direction of the car. Weren't they worried they might squash her against the limestone ceiling of the shaft? Or had Ohin had enough of her, and was just as glad for a way to get rid of her? She flung a quick prayer to the Infinite for Shakki's safety.

Then, thank the blessed Creator of the creators, she reached the surface level. Here was the tricky part—could she reach out far enough to snag one of the door handles? At least with the car rising she wouldn't have too far to fall. But then they'd catch her.

Holding onto the ladder with one trembling hand, she stretched as far as she could toward the door. She just managed to snag the handle with her fingertips. She broke three nails to the quick, but she tugged the door open far enough to get a better grip on the handle. Holding the door as tight as she could, she extended her leg and angled herself out of the shaft.

As she rolled across the floor to get clear, she felt hands grabbing her. Summoning her sket strength, she wrenched away, sending the GEN man who'd tried to capture her flying.

Another GEN, a woman, was approaching from the other side, but Kayla slapped at her, and sent the woman to her knees.

Guilt twinged in her that she might have hurt the GEN man and woman, but Kayla pushed aside her regret and just ran. She could see a pair of doors ahead, plasscrete set in an opening of the cavern. They were triple her height. They had to lead to the exit.

There was nothing more than a loose plassteel bar set in a pair of brackets keeping the door shut. She grabbed the bar and was about to fling it aside when an idea sparked in her mind. Gripping the bar, she ran back to the lift, which had still not quite cleared the surface level. She wedged the heavy plassteel bar between the roof of the car and one of the ladder rungs. Then she ran back to the exit and shoved open the doors.

She knew it was night, even without the confirmation of her internal clock, but she was still surprised by the utter blackness outside. Even isolated adhikar land was dotted with a little light from the lowborn managers' cottages. But ten meters beyond the two illuminators set on either side of Antara's entrance, not even starlight seemed to penetrate the darkness.

A few meters from the door, a wall of boulders four times as tall as she was towered over her, stretching to the left and right into the darkness. She could make out crevasses between the rock towers, black against the dark gray of the boulders. If there was anything living out there, even so much as a scraggly sticker bush, she couldn't see it. Even the most isolated northern adhikar had something growing on it, even if it was fallow with nothing but scrap grass. Where could she be?

Lingering just outside the door, she tapped into her locator software and waited for the program to access the nearest positioning signal. It would take longer in a remote area like this one seemed to be since the signals would be more widely spread. And it might only give her an approximate location in whatever sector it identified from her internal map.

But the locator kept searching and searching, sweeping the area over and over without result. She boosted the receiver as high as it would go, but still she got no answer. Her skin prickled with unease and instinct told her it would be safer to go back. But how could she without some clue of where she was?

The GEN man and woman would start to stir soon. And it wouldn't take her pursuers long to figure out the bar was wedged in the elevator shaft. Someone would either use the hatch, or the GEN man or woman would rouse and pull it away.

Maybe she had to get farther from the cavern and past that wall of boulders. They could be blocking whatever positioning signal was out here.

She stepped out farther from the doorway, and a blast of wind nearly took her off her feet. A storm? This was the month of Anceathru, well into Loka's spring. She'd never seen a spring storm this fierce, not even in the most northern sectors.

Where could she be?

Fighting the wind, she felt along the rock face with her hand, searching in the dimness for a space wide enough to squeeze into. At first she found only cracks she could barely wedge a finger into. But suddenly a space opened up, and she stumbled into it, falling to her knees.

Her shins were throbbing with pain, but at least she was protected from the wind here. She pushed to her feet and reached out to either side. The opening in the rock wall was maybe a hand's length wider than her shoulders on either side. How deep did it go?

Her back to Antara and the clearing around it, she walked along, feeling her way with her palms on either side. From the smoothness of the rock, she guessed that this opening was man-made. Which had to mean it led somewhere, otherwise why use energy-gobbling lase-powered equipment to create it?

She might be safer from the wind within the passageway, but its high walls cut off the light even more. There was only so much her circuitry could do to help her eyes take in more light, which meant she barked her already sore shins on every obstacle she came across. The path was littered with rocks, some wide enough she couldn't walk around them and had to climb over them instead. Even standing atop the tallest of the rocks, the top of her head came nowhere near the upper edge of the sheer granite walls on either side.

She continued doggedly on with nothing but faint starlight lighting her way. The trinity moons seemed to have abandoned this place. She touched into the lunar chart tucked away in her annexed brain. Avish and Ashiv had arced across the sky during the day. Abrahm wouldn't rise for another hour.

Just as she reached the top of another pile of rocks, a powerful gust of chilly wind thrust into the passageway and struck her hard. Losing her balance, she tumbled down the pile and banged into the rock walls on either side. When she hit the bottom, she lay there, dazed.

She'd been so sure at the beginning that the smooth sides meant this was a man-made path, that it led somewhere. But maybe she was wrong. Considering how difficult the going was, this couldn't be the way they'd brought in all those crates of kel-grain and synth-protein and dried soy milk. It seemed more and more like she was going the wrong way.

The boulders on either side increased in height the farther

she got from Antara, as if the stone was a live thing growing. There was no climbing them. She'd just have to keep pushing through the narrow passage and hope there was an exit somewhere. Thank the Infinite she was as small as she was.

Above her, the stars had grown more vivid to her light-starved eyes. At a slightly wider point in the passageway, she could see that the constellations looked different. The handful of stars that constituted the Enforcer was directly overhead instead of nearer the eastern horizon. The Prayer Mirror, a simple arrangement of four points of light, wasn't the rectangle she knew from her home sector, but a warped, sharp-angled thing.

Antara must be in Eastern Territory then. Kayla had spent very little time there, but had traveled quite a bit in Northeast Territory's most eastern sectors, Skyloft and Ret. The constellations looked different in Skyloft and Ret, but nowhere near as misshapen as here. Just how far east was she?

The path narrowed so that she had to travel sideways. Then five or so meters ahead of her, she could see it opened wide into a clearing floored with granite. She hung back, reluctant to confront the wind whipping by.

But she leaned out far enough to see what had been built in the center of the roughly fifty meter by seventy-five meter open space. It was an enormous plassteel enclosure, a good ten meters tall, thirty meters square. The sides were meshed, the squares of plassteel no larger than her palm. Haphazard piles of rock littered the floor within the meshed walls. Stacked against one side was a peculiar heap of pearlescent white globes, as big around as the circle of Kayla's arms. The enclosure's massive gate lay open.

What in the Infinite's name could they be storing in there? It was open to the elements with that mesh, so it made no sense to stage the crates of foodstuffs here. Shakki had mentioned a meat animal had gone into the night's dinner. Could this be a trap of some kind? But why so large a trap?

She stepped out of the passageway, stumbling a little as the wind hit her. Bracing herself against its power, Kayla moved until she'd put twenty meters or so between herself and the rock walls. This was as open an area as she was going to get.

A suspicion had crept inside her, bringing with it despair. Even so, she tested her locator, her hands tightening into fists as it came up empty. Even the most isolated sectors in Eastern Territory would have had enough positioning signals for her to pick up. Yet her receiver heard nothing.

There was only one part of Svarga where there were no signals at all. Her suspicions were growing more concrete.

She inched a little closer to the enclosure. What *were* those strange white globes? Some kind of fruit native to this area? Except she'd seen nothing like a plant growing, not so much as a sticker bush or a sprig of chaff heads.

She was halfway to the enclosure when some instinct froze her. A dry scraping sound approached from her left.

A *thing* was moving toward her—purplish-black, a good five to six meters long and as big around as she was. It slithered along the ground, looking like an enormous rat-snake that had lost its head and legs.

If it had eyes, she couldn't see them. Something like a tongue flicked out from the nearest end and it seemed to correct its course so that it was heading straight toward her.

Kayla backed up to the cage. She reached the gate and pulled it shut. There was a locking mechanism, but it was electronic, and without the code, she wouldn't be able to engage it. But surely she was strong enough to hold the gate shut against that slithering creature.

But it didn't try to pull the gate open. It just flattened itself no thicker than Kayla's hand and started squirming *under* the gate.

Kayla swallowed a shriek, then let go of the gate and ran to the other side of the cage. The ugly creature continued squirming under the gate, but it didn't move fast. She would only have to wait until it was inside, then she would run past it and out through the gate.

But as she watched it, the fat purple thing halted, two thirds of its body in, one third out. It changed course, moving left toward a ten-centimeter crack in the rock. It dove into the crack, compressing its body, as centimeter by centimeter it disappeared.

Kayla raced for the gate, wrenching it open again, putting distance between herself and where the snaky purple creature had disappeared. She turned in the clearing, searching for safety, but there was nothing but rock walls looming over her, and dozens of cracks that could hide more of the slithering menaces.

She jolted as loose rock tumbled to her left. She heard a new sound, like the tapping of a dry stick against a plasscrete wall. She'd heard that sound before, but it had never been so loud and heavy.

A bhimkay leapt into the clearing.

She'd seen young spiders that reached halfway up her thigh, the full grown variety that came to her waist. But this one towered over her, twice her meter-and-a-half height. It was blacker than the wind-whipped night, the red marking on its abdomen flashing in and out of view as the eight long, segmented legs scrambled across the boulders.

It had spotted her. It was heading her way.

The passageway. It was too tight for the bhimkay to fit, wasn't it? But she couldn't get her feet to move. Sheer terror rooted her in place.

She wept, because the bhimkay was creeping nearer. The wind drove the tears from her eyes. She would die here in this hell.

Suspicion vanished, settling into fact. She knew exactly where she was.

The Badlands. The impossible eastern half of Svarga continent. Barricaded from the habitable sectors of Western Svarga by an unforgiving mountain range called the Wall. Nothing lived in the Badlands.

Except squirming monster snakes and oversized bhimkay.

The spider had stopped, crouching head-down toward Kayla. Its myriad eyes seemed to take her in.

That was enough to shake loose Kayla's paralysis. Realizing the enclosure was nearer than the passageway, she took off running. The bhimkay wouldn't be able to slither under the gate.

But the spider was running too, its long legs eating up the distance. She'd nearly made it to the gate, was just centimeters from the safety of the enclosure.

The spider overtook her. It knocked her to the ground and sank its venomous mandible into her thigh.

11

Could you take another look?" Devak held up the five-by-five centimeter holo projection of Shun to the scowling lowborn man. "You barely glanced at it."

The lowborn man standing in the doorway of his Viata sector flat didn't shift his gaze from Devak's face. "I told you I've never seen him. I don't associate with trueborns. Avoid the whole lot of you if I can help it."

Now his scowl shifted to a sneer as his gaze strafed Devak from head to toe. Devak's clothes were filthy after eight days taking pub-trans from place to place and sleeping in crowded public houses. The lowborn man, clearly a prosperous businessman with his fine dromwool jacket and pants, made Devak feel as lowly as a sewer toad.

Devak took a breath to ask again, but the lowborn slammed his flat door in Devak's face, cutting him off. Devak clutched the thumb-sized holo projector, what he'd taken with him in lieu of the sekai that he'd left with Pitamah. The small HP belonged to Junjie, and had Junjie's only picture of his dead mother stored on it.

Devak had figured out a way to store three images on the device meant for one—Junjie's mother, Shun, and Kayla. Devak toggled the image now to Kayla and gave her a longing look. He wished desperately that he could talk to her, that he could tell her they were coming for her. Tell her about Pitamah. That his great-grandfather might be dying, that Zul might not be there when Devak finally got back home.

Switching off the hand-held HP, he stuffed it back in his carrysak and trudged toward the stairs. Junjie was making his way through the flats just above Devak on the warren's top floor. Maybe he'd had better luck.

Their three days searching for Shun in Creth sector had been fruitless. They'd then traveled to Wesja, a mixed sector to the south, and spent another two days with nothing to show for it. They were nearly to the end of their third day here in Viata, a mixed sector the size of Creth and Wesja combined, and still no sign of Shun.

Devak had been so smug thinking he'd found the boy, even more so with the image to show around. But despite the bait of the dhans, Shun must have gotten suspicious because he was nowhere near the flat Devak had been so sure they'd find him in. And everyone there denied ever seeing the boy.

As Devak pushed through the stairwell door into the top floor hall, he heard the sound of a slamming door. Junjie stood at the far end of the hall, mouth still open as if in mid-argument with some equally reluctant lowborn. Then, with slumped shoulders, Junjie trudged toward Devak.

"What about those other two flats on the end?" Devak asked.

"No one answers," Junjie said. "I hear voices inside, so someone is home, but I'm guessing they were warned about us."

Junjie took a last look at Shun's image on his wristlink,

then put the device into sleep mode. "What now? There's not another pub-trans down to Amik sector for two hours. It's nearly time for evening meal, and we ought to start looking for a place to spend the night."

Devak's stomach rumbled at the mention of evening meal. They hadn't eaten since morning, just before they left the public house, an unsatisfying meal of stale naan made of ground kelgrain, dipped into lukewarm kelfa.

They started down the stairs. Devak stopped at the bottom of the first flight and thumbed open the secret pocket in his carrysak to recount their remaining dhans. His heart fell at the tiny total.

"We have barely enough for a meal, let alone a public house." Devak stuffed the coins and bills back into the secret pocket and continued down the stairs. "I'm not even sure if it's enough for pub-trans fare to Amik."

Junjie let out a long hiss of air. "Which means we have no way of getting home, either."

At the next landing, Devak rounded on Junjie. "Do you want to give up? When we haven't even found Shun?"

"No, but if we haven't the dhans to go forward and we don't have enough to go back, we need more dhans."

"Am I supposed to make them out of thin air?" Devak snapped his fingers.

"Of course not," Junjie said. "And I know we've been as careful as we could be with the money. But all the traveling around we've been doing—"

"I thought he'd be in Creth sector!" Devak shouted, then he bit back his anger. "I know this is all my fault. I should have studied the data longer. I shouldn't have sent him that wristlink message. That's what scared him off."

Junjie took Devak's arm, and urged him down the stairs. Once outside, they started down the street in the direction of the pub-trans stop.

The first of the brother suns, Iyenku, had set. With Iyenku's brother, Kas, close to the horizon, the sky overhead had darkened to a deep green. The air had chilled, reminding Devak how cold the northern sectors could get even in spring. He'd had a fleeting idea that they could find a private place to sleep outside, but not in this weather.

Illuminators were coming on in the shops on the right-hand side of Xata Street, and in the flats on the left side. Merchant shops like the clothing and supply stores would be closing down soon, but the curry shops were starting to fill up with the evening meal crowd. Another hunger pang stabbed Devak's stomach.

"It's stupid to blame anyone for anything," Junjie said, drawing Devak out of his gloom. "It won't do us any good."

"You're right." Devak pulled Junjie out of the flow of the crowd. "I want you to know, I'm really glad you're with me. I'm lucky to have you as a friend."

"Me too. It's good that we're doing this together."

"I've been wanting to say . . ." A lump settled in Devak's chest. "But I don't want it to come out as some kind of big insult."

"I can't imagine you insulting me."

Devak let the words come out in a rush. "I'm glad I'm not high-status anymore, that I'm not even demi. It's a relief to just be minor-status like you."

Devak held his breath, waiting for Junjie's response. His friend smiled. "I just want you to be happy, whatever status you are. Even if you were lowborn or GEN, it wouldn't matter to me."

A warmth filled Devak. It felt like a thousand-kilo weight

had just floated off his shoulders. He clasped Junjie's hand. "Thank you."

They moved off again. Up ahead, Devak spied the pub-trans stop. "I don't know that we have enough dhans for passage. We could probably get a little food though."

"I have an idea about dinner," Junjie said.

He pulled Devak past the covered stop. As they went on, the bustling crowd along Xata Street thinned. The storefronts and flats ended. They passed a last set of street illuminators on either side of Xata Street. Then Kas dropped below the horizon and between the loss of that light and that of the storefronts, the going was nearly dark.

Devak could see the dimmest of lights in the distance. What was up ahead? He tried to envision the map of Northwest Territory. Because of a lack of water, most of Viata's settled areas were in the west of the sector. Right up against the eastern border of the GEN sector, Cati.

"Are we going into Cati?" Devak asked.

"I thought our dhans might go farther there," Junjie said. "If you're not squeamish about rat-snake stew."

Right now, he'd almost eat a rat-snake raw. They hurried along the rough, unpaved path, focused on the nearest glow of light.

"There'll be nothing like a curry shop here," Junjie said. "We'll have to ask for a meal in a private home. I've done it once or twice. Not too many GENs will say no to either a trueborn or the dhans."

What had been Xata Street in Viata sector became Niba Street in Cati. Unlike the well-kept, neatly painted multi-housing in Viata, the walls of the GEN warrens were pitted and cracked, the defects black shadows in the faint light of the illuminators along the street. Chin-high sticker bushes crowded close to the unpaved roadway, and the symbiotic fungus on the junk trees glowed blood red in the failing light.

On one warren wall, Devak caught a glimpse of a four-story-tall mural of a GEN woman with hands uplifted, a prayer mirror in her hands. Scrawls of GENscrib marred the mural. He'd learned a bit of GENscrib from GENs he'd met in the Kinship safehouses and could read part of the graffiti. Nothing but crass meanness, befitting this desolate place.

Clusters of GEN adults crowded around the two lit street illuminators, maybe two dozen in all. He wondered why these few GENs were loitering in the street rather than in their flats preparing evening meal for themselves or their nurture children.

Weirder still, there were no nurture children in sight, not an under-ten, nor an under-fifteen nearing a first Assignment, not even a babe in arms. Only those men and women, the youngest among them maybe a twentieth-year.

Devak could tell when his and Junjie's presence had been registered by the GENs—the murmur of conversation ended. One by one, then in twos and threes, everyone on the street turned their way.

As he got close enough to more clearly see the adults' faces, he saw their clear rage at his and Junjie's intrusion in their sector. Devak's forward pace stuttered and slowed.

"They don't want us here," Devak said softly to Junjie.

"Trueborns show up out of the blue," Junjie said, "they're probably worried about what we're doing here."

"Why no children?" Devak asked.

"Maybe they're all in the flats with their nurture parents," Junjie said.

Which would explain where the rest of the GENs might

be. Cati sector should be home to hundreds of GENs, not just these twenty or so.

A half dozen men and a few of the women—the tallest and most muscular—broke off from the crowd and strode toward Devak and Junjie. Devak put out a hand to stop his friend. "I don't think they're worried."

Just as Devak was considering turning and running, the GENs had flanked them, then surrounded him and Junjie. A pale-skinned GEN man so broad and tall he nearly blocked the light from the nearest street illuminator towered over Devak. The illuminator behind the GEN made a silvery halo of his near-white hair.

"What are you here for?" the GEN demanded.

"We . . ." Junjie's voice trembled and he had to start over. "We were hoping for a meal. We have some—"

Devak squeezed Junjie's arm tightly, stopping his words. "We took a wrong turn, went over the Viata-Cati border by mistake. We'll just go back the way we came."

Devak moved to turn around, but the massive GEN man yanked Devak back toward him, a handful of Devak's shirt in his meaty fist. "You're here to spy. Not happy just to use the 'cams. Have to walk your dirty selves into our homes."

Devak had never feared GENS, had learned from Kayla that all those superstitions about GENs and trueborns touching one another were nonsense. But as he felt the circle of GENs tighten, felt their anger heat the very air, his heart pounded in his chest.

"If you'll just let us go, we'll leave," Devak said, pressing as close to Junjie as he could, ready to defend his friend. "We didn't mean to cause you any trouble."

"Not enough to steal the food from our warehouses,

trueborn?" the GEN man said. "Have to come here to steal more of it to feed your fat selves?"

The big GEN pulled hard again on Devak's shirt and it ripped at the shoulder. His knuckles scraped Devak's chest as he brought up his other fist. "I think I ought to redecorate that fine trueborn face. See how *you'd* like spending some time in a gen-tank."

All these months, falling in love with Kayla, working with the Kinship for GEN rights, it shocked Devak how all the ugly, ingrained beliefs about tankborns flooded him. They were brutal, and stupid, and dangerous. He hated himself as the thoughts raced through his mind, but he couldn't control the response to his fear.

More hands grabbed him from behind, pinning his arms back. From Junjie's squawk of pain, Devak guessed they'd done the same to him. Elbows knocked into him, jolts of pain along his newly-healed back. Curious fingers tugged at the closure of his carrysak.

"Let my friend go," Devak pleaded. "You can do whatever you want with me."

The big GEN hesitated for just a moment, then he cocked back his fist. Resisting the urge to shut his eyes, Devak stared the GEN down.

"Cheffa!" a voice cried out beyond the circle of GENs. "All of you, let them go!"

Cheffa's fist loosened a bit, then tightened as new determination set on his shadowed face. Bootsteps crunched toward them across the dirt and gravel road.

"Cheffa, leave off," the man said again. Devak heard the authority in the voice, saw the rage drain from Cheffa's face.

With a growl, Cheffa dropped his hands and took a step

back. The circle of GENs broke up and they drifted back to the street illuminators. Devak quickly checked his carrysak. The little holo projector, the only thing he cared much about, was still inside.

Devak looked over at their rescuer. A young GEN man in a Brigade uniform, pale brown skin and light brown eyes. In his twenties, Devak guessed. After a few moments' struggle to retrieve the pre-explosion memory, Devak came up with a name. "Waji."

Devak had met the GEN enforcer in Nafi, a GEN sector. Pitamah had sent Devak there after the bombing of a warren above a Kinship safehouse. But the real tragedy had been the death of a sixth-year GEN girl in the explosion. That had been the first time Devak had seen the rumbling of insurrection in the GENs, had witnessed their anger.

"Good to see you again, young Mar," Waji said.

"Not a Mar any longer." *Thank the Lord Creator.* Devak turned his head to bring the sapphire bali into the light.

Waji shrugged. "I can escort you back to Viata. Or if it was truly a meal you were looking for, I can offer you a few modest bites."

Devak wanted to say no. He suspected whatever the GEN enforcer gave Devak and Junjie would be food out of his own mouth. But he remembered Waji's pride and didn't want to insult the GEN.

"Thank you," Devak said. "We would appreciate the meal."

Waji led the way, one hand on his shockgun. As they passed the knot of GENs, Devak kept Junjie between him and Waji. The men and women who had threatened them kept their distance, but Cheffa looked as volatile as an enraged seycat.

"Where are the rest of them?" Devak asked. "The warrens all look dark, just when everyone should be inside preparing evening meal."

"This is all that's left in Cati," Waji said. "Social Benevolence came for the children first. That's how Cheffa and his partner lost their fourth-year nurture daughter. Enforcers have come in randomly to pick off certain GENs with high-value skets like tech or medic. Word filtered back that the GENs taken have all been reset before they're given new Assignments. The ones left in Cati have mostly physical skets, but they know that eventually they'll be taken, with nothing but a reset to look forward to."

They passed the rubble of a destroyed building. Devak eyed the remains of what was likely a foodstores warehouse, considering the shards of crates that littered the piles of broken plasscrete.

"When did this happen?" Devak asked.

"Six months ago, before I arrived," Waji said. "Not long after the children were taken. I heard no was one killed this time, thank the Infinite."

Waji led them down an alley between two warrens. A few illuminators on the walls above lent the narrow space a faint light.

As Devak followed, he kicked something soft and heard the squeal of a rat-snake as it scurried away. "When were you re-Assigned here?"

"Not long after the Nafi bombing," Waji said. "Armed GENs like me are starting to make some trueborns nervous, even though the shockgun versions they give a GEN can barely kill a sewer toad. But they know they need some kind of Brigade presence in the remote GEN sectors."

"But not trueborn enforcers," Devak said.

Waji looked back over his shoulder, eyes glittering in the dimness. "You saw what it was like with Cheffa and the others. They're losing their fear of trueborns entirely. They're more willing to risk a reset because they know that's likely their fate anyway."

"They're not worried about being destroyed?" Devak asked. "There are enforcers out there that would just as soon burn a GEN to nothing with a shockgun." And for those GENs who believed in the prophets' liturgy, that meant they'd never return to the Infinite's hands.

"Enforcers know better than to destroy a tankborn these days. Not with the problems the gene-splicers have been having creating new GENs."

"You've heard about that?" Devak asked. The issues with poor quality artificial embryos wasn't widely known, even amongst the Kinship.

"And I've passed that information on to as many GENs as I can." Waji's voice took on a hard edge. "Knowing gives us at least a little power."

The enforcer turned left around the back of the warren, followed by Devak, then Junjie. Junjie said, "They should know that it isn't trueborns bombing their warehouses, leaving them and their families hungry. It's FHE. It's been their plan all along to start a GEN uprising."

Waji gave Junjie a sharp look. "No matter who's done it, it's strengthened our will. And I'm glad enough of that."

Waji stepped up to a door set in the rear of the warren's first floor. He tapped out a code on a keypad beside the door—the lock a luxury afforded an enforcer—then led Devak and Junjie inside.

He shut and locked the door again before slapping on an

illuminator and poking a finger in Junjie's chest. "You know a lot about FHE."

Junjie kept his dark gaze locked with Waji's. "I was part of them once. Not anymore."

Waji stared a long time, then finally said, "And I was part of the Kinship. But I think now neither group is a friend to GENs."

"My great-grandfather, Zul, still is," Devak said in Pitamah's defense. "But you're right about the Kinship. They've lost their way."

They left it at that. Devak looked around the small windowless flat, its living room just large enough for a sofa and a legged side chair. A hall led down to what Devak guessed was a sleeproom. The kitchen had been wedged in the corner opposite the living room, catty-corner to the sleeproom.

"Is there somewhere we could clean up?" Devak asked.

Waji took them down the flat's short hall to a door that opened to the warren's first floor corridor. The communal washroom lay just outside the flat's inner door.

Devak looked down the long, dark corridor. "No one will mind us using it?" He could just imagine Cheffa's reaction to finding him and Junjie here.

"I live alone in this warren," Waji said. "The only building that's occupied is the farthest one down, and that one is only half full. You shouldn't have any problems here."

Waji returned to the flat, and Devak and Junjie stepped inside the washroom. Devak scanned the utilitarian space. The washrooms in the public houses they'd been staying in had been bad, but none of them were as rough as this one. There were no doors on the three necessaries, and the plasscrete walls and floors were split with cracks.

Both Devak and Junjie made quick use of it, relieving themselves in the necessaries, then using the dribble of water from the faucet to wash up. Nothing like the luxury of the warm showers he'd enjoyed in the big house in Foresthill, or even the bath in Pitamah's small home in Ekat. But after the grubbiness of the last several days, it felt good to clear away some of the dirt.

They changed into their least-soiled kortas and chera pants, then used the thin stream of water to rinse some of the stains from their other clothes. They spread the wet clothes over the walls of the necessaries.

Waji was busy in the kitchen when they got back to the flat. Devak and Junjie both offered to help, Junjie peeling and slicing the patagobi root, Devak rinsing the kel-grain and measuring it into a pot. Waji pulled two long, skinny bodies from his coldstore. Their eight segmented legs had already been removed, but they were easy to recognize. Rat-snakes.

Devak couldn't suppress a fleeting nausea at the thought of eating them. But he was learning that meat was meat. Although Junjie had never spelled it out, Devak knew he'd eaten rat-snake already. It had been tasty enough.

"I can do one of them," Devak said.

Waji looked dubious, but he handed the larger one over, along with a second knife. The abdomen of the creature was the length of Devak's forearm. He watched Waji cut off the venomous head, then carefully nudge it into the mini-cin with the knife. Devak followed suit, then imitated Waji's cut along the underside of the abdomen, although more clumsily.

With the meat skinned and diced, Waji took over the meal. He tossed in what looked like dried chaff-head flowers, the blue of their petals faded to gray. The pulp of an overripe orangefruit, squeezed from its rind, added some juiciness to the rather dry meat. A little sprinkle of sakara added some sweetness.

Devak remembered Kayla telling him how GENs would add savor and variety to the food trueborns provided them. Sometimes they'd be allotted nothing more than the nutrition-packed but dull-flavored kel-grain. GENs would scour the empty fields and bare lots surrounding their warrens for anything palatable. The hour Waji had spent to make something to fill their stomachs was the least of it. How long did it take to find the chaff-heads, the wild patagobi?

Waji spooned up the stew over mounds of kel-grain, and they sat on the sofa, bowls balanced on their laps. Devak had to blank from his mind the look of the rat-snake as he'd skinned it, but he was so ravenous, he wolfed down the evening meal in silence. It turned out to be surprisingly delicious and filling.

The others shoveled the food into their mouths just as hungrily. It wasn't until Waji gathered the bowls that the enforcer asked, "Are you on Kinship duties? Is that why you've come to Cati?"

"Nothing to do with the Kinship," Devak said. "We're looking for someone."

Before Devak could reach the carrysak he'd left beside the sofa, Junjie brought up Shun's image on his wristlink. "We're looking for *him*, but only because we're hoping he'll lead us to Kayla."

Waji's eyes widened. "Kayla, nurture daughter of Tala? I thought she was killed in an FHE explosion." So GEN gossip of Kayla's heroism had reached Waji, as well.

"She wasn't," Devak said, fishing out the holo projector. He showed Kayla's image to Waji. "This is her *after* the explosion.

FHE has her. We think Shun might know where."

"Let me see the boy's image again," Waji said.

Devak swapped Kayla's image for Shun's on the HP. Waji took the device and gave it a long look. "I've seen him."

Junjie leapt to his feet, excitement brightening his face. "Where?"

"He's come in and out of this sector," Waji said, handing back the thumb-sized projector. "Keeps to the shadows, out of the way of Cheffa and the others."

"So he's here somewhere?" Devak asked.

Waji shrugged. "Last I saw him—maybe four days ago, close to nightfall—he was leaving Cati."

"Right after you sent that message." Junjie sank to the sofa again, enthusiasm deflated.

Devak wanted to kick himself for his stupidity. "So Shun's gone."

Another shrug from Waji. "He could have come into Cati again and I didn't see him. Being the only enforcer here, I can't be everywhere at once."

Junjie's fingers curled around the wristlink on his arm, the image of Shun his only connection to the boy. "Where does he go when he's here? Is he looking for food? Do you think he ever sleeps here?"

Waji shrugged. "He can't get into the empty warrens. Last time the Brigade was here, they boarded them up. I check them daily, and no one's been inside."

Junjie persisted. "What about the warren the GENs live in?"

"If he's gone in there, he'd better hope to the Infinite that Cheffa doesn't see him. I don't always feel safe in there myself. The Brigade uniform doesn't mean what it used to."

"Why wear it, then?" Devak asked. "I could take you off the

Grid. You could go anywhere you wanted."

"Maybe," Waji said. "For now, I feel like I can protect the Cati GENs at least a little as an enforcer."

"Except it seems like they don't want your protection," Devak said.

"I haven't been able to do much," Waji agreed. "I haven't been able to stop the Brigade when they show up to take GENs away. Or when they confiscate kel-grain and synthprotein from Cati's remaining warehouse."

"Why would the Brigade take GEN food?" Devak asked.

"To replace what's been stolen from trueborn foodstores," Waji told them.

"Stolen by whom?" Junjie asked.

In silent response, Waji raised his brow, gaze fixed on Junjie. "Ah," Junjie said. "FHE."

"We ought to at least check that last warren for Shun," Devak said.

Waji shook his head. "I don't see how that boy could make his way inside. There are plenty of empty flats, but they're all on the top floor. And Cheffa and his partner live on the first. They're nearest the front entrance, but even if the boy went in through the back, he'd risk Cheffa hearing him."

"He might use the fire ladder in the back," Junjie suggested. "To get into the upper floors without Cheffa seeing him."

Waji narrowed his gaze on Junjie, clearly considering. Then he let out a long breath. "I'd better come with you. Just in case you cross paths again with Cheffa."

Waji led the way again along the rocky, scrap grass-covered path behind the warrens. The first two of the trinity moons, Abrahm and Avish, had risen, Abrahm only a sliver, but Avish full and fat. They shone more light on the uneven ground than the illuminators had. Even so, long shadows cast by junk trees and sticker bushes could have easily hidden an attacker.

But they made it to the last warren without encountering anyone. Based on the lights in the windows, the crowd in the street must have gone in for their own evening meals.

A rear door identical to the one in Waji's warren unlocked into an empty, windowless flat like the enforcer's. It had the same short hall leading to an interior door that led to the first floor hallway just off the communal washroom.

"Best to start on the top floor," Waji said. "Avoid Cheffa as long as possible."

Waji led the way up the stairs. Once on the fifth floor, Devak and Junjie stayed out of sight while Waji knocked on doors of the flats he thought were empty. A couple times the enforcer encountered an occupied flat and had to soothe the irritated GENs inside.

The empties were all just that—empty. No one living there, no signs of anyone having been there in a long time—thick dust on the floors and food prep areas, rat-snake scat and nests everywhere.

They made their way down the floors, with fewer empty flats on the fourth, even fewer on the third and second, and only two on the first. Same results everywhere. No Shun.

The sweat of climbing stairs and the dust from the empty flats undid the cleaning up Devak and Junjie had done. They went into the first floor washroom and used the trickle of water from the spigot to clear away the muck.

Waji needed to use one of the necessaries, so Devak made a point of stepping aside to give the GEN some privacy. As he stood there, his gaze fell on the back corner of the washroom. Odd that the cracking there formed a perfect square. Odder still that a hand-sized piece of the plasscrete had broken out in the center, almost like a handle.

"Oh, sweet Lord Creator," Devak murmured.

He hurried over to the corner and fit his fingers into the broken out slot. Straddling the half-meter square of plasscrete, he pulled.

He'd expected the square to be heavy, but there must have been some counterweight on the other side because it moved more easily than he expected. It was hinged as well, lifting up and leaning against the wall. Chill air gusted up from the hole beneath.

Devak heard a scrabbling from the hole, clearly made by something larger and heavier than a rat-snake. He turned to Waji. "Do you have an illuminator?

Waji handed over a black metal tube marked with the black and red bhimkay emblem of the Brigade. Devak switched it on and shone it in the hole. It lit a ladder leading down.

Waji tried to take back the illuminator. "*I* should check it out."

Devak shook him off and swung down to the ladder, illuminator clenched in his teeth. Despite his bravado, he was praying to the Lord Creator that whoever was down there wasn't armed.

At the bottom, Devak turned, shining the illuminator down the tunnel at the ladder's foot. The light caught a boy backed up against a pile of rock that blocked the tunnel.

Even through the dirt on the boy's face, Devak recognized him. It was Shun.

12

Kayla lay in the uneven, jutting rocks, her body paralyzed. She tried to will herself to move, to run away, but all strength had left her.

The massive bhimkay stood over her, one front leg at her feet, the other centimeters from her face. The legs were as big around as the meaty part of Kayla's thigh where the creature had bitten her, shiny black and barbed with thick, sharp hairs.

Kayla's racing heart pounded so loudly in her ears, she couldn't hear the wind anymore. Was it just fear? Or was her speeding heart rate a side effect of the spider's venom? She'd learned about bhimkay in Doctrine school—the facts about bhimkay bites must have been stored somewhere in her annexed brain. But her GEN circuitry wouldn't respond, couldn't follow the path to the information she needed.

Her circuitry's warming function wasn't working either. The night cold had intensified until shudders rocked her body. Where she'd fallen after the bhimkay let her go, a fist-sized stone stabbed into her back, and with each shiver it scraped through her torn shirt.

The creature's body vibrated above her, its legs dancing. Kayla had only witnessed a bhimkay strike and consume prey once in her life—while she was traveling with the lowborn, Risa. They'd parked Risa's lorry outside the fenced adhikar in Central Western Territory, to rest for the night. The bhimkay had snatched a full-grown seycat that had caught its leg in a rat-snake trap. The bhimkay had dispatched the seycat quickly with a bite, then waited until its venom liquefied the six-legged feline's body. A few minutes later, the spider had folded its legs and sucked up the masticated tissue.

Oh, sweet Infinite, was that what was about to happen to her? Would the bhimkay venom dissolve her muscles, her organs, so the giant spider could eat her?

Her heart still thundered in her ears and she could still draw breath. Her shivering had slowed, which could mean she was so cold she was past that reflex. She tested her circuitry, and discovered she could warm herself again. Could her GEN healing be fighting off the bhimkay venom?

Just as faint hope rose in her, the bhimkay bent its legs and crouched lower. It grew near enough that if Kayla could have lifted her arm, she could have touched the mandibles, each one as long as her forearm. But she was still at the spider's mercy, still too weak to save herself.

The bhimkay's head and abdomen hovered less than a meter above Kayla. Two of its legs—the second of the four on the right, the third on the left—started to curl toward Kayla. The other six legs remained motionless.

The hooked feet moved slowly across the tumbled rock toward her body. Then she felt the legs sliding under her, one at her shoulders, one at her hips. The spider kept its barbed hairs close to its legs so they only lightly scraped Kayla's skin.

And then the bhimkay lifted her.

Kayla went wild with terror, the last of her strength spent struggling to get loose. But the creature didn't let go. It just danced a little on its six feet to keep its balance, then pulled her up close to its abdomen.

Fear won't help me. I have to think!

The spider started to move. Kayla could look to the side and saw the bhimkay was carrying her into the wire mesh structure. They were angling across the cage toward the white globes she'd seen before.

As they got closer, Kayla could see the globes were translucent, and within many of them, eight fragile legs wriggled on a body the size of her head. Bhimkay babies.

Dear Infinite, she wasn't food for them, was she? Was that what the spider was saving her for?

They stopped beside the pile of eggs. The way the bhimkay held her, Kayla was nowhere near the mouth parts. If she could just gather enough strength, she could slip free. She would run as best she could and close the gate.

If she could outrun a bhimkay.

Kayla readied herself. The paralysis seemed to have passed. She still felt weak, but if she could stand, if she could at least stagger away, maybe she had a chance.

The bhimkay started to bend its legs again, to crouch. Kayla tensed, wary of the sharpness of the hair barbs. The two legs holding her seemed to relax.

Then Kayla heard the distant shouts and the bhimkay shrieked and stiffened. Its grip tightened on Kayla, squeezing her hard enough that the point of the hair barbs pricked her skin. The creature stood there frozen, as if its own venom had turned on itself and paralyzed it.

People started spilling from the rock crevasse into the clearing—Shakki first, then Ohin, then a gang of eight well-muscled GEN boys. All the boys were armed with meter-long sticks.

Shakki ran across the clearing straight into the cage, seemingly fearless in the face of the massive bhimkay. But the bhimkay no longer seemed to be a threat. It stayed frozen, the legs on the ground half-bent, but trembling, the two surrounding Kayla still too tight.

Shakki shouted, "Tak, let her go." The GEN girl had what looked like a palm-sized sekai in her hand, and she tapped it. The bhimkay's legs finally unlocked and it lowered itself and Kayla to the ground.

Kayla crawled out from under the spider, cut all over by the barbs, the mandible strike oozing blood. Shakki tucked away the sekai-like thing and helped Kayla to her feet. Kayla leaned against the smaller girl.

As Shakki and Kayla passed through the gate, the burly boys started to enter the cage. "Leave off," Shakki ordered them. "Tak has had enough punishment."

She realized the boys were the same ones she'd seen playing violent games in the Bhimkay Lounge. They looked disappointed at Shakki's demand. Kayla took a close look at the sticks the boys carried. With that control panel at one end, and the boys' eagerness to use them, they must be a weapon of some kind.

The boys backed down, but Shakki muttered, "Wish I could keep them from playing their mean tricks with the others so easily."

"Others?" Kayla asked.

"I'll explain later," Shakki said.

"How did I survive the bhimkay's bite?" Kayla asked.

"Tell you that later too," Shakki said in a rush.

Kayla saw why when Shakki dipped her head at Ohin's approach. "Always one with you."

Kayla couldn't bring herself to either bow her head or say the words. Even so, Ohin's look was kind and caring. "Why did you run, Kayla? I'd hoped you were one of us now."

Never, Kayla thought. After they'd abducted her, kept her imprisoned, lied to her about Devak, how could she want to be part of FHE? Not even to save her own life could she give Ohin or FHE her loyalty.

"Let's get you inside," Ohin said. "The medics should take a look at you."

Kayla glanced at Shakki, and the girl's eyes widened slightly. Kayla tried to read whatever message Shakki was trying to pass. Then Kayla remembered she had blocked her roommate from speaking to her via the circuit-comm. She hastily removed the block.

No medics, was all Shakki would say on that inner comm.

Kayla nodded ever so slightly. She flung her arm around Shakki's shoulders and they headed toward the path back to Antara.

It was slow going. Every part of Kayla ached, not just from the bhimkay wounds and the residue of the venom, but the headlong rush to escape had overtaxed her muscles. She had to lean hard on Shakki. At the points when the going narrowed enough that Kayla had to sidle through, she clutched so tightly on Shakki's shoulder to keep her feet that the younger girl grunted with pain. Although Kayla could have used the help of someone bigger and stronger, she refused to let Ohin or the boys so much as touch her.

Once they got back inside Antara and the doors were locked behind them, the gang of boys trooped away to pile into the freight lift. Kayla felt so tired, she wished she could curl up on the stone floor right there. Her quarters seemed impossibly far away.

Ohin reached for Kayla's hand. "We should take her to one of the Maramatas. She might need a tank session to pull out the rest of the venom."

Shakki stepped between Kayla and Ohin, forcing Ohin to let go of Kayla. Shakki was half his size, yet she was clearly determined to protect Kayla from the FHE leader.

"She just needs a good night's sleep, in her own bed," Shakki said. "I'll clean her up. All the time I spent helping the GEN healer in my home sector, I've got enough med training to take care of Kayla."

Kayla could see Ohin's reluctance, but he nodded. "If her condition gets worse, take her to Medic Palla."

The freight lift was nearest, but the thick-headed boys had taken it and it was still descending to the lower levels. So Shakki guided Kayla past it down a gently curving corridor. "There's a passenger lift just up ahead," Shakki said.

As Ohin walked with them, he got that far away look on his face that told her he was using his circuit-comm. A vibration started up at the base of Kayla's skull and words started traveling along her circuitry, one-sided snatches of a conversation with the flavor of Ohin's voice. *She's fine . . . refusing to . . . can't force her.*

She tapped Shakki's circuit-comm. *Can you hear that?*

Hear what?

Nothing, Kayla said.

If she could hear Ohin, could he hear her? She didn't have his passkey, but could she backtrack along the path of her circuitry and speak to Ohin? Did she even want to?

Maybe it was worth the risk to be sure. She focused on the pathway Ohin's communication seemed to be using. Then she all but shouted, *Ohin! Ohin, are you there?*

The GEN leader didn't react, not a twitch of the shoulders, or a flick of his gaze toward her. He was still staring off into space as he walked beside them, caught up in his circuit-comm conversation.

Ohin! she called again, but again there was no response. Instead, more words zipped along her circuitry in the other direction, from him to her. *Need a plan . . . try again . . .*

Try what again? A chill prickled down Kayla's spine. Was it a reset he was talking about? Dear Infinite, if only she could hear the rest of what he was saying.

They reached the passenger lift. The car was waiting for them, door open, a trueborn man inside.

The man dipped his head. "Always one with you."

"Until the day, Aasif," Ohin replied.

Unlike the freight lift, this one only took them down one level to L1. They had to exit and wind around to a second lift that also only descended one level, then a third, before they finally got down to LL, the lowest level.

Even though Ohin shadowed them every step of the way, he didn't speak to Kayla or Shakki, didn't even look their way. The only thing he ever said aloud was to answer "Until the day," to all the himayati rattling out their oath of "Always one with you."

But he stayed busy on his circuit-comm and Kayla caught a few enigmatic phrases. *Keep to schedule . . . when they get there . . . complete the training.* Always only his side of the conversation, and not enough to make any sense out of it.

Shakki and Kayla finally parted company with Ohin outside the lift and made their way to Seycat. Slapping on the illuminator to their quarters, Shakki shoved the door shut with her foot and helped Kayla to her bed. Blessedly, Ohin's intrusion on her circuit-comm had stopped. Apparently whatever blocked anyone from listening in on her communication inside Seycat also blocked what she was picking up from Ohin.

"Can you undress yourself?" Shakki asked. "Or do you need my help?"

"I can do it." Kayla's hands shook so badly, she thought she'd have to take that back. But moving slowly, she managed to get her shirt, shoes, and leggings off. She left on her skivs and breast band, relieved that the bhimkay barbs hadn't shredded them.

Shakki, a packet of sani-wipes in her hands, whistled at the myriad wounds Kayla could feel all over her body. The mandible strike on her right mid-thigh was puffy and red from bhimkay venom. Her back felt riddled with tiny cuts from Tak's barbed hairs.

Shakki sat on the bed beside Kayla and swabbed at the leg wound. Kayla sucked in a breath at the excruciating pain. "Okay, tell me. Why didn't Tak's venom kill me?" she asked.

"Because when she was still in the egg, medics removed most of her venom sac." Shakki probed inside the wound with a sani-wipe and Kayla nearly knocked her hand away. "They only left enough of a sac for Tak to use to catch nagas, or hold off a wild bhimkay for a short time."

Kayla could feel sweat beading on her forehead. "I'm guessing nagas are those fat, nasty squirmy things?"

"That would be them." Shakki left off torturing Kayla's leg, shifting her attention to the wounds on Kayla's back. They stung, but not nearly as badly.

"I saw a naga," Kayla said. "It squeezed into a crack in the rock when the bhimkay came."

"I've seen the babies slide into openings no bigger than

your pinky," Shakki said, moving across Kayla's back, tossing aside bloody sani-wipes as she went. "There's nothing like them in the settled sectors, that's for sure. Tough and stringy, but they are tasty slow-cooked in a stew."

Now Kayla realized—that meat Shakki had bragged about, what they'd eaten last night—it was naga meat. "I guess I'd rather eat it than have it eat me."

"It couldn't have eaten you," Shakki said. "It barely has a mouth. They scrape lichen off the rocks for food."

"Then why did it chase me?"

Shakki laughed. "Body heat. It just wanted to cuddle up to you." Shakki patted Kayla's back lightly. "Done. Your GEN healing should do the rest."

Moving as creakily as an eightieth-year, Kayla went to the dresser for a sleep shirt. "So the medics remove most of the venom. But what was it you did that made the bhimkay freeze when she had hold of me?"

Shakki, busy gathering up sani-wipes, grimaced. "They install inhibitors in the bhimkay's brains." She pulled the palm-sized device she'd used earlier from an inner pocket. "We use these presakas to transmit commands. *I* only use it in an emergency, to keep a bhimkay from accidentally hurting someone. But some of those Bhimkay Boys go overboard, use the presaka to punish their spiders, in addition to the shocksticks."

"Spiders, plural?" Kayla remembered Shakki talking about *the others*. "How many are there that the medics have meddled with?"

"Ten in the original group." Shakki tossed the presaka on the dresser, then flung off her clothes. She fished a rumpled sleep shirt out of her blankets. "Two didn't tolerate the inhibitors and had to be killed."

Kayla lay carefully on her side to avoid the most injured spots on her back. "Can you switch off the illuminator? I'd like to sleep." Shakki did as Kayla asked. Kayla heard the other bed squeak as Shakki lay on it.

I'm hearing him, Kayla said without preamble. *Ohin. Through my circuit-comm.*

He has your passkey?

Aideen has had it for years, Kayla said, *but she promised she didn't give it to Ohin. I think I believe her. What I'm hearing . . . I don't think Ohin even knows I'm hearing. It's just bits and pieces of conversation I pick up when he's using his circuit-comm to talk to other people.*

Can you hear who he's talking to? Shakki asked.

No. That's what's weird. And I don't hear everything he says, although each time I hear more. I must have to be close to him, otherwise I guess I'd be hearing him all the time. And it doesn't seem like he can hear me. I tried calling to him in the corridor on our way here.

Are you sure it's Ohin you're hearing, and not pieces of old memories?

It sounds like him, the way you sound like you, and Aideen sounds like her. But I don't get why I can hear him and no one else.

I don't know if that's good or bad, Shakki said. *Might be good if you can figure out what he's planning, bad to have Ohin leaking into your head.*

They lay in the silent dark for a long time. Kayla drifted to sleep for a few seconds or a few minutes. When she woke again, she remembered her question about the bhimkay. *Are Tak and the others just used for hunting?*

Hunting and fending off the wild bhimkay, Shakki said, then she got an aggrieved tone to her voice. *And the Bhimkay Boys ride them. But I'm not allowed to. Ohin says I'm too small.*

It seems like small would be better.

To ride, maybe, Shakki said. *But Ohin intends the Bhimkay Boys to fight on spider-back. When Ohin says "Until the day?" He means when the big battle happens with the outsiders.*

Ohin's planning a war? Kayla asked, aghast. She thought wars were archaic things they'd left behind back on Old Earth.

I don't see how he can manage it. So many of the bombers get killed in the explosions, he's got to run out of martyrs sometime. And if he starts setting off bombs in the trueborn sectors, you can be sure the Brigade will put a quick stop to it.

Even so, knowing the damage Ohin could do, had been doing, made Kayla queasy. *How does Ohin even get the himayati out? Or bring new GENs in? The supplies, too—how does he get them past the Wall?*

Ohin had passageways excavated, Shakki said. *That's how Essali and I came in. The Brigade had caught us leaving a safe house in Jassa sector, and we were on a one-way trip to a reset. FHE operatives ambushed the enforcers before we could be stuffed into a Brigade Dagger. We were passed from one FHE operative to another until we got to Belk. That's where we picked up the first passageway.*

You walked all the way through the Wall from Belk?

It took three days, with rest stops and time to sleep. But the portable tank you were in would have been brought some other way. Not sure how. You can't exactly use a lev-cart over those boulders.

An idea sparked inside Kayla, bringing hope with it. *Then if we could find one of the passageways out—*

In the first place, Shakki said, *I don't know where they come into Antara. Probably into locked rooms you and I will never see. They may not have reset me before the trip, but when they brought me and Essali in, they blindfolded us for that last stretch so we never saw. In the second place,* Shakki went on, *don't you think the secret ways in would be well-guarded? Better than the surface?*

Kayla's hope extinguished. She lay on her bed, the dark adding to her gloom. It wasn't right to feel a little angry with Shakki, but she couldn't seem to help herself. *If you want to ride one of the bhimkay, why not just hop on? How could anyone stop you?*

You need a saddle, otherwise the hair barbs are too sharp. Ohin never gave me one. And there's no borrowing one. Those big hulking boys keep their saddles locked up in their quarters.

Not fair.

No. Shakki sighed. *The bhimkay are smarter than you'd think. They bond to the people who handle them.*

Is Tak bonded to you? Kayla asked.

No, another bhimkay is. A male called Pev. I taught him to carry me like Tak carried you. That's almost as good as riding.

Kayla, remembering how terrified she'd been wrapped in Tak's spike-studded legs, wasn't too sure that was something desirable. *Who is Tak bonded to?*

It used to be Essali, Shakki said. *They let us room together when we got here. She's the one who found out about Devak and told me.*

Could I talk to her? Find out what else she knows?

I don't know where she is, Shakki said. *One day she never came back to our quarters. I tried to find her on the circuit-comm. She didn't answer.*

Maybe she blocked you like I did, Kayla suggested.

No, Shakki said. *I can tell when I'm blocked. This is different. It's like she doesn't exist anymore.*

Foreboding weighted Kayla's heart. *Do you think she left? Escaped?*

Not escaped, Shakki said with certainty. *I've been wondering if they've reset her. Or . . . or, she's dead.*

13

Three days after Kayla's aborted escape, Aideen somehow persuaded Ohin that Kayla should be allowed outside. She knew Antara's location now, knew there was no escaping. Under Shakki's wing, Kayla would be just as safe outside as within the cavern, and she would be happier with the freedom.

Why Aideen had championed Kayla's cause, she had no idea. She couldn't help but be suspicious, wondering if this was Aideen's attempt to turn Kayla's heart toward her. But Kayla didn't look a gift drom in the mouth, and even thanked Aideen.

It had been Shakki's idea that Kayla take on Tak's care. The younger girl had performed some kind of magic on Ohin, managing to persuade him that Kayla would feel more a part of FHE if she could work with the bhimkay. Tak needed of a dedicated partner, and Shakki sold Ohin on the idea that Kayla was the perfect candidate.

Kayla thought they would just be giving the spider another chance to eat her. But Shakki assured Kayla that the fact that Tak had carried her to safety after accidentally biting her meant the bhimkay regretted what she'd done, at least as much as the creature could.

By the third day of her spider training, Kayla had stopped being completely terrified. She only felt the faintest fluttering in her stomach as she followed Shakki out of Antara's tall double doors, then along the passageway toward the clearing. The early morning sky above them was an intense emerald green Kayla had never seen in the settled sectors. It was cold enough to use her circuitry to warm herself, but Kayla had learned her first day out here that elevated body temperature would just bring out the nagas.

Shakki had thought it was hilarious when a baby naga, half its body squeezed into a crack, spiraled its way up Kayla's leg and pulled her up short. That one time with the naga lovingly hugging her leg, her sprawled on the rocks, was enough for Kayla to decide to endure the biting cold.

As they stepped clear of the passageway, the wire enclosure came into view. Kayla couldn't help herself—she froze, just as if another baby naga had taken hold of her. Every instinct in her told her to turn and run.

Eight giant bhimkay filled the enormous cage. They clung to the sides and ceilings, one of them spread-eagled across the inside of the gate. Tak huddled over her eggs, her clawed feet in constant motion, touching the egg coverings in turn. The spider tensed and hissed every time one of the other bhimkay got too close.

Shakki took Kayla's hand to urge her toward the enclosure. Kayla wanted to resist, but this being the third day visiting the bhimkay, it was time she finally got a little closer.

Shakki got Kayla to within a few meters of the cage, then Kayla's feet of their own accord planted themselves in the rocky dirt, halting her forward motion. The legs of the bhimkay that straddled the gate spanned a rough four-meter diameter circle. Its belly was a solid black, the trademark red design on its back not quite visible.

"These really aren't *genned* to be bigger?" Kayla asked. "Like the droms are?"

"Like I told you before, the Badlands grows them this big."

Kayla looked up at the bhimkay towering above her. "Tell me we don't have to walk in the gate with that thing there."

"We're not going in there at all," Shakki said. "Not without any of the other handlers here."

Kayla looked around her at the empty clearing. Yesterday and the day before, they'd come an hour or two later. The other six handlers had already been out here, presakas and shocksticks in hand, roaming the exterior of the cage. They were supposedly "training" the bhimkay, but their training seemed to consist of shouting and poking the shockstick through the wire mesh. Once they had their spiders in a frenzy, they'd freeze them with a presaka command, strap their saddles on, and take off on spider-back.

Shakki never came outside without the presaka, but she didn't carry a shockstick. She'd said the first day, "If I'm cruel enough to the bhimkay to get bit, I deserve it."

At the time, Kayla had agreed because there were six other handlers out here with the weapons. But with just her and Shakki here, Kayla wasn't so sure.

"I'm not sure I'm ready to go inside the cage," Kayla said. So far, she'd only sat outside and watched Shakki work with Pev.

"There's nothing to worry about, really," Shakki said. "Last night, I hacked into the bhimkay database, so I have all the spiders' frequencies. That will let us command any of the bhimkay if we need to, not just Tak and Pev. And anyway, there's an emergency stop command that freezes any of the spiders for several minutes, long enough to get away."

"Tak bit me pretty quick that night I tried to run away," Kayla said.

"I really don't think she'd do that again." Shakki tugged Kayla along the long side of the enclosure. "I'd like to see if we can get Tak to start bonding with you."

Tak didn't look like she had any intention of paying attention to anything but her eggs. She hunched even more tightly against the pile as Kayla and Shakki approached.

"How much longer before the eggs hatch?" Kayla asked, stalling.

"That's up to Ohin," Shakki said. "The eggs were treated after she laid them to grow thicker shells. The babies won't be able to get out without human help. So even when they're ready, they'll have to wait for Ohin to give the order. The hatching will take days because Ohin will want the gen-techs to install the controller circuitry in each one before he lets the next one come out."

Shakki splayed her hand against the thick wire mesh just above the bhimkay's head. "If I call him, Pev will come out in a heartbeat. That's him on the gate. If we get him out, it might encourage Tak."

"Why get her out at all?" Kayla asked.

"We need to bond her with someone else," Shakki said, hand still against the mesh, her eyes on Tak. "That's one thing we've figured out—they do that in the wild with another spider."

"You mean, take a mate?"

"Not the same," Shakki said. "Mating is very mechanical. A female like Tak lays eggs, a male like Pev comes over and fertilizes them. The females tend to want to bond with other females. Males don't care."

"But how did you get Tak and Pev and the others to bond with humans?"

"Like nurture parents bond with the children Assigned to them," Shakki said. "We raised them."

"Then how would you be able to get Tak to accept anyone new?"

"I was thinking we'd find someone similar to Essali." Shakki fixed her gaze on Kayla. "You're about her height and size. Her hair's almost the same, long and crimped curls. She was just a shade darker than you, but hardly enough to notice."

Halfway through Shakki's assessment, Kayla was shaking her head. "Not me. Find someone else."

"Tak picked you up and carried you," Shakki said. "She knew she'd hurt you and she had to keep you safe, so she carried you where she could protect you from the other bhimkay."

Tak had been so careful, keeping her hair barbs retracted. It was only the directive from the presaka that had made it impossible for the bhimkay to control those barbs such that they'd pierced Kayla.

Shakki took Kayla's hand and pressed it against the wire mesh in place of her own. "Let's just see what happens."

Kayla could have walked away. She could have gone back inside Mahala and resumed her work tour in the foodstores warehouse. But the thought of toiling there in the depths of the cavern system day after day filled her with despair. She'd rather be dispatched by a spider bite.

Tak kept up her nervous tapping of the eggs, but she'd turned her head toward Kayla's hand on the cage. "What am I waiting for?" Kayla asked.

Shakki's sigh told her that whatever the GEN girl was expecting, it wasn't happening. "Oh, well. Could you just stay there a little longer? I'm going to get Pev out."

Kayla spread her hand out just a little bit wider. She stared through the wire at the bhimkay, wishing—what? That she could read its mind, could somehow understand what it wanted.

Then Tak moved. With slow, careful motions of her segmented legs, she inched closer to the mesh. Her front feet grabbed about a meter up the enclosure wall, and the bhimkay heaved her head right up against the mesh.

Kayla watched, half-terrified, half-fascinated as the spider leaned close. What looked like two short legs on either side of her mouth extended.

They brushed her hand through the holes in the mesh. It was so gentle, it tickled.

"Shakki?" Kayla's voice sounded unnaturally high. "Is that part of her mouth? What she eats with? Is she wanting to take a taste of me?"

Shakki, about to open the gate, relocked it and trotted back toward Kayla. Shakki stopped several meters away. "Those are her pedipalps. Kind of like hands, or antennae. She's feeling you, not tasting you. At least, not tasting you to eat."

A second pair of legs rose to clutch the mesh. Tak positioned her myriad eyes in Kayla's direction. The bhimkay hummed faintly.

"Shakki?" Kayla asked.

"That's good. I think she's accepting you." Shakki moved slowly toward Kayla. "Here's a spare presaka just in case. Let's see if we can encourage her to come out to you."

Heart thudding like a hammer in her ears, Kayla followed Shakki to the gate. Pev was still waiting there, his eye-studded head bent down toward Shakki. The male bhimkay vibrated a little as Shakki tapped in the gate code, then he dropped to the rock floor of the enclosure as the latch released.

So did all the others, Tak included. But while Tak hung back by her eggs, the other six skittered to the door.

A tremor fingered its way down Kayla's spine. "Now what? Lock the gate again?"

"Watch," Shakki said.

Kayla thought Shakki might get out her presaka, but instead she spread the fingers of her right hand, flung it above her head, and made a pushing motion. Pev did an about-face, then rose up on his four hind legs. He hissed, waving his front legs at the other bhimkay.

They all retreated to the back end of the enclosure. All except Tak. Moving slowly along the mesh wall, she approached the gate. When Pev dropped to all eight, Tak moved more quickly, nudging the male bhimkay aside.

Shakki laughed. "She doesn't care much for him, but he's so sweet on her."

Shakki finally opened the gate, and Tak exited first. After Pev followed, Shakki locked the gate again.

Tak moved toward Kayla. Instinct sent Kayla a few paces backward. Gritting her teeth, she stilled and let the bhimkay approach.

Using her front two legs, Tak lightly tapped Kayla all over, just as she'd been checking her eggs. Those spider feet were tipped with twenty-centimeter-long claws, but Tak was so gentle, she never pierced Kayla's skin.

"Do I touch her?" Kayla asked.

"They like their pedipalps stroked," Shakki said. "And their abdomen between the hair barbs."

Kayla stretched her hand up, and to her shivering surprise, Tak bent low enough that Kayla could reach the pedipalps. They were as long as Kayla's forearm, and about as big around as her wrist. When Kayla ran her palm down the length of one pedipalp, she discovered the hair there was coarse but flexible, not stiff, dangerous barbs like on the bhimkay's legs and body.

The bhimkay crouched even lower. Now the long, segmented front legs were on either side of Kayla, and the pedipalps within easy reach. As Kayla petted them, the spider growled, the rumbling noise shaking its whole body.

Kayla hesitated. "Am I doing it wrong?"

"No." Shakki was stroking Pev's pedipalps. "That's like a seycat purr. It feels good to them."

Tak hunkered so low, her body was eye-level to Kayla. She moved under the arching legs to the creature's abdomen, running her fingertips cautiously between the sharp hair barbs. Tak wriggled a little, then growled softly. She tucked her middle legs in more tightly, like Risa's pet seycat, Nishi, would do with her paws when she didn't want Kayla to stop petting her.

Shakki gave Pev one last pat, then stepped back. "We need to get to work. First, you have to learn the hand signals. I made them up myself. I tried to teach them to the boys, but you can't tell them anything."

Shakki went through a dozen or so motions with Kayla. The pushing away motion she'd used earlier with Pev. A sweep of the fingers with the right or left to direct the bhimkay to either side. A throwing motion to send the spider out.

It was easy enough for Kayla to memorize what the pattern should look like and store it in her annexed brain. Getting her body to duplicate Shakki's fluid movements was another story.

Shakki let Kayla test her skills on Pev as well as Tak. If the bhimkay didn't understand, they tended to stand stock still. Sometimes they'd creep a little closer to beg for a stroke of their pedipalps. Pev seemed to have a shorter attention span than Tak. He wandered off in the middle of Kayla's practice session.

Poor Tak just stood there, head slightly cocked. Kayla's arms felt ready to fall off, but despite Shakki's invitation that they quit for the day, Kayla waved her off.

Tak moved to the left. Kayla stared at her left hand for a moment. What had she done?

Trying not to think too hard, Kayla waved her right hand. Tak sidled to the right. Kayla could almost see relief in the bhimkay's eight eyes that Kayla had finally learned to speak correctly.

Kayla offered her hand as she approached Tak and gave the pedipalps a firm rub. "Poor thing, stuck with such a stupid handler."

Mid-growl, Tak tensed. Pev did too, half-turning toward the passageway.

Now Kayla heard the approaching voices. "The boys are coming."

"We'd better get ours in," Shakki said.

Shakki was just starting the *Come on* motion with Pev when the bhimkay, anticipating her command, jumped ahead. But Pev's fear of the boys' imminent arrival made him clumsy. He stumbled over Shakki, and the barbs on his front right leg tore into her left side. The spider's awareness that he'd hurt his bonded human sent him into greater panic. He pulled the barbs free, but the impetus spun Shakki around and sent her tumbling into the barbs on his back two legs, cutting deeply into her right side.

"Denking hell!" Kayla shouted, terrified for Shakki and so angry at the boys she wanted to toss the lot of them into the nearest boulder. She made her own awkward gesture at Tak, and thank the Infinite, the spider understood. Tak started toward the gate, herding Pev with her.

Kayla knelt beside Shakki. Shakki's eyes looked glassy from the pain. "You have to get the bhimkay put away."

"I have to get you to the medic."

Shakki clutched Kayla's arm. "Bhimkay first. Boys are almost here." She reeled off the code for the enclosure, then pushed at Kayla.

Kayla ran for the gate, weaving through the spiders' legs. She tapped in the code, saw the caged bhimkay turning toward the gate. Tak hissed, and Kayla put her trust in the spider. She yanked open the gate, and stood out of the way of those dangerous barbs as Tak and Pev skittered inside, both of them hissing and warning the others to stay back.

The boys started pelting into the clearing just as Kayla latched the gate. Most of them ran right past Shakki, only a couple slowing to check her out. Kayla shooed them away, automatically using the same gestures she'd used on Tak.

Kayla lifted Shakki carefully, positioning her over her shoulder. She started for the passageway, but as she reached the opening, she heard a chorus of bhimkay shrieks.

Her head hanging midway down Kayla's back, Shakki muttered, "Denking boys. They don't have to."

Kayla looked back to see several of the boys had their shocksticks out, and were applying the weapons generously to the legs of their bonded bhimkay. The spiders were frozen, likely due to a command to their inhibitor via the presakas.

"What about Pev and Tak?" Kayla asked. The male and

female had taken posts beside Tak's eggs, their agitation clear from their hissing and shifting feet.

"They're afraid of Tak, so they won't bother her," Shakki said. "And even though Tak pretends to hate Pev, she'll protect him."

I'll kill those boys if they harm so much as one hair barb, Kayla said to Shakki as she entered the passageway.

It was difficult going in the narrow parts. Kayla had to shift Shakki to the ground so they could squeeze through, keeping her arm tight around the smaller girl to support her. At one point, Shakki fell so quiet that Kayla thought the girl might have passed out.

But then Shakki said, *Don't let them put me in a gen-tank.*

What if the medics say you need it?

Don't let them, Shakki said. *Promise me.*

I promise.

They got to the tall doors at Antara's entrance and Kayla pounded on the plasscrete with her fist. A small inset door slid open and the female GEN guard waiting inside took a quick look around.

"It's us, Faia," Kayla said with exasperation. "Hurry up, Shakki's been injured."

Her voice barely more than a whisper, Shakki said, "She's just checking for wild bhimkay. Can't have them following us inside."

Faia gave Kayla a dark look—she was the guard Kayla had struck during her attempted escape—and threw aside the bar from its brackets. Kayla slipped inside and hurried to the freight lift. Thank the Infinite it was still on the top level after the boys had used it.

"Faia, can you send us down?" Kayla asked.

Faia trotted toward them down the corridor, a shockgun

slapping against her leg. The GEN woman hadn't been armed the day of Kayla's near escape.

Faia tapped in the code to send them to L2 where Maramata 1 and 2 were. The door opened not in a corridor but in a lab. It was Kheta 3, the same hydroponics lab Lovise had worked in. The techs there looked over in surprise as Kayla toted Shakki through the long rows of kel-grain and soy.

The girl's body was lax over Kayla's shoulder. She *had* passed out. Better for Shakki, considering the pain she must be in.

Once clear of the lab, Maramata 1 was just ahead, around a curve in the corridor. A minor-status trueborn woman— Medic Palla—waited at the door, so someone must have sent a message ahead. Could it have been one of those useless boys? No, more likely Faia had alerted Palla by wristlink.

"Bring her here." Palla gestured toward a treatment table.

Beyond the table were gen-tanks, two rows of five, seven of them occupied. Other trueborns, medics or techs, moved through the room monitoring the tanks.

While Kayla carefully laid Shakki on the table, Palla pulled a privacy curtain shut around it. Now Kayla could see an alarming amount of Shakki's blood soaked both their clothes.

The medic picked up a pair of scissors. "Would you step out please so I can prep her for the tank?"

"No tank," Kayla said.

Palla looked up at Kayla. "With those injuries, I have to insist—"

"No tank," Kayla repeated. "And I'll be staying here to make sure."

Palla had tried to convince Kayla her true memories were hallucinations. She might be a good medic, but how good was her word?

Palla's pale blue eyes narrowed on Kayla, but she didn't press the issue of the tank or insist again that Kayla leave. She turned her attention to cutting Shakki's shredded clothes from her body to further assess the damage. Kayla was relieved to see the smaller wounds on Shakki's left side had already started healing.

Just as Shakki had done for Kayla, the medic methodically cleaned the GEN girl's wounds. Then she grabbed a vac-seal filled with a pinkish goo.

Palla broke the seal and was about to squeeze some into one of the deeper gouges when Kayla grabbed the trueborn woman's wrist. "What is that?"

"Pratija." The medic scowled at Kayla as she tried to pull her arm free. "It lessens the risk of infection and promotes healing."

"Put some on your own skin," Kayla said.

"That won't prove anything," Palla protested. "I'm not a GEN and I don't have a cut."

Kayla's gaze strayed to the lase-knife on a nearby tray. Palla must have seen the look because her voice shook when she spoke again. "I take my vow as a medic seriously. The pratija will help her."

Shakki stirred. "It's okay, Kayla. I've used it before on myself."

Kayla let go. She backed up to the curtain to stay out of the way. The pratija must have had some kind of painkiller in it too because Shakki sighed with relief as Palla applied it.

The medic handed Kayla a gown for Shakki, then left Kayla to help the girl sit up and put it on. Once Kayla had stacked a couple pillows for Shakki's head, the girl lay down again with a groan.

"Those denking boys," Shakki muttered. "I'd like to reprogram their shocksticks to zap *them*." She turned toward the curtain. "Palla's not watching. Who's in the gen-tanks? Anyone you know?"

"I didn't even notice."

"Open the curtain," Shakki said. "Down at that end so Palla doesn't notice. I want to see who was stupid enough to let themselves get dunked in gen-fluid."

Kayla pulled open a gap in the curtain wide enough for Shakki to get a look. The GEN girl was smiling at first—the boy in the far tank was Veshni, one of the Bhimkay Lounge game players who was always injuring something. But then Shakki's gaze froze.

"Dear sweet Infinite." Shakki grabbed for Kayla's hand. "The third tank down."

Kayla didn't recognize the girl inside with her near high-status skin color and long, dark hair twisting around her shoulders. "Who is it?"

"It's Essali," Shakki said. She lowered her voice. "The one who told me about Devak."

Kayla couldn't help herself, she took a step out from behind the curtain. Palla, glancing up from the sekai she'd been working at, looked alarmed. "Stay away from the gen-tanks. That fluid is dangerous."

Palla started toward Kayla, but Kayla stepped right up next to the third tank. Just like in Akhilesh's lab, tubes riddled Essali's body.

Then Kayla glanced across Essali's tank to the one in the row next to it. And her heart all but stopped.

It was Lovise.

14

As Devak dragged the boy from the dark hole under the washroom floor, the elusive Shun barely protested. The boy was filthy, and stunk so bad that Waji flatly stated the boy wouldn't be allowed into his flat unless they cleaned him up. So they did what they could in the washroom.

The trickle of water from the spigot was no substitute for a decent bath, but at least they lessened the stench from the boy's dirty body. The rank korta and chera pants Shun wore were good for nothing but burning.

The boy—Usi Haddad, he'd informed them, not Shun—could hardly walk back to Waji's warren. As Devak steadied him on one side while Junjie supported him on the other, Devak understood the boy's weakness. Usi was nothing but skin and bones under his disreputable korta. His dark eyes were huge in his gaunt face, his black hair shaggy, and his medium-brown skin had an unhealthy pallor.

Waji made the boy strip everything off at his doorstep and wipe the rest of himself with a handful of sani-wipes. Then Waji fetched a worn but clean korta, leggings, and skivs and they helped Usi dress. Junjie thought to fish Usi's identity chip from the hem of the old shirt and slip it into the new.

Usi didn't need any help wolfing down every scrap of leftover rat-snake stew and kel-grain. After the last bite, he collapsed on Waji's sofa and almost immediately fell into a coma-like sleep. With the boy shuddering from cold, Waji dumped all his blankets on Usi. Then Waji, Devak, and Junjie crowded together on the enforcer's narrow bed, warmed by body heat and the small radiant stove that Waji brought into the sleeproom from the kitchen.

The boy was dead to the world the rest of that night and all the next day and night. Junjie and Devak spent their time with Waji out in the fields behind the warren. Waji showed them the net traps he used to capture rat-snakes, identified wild patagobi plants, and taught them how to avoid chaff head and yellow scrub flowers that had been pissed on by seycats marking their territory.

Evening meal the second night was as tasty as the first, the scrub flowers adding a sharper flavor than the chaff head. Junjie had wanted to wake Usi to feed him, but Waji told him the boy needed rest more than food. He'd wake when he was ready. Junjie spent the second night sitting up, sleeping at Usi's feet.

A clatter jolted Devak awake the second morning before first sunrise. The bed beside him was still warm, but Waji wasn't there. Now he heard the enforcer shouting from the living room, Junjie's pleading voice, and a high tenor that Devak guessed was Usi's.

Still in nothing but his sleep shirt, Devak hurried from the sleeproom. Waji stood against the door in his own knee-length sleep shirt, brandishing a stout sticker bush branch, the business end studded with wicked, twenty-centimeter-long stickers. Junjie held his hands up at Waji, as if to placate the enforcer. Usi stood facing Waji, his trembling hands clutching the grip of the enforcer's shockgun.

Waji glanced beyond Usi and Junjie, but didn't let on that Devak was there. The enforcer glowered at Usi. "Is this how you pay me for feeding you and giving you a bed? Stealing my weapon while I'm asleep?"

"Just let me go," Usi begged. "Let me leave and I won't bother you again."

Junjie tugged at Usi's arm. "Please, put it down. Give the shockgun back to Waji."

"He'll kill me," Usi said, his voice wavering.

"Denking hell," Waji said, "I couldn't kill you with the shockgun if I wanted to. It's GEN-issue. But this—" Waji waved the club in his hand— "this could kill you. And I will if you don't give me back my weapon."

Junjie gave the boy's arm another tug. "We only brought you here to help you, Usi."

Well, Devak thought, they'd brought him here to see if *he* could help *them*. But Devak wasn't going to bring that up in the middle of this mess.

Usi still hadn't realized that Devak was there. With his feet bare on the cold floor, Devak walked silently up behind the boy and with a quick grab yanked the shockgun from Usi's hands. Stepping around the boy, he transferred the weapon to Waji.

As if Usi had used up all his strength with his brief rebellion, he swayed and would have crumpled to the floor if Junjie hadn't caught him and helped him to the sofa. Dropping to the cushions, the boy buried his face in his hands.

Junjie rubbed Usi's back. "Can we get him some food?"

Waji propped the sticker bush club beside the door. "If that boy will behave."

Usi looked up. "I will. I'm sorry. But I thought the shockgun would be good when they come for me."

Devak could see Waji was ready to launch into questions, so he took the enforcer's arm. "Let's get dressed. We can talk over morning meal. Junjie, can you start some kel-grain?"

Junjie jumped to his feet. "Right away."

Devak and Waji each took their turn in the communal washroom, then dressed, Devak in one of the sets of clothes he'd rinsed and laid out to dry, Waji in his uniform. Anticipating their departure, Devak made sure he had everything packed up again in his carrysak.

Despite Devak's intent to question Usi during morning meal, the boy was stuffing the sakara-sweetened kel-grain into his mouth so quickly that Devak could see he'd get nowhere until Usi was full. The boy downed three bowls of kel-grain and a half-glass of soy milk before finally sitting back with a sigh.

Usi's gaze then slid to the door, but Waji moved in that direction and leaned against it. "Who's coming for you?"

Usi gave the door a longing look. "Where are the other enforcers?"

"There aren't any others besides me," Waji said. "Not here in Cati."

"Oh," Usi said. "Then maybe . . ."

Before Waji could ask again, Junjie gave Usi a poke. "*Who's* coming for you?"

"The Brigade," Usi said. "Because they know about me and the bombs."

"You mean, they know you were a member of FHE?" Junjie asked.

"Yes," Usi said.

Junjie took Usi's hand. "How would they find out? You were way more underground than me. And no one knows I was FHE except Devak and Zul and Kayla. And that's only because I told them."

Usi shook his head. "They know because an enforcer saw me at the warren in Nafi sector. Right before it blew up."

"But that doesn't mean anything," Junjie persisted. "You could have had good reason to be there."

Usi yanked his hand out of Junjie's hold, his expression fierce. "I did have good reason! I'm the one who delivered the bomb!"

Horror filled Junjie's face and he leaned away from Usi. "A little GEN girl was killed in that explosion."

"Don't you think I know that?" Usi cried. "It was the only denking bomb I ever had anything to do with, and it killed someone."

"You set it?" Junjie asked quietly.

Usi shook his head. "I didn't even know what was in the crate, just that someone from FHE wanted it delivered. I thought, well, maybe they know how hungry everyone is with so much kel-grain destroyed, so they're sending food. I thought they were only blowing up warehouses, not warrens." Tears glittered in the boy's eyes. "I set the crate in the entryway, just like they told me."

It must have been especially powerful explosives, because it had brought down the entire warren. "I thought FHE usually sent out a warning," Devak said. "To keep anyone from being killed. Didn't you tell everyone to leave?"

"I told you, I didn't know it was a bomb!" Usi shouted. "Someone else must have been in charge of warning them, someone who knew what would happen. The little girl was the only one left behind." Now the tears spilled down Usi's face.

Outrage burned in Waji's light brown eyes as he pushed away from the door. "I want you out of here."

Usi got up and started to pull off the old korta Waji had given him. "I should give this back."

"Don't be an idiot, boy," Waji said. "Keep it. I don't want it back. You need forgiveness from your Lord Creator? Then I suggest you help Devak find Kayla."

Usi's eyes got big, then he quickly looked away. "I don't know where she is."

Waji grabbed a handful of Usi's korta and shook him. "You'll help him, or I'll escort you to the Viata sector Brigade myself."

Junjie jumped to his feet, wedging himself between Usi and the angry enforcer. "We should go, Devak."

Devak quickly cleared the table while Junjie grabbed the carrysak. Usi kept eyeing the door, but with Waji standing over him, the boy stayed put.

Devak nodded at the enforcer. "Thank you for your hospitality."

"I'm glad to help Zul's great-grandson," Waji said. "Do you have enough dhans?"

"I can't take your money," Devak said.

"I have nothing to spend it on," Waji said, moving toward the kitchen. "The Brigade provides my food and the flat, little enough as it is."

Waji dug through a drawer and came up with a small roll of dhans. He stuffed them into Devak's hands, then tugged open another drawer. "I have something else for you."

Waji scooped up handfuls of nutras, wrapped nutrition bars. Devak opened the fastening on his carrysak and held it out. Waji dumped the bars in.

189

"I can't stomach them myself," Waji said of the kel-grain-based nutras, "but if you're hungry, you'll have something to fill you up."

"Thank you again," Devak said.

"Stick to the pathway along the backs of the warrens," Waji said. "Just past the last building, there's a path through the sticker bushes that meets up with the road farther on. That should save you from Cheffa's notice."

They headed out, Devak leading, Junjie trailing, Usi in between. Devak was burning to grill Usi, to find out what the boy knew about Kayla. He said earlier that he didn't know where she was, but Devak was sure he knew something.

Devak wanted to wait until they were clear of Cati sector and safely back in a trueborn sector before questioning Usi. He didn't like the idea of running away from GENs, of seeing them as something to fear. But everything seemed to be turned upside down since FHE started their bombing campaign.

The memory of that dead little girl in Nafi stabbed Devak's heart again. When he looked back at Junjie, he could see the grim look on his friend's face. Maybe Junjie was thinking of that girl too and how this boy he had such strong feelings for might not be who he thought he was.

The tension in Devak's shoulders finally relaxed when they crossed the border back into Viata sector, where the streets were filling with trueborns and lowborns hurrying past. He spotted a serving house, third door past the border. "I could do with some kelfa."

He held the door for Usi and Junjie. The stench of burnt kel-grain hit his nose and he almost turned around and left, but the other two had already gone up to the counter. Devak followed them through the cheap plasscine tables and chairs cramming the floor. When he laid his hand on the counter, he regretted it. It was sticky with sloshed kelfa drink. No surprise the place was empty, despite the busy morning crowd outside.

The brown stains on the apron of the minor-status trueborn man behind the counter weren't encouraging, but Devak spared a half-dhan on three kelfa drinks. The first sip of his kelfa told him whoever worked the kel-grain ovens hadn't quite gotten the knack of proper roasting.

The table by the window at least was clean, and with the roasting ovens still going, it was warm. And despite the bitter taste of the kelfa, the drink was hot and Devak was glad for a place to sit and talk. The street outside cleared as the morning shift went to work and the night shift went home. Other than the trueborn man tending his ovens, they were alone.

There was sakara on the table, and Devak dumped a couple measures full into his kelfa to sweeten it. The others followed suit.

Devak took another swallow, then set his cup onto the table with a clunk. "I want to hear it from the beginning. Not just Usi, but Junjie too. How did you become part of FHE?"

Junjie exchanged a glance with Usi, then said, "After a Kinship meeting. I was angry about how things went at the meeting—you know, Devak, another session with everyone insisting we had to go slow with GEN rights or the world would end. Anyway, a minor-status trueborn was waiting for me outside. I didn't remember seeing him in the meeting, but he must have been there because he knew all about the arguments we'd been having."

Junjie tipped his head at Usi. "The minor-status gave me Usi's call ID. A week later I contacted him."

Devak turned to Usi. "And you?"

Usi slid his cup side to side. "My father joined back at

the beginning five or so years ago. He supervised GENs in a plasscine extrusion factory and believed they should have the same rights as trueborns. He found a few other people who thought the same way and they started FHE."

Devak took another bitter swallow of kelfa. "I'm surprised none of them knew about the Kinship."

"That's mostly for high-status," Usi said. "My father didn't keep company with them."

Devak asked, "Was Aideen Kalu one of those first?"

"You figured out her real name?" Usi asked. Then he nodded. "Yeah. Her, my father, two or three others."

"Where's your father now?" Devak asked. "Would he know where Kayla is?"

Now Usi's gaze dropped to his kelfa. "I don't know where he is. He planted the very first bomb in Esa sector. He never came home from that. I think he blew himself up."

From what Devak understood, the Esa bombing had happened before the one in Qaf that Kayla had witnessed, where one enforcer had been badly injured and another killed. Which meant the FHE strike in Esa would have been before last winter.

"You've been alone all this time?" Devak asked. Usi shrugged. "How old are you?"

"I'm a fifteenth-year as of two weeks ago," Usi said.

"How have you been getting by?" Junjie asked. "Has FHE been helping you?"

"They did for a while," Usi said. "All during that time you and I were talking via wristlink, Junjie, I'd get dhans from Aideen sometimes via a courier. Once she got Kayla's body, that stopped. I haven't heard from anyone from FHE since Kayla died."

Devak grabbed Usi's wrist. "Are you lying to us?"

"Lying?" Usi asked, trying to pull away. "About what?"

"Kayla." Devak gripped Usi's wrist tighter. "Do you know where she is, and that's why you're not telling us the truth?"

"What truth?" Confusion flickered in Usi's face, but behind the confusion was something else. He knew more than he was letting on. "Besides FHE taking Kayla's body?"

Devak leaned closer, lowering his voice. "Kayla's not dead. Don't tell me you didn't know that."

Usi's mouth dropped open. He shook his head slowly from side to side. "I didn't know. Honestly. Aideen told me she was dead."

"Why would she tell you that?" Devak twisted Usi's arm until the boy winced.

Junjie grabbed hold of Devak's fingers and peeled them off Usi's wrist. "Because she thought Kayla would be safer that way."

"Safer from who?" Devak demanded. "From us? From me?"

"Kayla killed at least one trueborn enforcer," Junjie said. "Injured Akhilesh. Better if the Brigade assumed she was dead."

"Even so," Devak said, "I think he knows where Kayla is."

"I . . ." Usi grabbed up his cup and downed the last of the kelfa. "I *think* I know how to find her."

"Then tell me," Devak demanded. "Or I'll find a way to get it out of you."

It made Devak a little sick to think about it, but in that moment, he would have beat the boy if he had to.

"I won't tell you," Usi said. "That's not how I want to do this."

Devak grabbed that skinny wrist again and tightened his fingers, all his anger lending him strength. "You're not the one making the rules here. I am."

Usi grimaced with pain. "I'll help you. I promise. But you have to take me with you."

15

We can't take you with us!" Devak's near shout caught the attention of the trueborn shopkeeper, who stopped his shaking of a pan of hot kel-grain to give them a narrow-eyed glare. Devak hunched over the table, lowering his voice. "We have barely the dhans for the two of us, let alone for three."

Usi sat back, the spindly plasscine chair creaking as he crossed his arms over his chest. "Then I won't tell you what I know."

If not for the glances the trueborn man kept casting them from behind the counter, Devak would have taken the boy and shaken him. "Why don't you tell us what you know, then we'll try to figure out a way for you to travel with us."

Usi shook his head. "You wouldn't need me then. You'd just leave me behind."

"We wouldn't," Junjie said, although that was exactly what Devak was considering.

Devak leaned back in his own chair, his gaze roving the cluttered room as he tried to tamp down his temper. He could bear the odor of burning kel-grain, the griminess of the serving house's undecorated walls, the slime-spider crouched over some unknown brown blob in the corner. But that this boy might know something about where Kayla was and wouldn't tell him—that he couldn't stomach.

Devak drew in a long breath. "You have to tell us something. Otherwise, how do we know you're not just telling us what we want to hear?"

The boy fidgeted in his seat. "I'd rather just lead you there."

"Lead us where?" Devak asked. "Where Kayla is?"

"Well . . ." Usi squirmed. "To people who can tell us where she might be."

Devak slammed his half-empty cup of kelfa on the table. The warm, sticky liquid sloshed on the back of his hand. "I don't think you know anything more about Kayla than Junjie and I do!"

"I know one thing," Usi said. "We have to get over to Ret sector."

Devak snatched a sani-wipe from a side table and cleaned the sakara-sweetened kelfa off his hand and the table. "Funny how you pick a sector clear on the other side of the continent from Viata. More than three thousand kilometers from here to there. We don't have the dhans for one person's pub-trans fare all the way, let alone the three of us."

Junjie said, "Maybe Zul could—"

"We've pretty much drained Pitamah dry." Devak turned to Junjie. "Maybe it's time we all parted ways. I could use the dhans we have to get as far as I can, then walk the rest of the way to Ret."

"You can't!" Usi protested. "You won't know who to talk to once you get there."

"Then tell me who it is," Devak demanded.

"It wouldn't do you any good," Usi said, "because they won't talk to *you*. Me, they trust."

Devak's temper bubbled up again. "But we have no way to get there! Not all of us!"

Behind the counter, the oven door banged shut, and the trueborn man looked ready to heave all of them out the door. Junjie put up a placating hand toward the man, then turned to Devak. "I have an idea. A way we could get partway there for free. Just give me a minute."

Junjie left the serving house. On the walkway outside the window, he tapped a call ID into his wristlink. The display was far too small to see who Junjie was talking to, but it was someone he knew well from his smile and relaxed posture.

Devak drank down the last of his kelfa, wincing at the bitterness the sakara couldn't quite mask. "What happened to your mother?" he asked Usi.

"Died giving birth to me," Usi said.

That took Devak aback. "How could that be? If she was having problems delivering, why wasn't she put in a tank?"

Usi laced his hands together on the table. "Our family has been clinging to minor-status by our fingernails since even before I was born. We weren't even supposed to be trueborn. One of my great-greats was a lowborn who saved the life of some really important high-status. As a reward, they made him minor-status, but no adhikar came with it. He worked hard to earn some, but over the years, our adhikar has come and gone."

"So when your mother was pregnant with you, she and your father didn't have the dhans for the gen-tank?"

Usi nodded. "And she was a long way from a medic, out working the kel-grain fields on high-status adhikar land. My father was at the extrusion factory, two hundred kilometers away. He didn't hear for two days."

Then Usi would have been raised in a crèche, Devak guessed,

maybe even in a center for lowborn children. Devak had heard of minor-status parents who saved money by letting their children be cared for with lowborns, usually by a GEN caregiver.

Junjie, still talking on the wristlink, looked through the window and smiled in apology. Then his gaze wandered to Usi, and Junjie's eyes softened.

Devak nudged Usi with his toe under the table. "I want you to know that Junjie's my friend. My best friend. You'd better not be making him think you like him just so you can come along with us."

Usi gave Devak a somber look, then he craned his neck so he could see Junjie through the window. "Sometimes remembering his voice was the only thing that got me through these last few months. To actually see him, to actually meet him face to face . . ." Usi's mouth curved into a smile.

Junjie tapped off his wristlink and headed back inside. He was grinning and looked very pleased with himself. Then his gaze locked with Usi's and the two of them just stared at each other as Junjie approached the table.

Junjie took his seat again, sliding the chair close to Usi's. "That was Risa Mandoza. She and Kiyomi will be in Amik sector in a couple of days. She can take us as far as Nafi sector in Northeast Territory."

Devak did a quick mental calculation. That would knock nearly half the distance off the trip. "Can she transport all three of us?"

"If we don't mind sharing the bay of her lorry with three thousand kilograms of kel-grain and her pet seycat."

As rough as their trip had been so far—riding in pub-trans with lowborns glowering at them, sleeping in public houses—traveling with someone he knew and trusted would seem like sheer luxury.

"How many legs on pub-trans between here and Amik?" Devak asked.

"Two, I think." Junjie tapped at his wristlink. "Yeah, two. One that goes from Viata to eastern Wesja, then we'd have to spend the night and catch the morning pub-trans to Amik."

Devak pushed his chair back. "How long until the next pub-trans leaves?"

Another check of Junjie's wristlink. "Twenty minutes. We'd better go."

Devak grabbed their carrysak. Old habits took hold of him, and he found himself searching for a coin to leave on the table for the owner. The man had his eyes on Devak, expectation clear on his face. Devak brought the coins out, but only to dole them out to Junjie and Usi for pub-trans fare. He couldn't spare so much as a quarter-dhan for the serving house owner. Devak's stinginess earned him a scowl from the man as they exited.

The big multi-lev pub-trans hadn't pulled in yet, but a big crowd of lowborns, a few with children in tow, had queued up at the stop. At the end of the line of lowborns, maybe fifteen GENs clustered together.

This was the part Devak hated. The moment the lowborns spotted him, Junjie, and Usi, they backed away, making room for the three of them to board first. Even though they stepped aside, the resentment was clear in the lowborns' faces.

Devak could read the silent message in their eyes. Public transportation was for lowborns, not trueborns. They could tolerate GENs—how else could the tankborns get to their Assignments? And besides, GENS sat on the crowded, smelly upper level.

But trueborns had no business being on pub-trans.

Trueborns had lev-cars—their own, or their friends'. Or they could rent one.

Except when they couldn't, when they barely had the dhans to ride pub-trans. But Devak couldn't tell the lowborns that. It wouldn't change their minds anyway.

The multi-lev rumbled up, sighing as it shifted its suspension engine to parking mode so it settled lower to the pavement. The doors opened, one in front by the driver and another in the middle of the vehicle's body. The queue of lowborns stepped back to let their brethren exit from the middle door. Then the middle door shut since everyone had to use the front to either pay or flash a travel chit at the driver.

But everyone in the queue just stood there, staring at Devak, Junjie, and Usi. They wouldn't step up into the multi-lev until the three trueborns had boarded.

So Devak climbed up the steps into the front door, dropped his fare into the till installed beside the lowborn driver, then took a seat in the first row. Junjie sat behind Devak, and Usi beside Junjie. After a gap of several seconds, the lowborns filed on, followed by the GENs.

Despite the open seat beside him, none of the lowborns sat with Devak. In fact, because trueborns were riding, the first four rows on either side of the aisle were now forbidden to lowborns. That didn't matter to the GENs, since they'd gone straight for the second level using the stairs at the rear of the multi-lev. But lowborns who would have otherwise sat in those first four rows might end up standing in the back.

The lowborns kept their eyes straight ahead as they hustled past, their faces set with anger. Just as Devak feared, there were four or five more lowborns than seats. The overflow had to stand. Devak considered going back and offering to one or two to share his seat, but the way they scowled and glared, he didn't think they'd appreciate the invitation.

Junjie leaned forward. "I don't understand why they don't behave like the lowborns in Ekat sector. They usually ask permission to sit up front with me. It's not a big deal."

Usi lowered his voice. "Southwest Territory must be pretty liberal. Up here in the north, the Brigade will sometimes board a pub-trans unannounced. It's bad news for any GEN or lowborn sitting where it's forbidden."

"Has it always been like that?" Junjie asked.

"Mostly since the bombings started." Usi made a face, no doubt thinking of his own part in FHE's doings.

"Lowborns shouldn't have to ask permission," Devak said, keeping his voice just as low as Usi's. "They should just sit if the seat is free."

The doors swung shut and the multi-lev rose as its suspension engine roared to full power. It traveled more than a meter off the pavement, much higher than a passenger-sized car.

The multi-lev turned widely at the next corner, then again to head the other way. A skyway was just up ahead to the right. Devak could see it through the driver's windshield. But he'd been taught early on by Junjie that only the express pub-trans used the skyways. You had to pay dearly for the extra speed and fewer stops of the express. Their dhans went much farther on the older and slower local transportation.

So they passed the skyway entrance and plugged along through the surface streets, stopping every time a pedestrian crossed the road or whenever a delivery lorry pulled out of an alley. It would be a long, dull trip to Amik. Devak figured it would pass more quickly if he caught up on his sleep.

Using his carrysak propped up like a pillow, he leaned

against the multi-lev's window. It was warm inside the vehicle and he was tolerably comfortable, so he quickly drifted off.

A lurch of the multi-lev nearly pitched him off his seat. It hadn't been the controlled braking the driver had used in the streets of Viata, but a panic stop. From the angle of Iyenku and his brother sun, Kas, it must be mid-afternoon, a good three hours since he'd dozed off.

Devak's head felt stuffed with drom wool. "What's going on? Where are we?"

Junjie was staring out the windshield, his eyes wide and scared. "Wesja, just across the border. Passed an allabain village five kilometers back, but now we're in the middle of nowhere."

Devak looked out the side window. It was nothing but empty countryside—scrap grass studded with sticker bushes and junk trees.

Then he looked through the windscreen, and he saw what had seemed to alarm Junjie. Three GENs stood in the road maybe ten meters up ahead, arrayed so that they blocked the multi-lev. Devak suspected if the driver tried to navigate around them, the sandy dirt on either side of the pavement wouldn't support the weight of the big vehicle.

"What are they doing on the road?" Devak asked, his mind still slow with sleep.

Then other GENs spilled out onto the road from behind sticker bushes and junk trees. A few dozen men and women, all of them with fierce looks on their faces, and every one carrying a sticker bush club similar to the one Waji had wielded earlier that morning in his flat.

A short, burly GEN man led the others toward the multi-lev, and they moved faster the closer they got. The burly GEN shouted and they all raised their clubs.

"What are they doing?" Devak asked again.

The burly man gestured to several of his compatriots and he and a half dozen others approached the front of the multi-lev. The burly man stepped on the front bumper of the vehicle, which trembled slightly as the suspension engines accommodated his additional weight. He scanned the interior through the windscreen, zeroing in on Devak, Junjie, and Usi up front.

The GEN dropped from the bumper again. The four men and two women with him backed away.

Was that it? Now that they discovered there were trueborns on board, they'd back down?

Then the burly GEN's club slammed into the windshield. From the ground, the man could only wield the club against the lower part of the tall, broad sheet of clear plass. But he struck hard, twice, three times, until a spider web of cracks riddled the windshield. Then he signaled to the others and the half dozen nearest swung their clubs as well. The cracks grew more numerous until the lower portion of the windscreen gave way, sheets of it sagging, holes gaping.

Then the burly man wrenched open the door and boarded.

16

Kayla stepped inside Seycat, the clean smell of morning and bhimkay lingering in her hair and clothes. After reflexively locking the door behind her, she looked over at Shakki. The girl had been sleeping when Kayla left to check on the spiders. But now Shakki sat cross-legged on her bed, still in her sleep shirt, a prayer mirror in her hands.

Shakki set the mirror aside. "How are Pev and Tak doing? Those sanaki boys haven't been abusing them, have they?"

"Our bhimkay are fine," Kayla reassured her. "Pev even let me pet his belly, although it made Tak jealous. And those boys know if they touch one hair-barb on either Pev or Tak, *I'll* bite them."

"One more day of rest," Shakki said irritably. "I feel fine now. Palla is a tyrant as a medic."

Palla was worse than that if she knew why Essali and Lovise were installed in those gen-tanks. Not to heal any injury or cure disease, Kayla and Shakki were both certain. They were being jailed in those tanks as surely as any trueborn up in Far North Prison.

Kayla crossed to Shakki's bed. "It's only been three days.

And you *do* need to regain your strength." Kayla twitched up Shakki's shirt and assessed the girl's wounds. "All scabbed over and clean, even the worst ones. Do you have that accelerated healing programming in your annexed brain?"

"FHE installed that and Infinite knows what else when I first arrived," Shakki said, then she switched smoothly to the circuit-comm. *That was when I still trusted them.*

Kayla thought of Essali and Lovise, floating in green genfluid. *Sweet Infinite, I wish there was a way to get them out of there.*

I wish there was a way to get us *out of here.*

I've been thinking about that. Kayla sat beside Shakki on the bed. *Why can't we just walk out?*

Shakki stared at Kayla as if she were the sanaki one. *How? Are you going to jump from boulder to boulder? Even if you could climb the rocks circling Antara, the tops are too narrow to be safe to walk on and too far away from one to another to jump across the gap.*

There must be paths like the one to the clearing.

The path to the clearing and the clearing itself, Shakki said, *all had to be blasted away, just like the underground passageways were. You might have noticed FHE is good at blowing things up. Everywhere else, the boulders are too squeezed together at the bottom so you can't fit between them.*

Kayla tried a different tack. *I'm* strong, *Shakki. If we had ropes, maybe we could scale the boulders. I could climb up and pull you up after me. Then use the rope to go from one to the next.*

Do you know how many kilometers we'd have to travel? Straight up this side of the Wall then down again? And even if you had the strength—Shakki put up a hand to stop Kayla's interruption—*you've forgotten another big, enormous problem.*

Kayla sighed. *The wild bhimkay.*

They're everywhere. They only keep their distance from the vicinity of Antara because they respect the territory our group has marked out.

If we could get one of the boys' saddles—

I told you, Shakki said. *That's not going to happen. They keep them under their beds.*

Then I wish Tak and Pev could carry us. Like Tak did that day she bit me, when she wrapped her legs around me.

Shakki shook her head. *It's one thing to carry you a few meters. Toting a forty or fifty kilogram human all the way across the Wall with their legs would hurt Tak and Pev. They might get partway and wrench something and not be able to go farther. Even if we could continue on and leave them behind, with only six legs, they wouldn't be able to get to the nagas or rat-snakes before they slipped away. They'd starve to death if they weren't killed by the wild bhimkay.*

Kayla's last spark of hope faded. *I don't want to hurt them. We'll have to find another way.*

Shakki's stomach rumbled. "I'm pretty much starving. I could eat a full-grown naga by myself."

"I haven't eaten yet either," Kayla said. "I'll go get us both something."

"I'll come with you," Shakki said. "It's not like a walk to Mahala will be a giant strain."

Shakki quickly dressed in shirt and leggings and they headed out. When they got to Mahala, a crowd had spilled out through the entrance into the corridor. Kayla and Shakki had to squeeze along the corridor walls to get to the door. Everyone was giddy with happiness, their gazes and attention all focused in the same direction.

"What's going on?" Shakki asked.

"Has to be Ohin."

Shouts of "Always one with you!" peppering the crowd made that guess a certainty. But why the sudden swarm of people? From what she could see of the tables, they were still filled with bowls and plates of food, but no one was sitting there eating.

Kayla reached back for Shakki's hand and forced her way inside Mahala, closer to the front of the mass of people. Sure enough, there was Ohin, at the center of them all. The Bhimkay Boys surrounded him, acting as bodyguards. With linked hands, they held back the adoring crowd that wanted to get closer to the FHE leader.

Close enough to hear, but far enough back so they wouldn't be noticed, Kayla positioned herself and Shakki behind a tall trueborn man. She recognized the trueborn as Aasif, the one who'd operated the lift that day Tak bit her. She hoped the man's broad back would hide her and Shakki from Ohin.

"Until the day!" Ohin shouted over the crowd. "Until the day!"

Ohin put up a hand and the shouts of "Always one with you!" quieted in a ripple from front to back. Aasif whispered that oath fervently one last time before he fell silent as well.

"The day comes closer," Ohin said. "Our himayati have taken the fight deep into outsider trueborn sectors. FHE's attacks have incapacitated the enemy throughout the five territories."

As cheers arose throughout the crowd, Kayla looked back at Shakki, her stomach churning. She didn't dare let one word slip via the circuit-comm, not when she knew they might be overheard.

"We've prepared a vid of some of the destruction," Ohin said, raising his voice above the crowd. "Take a look."

With the Bhimkay Boys escorting him, he moved closer to the wall just to the left of the door. Everyone turned in that direction, and those still in the corridor squeezed inside.

Now Kayla saw that some of the tables had been shifted away and a holographic projector had been set up to project on the wall. The illuminators dimmed in that corner of Mahala as the holographic vid started up.

At the first views of destruction and ruin, Kayla's stomach knotted even tighter. The vid was in tight enough that she couldn't see the surroundings, just the smoking rubble of an unknown building. There was no way of knowing what structure this was, or which trueborn sector had been hit.

What if this was Two Rivers sector? That was where Devak had been living with Zul when she saw him last. To her relief, it didn't look like it could be the remains of the small house in Two Rivers that she remembered. It had to be a larger structure, like a warehouse or factory.

Then with a shock, she saw FHE scrawled in GENscrib on one of the chunks of plasscrete. Those around her were muttering that the letters were a victory mark. But Kayla knew where she'd seen that kind of inscription before: on buildings where FHE posted it as a warning to those inside to evacuate. For *GENs* to evacuate.

Now she registered the inferior quality of the plasscrete in the vid picture. She recognized the slim view of the next building over as the side of a GEN warehouse and caught a glimpse of a ditch that was nearly out of frame.

This vid wasn't showing destruction in a trueborn sector. It was in a GEN sector. And from that brief image, Kayla realized it was likely Esa sector. She'd witnessed that destroyed warren herself, and had transferred the memories into her annexed brain. This vid and those memories matched exactly. It had happened months ago, not recently the way Ohin was telling the crowd.

Kayla had been so astounded by Ohin's fakery, she didn't realize that Aasif had moved aside enough for the FHE leader to spot her. Ohin gestured, and the Bhimkay Boys began to push the crowd back, more roughly than they had to. The crowd made room readily enough for Ohin's passage.

"Until the day!" Ohin called out one last time to the GENs and trueborns still gathered. Several cried out "Always one with you!" as they dispersed, many with longing gazes back at Ohin.

Ohin glanced at Kayla, then smiled kindly at Shakki. At least, it would have looked kind to any of his admirers. That gentle look just raised Kayla's suspicions.

"Shakki, I know you're recently healed and need Kayla's arm to lean on, but I'd like to speak with her."

"We can do that right here," Kayla said. "Shakki doesn't have to go anywhere."

"I'd like some private time with you," Ohin said. "It won't take long."

A reset wouldn't take long, not if he got her somewhere out of sight. Palla and her med-techs could be waiting to help.

Ohin would need the assistance, because Kayla would fight back. She was easily strong enough to overpower Ohin, and maybe two or three others if they were unarmed. She had never shown her sket to the Bhimkay Boys, so she'd have the element of surprise helping her.

But where would that get her? The netcams were everywhere, and since they seemed to be tracking her especially, they'd see her striking Ohin. Things would end up exactly the same for her—with a reset.

Behind her, Shakki let slip one word via circuit-comm: *Don't.*

Kayla made one last stab at an excuse. "Shakki is still on bed rest. She only came out for morning meal because I could help her."

"Perhaps the boys could help her," Ohin said.

Shakki's eyes narrowed. *Maybe the boys could jump naked into a wild bhimkay pit*, she directed silently at Kayla. Then she said, "I can get my own morning meal."

Now Ohin turned his smile on Kayla again. She could see why it worked—she didn't trust him one micro-gram, but she reacted anyway, softening inside despite her fear of what he had in mind for her.

"I really don't need you for long, Kayla," he said. "Then you can get back to your day."

Back to her day as herself? Or as a new version with a fanatical devotion to FHE?

"We're only going to my workspace," Ohin said. "I'll have Jadi bring your morning meal." Ohin hooked a thumb at the tallest, broadest-shouldered Bhimkay Boy, whose wild dark hair and near-black skin reminded Kayla of an older version of her eleventh-year nurture brother, Jal. "It'll just be you and me."

Was Ohin telling her the truth? If he was on his circuit-comm ordering Palla and a gen-tech or two to join them in his workspace, Kayla couldn't see the tell-tale look on his face, nor feel the vibration at the base of her skull. She listened hard for any communication, but she heard nothing.

She'd just have to be ready to defend herself as needed, she decided as she nodded in agreement. She said to Shakki, *Make sure the boy doesn't put rat-snake turds in my kel-grain.*

Jadi's all right, Shakki said. *Only one of them I sort of trust. But you're okay?*

I can deal with Ohin, Kayla said. *I'll see you back at Seycat.*

Kayla walked off with the FHE leader, looking one last time over her shoulder at Shakki to make sure the boys weren't harassing her. Maybe because they were still in sight of Ohin, the Bhimkay Boys seemed respectful, walking quietly alongside the younger GEN girl.

Things stayed quiet inside Kayla's head too. Just when she would have appreciated the vibration—and whatever words of Ohin's she could pluck from her circuit-comm like sewer toads from the Chadi River—Ohin was keeping that channel closed. Could he have figured out she was able to overhear?

As they moved along the corridor, every passerby turned toward Ohin like a mag-connector toward plassteel, murmuring *Always one with you.* Ohin didn't answer them, maybe because they kept a polite distance, so he could pretend he didn't hear them. Even so, their heads swiveled as they passed so they could keep their gazes on him as long as possible.

As they traveled down the corridor, the passersby dwindled to none. It made sense that Ohin's workspace would be as out of the way as possible. Otherwise he'd be plagued by interruptions, by adoring residents begging for his attention. But Kayla's unease increased with the solitude.

They stopped at a door nearly to the end of the corridor. "I'm glad you and Shakki have become such friends," Ohin said. "She wasn't my first choice to replace Lovise, but Shakki seemed to want so much to help you assimilate here."

"Why did you replace Lovise at all?" Kayla asked, curious as to what he'd say.

"No one told you?" he seemed surprised, but Kayla was sure that if Ohin had wanted her to know, he would have made certain of it. "There was an accident in Kheta 3. A shelf collapsed in a supply room and Lovise was injured."

Palla had to have reported to him that Kayla saw Lovise in a gen-tank, so it made sense he'd come up with an excuse to explain that. But Lovise injured enough to be tanked? Kayla wouldn't buy that story with a quarter-dhan coin.

"Will she be okay?" Kayla asked.

"Good as new when she comes out," Ohin said.

The word *new* sent a new tickle of unease through Kayla. "Did you have to reset her?"

She thought she saw wariness in the way Ohin's eyes narrowed, but then he smiled. "Why would I have reset her for a simple injury?"

"If it's a simple injury, why did she go into the tank?"

Now irritation flashed in his face. "There were complications."

He turned away from her toward the door, positioning his body to block her view of the keypad lock. Kinship habits were so ingrained in Kayla, she shifted slightly and got a partial view of his fingers. As he entered the unlock code into the keypad, she registered the pattern of his fingers' movements.

She tensed, fearing someone might be waiting inside, ready to help Ohin overpower her. But when he pushed open the door, no one was waiting in the small space. It was just a narrow room, maybe two meters by four, a cluttered workstation set up along one wall, two float chairs pulled up to the holo computer display.

It crossed her mind that he still could use a datapod or vac-seal with a sedative to try to put her out. But that would be risky with her strength far exceeding his.

So maybe he did just want to talk. She couldn't imagine what about.

He moved one of the two float chairs within easy reach. "Sit, please."

She eased herself onto the cushion, wondering why Ohin didn't use ordinary legged chairs. The power needed to operate float chairs seemed wasteful. All the lectures from Aideen and Lovise about conserving precious power didn't seem to apply to the FHE leader.

Freedom, Humanity, Equality rolled across the computer screen, the words written in GENscrib instead of Bhasha. Another way to sneer at outsider trueborns, by using the GEN-exclusive script rather than write it the way trueborns would.

He turned to her. "It seems you're settling in finally. Do you enjoy your work with the bhimkay?"

"Yes," she said cautiously.

His blue eyes fixed on her, seeming to pierce her soul. "I understand you've given Shakki your passkey, that you use the circuit-comm with her. But no one else."

"There's no one else I trust inside my head," she told him.

"Not even Aideen?"

"Especially not her," Kayla said.

"Or me?" Ohin asked. "You don't want to talk to me on your circuit-comm?"

Again she wondered if he knew she could hear him. And why would he want to talk to her, anyway?

She met his gaze, tried to guess from that placid expression. "It's just as easy to talk like this."

"But not as personal. You might not believe this, Kayla, but you're quite special to me."

That alarmed her more than if he'd called in the medic and

gen-techs to reset her. "You don't even know me."

"I know you better than you realize."

"You don't! You don't know me at all. And you won't get an oath out of me, either."

Fire flashed briefly in his eyes, then he said calmly, "I don't need it from *you*."

She didn't like his slight emphasis on that last word. "Because you think we're friends? Or because you hope I'll forget all about Tala? Maybe go as sanaki as the rest of the people here and start thinking of you as my nurture father?"

He took a breath, the inhalation almost a gasp. She thought she might have made him angry, but instead she saw hope in his eyes.

She shook her head. "That will never happen. You are nothing to me."

He slapped his hand hard on the workstation, and the computer's holo display picked up the vibration of the table. *Freedom, Humanity, Equality* vanished, replaced by an image of a bhimkay. To one side, someone had drawn a magnification of the spider's head, but it was as if the back of the head had been cut away.

Before Kayla could get a good look, Ohin's brusque movement minimized the image to an icon. Kayla's fingers itched to touch the screen again, to bring the image back.

"I'm not looking to be your nurture father," he said. "Nurture parents have no genetic tie to those in their care. If there is one thing about trueborns that I have come to appreciate, outsider and himayati alike, it's the value of common genetics. The connection between generations."

"I'm more connected to my nurture mother than a lot of trueborns are with their genetic parents," Kayla said, thinking of Devak and his problems with his mother and father.

Ohin flicked his hand dismissively. "Your attachment to your nurture mother is just an emotional artifice forced on you by outsider trueborns."

"No one forced me to love Tala," Kayla said.

"But think of the relationship you could have with your true parents, your genetic parents," Ohin said. "*They* gave you your DNA, not the gene-splicers."

"But the gene-splicers have changed me anyway. Installed the circuitry. Gave me these." She set her hands on the workstation. "Gave me my sket."

Her regenned left arm lay beside Ohin's and for the first time, she noticed that the pale brown skin color the gen-techs had given it matched Ohin's nearly exactly. A chill passed through her. Was he so arrogant that he'd demanded that the color of her arm be set to the same shade as his own?

Of course, the color on the regenned arm wasn't so much different than the shade of her face. Maybe Palla and her gen-techs had only been trying to match that. But if they *had* given her Ohin's skin color, what else could they have installed inside her? Could the gen-techs have inserted that same programming as in the himayati, and one day she'd suddenly adore him?

She couldn't even think about that.

Ohin's voice brought her back to their conversation. "Your trueborn-created sket is useful. Worth keeping. But of what use is any alliance between you and the nurture family you were placed with forcibly? Isn't your genetics a more powerful connection?"

"Is this all about Aideen?" Hot anger burned inside her. "Did she ask you to talk to me? I feel nothing for her or her genetics. You can't convince me otherwise."

He started drumming his fingers, the soft raps on the workstation again activating the screen. "It wouldn't hurt you to be kind to her."

She didn't understand why he was defending Aideen when he didn't seem to like the woman much himself. "Was it kind of her to kidnap me?" Kayla asked. "To drag me here?"

"If you hadn't been brought here, the Brigade would have confiscated your body. Your DNA would have been torn apart, used by Akhilesh or someone like him to create a hundred other GENs."

So he was still keeping to that lie that FHE had rescued her from GAMA rather than from the bombing in Two Rivers. It was bare comfort that he didn't realize Kayla knew the truth. "I had friends who found me—would have found me and saved me."

"Found you, maybe," Ohin said. "But in time? Aideen got you into a portable gen-tank within minutes. A gen-tank controlled by FHE."

A gen-tank they'd planned to use even if she hadn't been injured—to reset her.

Ohin went on. "There was no arguing with outsider trueborns over whether you were worth saving. No discussion of whether the best use of your body was to break it down for DNA. Your friends could never have gotten to you as quickly as Aideen did, and would have had to have those discussions, those arguments. Meanwhile, you would have died, and the question of whether to harvest your body's DNA would have been answered."

The truth of what Ohin had said cut deep. "They would have burned me first. They would never have turned me over to the gene-splicers to be used that way."

"Perhaps," Ohin said. "They might have saved you from that last indignity."

"And they wouldn't have reset me to heal me." She held her breath, waiting for his response to that.

"*We* didn't reset you, Akhilesh did." He must have seen a germ of her fear in her eyes, because he set his hand over hers. "No matter what we find necessary with some other GENs, Kayla, you are in a different class. I would never . . ."

His last word trailed off. She felt the vibration of him using his circuit-comm at the base of her skull.

She's here. But I don't think it's time yet.

For what? That reset he'd just promised her he wouldn't do?

Ohin frowned with irritation. *I disagree. I think we shouldn't rush . . .*

He listened a few moments more, then abruptly got to his feet. "We'll have to continue this later."

Continue what? Kayla wondered. More tests of her loyalty? More talk of how she should cut away the most important part of her life, her nurture family? More persuasion that Aideen should take Tala's place in her heart? Kayla would just as soon abandon those conversations forever.

"Should I wait for you here?" she asked. She wanted dearly to get back to checking those images of the bhimkay.

"I don't know how long I'll be. Better for you to get on with your day."

He rose and went to the door, holding it open for her. No chance he would leave her in here unattended. If she could just lose him, she could come back and use the memorized code to get back inside.

She exited, stepping well clear of him as he walked out. Where Aideen refused to touch Kayla, Ohin did it far more often than she felt comfortable. The fewer chances she gave him, the better.

He made sure the lock engaged when he shut his door. Then he eyed her, apparently expecting her to walk with him. She would have to make a show of going back to her quarters.

Her stomach rumbled and she wished Jadi had brought her breakfast as Ohin had ordered. She considered only briefly going to Mahala to get something to eat. No, she had to use the opportunity of Ohin's absence to see what she could discover in his workspace.

After a distance, the corridor turned sharply left. Straight ahead was an alcove with a door set deep inside it. To the right the corridor continued on. When they'd come in the opposite direction, she hadn't even noticed the alcove.

In the dimness, she could just make out the nameplate beside the door with *Aideen Kalu* inscribed on it. Her birth mother's quarters, a place she'd never been.

"I hope you'll give some thought to what I've told you," he said.

"I will," she said, although whatever thought she'd give his lecture wouldn't be the kind of consideration he was hoping for.

Kayla would have thought he'd knock, but instead Ohin typed in a door code. Kayla tried to angle to see the code, but this time he stood so close to the keypad and it was so dim, there was no hope of catching it. She nodded his way as he went inside, giving him a smile with no goodwill behind it.

Just before the door swung shut, Kayla caught a glimpse of Aideen inside and another woman nearer the door—Charf, from the Bhimkay Lounge. Charf caught sight of Kayla too and gave her an evil look.

The moment the door latch clicked, Kayla turned on her heel and hurried back to Ohin's workspace, grateful that it was so isolated. If she encountered anyone, she'd tell them she got turned around.

But that part of the corridor was empty. She got to Ohin's door and put her hand up to the keypad. Half-closing her eyes, she retrieved the pattern she'd saved in her annexed brain. With careful taps of her fingers, she duplicated the pattern on the keypad.

The click of the door lock told her she'd been successful. She quickly opened the door, slipped inside, and shut it behind her. Then she sat at the computer and swiped her hand past the holo display to wake it.

There was an array of twenty or so icons along the left side and five others along the bottom. She recognized some of the icons on the left. It had a networking function—would that allow her communications access to the outside like the sekai in the Kheta storeroom had? There was also a writing program, calculating program, and drawing program. All standard for any computer.

The networking program wouldn't open without a password, so she focused instead on finding that picture of the bhimkay. She tapped the first bottom icon.

It was a map of the lowest level. She scanned it quickly and realized it wasn't all that useful. There were rooms indicated that she hadn't seen before, but the layout was essentially what she already knew.

She dropped the map back to the bottom. The next icon opened to what seemed to be a list of residents of Antara. It was alphabetical, so she could easily find her name and Shakki's. Essali and Lovise were there, with a symbol next to their names. Because they were in a gen-tank? Other names had the same symbol beside them. Thank the Infinite, not too many of those. And likely some of them were genuinely injured, not just imprisoned like Lovise and Essali.

If she had a datapod, she could upload the names into her annexed brain. She quickly searched the workstation, but didn't find any lying around, nor did she come up with one after a quick search of the drawers beneath the table. Without that shortcut, she'd have to read each name and store it away manually. She didn't have enough time for that.

She swiped away that file and brought up the next. It was a rendering of the inner workings of a presaka, the device that controlled the bhimkay's inhibitors. Just a technical drawing.

The next icon was the one she'd been looking for—the drawing of the bhimkay with part of its head cut away. Now she could see the layout of the inhibitor within the spider's nervous system. The electronics reminded her far too much of GEN circuitry.

There was a tiny nub right at the base of the head, where the neck would be if a bhimkay had a neck. It was marked with a yellow circle, a symbol she recognized from what Jal, her nurture brother, had told her in his endless, impatient tech lectures. That bit was a solar cell. It was connected to a square that had a lightning bolt symbol—the power source.

Kayla had learned enough in Doctrine School to know that the electrical impulses in a GEN's nervous system, coupled with their blood circulation, kept their circuitry powered. But a bhimkay had a simpler nervous system, so the controllers needed an external power source—the suns' energy—to keep operating. She stared at the drawing some more, wishing she had Jal's sket—he could suss out the functioning of anything electronic. If Kayla hadn't seen the circuitry in action in a bhimkay, she wouldn't have a clue about what it did. She memorized what she could in a rote way, without really understanding it, then minimized the picture.

She was about to tap the last icon when a knock at the door sent her heart racing. It couldn't be Ohin because he wouldn't have knocked. But could it be someone else who knew the code?

She tapped the icon, distracted enough by whoever was at the door that she had to look twice at the image on the screen to register what she was seeing. It was a bhimkay with a rider on its back. Except the rider wasn't using a saddle like the Bhimkay Boys did. He was carefully positioned between two rows of hair barbs.

A voice called through the door, "Ohin?"

It was Jadi, at last bringing the morning meal for Kayla. Would Ohin have given him the entry code? Surely not.

She started to turn back to the screen, but then she heard the beep of the keypad. Denk it, Jadi *did* know the code.

Kayla's fingers flew to swipe away the last image. She ran to the door and opened it just wide enough to see Jadi holding a bowl of kel-grain.

Kayla edged out and shut the door firmly. "Ohin doesn't want to be disturbed." She plucked the bowl from Jadi's big hands. "Thank you."

She hurried off down the hall before Jadi could ask her any questions. He tailed her for a while, then thank the Infinite, stepped inside the nearest lift.

But now what? Go back to Mahala? To her quarters? One thing was for certain, she was starving.

She was nearly to that sharp turn where Aideen's quarters

were. Just as she was about to pass the opening to the alcove, Aideen's door opened and Charf strode out. She glared at Kayla before marching off down the corridor in the direction of Mahala.

At the door, Aideen met Kayla's gaze. The trueborn woman glanced at Ohin, barely visible behind her, then back at Kayla. Aideen mouthed the word, *Stay*, before shutting the door.

Stay? Why? And why didn't Aideen want Ohin knowing?

Kayla slipped into the alcove, moved along its short, shadowy length until she was close to the door. Her stomach rumbled again, so she started spooning up kel-grain, as much to fill her belly as to be done with the bowl and spoon. At one point, a pair of GEN girls passed the opening of the alcove, but because the passersby were looking ahead around the upcoming turn of the corridor, they didn't spot Kayla in the shadows.

She finished her kel-grain and set the empty bowl on the floor. As close as she was to Aideen's door, she could hear the buzz of conversation between Aideen and Ohin, but it was impossible to make out words. She could only hear the deeper sounds of Ohin's voice and the lighter tones of Aideen's.

Kayla pressed her ear against the door. Had Aideen moved closer? Because now Kayla could hear her birth mother speaking. "Please, Ohin."

Please, what? Kayla puzzled over Aideen's plea, then at the edge of her hearing, she caught Ohin's footsteps as he moved nearer the door as well. Had Aideen pleaded with him to come closer?

Ohin spoke. "Genetic connections mean nothing to her."

Ohin must be referring to the conversation they'd just had. Aideen murmured something Kayla couldn't make out, then Ohin said, "The connection with them is too strong. Eleven

221

years of conditioning. She'll never betray them."

Betray who? Eleven years . . . that was how long she'd lived with Tala. And Jal, now close to a twelfth-year, had been her nurture brother nearly that long. Surely Ohin didn't think he could shift her alliance from her nurture family to him and Aideen?

Aideen said something, her voice again too light to carry through the door, then Ohin's deeper voice said, "We're the ones she should love. We're the ones who gave her life."

Because they saved her after the explosion? She was glad to still be alive, but Zul could have done the same.

". . . doesn't remember," Aideen said.

She didn't remember her time in the tank? How could she? Aideen had told her both of them had been there at Kayla's side as she'd been healed, but Kayla hadn't seen either of them until she'd emerged from the tank, and so had nothing to remember. Besides a series of nasty dreams about the explosion, Kayla recalled nothing from her tank time.

There were older memories of Aideen, long before Kayla ever arrived at Antara. Ones Kayla had once thought were fantasy, and later learned were real, when she discovered she'd been gestated inside Aideen's womb, not in a gen-tank.

In spite of herself, one of those distant images resolved in Kayla's bare brain. She was a third-year, cradled in Aideen's arms. Her birth mother gazed down at her with such adoration, Kayla's heart squeezed tight.

She tried to shake off the old images, to focus on the now, to catch more of Aideen's and Ohin's words. But the past kept intruding. Kayla's third-year self stared up at that doting mother. And then the old image changed, shifted, and Kayla saw a man beside Aideen.

Something was trying to reveal itself in Kayla's mind. She fought it, refused to believe it. How did she know it wasn't planted when they'd uploaded her memories?

Whatever it was, it was battering to get in. And as Kayla huddled there in the alcove, it struck her for the first time that if she'd had a birth mother, she had to have had a birth father too.

The distant memory of a woman and man standing together gelled in Kayla's mind. Aideen and Ohin.

"You have to tell her!" Aideen suddenly said so loudly the words rang clearly through the door. "You have to tell her she's your daughter!"

For an instant, the world went black, and Kayla wondered if someone was somehow resetting her. Then clarity returned, and Kayla twisted away from the alcove. Stumbling at first, then catching her stride, she ran.

She pelted down the corridor toward Seycat. But there was no escaping that horrifying realization, no matter how implausible it seemed. Still, she tried to reject it. It couldn't be true. It couldn't.

Oh, please, let that memory be a lie. If it wasn't, how could she live with it?

How could she accept that Ohin was her birth father?

17

Devak watched warily as the burly GEN boarded the multi-lev. Devak could read nothing in the man's face, whether the GEN meant to ransom the three trueborns on board, or kill them.

As the GEN lingered in the doorway, the lowborn multi-lev driver immediately put his arms up in surrender. The burly GEN turned toward the force of men and women pushing in through the door behind him.

"Hold on," he shouted to the GENs behind him. "Let the driver pass."

The crowd relayed the order. "Let the lowborn driver go!" "Yasi says to leave the lowborn be!"

The driver scrambled off the multi-lev past Yasi. His bobbing head was just visible through the side windows as he ran the length of the vehicle toward the back end. Then Devak saw him through the rear window trotting down the road in the direction they'd driven from. Likely he was heading for the allabain village. The nomadic lowborns would take him in.

Yasi grabbed Devak's right hand, pushed up his sleeve, then

did the same for the left. He wasn't quite as rough with Usi and Junjie—maybe it was Devak's high-status looks that irritated the GEN—but he quickly found Junjie's wristlink. The GEN unlatched it and slipped it into a hidden pocket in the hem of his shirt.

Yasi growled, "Now, get off. All three of you."

Junjie and Usi started to push to their feet. Devak waved them back down. "I think we're safer here."

"Think again, *Mar.*" Yasi thrust out with the club, just close enough that a sharp thorn on the end dug a scratch in Devak's cheek.

Devak sucked in a breath at the pain. He felt the track of blood dripping down his cheek.

Yasi leaned a hand on the back of Devak's seat, and put his face inches from Devak's. "We're setting this multi-lev on fire. Destroying it like you trueborns blew up our food and shelter. Stay if you want to burn to death."

He turned to the multi-lev controls and put the vehicle into parking mode. It sank lower with a hiss.

Yasi strode down the aisle, the seated lowborn passengers shrinking back as he passed. "GENs get off first!" he shouted. "Then lowborns."

The lowborns standing in back scrambled out of Yasi's way as he went partway up the stairs to repeat the order to the GENs riding on the upper level. Then he stood at the back as the GENs thundered down the stairs and up the aisle. Someone had opened the middle door and the GENs left that way. A few of the armed GENs outside approached them and escorted them away from the multi-lev.

Yasi took a last look at the upper level, then nodded at the lowborns. They quickly grabbed their carrysaks, took children by the hand and hustled up or down the aisle to the middle door. Following their lowborn driver's example, they moved off in the direction of the allabain village. The GENs outside let them go.

Now Devak, Junjie, and Usi were the only passengers remaining on the multi-lev. Yasi started up the aisle toward them.

Usi's voice trembled as he spoke. "Are they going to kill us?"

"If we were high-status, they might be angry enough to," Devak said. "But we're not worth much, being minor-status." At least he hoped Yasi thought a trio of minor-status boys were too insignificant to harm.

Now Yasi stood over them. "Well? Getting off or will you stay and fry?"

Devak glanced back at Junjie and Usi, then the three of them rose in near unison. Devak waited for Junjie and Usi to go first. Then he snagged the carrysak from under the seat, clutching it tight. But as he edged past Yasi, the GEN wrenched it from him. He gave Devak a nudge off the multi-lev, then followed.

While Devak watched, anger bubbling up inside, Yasi pawed through the carrysak. Apparently, his cursory look missed the dhans in their hidden pocket, but he plucked out the holo projector and switched it on. He flipped through the three images, lingering on the one of Kayla.

Yasi turned Kayla's image toward Devak. "How do you know her?"

"She was Assigned to my great-grandfather."

"Why do you have her image?"

Devak speared Yasi with his gaze. "Because I love her."

Whatever opinion Yasi had of Devak's declaration, he didn't say. But he dropped the HP back into the carrysak and handed it back to Devak.

Yasi shouted at the crowd, "Get to work!"

Twenty or so GENs set aside their clubs and moved toward the multi-lev. As they swarmed the vehicle, Devak noticed that nearly every one had physical problems—hand tremors, a shambling walk, their heads tipped to one side or forward. It was impossible to imagine GENs purposefully engineered with those disabilities. Had these GENs, who should have been disease resistant, been sickened with the same ailment?

Despite their physical difficulties, some squirmed underneath, others surrounded the outside, the rest climbed on board. The ones under the multi-lev came out with pieces of the suspension engine, the ones on the outside pried off sheets of lightweight plasscine, and the ones on board stole what they could of the driver's controls—interfaces and electronics alike.

Most of the GENs who'd been riding on the multi-lev had been enfolded seamlessly with the armed GENs, but a few had broken away and were hurrying after the lowborns. Devak suspected they feared their trueborn patrons and the Brigade more than they trusted this GEN band.

The GENs breaking down the multi-lev distributed what they'd salvaged into carrysaks, or onto their own backs and those of their companions, then headed off toward a thick grove of sticker bushes edged on two sides by tall boulders. They took with them the GENs from the multi-lev who had stayed, but they left Devak, Junjie, and Usi standing in the roadway.

Only Yasi and a single GEN woman remained standing in the roadway. She was tall and beautiful, her eyes kelfa brown, with dark hair hanging past her waist. Devak didn't remember her from the multi-lev, so she must have been a part of Yasi's band.

The woman approached the multi-lev. Like so many of the

other GENs, she couldn't seem to walk quite straight as she moved along the pavement.

She carried a plasscine bottle leaking a stinking fluid. From the sweet-acrid smell, Devak guessed it was nasaka, waste fluid from a plasscine extrusion factory. It was nasty, poisonous stuff, and extremely flammable.

How in the name of the Lord Creator these GENs had gotten their hands on nasaka, Devak had no idea. Plenty of GENs worked in the extrusion factories, but their lowborn and trueborn supervisors kept a sharp eye on their every movement.

Yasi nodded at the woman. "Thank you for your good work, Shima."

Shima set one foot on the bottom step of the multi-lev and braced a hand on the doorframe. She seemed to lack the strength to climb up. When Devak reflexively moved forward to assist her, Yasi caught his arm.

"She has to do it herself," Yasi said.

Finally Shima levered herself up into the multi-lev. As she walked to the back of the vehicle, Devak could see her through the windows, staggering, using the seat backs to steady herself. As she returned to the front, she flung drops of nasaka on the seats and aisle. Some of it must have sprinkled her too.

"That stuff is not safe," Devak said. "She should be more careful."

"She's already dying," Yasi said. The way his voice broke, the intense way he looked at Shima, told Devak the woman meant something to Yasi.

When she reached the front door, she tossed the empty bottle, then pulled a pair of palm-sized rocks from a pocket in her leggings. Devak recognized them as dhatu, fairly rare on Loka, with its limited metal resources. Again, something not easy for a GEN to come by, since pieces of dhatu even that small would be difficult to smuggle out of a plassteel factory where the metal-containing ore was used.

Shima struck the two rocks together, and now Devak understood. She was attempting to make a spark to ignite the nasaka. A risky way to light a fire, especially when she'd probably soaked herself with the flammable liquid. Why was she still in the multi-lev? Devak willed her to get off the pub-trans before her clothing lit.

Three tries, four. Five. Then with the sixth, a spark flew. A flame blossomed on a seat back, licked eagerly at the plasscine. Consumed the entire seat, then raced to the aisle and jumped to the other side.

The fire was growing quickly, the two walls of flame in a race to the back. "She should get off now," Devak said. "Or she'll catch fire herself."

"She's already dying," Yasi said again, his words choked and rough. He lifted his club toward Shima in a salute and she raised her hand in return.

Then she dove into the fire.

"No!" Devak cried out as her clothes and long dark hair immediately burst into flames. She screamed, an animal sound of pain that tore deep inside Devak. Without conscious thought, he took a step toward the burning multi-lev. Yasi wrapped his strong arms around Devak and dragged him back.

It didn't take Devak long to realize the futility of trying to save the GEN woman. He couldn't bear to watch her burn either, or listen to her screams. But he forced himself to, because a part of him felt responsible, because he was trueborn, because despite his love for Kayla, despite his work with the Kinship, he hadn't done enough for GENs. His neglect had somehow contributed to the suicide of that beautiful woman, and his heart felt torn from his chest at the thought of it.

When it was too late to do anything, Yasi let go of Devak. Tears spilled down Devak's cheeks, their salt stinging in the scratch Yasi had dealt him. He looked back at the GEN man, saw Yasi's tears. Once more Yasi said in a bare whisper, "She was dying anyway."

"Why?" Devak asked.

"From breathing nasaka fumes," Yasi said. "I gave it to her myself to inhale."

"Why would you?" Devak asked. "The fumes don't make you feel good, like a lifter does. Just sick. And you had to know it could kill her."

"But it was the only way to break the Monitoring Grid's hold on us," Yasi said. "The fumes damage our neurological systems. That scrambles the signals the circuitry sends out to the Grid. We try to inhale the right amount, to affect the signal transmission and nothing else. But it's hard to know how much."

It reminded Devak of Pitamah, of how his great-grandfather had experimented on himself and the scientists who'd worked with him as they were inventing the first GENs. The experiments wrecked Pitamah's nervous system the way Shima's was ruined, although in his great-grandfather's case, time in the tank and punarjanma injections had extended his life.

"You didn't have to use the nasaka," Devak said, heartsick. "I know a way to reprogram GENs to take them off the Grid."

Yasi looked over at him, his expression bleak. "But have you been here before today to help us with that, Mar?"

The heat of the flaming multi-lev drove Devak back, thick black smoke burning his eyes. Yasi hung close to the multi-lev for a few moments more, maybe paying tribute to Shima, then he retreated to Devak's side. The other GENs had nearly disappeared amongst the sticker bushes.

"What about you?" Devak asked. "And all the others? Has everyone used the nasaka?"

"All the vidrohi have breathed the fumes," Yasi said. "Some of us are doing fine, some are dying like Shima. The Brigade hasn't found us yet, but there's no way to know if we're truly safe from the Grid."

The vidrohi—a Bhasha word for rebellious. But their rebellion, their tearing themselves away from the Grid, had exacted a high price. Sickness and death.

Devak glanced over at Junjie, catching his eye. "Can I speak with my friends?"

Yasi, still staring at the fire, waved a hand in permission. Devak crunched across the rocky roadside dirt to the pavement where Junjie and Usi were.

"Junjie, do you still have the Grid password app on your wristlink?"

"Never deleted it," Junjie said. "But I haven't hacked into the Grid for months. Not since the Kinship stopped sending updates for the Grid programs. Besides, those GENs—"

"The vidrohi," Devak put in.

Junjie shrugged. "Either way, they took my wristlink."

"Vidrohi," Usi said. "A pretty sad rebellion. Some of them can barely stand. They have to lean on other people for help."

"That's because they're using nasaka fumes to compromise their nervous systems," Devak told them. "To stop the Grid from finding them."

Junjie glanced toward the retreating GENs. "I wondered. They remind me of the trueborns I'd see coming in for treatment in Akhilesh's GAMA lab with neurological diseases, rare ones that were mostly engineered out back on Earth. It took a long time in the tank to rebuild them."

"You know no one's going to put the vidrohi in a tank except to reset them," Devak said. "But the GEN restoration treatment—"

"No one's making the treatment anymore," Junjie said. "Not with all the turmoil that's been going on. Not with some of the Kinship thinking it's maybe safer to keep GENs as GENs."

"That's what Kayla chose," Devak said, "to stay a GEN. It's not a terrible thing."

Of course, at first, it had been so difficult when she'd told him she didn't want to be restored, even though she'd been born a trueborn. But he'd come to realize it was the right choice for her. In fact, her circuitry and annexed brain were an advantage for her in many ways.

"She did choose that, and it was a good decision for her," Junjie said. "But she figured she would eventually be freed from slavery with the Kinship's help. Except the loudest members of the Kinship think it would be for the GENs' own good to be left as slaves to trueborns. Trueborn patrons will just start treating GENs *nicer*. Be more *compassionate*. Like that would make up for being enslaved."

Disgust burned in Devak's stomach. The Kinship had completely reversed direction during his time in the tank. "If no one cares enough to give GENs their freedom, then it's not the Kinship anymore. Maybe FHE has the right idea. Make GENs angry enough to fight for themselves because the trueborns won't."

Usi shook his head. "Killing people isn't right either. The Kinship and FHE are both going wrong."

An idea sparked in Devak's mind. He looked over at Yasi. "The vidrohi are risking their lives with the nasaka to be free. The least we can do is help them see if their risk is working, that they're off the Grid. If I can get in, I should be able to search, since that's read-only."

"If my password app still works," Junjie said. "And if you can persuade that vidrohi leader to give back my wristlink."

"I think I can." Devak handed Usi the carrysak and returned to Yasi, who was watching the flames die down.

"I can tell you if you're off the Grid," Devak said. "Any of the vidrohi that want to know. I'd need the wristlink back, and you'd have to tell me your GEN ID and nurture line."

Yasi gave Devak a long look. "Why would I tell you anything more about me?"

Devak shrugged. "Believe me or not. I'm more on your side than you think. I told you, I'm in love with a GEN girl, and she would want me to help you."

Yasi's gaze narrowed on Devak for a long moment, then he finally retrieved the wristlink and handed it over. "Yasi 3178, nurture son of Te."

Devak started the password app, and the wristlink display blurred as the app created and tried hundreds of passwords. The program hit a brick wall with each one and Devak realized he should have checked before he made that promise to Yasi. With the GEN man staring at him expectantly, Devak's hopes sank lower and lower with each denial.

Then the wristlink beeped softly and Devak was in. He smiled up at Yasi and entered the GEN's information into the Grid search form. *Entry not found*, the wristlink returned. Thank the Lord Creator.

He showed the display to Yasi. "You're safe, unless a Grid

tech starts poking around. Sometimes they get bored and dig old databases out of archive, just to search for GENs that have been overlooked."

That was why the Kinship ghosted in valid entries for the GENs they removed from the Grid. It would look to a Grid tech that a GEN was right where he or she was supposed to be, working at their Assignment.

Was anyone in the Kinship even doing that anymore? If no one was tracking Grid updates, uploading them to make sure the ghosted locations were valid, were there Kinship GENs now in danger of being tracked?

"There is one other thing I can check," Devak said. "The Grid might have declared you dead. It does that with GENs who were once in the database, but when they're pinged, don't ping back. How long since you used the nasaka fumes?"

"Two months," Yasi said.

"How long for it to take effect?"

"No idea," Yasi said. "But I started feeling . . . *wrong* . . . within a week."

"That should be long enough. The Grid might have registered you as dead," Devak said. "But to check, I'll need your passkey."

Now Yasi scowled at him. "Do you think I'm sanaki enough to give you a chance to reset me?"

"I don't even have a datapod with the right program," Devak said. "Besides, as messed up as your circuitry is, you might not be able to be reset."

Yasi's eyes lit at that. To no longer have the threat of losing his personality, having his self wiped away with a reset, had to be a liberating thing.

Even knowing he was safe from that fate, Yasi leaned close

and whispered his passkey. Devak entered the twenty-digit string into the Grid.

He held out the wristlink to Yasi. "Congratulations. You're officially dead."

Yasi laughed, lightening some of the sorrow still in his eyes. "Will you check the others?"

"If you let us go afterward," Devak countered.

"If I do, will you send the Brigade for us?" Yasi asked.

"You've already put yourself at risk for that," Devak said, nodding in the direction the lowborns and GENs had gone.

Yasi sighed. "The lowborns have never done any of us harm. How can I retaliate against them? And I can't force GENs to stay with us if they choose otherwise."

They all started off toward the vidrohi encampment. It was as good a hiding place as the GENs could hope for in flat, open Wesja sector. A line of boulders four and five meters tall formed a wall about a half-kilometer from the road and parallel to it. Where the boulders tailed off, the sticker bushes, nearly double Devak's height, grew thickly enough to completely conceal anyone behind them.

As they neared the encampment, Devak told his friends that they'd be staying long enough to check the status of the other vidrohi GENs, then they'd wait for the next pub-trans to come through. Yasi didn't make any objection, so Devak assumed the GEN man agreed.

They reached the grove, entering single file between two thorny bushes. There were twice the GENs here than the number who had attacked the pub-trans vehicle, children among the forty or fifty present. Some were tending fires and cooking rat-snakes on spits, others lay up against the back of the boulders on worn plass blankets, or directly on the hard-packed dirt.

"Not much of a shelter," Yasi said, "but it keeps us from notice until the nasaka takes effect."

"What about bhimkay?" Devak asked. It looked like prime territory for the giant spiders.

"They've taken off a few of us," Yasi said. "But better to die of spider venom than serve trueborns again."

And some of the people lying on the ground looked close to death from nasaka poisoning. There were children among the ill, small pitiful bodies with eyes full of pain.

"The children breathe it too?" Devak asked, sick at the thought.

"The nurture parents choose," Yasi said. "Most say yes. We restrict how much they inhale, but their systems are so vulnerable."

Slavery or death. Devak could see no right answer.

Before Devak could start the status check on the vidrohi, Junjie asked for the wristlink. "I have to contact Risa. Let her know we won't be in Amik."

The realization sank like a stone in Devak's stomach. "By the time we get out of here, back to the allabain village, catch another pub-trans . . ."

"She'll be gone before we can get there," Junjie said. "She can't wait for us, or the Brigade would wonder why."

Even if Devak went back on his promise to Yasi, didn't take the time to search the Grid for all these GENs, they would only save half a day. With the new tighter Brigade security, Risa would have had to file a schedule. It wasn't as easy for her to switch things around like she used to for Kinship business.

Junjie made his call while Yasi let the group of vidrohi know what Devak would be doing. The ones who were well enough would go to Devak, the ill GENs he would visit. Although he suspected most of the sick would die before there was ever a chance that the Brigade would come and take them away.

Junjie returned with the wristlink. "Risa's sorry she can't help us. She could make a side trip through Dika sector to pick us up when she's done in Nafi, but that won't help us. She goes down to Saya in Eastern Territory after that."

Devak couldn't think about how the three of them would get to Ret. He just started checking the line of sick vidrohi, adults and children.

He asked for their passkey first—if they'd already been declared dead, there was no reason to search further. If the passkey didn't return favorable results, he'd ask for their GEN ID and nurture line.

The adults he could bear interacting with because he could see the acceptance in their eyes. But the children, hurting but not understanding why, broke his heart.

One little girl named Mey, no more than a fourth-year, didn't want Devak to leave once he'd figured out she was safe from the Grid. From her blanket on the ground, she took his hand and whispered, "Can I sing you a song?"

His chest squeezed so tight, he almost couldn't speak. "Please," Devak whispered back, then he bent close to hear.

She barely had the breath to voice the words to a simple spelling song that GENs were taught in Doctrine School. After one verse, she sighed, "I'm sleepy now."

Devak waited until her grip on his hand relaxed as she fell asleep. Then he pulled the rough plasscine blanket up to her chin and found a warm place by the fire to wait for the other GENs.

They filed past him, each hesitating only briefly before revealing their passkey. Only a few lucky ones had been gone long enough that they'd been declared dead. The others had to take the second step to get their status.

Of course, all the new GENs who had been on the multi-lev were still accessible to the Grid. But a few of the vidrohi were still being tracked as well.

Devak wished he could just "ghost" in all of them so that they'd look like they were exactly where their Assignments said they should be. But he could only read from the Grid, which meant he couldn't write the ghosting code into the database for any of the GENs. Not to mention the Grid programming was updated often and the ghosting code had to change accordingly. He didn't have the access or the updates.

Yasi gathered the new GENs and told them it was either nasaka fumes or they'd have to leave. A handful did leave, heading out while it was still light enough to avoid the bhimkay, but most of them were willing to risk the nasaka for freedom. The vidrohi who had already breathed the neurotoxin once and would have to again took the news with stolid acceptance. They'd probably thought they were safe—both from the Grid's monitoring and further nerve damage from the nasaka.

Devak had gotten three-quarters through the vidrohi and dusk was falling when the wristlink beeped. He was hopeful it might be Risa calling back to say she could transport them after all, or even Pitamah saying Jemali was on his way with his WindSpear.

But the face that appeared in the wristlink's display was Mishalla's—Kayla's long-time closest friend. "Devak?"

"Yes. Hello." He moved away from the fire to a relatively private nook between two boulders. "How are you?"

"Good. Eoghan and me both. But I've got some news for you."

"Is it Pitamah?" Devak said in a panic. "He was ill when we left, and we haven't heard from him."

"No, I think he's fine," Mishalla said. "I saw him at a Kinship meeting. He looked tired, but okay. I'm calling about a wristlink message."

"From who?"

She lowered her voice. "Did you know Kayla is alive?"

Now guilt pricked him. "I should have told you. I've known for a while."

"I knew," Mishalla said. "I *knew* without anyone telling me. But I got a garbled message, and I'm pretty sure it was from her. It came more than a month ago, but it was only today that Eoghan was finally able to decipher it."

Devak's heart thudded faster in his chest. "What did she say?"

"Not much," Mishalla said. "Just 'need help,' then she signed it with a K. It took some hard work, but Eoghan figured out the nearest comm-site the transmission pinged, which tells us where she was when she sent it. It pinged through Belk."

Belk. In the southeastern corner of Eastern territory. More than five thousand kilometers from Nafi, where Usi said Kayla would be.

evak finished checking all the vidrohi before confronting Usi. The boy was sitting beside the fire with Junjie, entertaining a few GEN children by juggling sandrocks, the unstable stones crumbling in Usi's hands after two or three tosses. But the children thought that was hysterically funny, particularly when the beige dust rained down on Usi's head.

Devak nudged Usi with his foot. "Come talk to me."

He looked up at Devak warily, but he rose. Junjie popped up too, and as Devak poked Usi toward the outer edge of the light cast by the fire, Junjie stayed close.

This far away from the flames, the chill of full night had settled upon them. Though it was mid-spring with summer just a month or so away, as far north as Wesja was, the day's heat didn't linger.

Devak turned to face Usi. "I just got information from someone I trust—more than you, anyway—that tells me Kayla is near Belk, not Nafi. So I want to know why you lied to us."

"I didn't," Usi protested.

Devak pulled the boy around so the faint firelight cleared

the shadows in Usi's face. "Kayla sent a message. From Eastern Territory, not Northeast. So you've been lying to us."

Usi looked flabbergasted. "No. I thought it was true."

Devak gave him another poke. "I think it's time you told us everything you know. Or we're leaving you here with the vidrohi."

"We can't, Devak," Junjie said. "I won't—"

"Then I'll leave you both," Devak said, his heart wrenching a little at the thought of abandoning his friend. "I'll find Kayla on my own if I have to."

Devak could see how his declaration was tearing his friend apart. Junjie finally took Usi's hand and squeezed it. "Tell him what you know. Please."

"Okay," Usi said. "But it isn't that much. Not as much as I led you to believe."

Unsurprised, Devak waved at him to continue.

Usi shrugged. "Aideen always told me FHE headquarters was in Northeast Territory."

"She told you this," Devak said.

"Yes . . . well . . . she hinted," Usi said. "She mentioned Nafi a lot. And since FHE's headquarters is in a cavern—"

"She told you that?" Devak asked.

"She hinted at it, would complain that it was hard to get a signal out with all that rock overhead." Usi shrugged. "Nafi is in Northeast Territory and there are caverns in the northern part of the sector, so that was my guess."

"Then you only guessed that Kayla was there," Devak said, letting his irritation spill out.

"It was a good guess," Usi protested. "I made it in good faith. It's what I believed was true."

"Belk is riddled with caverns too," Junjie reminded Devak. "That part must be true. Aideen just misled Usi, made him think FHE headquarters was north when it was south."

Devak wasn't sure what to believe, except he had a lot more faith in Mishalla than this trueborn boy. "Go back to the children," he told Usi.

Usi smiled in tentative relief. He reached out a hand to Junjie. But Devak said, "Just you, Usi."

Once Usi was out of earshot, Devak said, "I know you care for him—"

"I love him," Junjie said.

"You hardly know him," Devak said. "You love the boy you thought he was all that time you were part of FHE."

"But he *is* exactly who I thought he was," Junjie said. "And I think he's telling the truth. FHE told me hardly anything. I think Usi knew a little more because his father brought him in. But I bet they didn't tell him everything, either."

Devak wished he could see Junjie's face better in the twilight, to see if it looked like his friend was just clinging to false hope about Usi. Was Junjie fooling himself? "You think Usi guessed wrong."

"I don't think he's trying to trick us," Junjie said. "Yes, he wants to stay with us because he's afraid of the Brigade. But if he can help us, he will."

"Well, for now, I don't think he can help us at all if Kayla is five thousand kilometers from where he thought she was."

"What do we do now?" Junjie asked.

"We call Risa again and see if we can connect with her in Dika sector, get a ride on her lorry to Saya in Eastern Sector." Devak rubbed his eyes. "No idea how we'll get to Dika."

"Another pub-trans has to come through here at some point," Junjie said. "Do we have enough dhans for Dika?"

"Barely," Devak said. "If we don't eat until we meet up with

Risa. Thank the Lord Creator for those nutras Waji gave us."

Junjie made the call to Risa, pacing as he spoke to the lowborn woman. He mostly listened, nodding occasionally.

When he disconnected, he handed the device back to Devak. "We have to let her know when we've caught a pubtrans. She won't have a reason to sidetrack to Dika if we're not there, and she won't be able to wait for us for long."

They started back toward the fire. Devak asked, "Do you know why the vidrohi hijack the multi-levs? What they do with what they strip off it?"

"The metal they trade to the allabain for sticker bush root pulp and wild kel-grain," Junjie said. "The suspension engine parts they reconfigure to make a crude comm device. No idea how, but I guess some of these escaped GENs have hyper-tech skets."

They'd reached the fireside. On the other side of the fire, two cooks, a GEN man and woman, tended to four spits that looked as if they'd been made from multi-lev salvage. Each spit was loaded with several rat-snakes. Another cook had her eye on a pot of what smelled like kel-grain, although it was more aromatic than what Devak was used to.

Despite the crowd around the fire, its roar was loud enough that he and Junjie could have a fairly private conversation. Devak sat on a half-meter tall boulder jutting from the sand. The top was chilly, but the front of the stone was hot from the fire.

"What do they use the comm for?" Devak asked. "Who do they communicate with?"

Junjie sat on another rock beside Devak. Junjie's gaze immediately went to Usi, just beyond the rat-snake cooks. Usi had a second-year GEN boy on his lap, and several boys and girls were clustered around him, rapt. Usi seemed to be telling a story, gesturing wildly with his hands.

Junjie looked back at Devak. "They talk to other vidrohi bands that split off from this one when it got too big. They try to keep each band to no more than thirty, so they're less likely to be noticed by the Brigade, and because it's easier to feed a smaller group. They add more GENs when they hijack a pub-trans, then split off as needed. This one is due to split once they know who's going to recover from the nasaka."

Devak eyed the line of sick lying close to the fire. Mey, her inhalations noisy and too far apart, seemed to be struggling to breathe. She probably wouldn't make it through the night. None of them looked likely to.

Yasi approached, then settled in the sand beside Devak without asking permission to join them. Devak supposed the man didn't need to ask. He was the leader of this group.

Rather than change the subject, Devak brought the GEN man into the conversation. "Junjie's been telling me about the pub-trans. You stop them, salvage whatever is valuable or useful, make the comm devices," Devak said. "And keep in touch with the other vidrohi bands. But are you coordinating?"

"We let each other know where sympathetic allabain villages are," Yasi said. "If friends have been parted, they have a chance to talk. We warn about any news we hear about the Brigade. Other than that, we're all independent. It's safer that way."

"That isn't what FHE was hoping for," Devak said. "They wanted to make life miserable for GENs in hopes they'd rise up in a revolution against trueborns."

"We just want to survive," Yasi said. "Avoid the Brigade."

"Don't you want things to change?" Junjie asked. "Don't you think GENs should have all the same rights as trueborns?"

For a moment, Yasi seemed thunderstruck. "Of course I do. I never thought a trueborn would think the same."

Devak considered the shambles that the Kinship had become. "Most don't. We do. We used to be part of a network that did as well."

"The problem with a revolution," Yasi said, "is that it takes too long. There's no way to know which side will win. We want to be free *now*. If that means we have to scrabble in the wilderness like the allabain do, we will. Let someone else fight the revolution. We're already free."

"But so many of you are dying from the nasaka," Devak said, glancing again to Mey in that line of suffering GENs.

"Fewer than would die in a revolution," Yasi said. He got to his feet. "Cooks are serving. Better get some. The food goes fast."

Devak joined the line behind Yasi. He might be the leader, but he got no special treatment—there were twenty hungry GENs in front of them. The children were fed first. Two older boys, maybe twelfth-years, took two bowls each and headed over to the dying.

Devak watched them as he waited in line. The boys feeding the sick would take a mouthful of the kel-grain and rat-snake meat, then offer a bite to whoever they were tending. Once they'd coaxed a little food into one of the dying, they'd move to another blanket.

One of the boys lingered over Mey's sleeping body. He stroked her hair back, but didn't wake the little girl before moving on.

The food held out until Devak reached the spits and pot, although Junjie and Usi had to share the last scrapings of kel-grain. When he took his place by the fire to eat, Devak saw why the kel-grain had a stronger fragrance—it was wild, no doubt gathered by the allabain lowborns that the vidrohi traded with.

Unlike the bland genetically-engineered version, the

wild kel-grain was fragrant with a rich, almost meaty flavor. The gene-splicers who had altered the native kel-grain had apparently sacrificed its taste in exchange for greater yield and higher nutrition. Another way trueborns devalued GENs, since kel-grain was mostly meant for the tankborns.

After evening meal, several of the GENs built up the fire with oily sticker bush branches. The cooks passed around hot kelfa drinks, the cups carved from junk tree wood. They came up short on cups, but Yasi made sure Devak, Usi, and Junjie got some.

Devak didn't drink, too glad for the way the cup warmed his hands. All around him, GENs lay together in pairs and trios, no doubt to conserve body heat. Several of the younger vidrohi boys and girls paired up to lie on either side of the dying GENs. If they couldn't do anything else, Devak guessed, they would keep the pain-wracked warm on one of their last nights. The boy who had paused to stroke Mey's hair curled up beside her.

In the near darkness beneath two sticker bushes, Junjie and Usi shared a blanket. Devak could barely hear their whispering to one another. Devak didn't want to intrude on their private moment, but the cold night air would be difficult to bear alone without a blanket.

As the crowd quieted in preparation for sleep, Yasi came into the firelight a few meters away from Devak. The GEN man stared into the flames, a thin ragged blanket hanging around his shoulders. He brought a GEN prayer mirror close to his face, and his lips moved as he prayed.

Then he kissed the mirror and threw it into the fire. Devak moved to step further away, but Yasi must have heard him because he beckoned.

Devak asked, "Was the prayer mirror Shima's?"

"She left it behind, but to my shame, I couldn't bear to keep it," Yasi said. "The liturgy forbids destruction by flame, but I'm not as much of a follower as Shima was."

It crossed Devak's mind to tell Yasi that the liturgy was a false document, created by trueborns to control GENs. But what did he know about what was true and what wasn't?

"I think the Infinite would understand," Devak finally said.

Yasi nodded, then silently watched the fire for a long while. "Did you get enough to eat?"

"Plenty. Thank you." Devak hesitated, then asked, "Were you and Shima joined?"

"Back when we were still Assigned in Mendin sector," Yasi said, "her as a Doctrine School teacher, me as an electronics tech. They were going to re-Assign her to Giaqi in Southwest sector. I think sometimes the trueborns do that just so we can't make strong bonds."

Devak put his hands out to the fire to warm them. "That might be true sometimes. But usually it's about the dhans. Shima must have shown herself to be particularly valuable. The patron who sponsored the Doctrine school would have thought more about the profit in selling her Assignment than who Shima had joined with."

"You know a lot about how Assignments work." Yasi appraised Devak. "Too young to be an Assignment specialist. And I thought the specialists were all demi-status, not minor."

Only a few weeks ago, Devak would have felt mortification at the reminder of his loss of rank. Instead he felt such gratitude, such a lightness of heart now that all the trappings of *Mar* had been stripped away.

"I was high-status until we lost nearly all of our adhikar," Devak said, then hesitated before revealing the rest. "My father was director of the Monitoring Grid for all of the Western Territories."

"Director of the Monitoring Grid." Yasi bit out each word, shadows of anger forming and shifting with the light cast by the fire. "If not for that Infinite-cursed Grid chasing us across Svarga, we would never have poisoned ourselves."

Guilt stabbed at Devak, as deeply as if he'd created the Grid itself. "If it's worth anything to you, if I could reach in and destroy it, I would."

"That's not worth much," Yasi snapped. "Could wrecking the Grid bring back Shima? Or restore little Mey?"

The answers to those questions were clear. Now mixing with his guilt, Devak felt shame and helplessness.

Yasi's rage burned a few moments more in his eyes, then faded to resignation. "Nevertheless, I'm grateful to you for what you have done." He nudged the cup Devak still held. "The wild kelfa makes a much better drink. You shouldn't waste it."

Devak took a sip and had to agree. It was stronger, and with a spicy aftertaste he couldn't identify. He drank it all as they stood beside the fire, as it popped and crackled, as the dying moaned and sighed.

Once the cup was empty, Yasi took it from Devak and handed him the blanket. "It's not much, but it should keep you warm enough if you stay close to the fire."

Yasi walked off toward where the dying lay. The GEN man stretched out on the other side of Mey, opposite the twelfth-year boy warming the small girl.

Devak lay as close to the fire as he dared and wrapped himself tightly in the blanket, the carrysak under his head. He imagined Kayla lying at his side, her circuitry-generated heat keeping him warm. Then he dropped into sleep so quickly it was like falling off a cliff. His fantasy followed him into his dreams. He held Kayla close, murmuring his love for her in his sleep. She felt hot as the fire at first, but then her warmth slowly cooled. By the time she pulled away from him, her body felt icy. She touched his wrist one last time, then seemed to speak in Yasi's voice, murmuring an apology before she walked away.

The first light of Iyenku glaring in Devak's eyes woke him. A sour, metallic taste lay on his tongue, and all the strength seemed to have seeped from his body.

He pushed himself up to a sitting position and stared stupidly at the cooling embers of the fire. The GENs were gone. The cook pot and the spits were gone. The dying had been taken away, Mey with them. Only Devak remained, and Junjie and Usi, half-hidden under the sticker bushes.

Devak got woozily to his feet, tripping over his carrysak as he staggered over to where the other boys still slept. "Junjie! Usi!"

Devak dropped to his knees and shook their feet. They stirred, but didn't wake. He slapped their legs, shouting their names.

Junjie sat up, squawking when a sticker bush thorn scratched his ear. Junjie looked as muzzy as Devak felt. "What's going on?" Junjie asked, his words slurred.

"They're all gone," Devak said. He gave Usi another shake and the boy sat up slowly. "They all cleared out and left us behind."

"Why shouldn't they?" Junjie asked.

"I think they drugged us," Devak said. "Maybe so we wouldn't know where they went."

Usi yawned and rubbed his eyes. "What time is it? When does the next pub-trans come through?"

Devak pushed his sleeve up. "I'll check—"

His wrist was bare. Yasi had stolen the wristlink. Now they had no way to contact Risa.

19

Within hours of Kayla overhearing the conversation between Ohin and Aideen, a storm struck the Badlands. Its powerful fury matched Kayla's internal turmoil and kept her and Shakki trapped inside Antara all day.

Even worse than missing Tak and Pev and losing the chance to try what she'd seen on Ohin's computer display, Kayla was forced to return to toting crates for Penba rather than be left idle. During those long hours working, she thought she would die with the waiting, anger and hatred for Ohin mixing inside her with fear for the bhimkay's welfare.

At least the time indoors gave her and Shakki the chance to gather and hide supplies. Shakki discovered a stash of small plasscine bags in the Vijnana Center where she worked, the bags emptied of their former contents of computer components. Shakki slipped the bags to Kayla at midday meal and Kayla filled them with kel-grain when Penba wasn't looking.

Water was easier since they were allowed to keep jugs of it in their quarters. They also collected the empties left behind by the boys in the Bhimkay Lounge. Kayla and Shakki refilled them in the washroom and tucked them away under their beds. They also filched forgotten carrysaks from the lounge so Kayla and Shakki each had two. They threw out the trash from the boys' carrysaks, kept the illuminators and sealed nutras, then loaded them with the kel-grain, water, and a couple changes of clothes. Shakki added a medic kit stocked with bandages, wound glue, and a pain killing ointment made of sticker bush root.

They'd also spent a few hours looking for Lovise. Kayla had told Shakki what Ohin had said about Lovise's supposed injury. They went to Maramata 1, sneaking in while Medic Palla was distracted.

But before Palla chased them out again, they discovered that neither Lovise's nor Essali's gen-tanks were there. Palla insisted she had no idea where they'd gone, which Kayla didn't believe for a moment. Palla walked them to the other Maramata room, just to prove the two girls weren't there, either.

By evening meal, word had filtered down to the lowest level that the storm was short-lived and had already passed over Antara. Kayla and Shakki got permission to visit the bhimkay the next day.

That night in bed, what Aideen had said about Ohin invaded Kayla's thoughts again and again. Her stomach turned every time she thought that the FHE leader might be her biological father. Her restlessness woke Shakki.

What is it? the GEN girl asked. Even her comm voice sounded sleepy.

Kayla had to confess some of it, or she'd burst. *I heard something today about Ohin. I can't tell you yet, but it upset me.*

Are you in danger?

No. You either. I just have to think it through.

Okay, Shakki said with an audible sigh. She fell back asleep quickly and Kayla made an effort to lie still.

Hours later she finally convinced herself it couldn't be true. Ohin couldn't be her father. GENs were sterile. What she'd thought was a true memory of him looking down at her when she'd been a child had instead been a lie uploaded into her while she was recovering from her injuries. She drifted finally to sleep.

It seemed moments later that Shakki was calling her name to wake her. Shakki had a carrysak hooked over her shoulder.

"We have to get out there early," Shakki reminded her. "Try your experiment before the Bhimkay Boys arrive."

"Right," Kayla muttered, jittery with exhaustion. She dressed quickly, then followed Shakki down to Mahala.

As they walked along the empty corridors, Shakki nudged Kayla. *You'd better put away that anxiety. If I can pick it up, you know the spiders will.*

Kayla took a calming breath. *You're sure about trying this today?*

It'll be fun, Shakki said, but an edginess to her comm voice betrayed her nervousness.

Kayla's stomach twisted. This was only a trial run today, a practice session. But if it went wrong, they might both get spider-bit. And she would feel terrible if she were responsible for Shakki being injured again.

As they reached Mahala, Shakki took an appreciative sniff. "Always good to get to morning meal early when the kel-grain mush is fresh."

They each grabbed a bowl full, sweetening the mush liberally with sakara, then took one of the tables behind the sound dampeners. The tables were empty, so Kayla figured anyone could sit there, not just the high-and-mighty like Aideen and Ohin.

A surface guard arrived, just coming off duty. It was Faia,

the GEN woman Kayla had struck on her first escape attempt.

Faia gave Kayla a sour look, but she confirmed the weather report—all clear up top. Kayla gulped down her kel-grain, then stared at Shakki as the girl ate her breakfast far too slowly. *Calm. Patience*, Kayla told herself.

That early in the morning, there wasn't a ready escort to the surface. Ohin had changed the lift codes after Kayla's attempted escape and had never given the new ones to Shakki. Despite the story they'd told Ohin—that Kayla had forced Shakki to help her—the FHE leader didn't seem to want to trust Shakki anymore. So they had to cajole Faia to take them up, which she did with plenty of complaining.

Once outside, Kayla led the way along the narrow passageway. New piles of dirt and gravel littered the path, apparently blown in by the gale. Even more surprising were rocks the size of Kayla's fist, lifted by the windstorm and blasted into the passageway as if hurled by the Infinite's mighty hand.

In the clearing, they found a dead naga that had tried to escape the storm, but only got half-way into a crack before its body was slammed against the rock floor. Tangled with the naga was a chilling sight—a bhimkay leg, broken off at the top joint.

Kayla quickly checked the cage. Seven bhimkay had returned, including Tak and Pev. The gate, programmed to swing shut and lock when it counted the entrance of eight spiders, still hung open. All the bhimkay except Tak crouched low, bodies near the ground, legs curled under them. Tak lay sprawled across her eggs, Pev as close beside the sacs as Tak would allow.

Relief washed through Kayla, seeing Tak and Pev with all their legs intact. "Who's missing?" Her and Shakki's spiders she knew on sight, but the identity of the others still baffled her.

Shakki pulled a presaka from her carrysak. Thumbing the

frequency selector, she sent out a simple command to each of the other five bhimkay—raise your left rear leg. One by one, the spiders complied, four of them standing to perform the task, the fifth just giving his leg an indolent twitch.

Shakki reset the presaka to Pev's frequency. "It's Caya."

Jadi's bhimkay, a female about to lay. "She could still come back," Kayla said.

"If she was injured here, why wouldn't she come into the enclosure? They're all trained to see it as their nest, where they're safest."

"She might not have been injured here," Kayla said. "Her leg could have been torn off somewhere else and blown with the other debris."

The bhimkay were starting to stir, a couple of them edging toward the open gate. Kayla swung it nearly shut, counting on her strength to hold it if a spider rushed her. "Tak!"

She could have asked Shakki for her presaka, but she didn't like using the controller if she didn't have to. Tak shifted a little, turning her head toward Kayla. She called again, "Tak!"

This time Tak straightened her legs and started toward the gate. As Kayla expected, Pev followed. An aggressive shake of Tak's front left leg warned off the other bhimkay. They retreated back to the rear of the enclosure.

Tak and Pev marched through the gate and Kayla shut and locked it behind them. The pair of bhimkay stood obediently enough, but both of them were eying the dead naga.

"Do we let them eat?" Shakki asked.

Kayla considered. "That might distract them enough to let us climb on."

Kayla signaled to Tak to go ahead and feed. She still wasn't as fluent at the hand motions as Shakki, but Tak seemed to forgive

Kayla's clumsiness, and usually figured out what she was asking.

Both bhimkay crouched to bring their mouth parts close to the naga. Pev waited for Tak, which seemed gentlemanly, but in reality he wanted to be far enough from her in case she objected and bit him. He positioned himself a few meters away and at right angles to Tak to have the best view of her.

Crouched to feed, Tak's back was about at Kayla's hip height. Easy enough to stroke the top of Tak's large abdomen. As Kayla drew her fingers side to side, the hair barbs there rose slightly in response. The abdomen barbs weren't as thick as the ones on the spider's legs, more finger-diameter than wrist-diameter. And each row was about a double arm's thickness from the next. But their needle-sharpness made straddling Tak's and Pev's backs problematic.

"Are you sure that picture showed someone riding *between* the hair barbs?" Shakki asked.

"It did," Kayla said.

"Maybe we should have brought a blanket," Shakki said.

Kayla slid her hand along the space between a row of barbs. "I don't know how many chances we're going to have. Ohin could take away our privileges to visit the bhimkay any time." Tak picked up on Kayla's agitation and she trembled, reminding Kayla to keep her emotions in check and to herself.

Kayla noticed that as she stroked along that space between the barbs, Tak's hairs lifted almost straight up. "We can fit in here. If we're careful. The trick will be getting the hair barbs up straight, then sliding in so they flatten under us when we sit. Try stroking Pev."

Shakki looked dubious, but she ran her hand between the hair barbs on Pev's back. The same narrow space opened up. "Well, good thing we're both small." Shakki eyed Kayla with a wry smile. "Some of us smaller than others."

Moving carefully, Kayla rubbed Tak's back, at the same time lifting and sliding her foot across between the barbs. Tak, still sucking at the naga, didn't seem to mind. As Kayla settled her weight, straddling the bhimkay's abdomen with her legs, she smoothed the hair barbs flat behind her.

The barbs in front of her still stood vertical. She carefully grabbed two in each hand for balance.

Shakki followed Kayla's lead, climbing on and taking hold of Pev's barbs. With Tak still crouched, Kayla's dangling feet just barely touched the ground on either side. Shakki's shorter legs didn't quite reach.

"Now what?" Shakki asked.

"We ask them to stand up," Kayla said.

"With the presaka?" Shakki asked.

"I don't want to. I'd rather use the arm and hand signals."

"But how is Tak going to see your signals when you're on her back?" Shakki asked.

"She'll be able to see them." The bhimkay's range of vision was broad. "But they might look different to her. She might not understand."

She should have thought this part out before they started. But she was so eager to try to ride her bhimkay.

Tak had finished what she wanted of the naga, but greedy Pev was still eating. Kayla realized that with Pev facing her and Tak, she was squarely in Pev's line of vision.

"Do you think Pev would follow my signal?" Kayla asked.

"Maybe, if it's clear enough," Shakki said. "He's not as good at interpreting you as Tak is."

"I'm going to try signaling Pev to stand. While I signal, you tug on his hair barbs. Maybe if we do that enough, they'll understand that pulling on the barbs means stand."

Kayla moved her arm across, then up—the signal for stand. The motion upset her fragile balance on Tak's back, so she had to grip the bhimkay's hair barbs with her right hand for dear life. Her unsteadiness made her signal to Pev less clear, so the spider ignored it.

After a couple more unsuccessful tries, Kayla admitted temporary defeat. "I think you better try with Tak."

Shakki's crisp visual signal to Tak and the bhimkay's prompt response caught Kayla completely off-guard. She was glad for the suggestion she'd made about tugging the hair barbs, because when Tak straightened quickly to her three-meter height, Kayla yanked the barbs hard in panic. Tak hissed in pain and irritation.

"That worked," Kayla said in a thready voice.

She turned to sketch out the arm signal to Pev. This time the spider popped up, but Kayla suspected it was more due to Tak's movement than any communication skill on Kayla's part.

Shakki was grinning, a mix of delight and terror on her face. "How do we get them to walk?"

"Same way," Kayla said. "I think squeezing their sides with our legs is a good alternate signal since we'll be doing that anyway to stay on."

At least Kayla had done a better job mastering the "walk" hand signal. Even Pev accepted that cue, taking a tentative step before freezing.

Shakki tried squeezing her legs against Pev's sides, then thumped him lightly with her calves. He didn't budge.

Kayla noticed he'd swiveled his head toward Tak, and his multiple eyes were focused on her. "Let's see if Tak will move. Maybe that will encourage Pev."

Shakki signaled with her hand, and Kayla timed her leg squeeze to be nearly simultaneous. Tak stepped carefully forward, back right leg first, which tipped Kayla slightly backward. Tak froze while Kayla got herself upright again, then the bhimkay moved her third right with her fourth left, each step bobbing Kayla from side to side.

She had no idea how to ask the spider to go in any particular direction. She tried tugging on the hair barbs in her left hand to see if she'd turn left, but Tak just hissed. She'd have to figure out later how to turn. For now she'd let the bhimkay decide, which meant zigzagging back and forth across the clearing.

"Is Pev moving?" Kayla called out. She didn't want to unbalance Tak even worse by turning to see.

"Yes," Shakki said, her voice shaky. "He's staggering a little."

Tak wasn't staggering, but her movements were clumsy with Kayla aboard, not the bhimkay's usual graceful sequence. Kayla relaxed her lower back and let her hips move with Tak's motion. The spider's gait evened out, still swinging, but in a regular pattern.

"Move with him," Kayla told Shakki.

Shakki gave her a dubious look, then shut her eyes and let her shoulders relax. Her body began to move with Pev's.

"Oh! I see," Shakki said. Pev came up beside Tak, although he kept a spider-width between them.

Then Tak stepped into a crack in the rock, and Kayla tipped before she could match the sudden dip of movement. Tak stopped, her body seeming to shift to keep itself under Kayla. When Kayla got her balance again, she squeezed her legs tight, and Tak marched forward again.

She heard a little shriek from Shakki. Kayla chanced a look back. "Are you all right?"

"Just slipped a little," Shakki said, righting herself. "I could sure use one of the Bhimkay Boys' saddles right about now."

"I guess they'd make it easier to balance, and you wouldn't have to worry about the hair barbs." Kayla let her left hip drop as Tak's left side walked over a low rise. "But you wouldn't be able to feel the movement as well."

If Tak was understanding that a leg squeeze meant walk, what would happen if Kayla pulled her legs away entirely? She tried it, lifting them away from the bhimkay's sides. Tak kept walking, although more slowly. Kayla took a chance with her precarious balance and stretched her arm far enough to bring her hand, fingers spread wide, as close to Tak's eyes as she could.

Tak stopped promptly, nearly sending Kayla tumbling over her head. Having the stop signal shoved in the bhimkay's field of view like that must have seemed like Kayla was yelling at her. Kayla would have to figure out a way to tone that down.

She squeezed and Tak moved forward. How much peripheral vision did the spider have? Kayla tried the spread-fingers signal first close to her body, then moved it closer to the bhimkay's head a few centimeters at a time. About a thirty degree angle from her body did the trick.

Shakki had been experimenting too, with turning Pev left and right. They compared notes, Kayla sharing the positioning of the stop signal, and Shakki explaining that pressing a right leg moved the spider left and vice versa. Kayla practiced the movement, turning Tak in small loops across the clearing.

Each time they were closest to the enclosure where Tak's eggs lay, the bhimkay would swivel her head toward them. "Do you think she'd leave them behind?" Kayla asked.

"She has to when she hunts at night," Shakki said.

Voices echoed from the direction of Antara. Shakki looked toward the passageway, disappointment clear in her face. "The Bhimkay Boys are coming."

Kayla eyed the high wall of boulders encircling them. She turned Tak toward Pev and stopped her. "We either get off before they arrive, or we try climbing. They won't be able to see us up there."

Shakki looked dubious. "The bhimkay don't climb something that steep. They jump."

Fear and excitement burst inside Kayla in equal measure. She grinned at Shakki. "I'm game."

The voices were drawing closer, raucous shouts and catcalls from the boys. Her eyes wide, Shakki nodded.

Kayla squeezed her legs, directing Tak toward the wall of rock. She wasn't sure what the bhimkay would do when she reached the wall. Tak might refuse to go forward. She might think it would be too hard to scale with Kayla on board.

The boys would emerge into the clearing any moment. Tak and Pev had both reached the ten-meter wall. Kayla doubled her grip on Tak's hair barbs and squeezed hard with her legs, using her heels to lift up.

In one heartbeat, Tak bent her legs, lowering her body nearly to the clearing floor. In the next, they were flying.

Tak landed a couple meters from the top where the rock sloped less steeply, then skittered the rest of the way up. As Kayla continued to squeeze, Tak scrambled across the boulder tops, leaping easily from one to another. Kayla could hear Shakki gasping for breath to her left, and caught glimpses of Pev's legs flashing in and out of view.

Finally, Kayla put up the stop signal. Clever Tak had learned to smooth her halt, and Kayla's balance was improving, because she barely tipped forward. Shakki and Pev's stop was a little shakier, but Shakki stayed on board.

Kayla suppressed a whoop of joy for fear the boys would hear her. Shakki let go to shake a fist into the air, then teetered as Pev danced under her.

Shakki laughed. "I wish we could just go now. Just take Pev and Tak and leave them all behind."

Kayla sighed, ardently wishing the same. She was desperate to get to Devak. "We don't have any supplies."

"The bhimkay could probably catch nagas for us to eat," Shakki said.

"We didn't bring our water," Kayla reminded her.

"Yeah," Shakki said. "And as bad as the Badlands storms are, I don't think even our GEN circuitry would keep up with the cold, not to mention the wind."

"And I can feel Tak wanting to turn back, to return to her eggs," Kayla said. "We're only a few kilometers out, so I can control her, but I don't know that she'd keep cooperating if we went on."

They walked on more slowly, still leaping from boulder to boulder, but in a more controlled way. Then Tak came to a stop, Pev just behind her. The spider started to tremble.

Kayla urged Tak forward again. A few leaps more and she could see what had upset the bhimkay. Up ahead was a dead spider sprawled on the rock, three of its eight legs gone.

"Is it Caya?" Shakki asked.

Kayla kept squeezing her legs to drive the reluctant Tak forward. When they got near enough, Kayla could see where the back of the spider's head had been torn away. The electronics of the inhibitor were exposed, just like in that drawing Kayla had seen.

"It's her," Kayla said.

The rock Caya was on was wide enough for Tak as well, so Kayla urged the spider to jump the gap. Once they'd reached Caya's side, Kayla relaxed her hold on Tak's hair barbs, trusting in her own balance as she wondered how she'd persuade her bhimkay to crouch.

Whether it was Kayla releasing her hold or the sight of dead Caya, Tak bent her legs so Kayla could slide off. She moved close enough to get a better view of the inhibitor.

She compared the image from Ohin's computer that she'd stored in her annexed brain with the actual bhimkay lying before her. Part of poor Caya's head had been split, so Kayla could see the corner of the box that she recognized as the power source. Most of the rest of the electronics were hidden and that made it easier to spot the only other thing she'd understood from the drawing.

"That's the power source." Kayla pointed to the silvery metal. "It's implanted right under the surface of the carapace. And look here. There's the little solar cell hidden in the smaller hair barbs."

Kayla turned back to Tak. Stroking the spider's head, she felt amongst the hair barbs. There was the solar cell.

She looked over at Shakki. "Are you ready for the rest of it?"

For a long moment, Shakki just stared down at Caya. "Why can't we just leave the inhibitors alone? We don't even know what the bhimkay will do if we tear out the solar cell. They might forget they like us."

"Do you know for sure how far away we'd have to be for Ohin's presakas to stop working on Tak and Pev?"

Shakki lifted her gaze to Kayla. "What if I changed their frequencies? Erased them from the database?"

"There's still the emergency stop. Ohin wouldn't have to know the frequencies to use that. The only way to avoid him controlling our bhimkay, stopping our escape, is to disable the inhibitors."

"Except why out here, where if something happens, there's no one to help us?"

Kayla brushed her thumb against Tak's solar cell. "Because we don't know how many more chances we'll get. And I'm more afraid of Ohin's *help* than I am of getting injured. I'd rather die out here than end up in one of Ohin's gen-tanks."

Shakki sighed. "I guess I would too."

"Besides, if I do it first, and Tak goes crazy and hurts me, you can still get away. Back to Antara."

Shakki scowled. "That's not much of a choice. Antara's bad enough, but without you . . ."

Kayla had to do it now, before she lost her nerve. She grabbed hold of the solar cell between her thumb and index finger. "Get ready to run with Pev. Don't worry about leaving me."

Shakki's set, determined expression told Kayla the girl would likely hold her ground. Kayla sent off a swift prayer to the Infinite that they would all stay safe. She tugged gently on the solar cell, not using her sket strength. It didn't budge. Then she tried twisting it.

With almost no effort, the solar cell broke off between her fingers. Tak jolted and for a moment, Kayla feared she'd badly damaged the bhimkay. Then Tak unbent her legs and danced in place, before she settled down in her crouch again.

Only one way to be sure it worked. "Can you toss me Tak's presaka?"

Shakki pulled it from the carrysak and lobbed it over

to Kayla. Kayla made sure the frequency was right, then she entered the *lift leg 3R* command.

Tak raised her right leg, third one back. Disappointment settled inside Kayla. "It didn't work."

"Maybe . . ." Shakki said. "That power source is probably a battery that stores up what the solar cell feeds it."

"So the battery has to run down," Kayla said.

"If you keep sending commands with the presaka—"

"I'll wear down the battery."

Kayla hated forcing Tak to perform using the presaka, but if it ultimately meant she would be free of its control, it would be the right thing to do. So she ran through every command she could think of, asking Tak to lift each leg in turn, straighten all, lean left and right.

After twenty or so requests from the presaka, it took longer for Tak to respond. Then Kayla entered a command to lift 2L and the bhimkay didn't move. Kayla went through a handful of other options—stand, crouch, look at me. Other than tapping a front leg as if she were bored, Tak didn't comply.

"I think that's it," Kayla said. "The battery is worn down."

Kayla stuffed Tak's presaka into her breast band, then with her hand signals, she asked Tak to crouch. She slid onto Tak's back with a little more grace than she had the first time. Grabbing the two handfuls of hair barbs, Kayla tugged gently up.

Tak rose. Kayla used her right leg and Tak turned around toward Pev. Kayla squeezed, and Tak leapt to the boulder next to the one Shakki and Pev stood on.

Glowing with her success, she smiled at Shakki. "Your turn. Can you see the solar cell for Pev's inhibitor? Twisting works best."

Chewing on her lower lip, Shakki smoothed aside the smaller hair barbs on the back of Pev's head. Kayla could tell when Shakki found the cell, because she stared at it as if it were the poisonous mandible of a wild bhimkay.

"You have to trust him, Shakki," Kayla said. "Trust the bond between you. Or else, don't do it. But then you'd have to stay behind."

Shakki nodded, and with a determined set of her mouth, she twisted the cell and plucked it free. Pev jumped nearly a half-meter, tipping Shakki to one side and nearly off. Shakki kept a firm grip on the hair barbs and pulled herself back on top.

Shakki's eyes were huge when she looked over at Kayla. Her whole body shaking, she fished Pev's presaka from the carrysak, then put Pev through the same paces as Kayla had Tak until the male bhimkay's battery ran down.

Triumph burst inside Kayla and without thinking, she pulled Tak's presaka from her breast band and threw it, her sket strength taking it far away across the rocky landscape. Shakki flung Pev's as well, watching as it shattered on a boulder and disappeared into a crevasse.

"We shouldn't have," Shakki said, even as the smile lingered on her face.

"No," Kayla said. "But it was like poison in my hand."

Using legs and hands, Kayla turned Tak back toward the clearing. Shakki followed on Pev, and the two bhimkay raced each other. As the wind whipped at them, Kayla threw back her head and shouted with joy.

They'd freed their bhimkay. There might be hell to pay with Ohin for destroying the presakas, but she and Shakki were one step closer to escape. One step closer to seeing Devak again.

20

When Devak, Junjie, and Usi returned to the vidrohis' dead fire, they discovered a plasscine jug filled with water beside Devak's carrysak. A packet wrapped in a scrap of blanket also lay near where Devak had been sleeping. Inside the blanket swatch were three cakes made of pounded wild kel-grain and several strips of dried rat-snake. That was all the apology they got from Yasi for drugging them, stealing Junjie's wristlink, and sneaking away.

A quick check of the carrysak revealed that of the three changes of clothes Devak and Junjie had brought with them in the carrysak, Yasi had taken two, leaving them each with one extra korta and pair of chera pants. All of the nutras were gone, but the little holo projector was still there. It might not be as crucial now that they'd found Usi, but Devak would have hated losing Kayla's image.

"They didn't take the dhans?" Junjie asked.

Feeling like an idiot for not checking before, Devak dove into the carrysak again and used his thumb to release the hidden pocket. Relief washed over him when his hand closed on the wad of paper and stash of coins.

"Thank the Infinite," Junjie said. "Yasi could have taken the carrysak, dhans and all. He must have known how badly we needed that money."

Devak laughed harshly. "He must have known that dhans wouldn't do him much good. The allabain don't want money. They'd rather trade labor or goods. And where else would the GENs spend them? At the nearest lowborn Streetmarket?"

Devak felt angry and betrayed, not the least inclined to see anything good in Yasi or the rest of the vidrohi. Between the bitter taste still on his tongue, the helplessness of knowing that once again they'd lost their chance to meet up with Risa, and the fact that he'd come to like Yasi in those few hours he knew him, Devak just wanted to chase after the GENs and shout at them.

A useless notion. Yasi was only doing what was best for his people. He couldn't have known how crucial that wristlink was to the three of them.

"With the nutras gone, I guess we'd better make this food last," Devak said, breaking one of the palm-sized cakes into three portions. "No telling when we can buy more."

Devak started nibbling on his kel-grain cake, again surprised at how much more flavorful it was than the nutras made with genned grain. "We'd better keep an eye out for another pub-trans."

"Do we even have the dhans?" Junjie asked.

"Barely enough for Amik, I think," Devak said. "If we don't, we'll have to tell the driver what happened to us on the other multi-lev and maybe he'll take us anyway."

"Should we wait by the road?" Usi asked. He'd finished his bit of cake and was eying the other two lying on the scrap of plasscine.

"It's warmer here," Devak said. "And we could crawl inside the sticker bushes if we see bhimkay. But we'll still be able to hear a pub-trans coming."

Devak tied up the food packet and tucked it in his carrysak along with the two thin blankets they'd been left. Usi found a spot beside the wall of boulders with both a clear view of the road and some concealment thanks to the thicket of sticker bushes. They all sat cross-legged on the hard-packed dirt, Devak's stomach protesting the meager breakfast.

Usi, closest to the boulder wall and leaning against it, fell asleep. Junjie dozed off and on, and Devak wanted to do the same. He could still feel the drugs he'd been fed lingering in his body. If not for the sticker bush spines threatening to pierce his back if he relaxed against the branches behind him, he might have nodded off too.

The sound of suspension engines jolted him fully awake. He poked Junjie, who roused Usi.

"Something's coming from the south," Devak said, peering down the road.

Junjie rubbed his eyes. "Sounds too small to be a pub-trans."

They all stared south. It took a full minute for the vehicles to reach the bend in the road where they came into view.

"The Brigade," Devak muttered as three Brigade Daggers closed on the burnt-out multi-lev.

Junjie turned to him. "Do we show ourselves?"

There was no reason why not. They were victims here, trueborns whose transport had been hijacked and destroyed by renegade GENs.

"They'll want to know where Yasi and the others went," Devak said.

"We don't really know the answer to that," Junjie said.

"But we know what they looked like," Devak said. "We know about the nasaka."

"We don't have to tell them that," Junjie said. "We can say they attacked, then ran away with my wristlink. That's true enough."

Devak watched as the first of the Daggers reached the black shell of the multi-lev. "This isn't the first time this has happened. Don't you think the enforcers will do whatever they can to find out what they can? Trueborns or not, me being Zul Manel's great-grandson or not, everything is changed now. I don't think we can count on being safe with the Brigade."

Usi stirred. "And you're forgetting me. They might not know who I am at first, but it wouldn't take them long to make the connection between me and the Nafi sector bomb."

"Right," Junjie said. "We can't let them know you're with us."

The remaining two Daggers had pulled up alongside the multi-lev. Devak could hear their voices drifting toward them, although he couldn't make out the words.

"I'm still mad as blazes at Yasi," Devak said softly. "But we have to protect the vidrohi." Because of Mey. Because Kayla would want him to. Because it was the right thing to do.

Junjie tipped forward to get a better look. "What if they're still there when the pub-trans comes by?"

"We have to hope they won't be," Devak said.

Then Usi spoke up. "What if the pub-trans that comes is going the wrong way?"

Devak didn't want to even consider that. "We'll have to take it. Try to get somewhere we can beg the use of a wristlink."

The hours seemed to drag on after that. They each took a

swallow of water from the jug, and chewed on a strip of dried meat. It worried Devak that the water smelled faintly of nasaka. He guessed that was what the jug had held before it had been emptied, rinsed, and filled with water.

At one point an enforcer started over in their direction and they had to scramble behind the boulders out of sight. As they huddled in a half-concealed niche where two of the boulders overlapped, Devak prayed silently to the Lord Creator to make them all invisible. He caught the glint of Junjie's prayer mirror and saw his friend's lips moving in quiet entreaty to the Infinite.

The enforcer came as close as the screen of sticker bushes. The man, a pale-skinned minor-status, started to press through and immediately got snagged on thorns. He cursed under his breath, muttering something about his chutting Brigade captain, then extricated himself from the thorns and backed out of sight.

Devak heard the enforcer report on his wristlink, "All clear!" as his footsteps retreated.

Late in the afternoon, a ten-meter-long tow vehicle arrived, hitched up the burnt multi-lev, and hauled it away. The Brigade Daggers departed soon after. Devak, Junjie, and Usi returned to their lookout in the sticker bushes.

Still no pub-trans. They each took another swallow of water, but Devak wouldn't allow them any more food. They had at least two days before they got to Dika—that is, if a pub-trans showed up today. They'd need all their dhans for the two legs to Dika, so they had to make the food last.

The primary sun, Iyenku, had set, and Kas was sinking toward the horizon. They had the two thin blankets between them if they had to sleep outdoors another night. Maybe they could find a couple of dhatu rocks to start a fire, but they'd have to gather tinder and firewood if they could even get lucky enough to stumble across the dhatu in the growing dusk.

Junjie grabbed Devak's arm. "Do you hear that?"

Devak listened. "Is that just wind?"

Usi jumped to his feet, shoving aside a spiny branch. "No, look! Can you see the lights? And it's coming from the north."

Devak could see the lights now, and from the growing roar of the suspension engine, it was clearly something big. "Has to be a pub-trans."

At that point, he almost didn't care if it turned out to be a Brigade Jahaja come to scoop all three of them up. He couldn't sit another moment in the sticker bushes. He hooked the carrysak over his shoulder and got clear of the spiky thorns.

With the other boys beside him, Devak started trotting toward the road. "If it's not a pub-trans, we run the other way. If we have to fight, it'll be just you and me, Junjie. Usi has to get clear."

Usi started to protest, but by then the vehicle had gotten close enough for them to see the lit pub-trans markings on its side. They reached the road only a couple hundred meters from the multi-lev and waved their arms. They had to look grubby and disreputable, but thank the Lord Creator, the driver hit the air brakes and the multi-lev came to a stop.

Pasting a smile on his face, Devak rehearsed in his mind what they'd say to the driver. *GENs ambushed our pub-trans. Stole my wristlink, then ran. The Brigade wouldn't take us back to Viata, or even let us use their comms.*

The multi-lev settled into boarding height and the driver opened the door. The lowborn driver looked worried— because he'd have to scramble his passengers to accommodate trueborns?

Keeping that bright smile on his face, Devak climbed the steps. Halfway up the third and last, he jolted to a stop when he saw a pair of enforcers sitting in the front seat, right behind the driver. Their black-tricked-out-with-red uniforms glittered menacingly.

Junjie bumped into Devak from behind. Devak could hear Usi suck in a breath.

Trying not to return the enforcers' stares, he asked, "How much for three to Amik?"

The driver named the fare and relief washed over Devak. It would take them down to their last quarter-dhan or so, but they had it.

He counted out the fare and dropped it in, then glanced behind him. Junjie was clutching Usi's hand so tight, it had to hurt, but Junjie wasn't taking any chances that Usi would make a break for it.

Devak caught Junjie's whispered words ". . . only make it worse . . ." as he sidled past the enforcers. The two Brigade men turned to follow Devak's passage to the empty seat farthest from them, three rows behind. Devak wished they could take some of the vacant seats scattered amongst the lowborns in the back two-thirds of the multi-lev, but that would upset the lowborns and raise even more suspicion with the enforcers.

Devak backed out of the way so Junjie could push Usi into the window seat. Junjie squeezed in next to Usi, scooting over far enough that Devak could sit beside him. Devak set the carrysak on the floor and nudged it under the seat behind his feet.

The taller of the two enforcers rose, grabbing a seat back for balance as the multi-lev pulled out. Devak tossed the blankets from the carrysak over Usi and the boy leaned against the window, face buried in the blankets.

The enforcer loomed over them, his nametag just visible in the dim light—Keft. "What were you boys doing out here?"

About to launch into his practiced excuse, Devak winced as Junjie dug his fingernails into his arm. "We're kind of in trouble," Junjie said. "I work in a gen-lab down in Amik and borrowed my supervisor's AirCloud to pick up some GEN DNA here in Wesja. I wasn't supposed to bring my friends with me. Then we broke down a couple of kilometers north of here."

Keft scanned the three of them, his gaze lingering on Usi's huddled form. "We didn't pass a broken down AirCloud."

Junjie's jaw dropped and he looked truly horrified. "No! We left it right by the road."

"It's gone now," the enforcer said. "Some tat-face scum likely stole it."

Devak's stomach burned at the enforcer's use of the GEN slur. "What would a GEN be doing out here?"

"Never mind that," Keft said. "You shouldn't have left the lev-car."

"But no one came through to help us," Junjie said, whining a little. "Not even the northbound pub-trans."

"There was a problem with the pub-trans," Keft said. "You didn't see it?"

Junjie shook his head. "By the time we got to where you saw us, there were only Brigade Daggers just leaving. We tried to wave them down but they didn't see us."

"Why not use your wristlink to call for help?" Keft asked.

"I forgot it back at the lab," Junjie said.

Keft nodded, although he didn't look completely convinced. "And what about your friend?" He stuck his chin out toward Usi.

"Sick," Junjie said, and Usi moaned on cue. "He shouldn't have eaten that allabain meat pie." Usi groaned even louder, as if at the memory of it.

Keft drummed his fingers on the back of the next seat up. "I suppose you ought to contact your supervisor." He unlatched the wristlink from his arm, then tapped a code into it.

He held it out to Junjie. Junjie eyed the wristlink the enforcer held out as if the thing were a bhimkay in miniature.

Any call ID Junjie entered into the device would undoubtedly be traced. Their false story would fall apart in the moments it would take to check it.

But refusing the offer would look just as suspicious. Devak lifted the wristlink from Keft's open palm.

"If you won't call him, I will," Devak said. "I work for him too and I'm in just as much trouble. And he ought to know that Shun is sick."

Usi seemed to take the hint because he started gagging, sounding like he was about to lose the fictional meat pie he'd eaten. He made enough noise for the enforcer to think he was about to vomit up his stomach and half his intestines.

With Keft briefly distracted, Devak let his thumbs fly across the entry pad of the enforcer's wristlink. The string of numbers he tapped in would later look like he'd called someone physically located in Amik, but it would route to someone else.

To Pitamah. If he even answered. If he wasn't lying sick somewhere, or dying. Guilt battered Devak from all directions—that he hadn't spoken to Pitamah since they'd left, that he was only contacting him now that he and Junjie and Usi desperately needed help.

Bless the Lord Creator, Pitamah's face appeared in the wristlink display, haggard but still alive. "Hello? Devak?"

It would have been better not to have his real name spoken, but there was no help for that now. "Mar Sharma," Devak said, using the last name of his long-dead half-brother, Azad. "There was a problem with your AirCloud, and Junjie was afraid to call you. We never made it to the Wesja lab for the DNA."

Only a moment of confusion on the old man's face, then he said, "I don't recognize the ID you're calling from."

"An enforcer is helping us out," Devak said cheerfully.

He tipped the display toward Keft long enough for Pitamah to register Keft's uniform. Hopefully those few seconds were short enough that Keft would neither get a good look at Zul's distinctive face with its near GEN-like tattoo, nor see the old man's sapphire bali and realize he was no high-status Mar, but a minor-status.

Devak added, "We told him you supervise all three of us at the Amik gen-lab—me, Junjie, and Shun."

A light of clarity shone in Pitamah's eyes, then his brow furrowed and his voice took on an angry tone. "What have you done with my AirCloud, Junjie?"

Devak handed Junjie the wristlink and his friend repeated the made-up story. With the enforcer listening to every word, Junjie was clever enough not to elaborate, so he wouldn't be caught in some duplicity Keft could pounce on.

Junjie was about to hand back the wristlink to Keft, but Devak intercepted it to add another message. "Someone should track down that allabain who fed Shun the bad pie." Devak stared intently at Pitamah as he spoke. "She was serving them out of the back of someone's lorry. We told her we'd come by for another serving next time we came through Dika, but that old woman shouldn't be let anywhere near food."

Devak could see the moment his message clicked with Pitamah, that he should get hold of Risa. "I've heard of that woman. I'll make sure she's found." Then he added, "I would hope you at least still have the funds I sent you with?"

That was Pitamah's way to ask if they needed more dhans. Devak couldn't bear to ask more of his great-grandfather, but as late as they'd caught the pub-trans, they were going to have to stay overnight in Amik to wait for tomorrow's to Dika. So they would need more money.

While Devak tried to figure out a way to ask, not to mention think of a place for Pitamah to send dhans, Junjie leaned over so he could be seen in the wristlink.

Junjie's expression was a study in shame. "I left all the dhans you gave us in the AirCloud, Mar. So they're gone too."

Pitamah bristled in pretended rage. "I should let you three go hungry tonight. Teach you a lesson."

Junjie lowered his eyes, as if in supplication to his superior. "If you choose to, Mar, you could send the funds to the lab in Amik. We'll be there later tonight." For Junjie to mention it, he must know someone at the Amik gen-lab that they could trust to pass on the money they needed.

"I will consider it." His wink was so quick, his smile so faint and brief, Devak almost missed them.

Then Pitamah grew somber again. "You should know we've had another problem. Like the one in Nafi and in Fen."

At first, Devak didn't understand the connection. Then it hit him. FHE had set off bombs in both those GEN sectors.

"Where?" Devak asked, fearing the answer.

"Ekat," Pitamah said.

Junjie leaned in. "Did it happen at the lab?"

A slight shake of Pitamah's head. Devak said, "Not at the central green, I hope."

"Closer to home," Pitamah said as softly as he could.

Horror washed over Devak. FHE had set off an explosion at Pitamah's house in Ekat? "Were you there?"

"No," Pitamah said. "But nothing could be salvaged."

Devak longed to say something to comfort his great-grandfather, but Keft was shifting with impatience, glaring down at Devak. Devak's goodbye was too abrupt. He hoped Pitamah understood.

Devak wished he could erase the call ID path entirely, but he couldn't do that under the enforcer's nose. Keft took back the wristlink.

Devak expected the enforcer would return to the front, but he stood over Devak, eyeing him and the other two boys in turn. "I want to see your identity chips."

Ice flooded Devak's veins. He could feel Junjie's gaze on him, could almost read his friend's mind, because he was thinking the exact same thing. *We can't let the enforcer see Usi's chip.*

Usi, hunched under the blanket, didn't move, as if he was so ill he hadn't heard Keft's request. Devak took his time picking up the carrysak and fishing the two-centimeter diameter chip from the secret pocket. Junjie felt along the hem of his shirt methodically as if he couldn't remember quite where he'd tucked his.

Finally they turned the chips over to Keft. As the enforcer snapped them one at a time into the sekai he'd pulled out, Devak was grateful they'd used their real first names and hadn't made up surnames.

Keft handed the identity chips back and gestured to Usi. "I need his too."

Usi stirred, fumbling under the blankets. Then suddenly he folded, head over knees. Heaving, Usi threw up the miserly breakfast they'd eaten.

Keft jumped back, mouth twisting at the rank smell. "Never mind. I'll let that one pass." The enforcer returned to his seat.

Usi was shaking now, looking truly sick. Junjie took one of the blankets and tossed it on the floor to clean up the mess. Since Usi had eaten so little, there hadn't been much to clean.

Junjie opened the window to freshen the air and threw the smelly blanket out. That left one blanket between the three of them.

Devak handed Usi the water bottle. "Are you okay?"

Usi swished a mouthful of water, then went up on his knees to spit it out the window. He sank back in his seat. "Not the kind of talent you brag about," he muttered, low enough that the enforcer couldn't hear. "But it's helped a couple times before."

Junjie put his arm around Usi and pulled him close. Devak had nothing but the carrysak to hold. He stared out the window at the dark, wishing he could get out the holo projector to look at Kayla's image. But what if the enforcers saw him admiring an image of a GEN?

As the pub-trans made its ponderous way down the road, Devak wished he could leap out the window and fly to Belk sector and Kayla. The distance and days between them seemed impossible to travel, and he felt an urgency to get to her now.

An endless two hours later, the multi-lev pulled into a large pub-trans stop in Amik. Since Amik was a hub sector, there was more here than just a pub-trans shelter out on the street. There were three or four lines of multi-levs, some empty and shut down for the night, some disembarking passengers.

Several shops ringed the hub, most closed for the night, but a curry house wafted an appealing fragrance. There was a

Brigade sub-station here too, which must have been where the two enforcers would be headed.

Devak waited until the two enforcers left the multi-lev, lifting a hand in return when Keft waved goodbye. Then he, Junjie, and Usi left via the front door. The lowborns who had ridden behind them and the handful of GENs up top departed by the middle door.

"We should get our room at the public house first, then go to the lab," Junjie said.

"We only have a quarter-dhan left," Devak said. "Not nearly enough for a room."

"We could let the manager know we're getting more money later," Junjie suggested. "Maybe leave the carrysak with him or her as a guarantee."

"This is all we have left," Devak said. "I hate to leave it with a stranger."

"But if it gets us a room . . ." Junjie said.

"You're right. It's not like we have much choice." Devak headed off, leading the way across the hub.

They'd not gone more than a few meters when Keft stepped into their path. "I can give you three a ride home. We can use my Dagger."

A line of Daggers were parked along the street, outside the Brigade sub-station. Devak fumbled in his mind for an excuse. He couldn't tell Keft they were sleeping in the public house. If they were working in the gen-lab as they'd told him, they'd have a flat somewhere in Amik.

Keft gave Devak a nudge and motioned the others to follow. A few moments later, they were locked away in the back of a Brigade Dagger.

21

Kayla leaned against a wall of kel-grain crates in Godama 2, her arms finally empty. She supposed being forced to work in the foodstores room wasn't as bad a punishment as being reset, but over the last several days she'd spent so many hours shifting crates, she was beginning to think she might go sanaki.

Today, Penba had had her in motion for her entire work tour. Even now the GEN man was trotting over to her with that false smile on his dark face, no doubt with more labor in mind. But Kayla's internal clock had just ticked over to the end of her sixth hour of work and she was breaking for the day, no matter what Penba had planned for her.

"Another load has just arrived in the lift," Penba said cheerfully, the look in his dark eyes not quite matching that smile.

"It will keep until tomorrow," Kayla said. She turned at the sound of footsteps and to her Infinite-blessed relief, she saw Shakki entering. "I have to meet with Ohin."

"Of course, of course," Penba said, waving Kayla off toward the door where Shakki waited.

Kayla and Shakki walked along the corridor, arms linked,

both their faces bright with smiles as false as Penba's. If she and Shakki spoke out loud at all, it was mindless chatter about what might be served at evening meal, or whether there might be a new shipment of clothing in that last lift load. Every day they'd become more cautious about using their circuit-comms, speaking only in Seycat.

Kayla's and Shakki's punishment—in addition to Kayla returning to her work tour, Shakki was back in the Vijnana Center—was thanks to the Bhimkay Boys. By the time Kayla and Shakki returned on Tak and Pev, the boys had already saddled their own spiders and jumped free of the clearing.

When the boys saw Kayla and Shakki, they kicked their own spiders into such a frenzy that Shakki lost her grip on Pev and twisted her ankle falling. Pev's fussing over Shakki had riled up Tak, and she'd hissed and driven the other bhimkay back. Then Ghia, a female spider ridden by sour-faced Feshi, had challenged Tak.

Luckily Feshi had had enough sense to use his presaka to hold back Ghia before a full-fledged fight had broken out. And thank the Infinite Feshi hadn't gotten the notion to use the emergency stop to try to control Kayla's bhimkay instead of his own. It would have been a disaster if the Bhimkay Boys discovered what Kayla and Shakki had done with the solar cells.

Kayla and Shakki had told Ohin the story they'd rehearsed. They'd encountered a pack of wild bhimkay. In their mad rush to get back to safety, the presakas must have slipped from the carrysak into a crevasse, and it wasn't until they got safely into Antara that they realized the controllers were gone.

As angry as Ohin was that they'd taken the risk of riding the bhimkay without permission, the loss of the devices was the last straw. He forbade Kayla and Shakki to leave

Antara. They were not allowed to work with the bhimkay until further notice.

Kayla did tell Jadi where they'd found Caya. It was only fair that the kindest of the Bhimkay Boys should know how his spider died. Feshi and another boy named Maf went out to burn the body, but without a spider to ride, Jadi couldn't go with them.

The Bhimkay Boys weren't to work Shakki and Kayla's spiders, but Ohin made it clear they could use the emergency stop command if needed. Kayla's stomach was in knots worrying that one of the boys would take advantage of that permission, using a presaka on Tak or Pev. The moment the spiders didn't obey the controller, the boys and then Ohin would figure out why.

Shakki's nudge brought Kayla out of her turbulent thoughts. She'd been just about to collide with a mixed group of GENs and trueborns emerging from Mahala.

Shakki dragged Kayla to one side while the crowd passed. "How much kel-grain did you shift today?" Shakki asked loudly. "You look ready to drop."

"I stopped counting after the thirtieth stack of crates." Kayla sidled into the massive cavern, pulling Shakki after her.

"At least you don't have to inventory the stuff on the computers," Shakki said. "I swear they're making me count every last grain."

Shakki started off toward the packed tables of the main room. Kayla captured her friend's hand before she could go. "Come and eat with us."

"You know they won't let us. We're lucky they haven't separated us as roommates."

Kayla lowered her voice and leaned close to Shakki. "I just hate being alone with him."

"You're not alone," Shakki said. "Aideen's there."

It surprised Kayla that her birth mother's presence was more comfort to her than the annoyance it used to be. She hadn't forgiven Aideen for her abandonment twelve years ago; she probably never would. But Kayla was beginning to suspect the woman was on Kayla's side more than Ohin's.

Shakki cleared her throat and tilted her head toward the nearest netcam. The message was clear. They might not be heard, but that omnipotent eye could see them.

"We'll be okay," Shakki said, giving Kayla's hand a squeeze. She moved off, diving into the cacophony of a thousand voices. Kayla headed toward the dampeners.

Ohin was there, next to Aideen, but turned on the bench with his back to her. Jadi stood beside the table, looking somber and serious. The Bhimkay Boy—or was he still a Bhimkay Boy with his spider, Caya, dead?—bent close to Ohin as they spoke.

As Kayla approached, Ohin turned to face the table, nodding a greeting to her. Jadi still stood there, shifting from foot to foot as if he wasn't sure if he was dismissed or not.

Kayla took pity and asked him, "How are Tak and Pev doing?"

Jadi glanced at Ohin. Were she and Shakki also not allowed to get news of the bhimkay in addition to being forbidden to work with them? Kayla's anger at Ohin twisted up a notch.

Then the GEN leader nodded, giving Jadi permission to speak. "I've only just today been able to check on them," the boy said. "Pev is as lazy as usual."

He rubbed his arm where Kayla had heard Tak had bitten clear through. The bhimkay had apparently scraped the bone with her mandible and Jadi had had to spend half a day in the tank for healing.

"I'm sorry for what Tak did," Kayla said.

"Not your fault, or hers," Jadi said. "It was my clumsiness, especially with Tak so worried about her eggs."

"I'm sorry about Caya too," Kayla said. "I do think it was a quick death."

"Thanks," he said, then he fixed his gaze on her, like Shakki did when she wanted to use the circuit-comm, wanted to say something she wanted no one else to hear. What could Jadi want to tell her in secret, that he couldn't say in front of Ohin and Aideen?

"Kayla," Jadi said, eying her intently. "Can I—"

Ohin rose abruptly. "Come with me, Jadi."

Unease flickered in Jadi's eyes, but he followed Ohin. Just before they passed through the dampeners into the larger dining area of Mahala, Jadi gave a last look over his shoulder at Kayla.

"What's he up to?" Aideen stared through that space between the dampeners at Ohin making his way through the crowd.

Kayla looked as well, watched as Ohin stopped at a table filled with the rest of the Bhimkay Boys. Then the kitchen helpers arrived, bringing out three plates piled with food, and blocking Kayla's view of Ohin.

As the kitchen helpers left, Aideen narrowed her gaze, still focused in the direction of Ohin. "Don't like this." She glanced back at Kayla. "Just eat. For now."

Kayla would have argued, but Aideen had bent her head to her food. Kayla didn't like the troubled look on her birth mother's face.

The fragrance of the naga meat on Kayla's plate finally tempted her to pick up her fork and take a bite. It had been well seasoned and so thinly sliced it almost melted in her mouth. The kel-grain was flavored with exotic spices—cardamom, turmeric, cinnamon—and dotted with bits of patagobi root and finely diced dried redfruit. Not for the first time, Kayla wondered how FHE got their hands on such expensive foodstuffs.

"Is this what everyone is eating tonight?" Kayla asked. "Shakki, Jadi, and the others?"

"They're having naga stew," Aideen said.

"Then this is like what the outsider trueborns do," Kayla said. "Serve themselves the best, and give the GENs the dregs."

"This was Ohin's idea. He asked the cook to prepare this for you." Aideen's mouth tightened. "Don't like this," she said again.

"I'd rather he didn't do anything special for me," Kayla said.

Aideen reached across the table, as always not quite touching Kayla. "But Ohin sees you as *special*." It sounded more like a warning than something Kayla should feel good about.

She stared at Aideen. "What does that mean?"

Aideen reached a few centimeters more until her fingers pressed against Kayla's, touching Kayla for the first time since she'd arrived in Antara. "I know I've done the worst wrong a mother can ever do to her child. I don't expect forgiveness. I don't deserve it. I don't *want* it."

It was the last thing Kayla had expected Aideen to say to her. Grief and rage burst inside her. "You threw me away. Let them put circuitry into me. Made me a slave."

Aideen took the words like a physical blow. Color rose in her birth mother's cheeks as if Kayla *had* struck her. "I have no excuses," she choked out. "I am as much of a monster as you think I am."

In spite of her anger, tears burned Kayla's eyes. The question she'd wanted to ask burst out. "Why? Why did you—"

Aideen's glance toward the dampeners behind Kayla alerted her that Ohin was returning. He smiled warmly at Kayla, looking like a man about to bestow a great gift. "I have some news for you. I'd wanted it to be a surprise when they arrive, but it would be better for you to know. We're bringing your nurture family here to Antara."

For an instant, she felt pure joy, then horror washed over her when she realized her family would be trapped here with her. "I think the trip would be too hard for Tala. I'd rather they stayed in Chadi."

"It's too late," Ohin said with just a trace of irritation. "Bez, one of my operatives, has already spoken to your nurture mother. I'm sure Tala would be disappointed not to be allowed to come. She even recorded a message for you."

Ohin handed over a sekai. Kayla had to swallow back a sob as Tala's face filled the display. An unfamiliar gray streaked her nurture mother's golden hair, as if sorrow had marked her. Lines that had never been there before creased her brow and bracketed her mouth.

Ohin reached over to start the vid. "Kayla," Tala said, "Bez tells me you're well. Thank the Infinite! And he tells me that Jal and I can come see you. I'm counting the days."

The moment the vid ended, Ohin snatched the sekai out of Kayla's fingers. "Could I see it again?"

Ohin tucked the sekai away in a pocket. "Maybe later."

Everything about the vid seemed odd—the look on Tala's face, her nurture mother's odd choice of words. Tala had spoken almost mechanically, as if she'd been reading from a script.

Dread settled in her stomach over the strangeness of it all. "When are they coming?"

"It might take a couple weeks," Ohin said.

Could he be lying about all of it? Oh, sweet Infinite, please let that be the case. As much as it would ease Kayla's heart to have her nurture mother here with her, she couldn't bear the thought of Tala and Jal imprisoned here. Kayla was working on escape, but how could she leave knowing they were coming?

Ohin's gaze grew distant, and Kayla felt the vibration at the base of her skull. *I thought he handled it! Denking hell, he's incompetent! Track him down. I'm coming.* He pushed to his feet without so much as a goodbye and strode off toward one of the meeting rooms in the back of Mahala.

Aideen was staring at her. She lowered her voice. "You can hear him."

"I don't know what you mean," Kayla said warily.

"I could see it in your face," Aideen said softly. "You were listening. You wouldn't have given him your passkey. And he would never give you his without an even exchange. So how?" Aideen reached across the table, no reluctance now as she urgently took Kayla's hand. "Can he hear *you?*"

"I don't think so."

"You hear him, but he can't hear you. Neither of you has the other's passkey. How could . . ." Understanding lit Aideen's face. "Oh, sweet Infinite Lord Creator."

The tangled oath heightened Kayla's fear. "You know how?"

"His DNA," Aideen said.

Now Kayla felt sick as the truth slapped her. "He *is* my father then?"

"Yes."

"How? When GENs are sterile?"

"Girls are sterile," Aideen said. "GEN boys, not necessarily."

"Then you and he . . ." An ingrained revulsion filled Kayla, catching her by surprise.

"He was Assigned to a warehouse near us. We were both sixteenth years. It happened." Aideen shook her head, as if to cast off the old memories. "But that's not the DNA I'm talking about. It's what he put into you here in the gen-tank."

Kayla's skin crawled, and she could barely keep her dinner down. "He put more of his DNA in me?"

"Because you'd been changed so much when you were converted to a GEN. He wanted you clearly stamped as his daughter. Enough DNA that you virtually have his passkey programmed alongside your own." Aideen got up from the table, paced along it restlessly. "Can you hear everything he says?"

Aideen's agitation pushed Kayla to her feet as well. "More now than I did at first. But only when I'm close enough. It doesn't work at a distance like the regular circuit-comm. When I was in Akhilesh's lab, I could hear you all the way from Antara, but more than a few meters away, Ohin's comm fades to nothing."

"So you can't hear him right now, with him in the meeting room," Aideen said.

Kayla shook her head. "I don't feel the vibration, either." At Aideen's look of confusion, Kayla gestured to the base of her skull. "When he uses his circuit-comm near me, my circuitry vibrates back here."

Aideen took Kayla's hand. "Then we have to get you closer to the door."

"Just stand there? Won't someone start wondering what I'm doing?"

"Have to take the risk. I'm afraid he's going to . . ." Aideen shook her head. "You have to try to hear him."

Aideen drew Kayla toward the meeting room where Ohin

had gone. As they passed the tables in the quiet area, Aideen raised her voice loud enough for those seated to hear her. "Would you wait over here for Ohin? Let him know I'll be right back."

Aideen gave Kayla one last anxious look, then left her by the meeting rooms and hurried off. Kayla leaned against the wall nearest the door Ohin had gone through.

For several minutes, she heard nothing, and she wondered if this was a lost cause. Then, as if her circuit-comm had needed time to tune in to Ohin through the door, she heard him.

—*Devak Manel.*

Kayla couldn't breathe as she waited to hear more.

You were supposed to have taken care of both of them by now. How could you miss killing Zul?

Ohin had had someone try to kill Zul? And he intended to have Devak killed too? Kayla wanted to use her sket strength to pound the door down. But she had to choke back her rage so she could hear the rest of it.

Denking hell, the old man has probably gone underground to a safe house. Tell me you got the boy.

Kayla felt as if she were choking. Sweet, sweet Infinite, please . . .

Then do you know where he is?

She nearly collapsed with relief.

When you've done it, bring me the body. I want her to see with her own eyes that he's gone. That there's nothing left for her in the outside world.

22

Crammed in the rear seat of the Brigade Dagger with the others, Devak struggled to keep the terror from his face. Beside him, Junjie and Usi held hands, leaning toward each other for comfort. Devak would have given anything to have Kayla there with him, to hold her in his lap, his arms around her. To whisper in her ear how much he loved her, the way Junjie and Usi were doing.

Of course, if Kayla were really there in the back seat of that Dagger, she would almost certainly be on her way to a reset. Keft might end up putting Devak and Junjie and Usi into a jail cell once he discovered their lies, but a GEN like Kayla would have her personality wiped away. Just as well she wasn't here, no matter how much Devak longed for her.

Junjie kissed Usi and leaned his forehead against the other boy's. Devak could see Keft eying Junjie and Usi in the rear viewer and the enforcer's scowl of disgust. Devak had heard some people worshipped a version of the Lord Creator that had a very narrow view of love. A man should only be with a woman, and trueborns should stick to their own class—high status with high status only, and so forth. The way Keft was reacting to Junjie's and Usi's love, if the enforcer saw Devak and Kayla expressing what they felt for each other, Keft wouldn't just reset Kayla, he'd use his shockgun on them both.

Junjie turned to Devak. "We're almost to the lab."

So they'd be found out very soon. Junjie had told Keft that on the top floor of the building that housed the GAMA lab there was a flat that the three of them shared. Junjie *had* once worked in the Amik gen-lab, but Devak was pretty sure his friend was just making up the part about a flat.

The gen-techs would all be gone this late at night, but there would be a guard up front. Maybe he or she would be someone who knew Junjie. Maybe Junjie would be able to persuade the guard to buzz them in through the outer door so they could make Keft believe they belonged there.

The enforcer pulled the Dagger right up to the front door. "Do you go in this way, or through the back?" he asked.

"Either way," Junjie said glibly. "Thanks for the ride."

Junjie poked Usi, who reached for the door latch. Devak grabbed the one on his side. Neither one opened. Keft had locked the doors when they'd first pulled out, and he didn't seem to be in a hurry to release them.

The enforcer turned around toward them. "I'll just walk you in. Make sure you get into your flat okay."

Devak's heart sank to the vicinity of his toes. In the few seconds between the click of the latches unlocking and them all opening their doors, he tried to come up with a way to signal to the others that they should run. But Keft exited the Dagger so quickly, his hand lightly resting on his shockgun, Devak knew they didn't have a chance.

They all walked toward the lit entrance of the three-story

GAMA lab. Compared to the one Junjie had worked at in Plator, and even the Ekat lab, it was small, which made sense because Amik was such a small, less-populated sector.

Keft rapped on the glass front door, standing so the guard would have a clear view of the enforcer's red and black uniform. With a buzz, the door unlocked and Keft ushered them inside.

A minor-status man with midnight dark skin and close-cropped gray hair sat at a desk, the name Fahim stitched on his front pocket. He was clearly uneasy with the presence of an enforcer, his gaze dropping to Keft's deadly, full-power shockgun. The weapon Fahim carried on his own hip could only incapacitate a man for several minutes. Keft's could kill.

The five of them were all minor-status, but Keft was Brigade, and that meant he had power over them all. Even demi- and high-status trueborns had to bow to enforcer authority.

Junjie met Devak's sidelong glance behind Keft's back. *Do you know the guard?* Devak mouthed. Junjie shook his head and Devak's last hope died.

Keft stepped forward. "These boys say they work here. That they live in a flat upstairs."

Fahim's eyes snapped with anger as he fixed on Junjie again, then Usi, finally settling on Devak. Devak braced himself for their lies to be stripped bare.

But then Fahim said the most outrageous thing. "Mar Sharma is *furious*. Bad enough you let his lev-car be stolen, but to stumble in here so late."

To hide his shock, Devak bent his head to stare down at his feet. "It was Junjie's idea."

Fahim sneered with contempt. "You can tell that story to Mar Sharma."

Keft stared at them all in turn, as if trying to ferret out the trick. "I could take them, give them a night in the jail to consider the consequences of their actions."

Alarm passed over the guard's face, then he got himself under control. "*Mar* Sharma will handle them." The emphasis on the high-status title *Mar* broadcast to Keft that even he might be overstepping his bounds.

Keft tipped his head at Fahim. "I'll leave them to you, then." One last scan of Devak and his friends, as if memorizing their faces, then he strode out of the lobby.

Fahim pressed a control under his desk to release the inner door lock, then rounded the desk. "You're lucky. Zul contacted me less than twenty minutes ago." He flicked a glance at Devak. "You look enough like him I might have known you even without the call, but I might not have made the connection."

Fahim herded them through the inner door and shut it behind them. Now that they were beyond the watchful eye of Keft, the guard reached in his pocket and dug out a fat roll of dhans.

"How did Pitamah get the money to you so quickly?" Devak asked.

"He didn't," Fahim said. "Not even the great Zul can perform that kind of miracle. My wife cleaned out our emergency money and brought it by. You just missed her."

Devak stared at the roll of paper Fahim set in his palm. "We shouldn't take this."

"It's not as much as it looks like," Fahim said. "Mostly small notes."

"Even so," Devak said, "it's not right."

Fahim waved them down a long corridor lined with doors on either side. "Zul will replace it tomorrow. I know he'll keep his word. Oh, and here . . ." The guard unstrapped a wristlink and held that out to Devak. "It's old and full of static, but it works. We have another."

Devak suspected that was a lie, because most minor-status couldn't afford even one wristlink. They were usually passed down from a family member.

"And it's not a flat," Fahim went on, "but I thought I should be prepared in case you needed a place to sleep. Just a storeroom with a couple blankets from home that Camia brought with the money."

Devak followed Fahim up the stairs at the end of the corridor, Junjie and Usi behind him. "Then you're Kinship?"

"Was," Fahim spat out. "I'm not sure I feel welcome in the new Kinship." As they reached the second floor landing, Fahim eyed Devak over his shoulder. "I've heard you want to be with that GEN girl, Kayla."

"Yes. I love her," Devak said.

Fahim nodded as he continued up the stairs. "I feel the same about Camia, a lowborn woman I met at one of the Kinship meetings. Your great-grandfather arranged for Councilor Mohapatra to marry us. Not currently legal, but since the councilor performed it, someday it could be. Meanwhile, the outside world thinks she's my house manager, as if I could afford such a thing." He laughed. "I guess she is, although she shares my bed too."

They reached the third floor and stepped into a corridor identical to the one on the first floor. Fahim opened the second door on the right to reveal the storeroom.

"The washroom is right there." He hooked a thumb back toward the first door they'd passed. "With the Scratch scare over, we're not using the third floor labs, so you shouldn't cross paths with anyone. I'll just have to sneak you out in the morning."

"Thank you," Devak said. "You've saved us."

"Anything for Zul's great-grandson." With another friendly smile, Fahim left them.

The storeroom was lined on either side with floor to ceiling shelves. The shelves were loaded with supplies and equipment—boxes of sani-wipes, laserscope slides, jugs of green gen-fluid, small hand-held illuminators, and spare holo projectors. Various lengths of plassteel were jammed into the far end of the room, leaning against the wall.

Two blankets were neatly folded on the floor next to the plassteel rods. On top of the blanket were three plasscine bottles of what looked like redfruit juice and a half dozen nutra bars. Curious, Devak went over to get a closer look at the lengths of plassteel. Looked at on end, they were L-shaped, like the sort of thing you'd install on the corners of your house to protect the plasscrete from getting chipped.

"What are these for?" he asked Junjie.

"They're used to construct gen-tanks," Junjie said. "The glass sides must be in another storeroom."

Devak looked from the plassteel lengths to the row of jugs. "And gen-fluid to re-make GENS." Or to heal a trueborn, although that made Devak shudder even more than the thought of a hapless, reset GEN dumped into a gen-tank. He set aside the heavy rod. "You two can use the washroom first."

While they were gone, Devak tucked the dhans into his carrysak and strapped on the wristlink. He helped himself to a half dozen handheld illuminators from one of the boxes and added those to his carrysak. Then he pulled out the little holo projector. He hadn't had a private moment all day to look at

Kayla's image. He turned on the device and drank in the lines of her face.

Usi and Junjie returned and Devak put away Kayla's image. In the washroom, Devak sighed with relief as he washed the grime from his face and hands with the ample supply of sani-wipes. He wished he could change into his remaining korta and chera pants, but they were just as dirty as the ones he was wearing. Junjie had used the spigot and sink to rinse his extra clothes and had hung them up. Devak did the same. At least he'd have a cleaner korta and chera pants for the morning.

When he returned to the storeroom, Junjie and Usi had squeezed together under one blanket and left Devak the other. Devak lay head to head with the other boys, sharing out the juice and three of the nutras, putting the other three bars in the carrysak. Devak doled out a strip each of rat-snake meat, grateful they could go to sleep with full bellies.

At least it was plenty warm indoors, unlike the chill night they'd spent in Wesja sector. Devak shut off the illuminator, tucked the carrysak under his head with one arm through the strap. Exhaustion and the cozy warmth pulled him into unconsciousness.

A clap of thunder jolted him awake. His first muzzy-headed thought as he blinked into the darkness was that he'd dreamed the sound, but it still rang in his ears. Another explosion of noise hit, then the floor shook and went out from under him, and he was falling.

Supplies and equipment spilled from the shelves, tumbling with him. He tried to grab for something, anything to slow his fall, but everything else was sliding and crashing with him.

Then with a jolt, he slammed his right arm into something solid and stopped moving. Everything around him creaked and groaned. Something must have made a little space around him, keeping him from being completely buried.

He discovered he couldn't move and panicked for a moment before he realized he still had his arm hooked into the carrysak. It must have gotten wedged in debris and that was what had Devak pinned. Wriggling his arm and wincing against the pain in his right wrist, he freed himself.

"Junjie?" he rasped out, dust coating his mouth and throat. "Usi?"

At first, his only answer was a groan, then Junjie answered, "I'm okay. But Usi . . ."

"It had to be another bomb," Devak said.

Junjie's voice rose in panic. "I can't tell if Usi is breathing."

Devak found the carrysak again in the dark and tugged it carefully. But even that small movement was enough that whatever was pinning it down trembled, sending rubble onto his head. He wouldn't be able to pull the carrysak out completely without risking everything coming down.

With careful fingers he opened the carrysak enough to find two of the handheld illuminators and switched them on. He squinted through the dust at broken walls leaning at crazy angles and crushed plasscrete piled everywhere. Shelving, equipment, and supplies had come down with them. They'd ended up in a fortunate triangular shaped hollow formed where two slabs of plasscrete had jammed into one another, further supported by the plassteel rods. Plasscrete chunks, bottles of gen-fluid, and shattered gen-tanks littered the floor around them.

He could barely make out where Junjie was, even though he was only a few meters away. His friend was so covered in dust he blended into the rubble. Usi, lying in Junjie's arms, was just as dusty except where dark red blood dripped from his head. Devak didn't like the way Usi's head lolled to the side.

"He's not—" Devak managed.

"I found his pulse. And he *is* breathing," Junjie said, the edge of tears in his voice. "But he won't wake up. We have to get him out of here."

"We have to get *ourselves* out of here." Devak carefully insinuated his fingers as far as he could into the carrysak again. "I can't reach the dhans. And if I pull out the carrysak, whatever's pinning it might collapse on us."

"Then leave them," Junjie sobbed. "What does it matter?"

"It doesn't," Devak said. Nothing mattered if they couldn't get clear of the wreckage. If they couldn't get Usi to a medic.

He also couldn't reach far enough inside the carrysak for the holo projector with Kayla's image. Such a little thing to worry about with Usi injured and no telling how badly. But it was just one more gram of grief.

Devak abandoned the carrysak and any hope of getting it out safely. He surveyed the space they were in, looking for an escape. But he didn't know which direction they should go, let alone see a space large enough for a human to slip through. Junjie stroked Usi's head tenderly. "He's sweating. I don't know if that's good or bad."

"I'm sweating too," Devak said. "It's getting hot in here."

Hot and brighter. A red glow had added itself to the illuminators' pale white light.

"Great Lord Creator," Devak whispered. "The building is on fire."

Devak caught a glimpse of the terror in Junjie's face and looked away. It would only make him even more afraid. Would only make the truth more real.

They were trapped. They were all going to burn to death.

23

When you've done it, bring me the body. I want her to see with her own eyes he's gone.

Ohin's words rang in Kayla's ears as she ran from Mahala. She shouted for Shakki in her mind, praying her friend would hear her. Shakki caught up with her just as Kayla approached the last turn of the corridor before Seycat.

"What's wrong?" Shakki gasped, out of breath.

Kayla shook her head. "When we get inside."

They rounded the curve. Kayla stared at the limestone floor, sick inside with the knowledge she'd just absorbed, fervently wishing it wasn't true.

"What's she doing there?" Shakki asked.

Kayla lifted her gaze. There was Aideen, standing outside the door to Seycat.

Kayla's birth mother waited until they reached the door, then pitched her voice so low it was unlikely the netcams would catch her words. "Let me help you escape."

Only the slightest indrawn breath from Shakki. Kayla gave her a sidelong glance, willing her friend not to betray them.

"Let's go inside," Kayla said.

Shakki tapped the code on their door, then stepped aside for Kayla and Aideen to enter. Once they were all inside, Aideen pulled Kayla into the blind spot within Seycat. Shakki slipped her small body in behind Kayla's.

"We're not completely hidden," Kayla said softly. "You'd better be quick."

"Give me permission to use your circuit-comm," Aideen said.

"So you can just pass everything I say on to Ohin?"

"You ought to have figured out by now I wouldn't do that," Aideen murmured. "Anyway, Ohin has already guessed about your escape plan with the bhimkay. That's why he won't let you anywhere near the spiders again. But I can get you outside. What did you overhear on Ohin's comm?"

Kayla's heart stuttered as she remembered. "Ohin has sent someone to kill Devak. I have to try to find him before they do."

"Not what I thought you might hear," Aideen said. "But in either case, there's no time to waste. You have to decide quickly. Ohin will wonder where I am."

Kayla's desperate need to get to Devak, to keep him safe, urged her to say yes. But she held back that impulse. "Why would you help me? I've seen the way you look at Ohin. As if the suns rose and set by his command. As if you'd do anything for him."

"There was a time I would have done anything for him," Aideen said. "But he was a different man then. Now he's nothing but a tyrant. He's done some wicked, wicked things to his own people."

"Even so, why help me leave when he wants me here? When he'll punish you when he finds out?" And Ohin *would* find out.

"Because you're my daughter," Aideen said. "Because I love you."

"Now you love me?" Kayla said, wishing she could cut this woman with her words. "What about twelve years ago? If you'd loved me then, you would never have given me up. No matter how deformed I was."

Tears rimmed Aideen's eyes. She lifted a shaking hand to press it against Kayla's tattooed face. "I didn't give you up because you were deformed. My parents took you when they found out you'd been fathered by a GEN."

Behind Kayla, Shakki gasped. *Ohin's your father?*

Yes, Kayla told her.

Aideen swiped at her eyes. "I thought I'd die the night they tore you from my arms."

Her birth mother's revelations seemed to turn Kayla's world inside out. She shook her head, not liking the twinge of sympathy she felt for Aideen. "That's old history. Why help me now?"

Aideen's eyes flashed with anger, but Kayla sensed it wasn't directed at her. "Because Ohin is tired of your rebellion, Kayla, and he plans to start over with you."

"Start over . . . ?" Kayla asked, although she suspected.

"Reset you! Remake you in a gen-tank. That's what I thought you would have heard, listening at the meeting room door."

Fear settled cold and tight within Kayla. She glanced back at Shakki. *I'm letting her use my circuit-comm.*

Shakki said, *If you're taking the risk, then so am I. Give her my passkey too.*

Kayla squeezed her friend's hand, then released the block on Aideen. Once the connection to her birth mother was made,

Kayla sent Shakki the code to Aideen's comm, the equivalent to a GEN passkey. Shakki sent her passkey to Aideen in return. They sat together on Kayla's bed and the three of them locked onto one another's circuit-comms.

Can anyone else hear you? Kayla asked Aideen. *The others you have passkeys for?*

I've blocked everyone but you two.

Kayla had to take her birth mother's word for it. They were running out of time and couldn't argue the point anymore.

When can we go?

Tonight, Aideen said. *Before they let the spiders out to feed.*

Kayla's internal clock told her they had two hours before the Bhimkay Boys went out to unlock the enclosure gate. Even Tak would leave to hunt, and calling the spider to get her back would take precious time.

How do you know about the reset? Kayla asked.

I got it all from Jadi, Aideen said. *When Ohin went to speak to the other Bhimkay Boys, he was telling them his plan. They'll likely take you while you're sleeping.* Aideen's face set with determination. *I won't let that happen to my child again.*

The pieces of Aideen's story all seemed to tie together. Her behavior earlier in Mahala, the things she'd said about Ohin, had changed Kayla's picture of her birth mother, enough that Kayla thought she might be able to trust her a little bit.

But Aideen could still be lying about everything. Her coming to Kayla could still be a trick of Ohin's. Yet Kayla couldn't risk waiting to test the truth of what Aideen had said.

Kayla sifted through her doubts and made a decision. *Okay. We could use your help.*

Have you made preparations? Aideen asked. *Gathered supplies?*

302

Water and food, Kayla said. *Blankets. We could use illuminators. Presakas so we can control the other spiders until we get away.*

I can get those, Aideen said. *I'll take you up in the freight lift in Godama 2. I know the code to the room and the lift.*

What about the surface guards? Shakki asked. *Even with Aideen escorting us, they won't let us pass, not without checking with Ohin.*

Can you get a shockgun? Kayla asked Aideen.

She shook her head. *Ohin keeps them locked up.*

I'll have to overpower one of the guards then, get their shockgun, Kayla said. *If I'm quick enough I can shoot them both before either one gets a circuit-comm message off to Ohin.*

Shakki's brow furrowed. *But if the shockgun is set to kill, you won't have time to change it.*

Which meant she'd have to kill the guards. *It won't be,* Kayla said, although she wasn't the least bit sure. *When do we leave?* she asked Aideen.

As soon as I can get the presakas and illuminators, her birth mother said. *I'll knock three times, then pause and knock twice. But if I haven't returned and he comes for you . . .*

I'll do what I have to, Kayla said. Could she kill Ohin? With the guards she might hesitate, but if it was a choice between being reset as Ohin's obedient daughter and killing him, she knew which way she'd choose. Even knowing she would die herself at the hands of the Bhimkay Boys.

Aideen let herself out. After she left, Kayla and Shakki stared at each other.

What do we do about Tak's eggs? Shakki asked. *What if she won't leave them?*

I have to pray to the Infinite she will, Kayla said. *That her bond with me is strong enough.*

Maybe we should get out our supplies, Shakki said. *Be ready to go.*

To conceal their actions, Kayla dimmed the illuminator to the lowest setting it would go, then as quietly as she could, pulled out the two bulging carrysaks she'd stuffed under her bed. She could hear Shakki doing the same, then the squeak of the plasscine straps of the bed as Shakki sat.

I always thought, Kayla said as the quiet stretched, *that since GEN girls were genned without a womb, since we couldn't get pregnant, that GEN boys were the same. I mean, that they couldn't get a girl pregnant.*

But Ohin did, Shakki said, with just a hint at a question in her comm voice.

Aideen said some GEN boys can. I guess it usually wouldn't matter because—at least according to how it's always been—a GEN would never mate with a lowborn, let alone a trueborn. Kayla shuddered. *It seems so disgusting.*

But your Devak is—

A trueborn.

And you're a GEN, Shakki pointed out. *How is this different?*

Because it's Ohin and I hate him, Kayla said. *He thinks I should love him because we have genetics in common. He thinks his genetics should be more important to me than my nurture mother is.*

He's wrong about that.

And when I was in the gen-tank he had the techs add his DNA to mine. That's why I hear him, because his passkey is encoded alongside my own. And, sweet Infinite, he might have already had Devak killed.

Kayla was sobbing now, silently so she wouldn't make noise that the netcam could pick up. She doubted that would get them into trouble—she'd cried so many times before, grieving over Devak. But she hated the thought of someone seeing her so weak.

More than an hour had passed before Aideen signaled her return. Kayla and Shakki slipped out of Seycat, shutting the door behind them as quietly as they could. The corridor lights had been dimmed for evening, but there was enough light to see. That was worrisome since if they could see their way along the corridor, the netcams could see them too.

With her back to the nearest netcam, Aideen handed over a presaka. *I got a half dozen illuminators, but I could only get the one controller. I had to steal it from one of the Bhimkay Boys' quarters. I didn't realize Ohin had locked up the spares.*

Only need one to shut down the five other bhimkay. Kayla tucked the presaka in her breastband.

They hurried off to Godama 2. With most of Antara's residents in their quarters, Kayla, Shakki, and Aideen only passed a few stragglers. The few they encountered seemed tired and distracted, and anyway, most knew that Aideen and Kayla were favorites of Ohin. As long as Aideen mumbled *Always one with him,* and Kayla at least moved her lips the proper way in silent oath, no one questioned why they were wandering the corridor.

At Godama 2, Aideen unlocked the door, then locked it behind them. *Ohin will likely be at your door soon. We haven't much time.*

They ran for the freight lift. The inner and outer doors were open and the three of them were inside in seconds. Kayla and Shakki got the doors shut while Aideen entered the lift code, plus an extra code to take the place of a GEN tattoo. The lift shuddered and began to rise.

He could still stop us, Shakki said. *Once he figures out that Kayla's gone.*

And there are still the surface guards to deal with, Kayla said. *Someone who saw us might have already notified them.*

But when they pushed open the doors, neither guard was near the lift. They must have heard it coming, though, because they'd both started in that direction. Aideen planted a hand on Kayla's back to urge her forward.

"Aideen?" called Faia, as she neared the lift. "Can we help you with something?"

"Ohin asked me to come up," Aideen said, clearly stalling. "He's meeting us here."

"He never told me." Faia looked puzzled, but she kept coming nearer.

Aideen gave Kayla a shove. "Go!"

Kayla flung herself across the space between her and Faia and struck the guard so hard they both went stumbling. Faia must have already snapped open her shockgun holster, because the impact of hitting the floor sent the weapon flying.

Aideen snatched up the shockgun and aimed at the other guard, a GEN man, striking him with the energy bolt before he got his hand on his own weapon. Then, as Kayla rolled away, Aideen shot Faia too.

Kayla scrambled up, gasping out, "What . . .what setting?"

Aideen looked at the shockgun and the relief in her face gave her the answer. "Low power. They'll be okay. But only out for an hour at most." She dropped the shockgun beside Faia.

"Shouldn't we take the weapons?" Kayla asked.

"Ohin has transmitters installed in them," Aideen said. "Good on a battlefield, not good if we want to keep him from tracking you."

Shakki, who had stayed out of the way in the lift until the guards had been subdued, caught up with them as they ran for the door. Kayla slid the plassteel bar out of its carrier and pushed the doors open. They all stepped outside into the blackness of the Badlands.

Kayla was about to walk away when Aideen clutched her hand. She pulled Kayla close, hugging her tightly, her body trembling. Then she set Kayla away from her. *Goodbye*, she said before slipping back inside and shutting the doors.

Kayla and Shakki ran for the passageway to the clearing, Kayla's heart aching inexplicably at leaving Aideen behind. She put those emotions aside, focusing on the tricky passageway, blessedly brighter than usual due to the rise of two of the trinity moons. They went single file, Kayla first, then Shakki. Kayla's heart pounded from the exertion, the fear.

They burst into the clearing, strange shadows cast by Ashiv's and Avish's moonlight stretching across the bhimkay enclosure. Tak stood over her eggs, legs spread wide. Pev crouched beside her. The other spiders restlessly crisscrossed the cage, anxious to be released for their nightly hunt.

Well, they'd be out soon. Kayla planned to leave the enclosure unlocked and once the emergency stop wore off they'd be free.

She scanned the eggs underneath Tak. In the shifting shadows, she could see them pulsate and writhe.

"A good thing they can't hatch on their own," Kayla said. "They look ready."

Kayla dug out the presaka and got all the spiders except Tak and Pev frozen in place with the emergency stop command. Despite the necessity, Kayla felt a sharp sense of guilt at what they'd done. The bhimkay were clearly agitated, and being immobilized and not being able to work off their frenzy, they looked miserable.

Kayla stuffed the presaka into one of her carrysaks. She

was about to unlock the gate when a shout pulled her around. Jadi emerged from the passageway into the clearing. "Take me with you!"

"Oh, sweet Infinite," Shakki moaned. "Are the other Bhimkay Boys with him?"

Gasping for breath, Jadi trotted over to them. "It's only me. I brought my own supplies." He held up a carrysak.

"How did you even know we were here?" Kayla asked.

"I was going to try something tonight too," Jadi said. "That's what I was trying to tell you at dinner. I went up in one of the other lifts, and I saw Aideen on the surface. Saw the guards. I guessed where you were. She didn't tell me."

"We're going out of here on bhimkay, Jadi," Kayla said. "Who do you expect to ride?"

He scanned the edgy spiders inside the enclosure. "Moff. He's always been pretty quiet."

Except even Moff looked ready to explode. "Can you ride without a saddle?" Kayla asked.

"I have to," Jadi said. "I have to get free of him. Asking us to hold you down so he could reset you—that was the last kernel of kel-grain. I have to get home to my family before it all happens."

Kayla narrowed her gaze on him. "Before what happens?"

He got that look on his face that Kayla had come to recognize. As if he were struggling to say something, but someone had frozen his tongue.

"He programmed you, didn't he?" Kayla asked. "So you can't tell me his plans."

Jadi couldn't even nod. He was as inhibited as a bhimkay.

"Just bring him with us," Shakki said. "We don't have the time to argue."

What choice did she have? She couldn't bring herself to leave him behind. She unlocked the gate and entered quickly, stepping aside so Shakki and Jadi could slip in behind her. She shut the gate, knowing the moment she released Moff, he'd run out to hunt.

She selected Moff's frequency and set the bhimkay free. He straightened his legs, rising to his full height.

"Use a calming gesture with him." Kayla demonstrated for Jadi. "Shakki and I have used it on him, so he knows it."

Shakki had already started the open-palmed stroking movement even though Pev looked relaxed and sleepy. Jadi's motion wasn't as smooth, his hand shaking through it. But Moff was forgiving enough to get the gist of what the Bhimkay Boy was trying to convey. The bhimkay relaxed his legs again, lowering himself slightly.

Broody Tak was giving Kayla a more suspicious look. Kayla was confident the bhimkay would let her mount. The trick was to get Tak far enough off her mound of eggs that Kayla wouldn't have to step on the shells to reach Tak's back. They might be treated to keep from breaking easily, but she could still damage the babies by walking on them.

From the corner of her eye, Kayla could see that Shakki had already slipped between Pev's hair barbs and mounted him. Beyond Shakki and Pev, Jadi had managed to persuade Moff to crouch low enough, but the Bhimkay Boy just stood there.

"Use your arm to part the hair barbs, Jadi," Kayla said, "then slide your leg over. Like you're straddling one of the benches in Mahala."

"Can you show me?" His voice shook with nerves.

If she could get Tak away from her eggs a moment. As close as Kayla was, she could see the squirming of Tak's babies against the now near-transparent egg casings. Their folded legs wriggled and pushed, the sharp hair barbs drawing lines on the inside as the babies tried to break free.

"Kayla!" Shakki said urgently. "We have to go. The other spiders are going to start moving soon."

Kayla made the *come to me* gesture more insistently, but Tak, so preoccupied with her eggs, didn't budge. Another try, Kayla making the motion as precisely and clearly as she could, had the same result.

Could she climb on the eggs? She hated the thought of injuring a young spider or worse, breaking through a casing and getting bitten. She'd heard the venom from a newborn bhimkay was the worst since the babies didn't have the experience to know how much to release. They would use it all with one bite. It would kill her instantly.

"Kayla!" Shakki said again. "I think I hear voices."

Kayla's panic gave birth to inspiration. She used her *come to me!* gesture once again, even more imperiously, this time accompanying it with an imitation of Tak's angry hiss. Kayla drew it out, investing all of her human ire into the sound.

Whether it was Kayla's authority, or Tak thinking that the eggs were finally hatching, the female bhimkay scurried down from the nest. She immediately crouched without even waiting for Kayla's request. Her heart thundering in her chest, Kayla made a track between the hair barbs across Tak's back.

"Jadi! Like this!"

She hardly waited for him to attend to her, she just slid her leg across and straddled Tak. A tug of the hair barbs and the spider rose to her full height.

His face set and determined, Jadi copied Kayla's movements. Making a place for himself to sit went well enough, but he was awkward throwing his leg over. He finally slid himself into place, crying out a couple times as he jabbed himself on hair barbs.

Moff staggered a little as he tried to balance Jadi's awkward, bareback weight. "Get handfuls of the hair barbs," Kayla said. "Like me and Shakki."

Jadi clutched at the barbs, but Moff objected, skittering to one side and then the next. Jadi tipped and rocked, his expression terrified as he tried to stay on.

"I can't balance without the saddle!" he cried.

The boy clutched hard with his legs, making Moff even angrier. The male spider kept spiraling closer and closer to Tak's nest. Under Kayla, Tak danced, trying to surge toward her eggs to save them from Moff.

Then the male bhimkay leapt sideways, raking his hair barbs against several eggs on the periphery of the nest. The babies might not be able to free themselves from inside, but Moff's mature barbs sliced through the casings like a sharp knife through a rat-snake belly. In another moment, twenty or more babies were wriggling out and down the pile.

Shakki urged Pev backward several meters. "Let's go!" She swung her spider around toward the gate, unlatching it and swinging it open.

That was all Moff needed. He lunged across the enclosure for freedom. Caught by surprise, Jadi flew off of Moff. When he hit the ground, Kayla heard the snap of bone.

Jadi's right leg was bent wrong. He couldn't get to his feet. He tried dragging himself toward Tak and Pev, but Kayla could see the hopelessness in his eyes.

A dozen babies, wet and shiny, crawled toward him across the enclosure. Nearly the size of the smaller full-grown bhimkay in the settled sectors, they staggered at first, clumsy on their long legs, then they seemed to gain strength and grace within moments.

"Get out of here, Shakki!" Kayla shouted, then tried to turn Tak toward Jadi. But Tak seemed to have lost all her maternal instincts now that the babies had started emerging. She struggled against Kayla, trying to move toward the gate after Pev.

"You can climb on Tak!" Kayla yelled, legging the resistant female bhimkay over to Jadi.

Jadi just shook his head. The baby spiders had sensed him and were ambling over. Jadi stripped his carrysak from his shoulder.

"Take it!" He threw the carrysak at her and she barely caught it one-handed. "There's . . ." He struggled with the words, his pain or programming holding him back. ". . . something inside. You'll . . . know when you see it. . . . have to stop him." He lay back, his eyes rolling toward the approaching babies.

"I won't leave you!" Kayla kicked Tak's sides again, urging the bhimkay to stand over Jadi. Could she convince her bhimkay to pick up Jadi with her legs?

Then she heard the crash of running footsteps from the passageway. Shakki called out, "They're coming!"

Below her, one of the babies dashed between Tak's legs. Jadi's scream told her the newly hatched spider had hit home with a mandible.

"Go," Jadi whispered, his voice fading to thin air as the venom took effect.

Tak had had enough. She skittered backward, and Kayla, still holding Jadi's carrysak with one hand, slipped sideways, nearly off Tak. Kayla hooked the carrysak over her shoulder, then crawled back on top of her bhimkay.

Kayla looked back at Jadi one last time as Tak edged toward the gate. The former Bhimkay Boy was silent and still, swarmed by a half dozen baby spiders. If the creatures filled him full of poison and sucked him dry, no gen-tech would ever be able to use Jadi's DNA. That was small comfort.

The four remaining grown bhimkay were starting to move, the stop command losing its control over them. Kayla thumped her legs against Tak's sides, which gave Tak leave to run across the clearing, a swarm of babies and grown spiders in their wake. One of the Bhimkay Boys had just emerged from the passageway when he spotted the eager stream of newborn bhimkay. He ducked back into the passageway, and a commotion followed as the rest of the boys retreated into a narrower part of the passageway.

Some of the babies tried to get in to attack the newly arrived prey, but even they were too big to squeeze through. Whoever had excavated that passageway knew exactly what size newly hatched bhimkay were and what space would be narrow enough to keep them out.

As she and Shakki dashed across the clearing on Tak and Pev, Kayla heard Ohin shouting her name. Kayla ignored the calls from her despised birth father, driving Tak to the rock wall.

Then they were flying, Tak jumping to freedom, Pev a moment later. Atop the granite, they ran, leaping over crevasses and rock barriers, bhimkay and GENs escaping their prison at last.

24

Devak frantically looked around the wreckage for any possible escape, the heat rising steadily. For the moment, the fire hadn't breached the space he and the other boys were in, but they couldn't count on that for long.

"Can you call for help?" Junjie asked, his voice vibrating with fear.

Devak had completely forgotten the wristlink. He tried to tap out the code for a call, but the display wouldn't respond.

"The transmitter's not working," Devak said. "I hurt my wrist when we fell. I must have damaged the wristlink at the same time."

"What about the emergency signal?" Junjie asked.

Devak pressed the two buttons on opposite sides of the device. A light flickered on the display.

"I think it's set," Devak said. "It should be broadcasting."

At least they'd know where to find their bodies, Devak thought. He kept that to himself, though.

He rose, bumping his head on the slanted wall as he strafed the small space with the illuminator. The light couldn't penetrate the dense debris, so he crouched to explore another layer down. Finally he lay flat on his belly and scooted side to side as he pointed the illuminator in every direction.

The light caught a depression in the rubble. He reached in as far as he could with the illuminator and realized it looked almost like a narrow tunnel through the debris.

"There's an opening there." Devak pointed. "No idea how far it goes, but it might take us out. I could check it and come back for you."

"I think we'd be in the hands of the Infinite by then," Junjie said, "dead from the fire or crushed. We might as well all go. At least we'd die together."

Devak saw the sense of that. "You go first. Lead the way."

"Usi—"

"I'll follow and pull him since I'm a little stronger than you."

"You won't leave him?" Junjie asked. "Because of him setting the bomb in Nafi?"

"No matter what. We're not leaving him behind."

Nodding agreement, Junjie gave Usi a last tender kiss on the mouth and climbed into the space head first, an illuminator lighting his way. A few moments later, he called out, "I fit just fine and it goes a ways. Come on in."

Devak tucked the illuminator into the strap of the wristlink, tightening it as snugly as he could. Once he got Usi positioned close to the opening, Devak backed into it feet first. His body filled the small space. He had just enough room to squirm inside with his arms outstretched to get hold of Usi. He wouldn't think about the whole thing collapsing, or worse, the fire catching up to him.

Devak gripped Usi's shirt at the shoulders, letting the boy's head rest on his forearm, ignoring the pain in his right wrist.

Devak pulled Usi as close as he could, then inched backward himself. In some spots it grew tighter, and at one point Devak's chera pants got caught on something. After several moments of panic until whatever it was tore both fabric and skin, Devak shoved past.

He could just make out the shiny stickiness of the blood on Usi's head, could hear Junjie's gasping breath. "Where are we going?" Devak asked, hating that he was moving so blindly.

"It doesn't matter," Junjie said. "We just have to keep going."

"It's getting hotter," Devak said. Could they be going deeper inside, closer to the fire?

"I feel like I'm burning up," Junjie said. "Is Usi okay?"

Other than his head lolling from side to side from Devak's pulling motion, Usi hadn't moved. "He's fine. We'll get him out. I promise." Except Devak shouldn't be promising anything.

There was nothing but silence for what seemed like forever, then Junjie's voice drifted back to Devak. "Oh, no."

Devak squeezed his eyes shut. "What?"

"We're blocked. The tunnel is crushed by debris."

Devak lifted his wrist and swung the illuminator as far as its light would reach along the tunnel. He caught what looked like a gap. "I'm backing up. There might be another way out."

He doubted it would go any further than the first route, but they had to keep trying. Pushing Usi was harder, but crawling forward was easier. Even when he reached the new opening and saw it went quite a ways, Devak had to keep going to make room to let Junjie lead.

Finally they were in the new tunnel. Devak felt he was melting with sweat as he squirmed along. "Watch for other escape routes, just in case."

It was just as well they did since this new path ended too.

The backtracking was almost more than Devak could bear, but he blanked his mind to how exhausted he was.

"I think it's cooler in here," Junjie said when they slid inside a fourth tunnel. "Maybe we've gotten farther from the fire."

Devak couldn't feel the difference, but maybe it was because of the extra work of dragging Usi. What did it matter? They just had to keep going until they were truly trapped. That would just be a matter of time.

At first the beeping on Devak's wrist baffled him. Then he realized it was someone picking up the emergency signal. A faint shriek sounded in the distance, slowly growing louder. The local fire crew, no doubt. They'd probably picked up the wristlink's transmission. Did that mean they were nearing the outside?

Suddenly Junjie grunted. Had he been hurt? "Junjie? Are you okay?" No answer. "Junjie?"

When Devak first felt the coolness fluttering against his legs, he thought he must be hallucinating. But as he continued to worm his way backward, the coolness seemed to spread upward along his body.

Usi's head felt like a dead weight on Devak's arm. He had to keep adjusting to keep Usi's face out of the dust and sharp-edged debris.

The alarm from outside was growing louder. Would the rescuers come looking for him and Usi? Would they be in time for Usi? Devak couldn't count on that. He had to keep moving toward that coolness and get him out himself.

Suddenly, hands fell on his ankles and a voice called out. "Devak? I'm going to pull you out."

It was a woman's voice, and for a short, crazed moment, Devak thought it was Kayla come to rescue him. "I've got Usi.

I don't know what happened to Junjie."

He felt a pair of hands around each leg. He didn't even know who was pulling him free, except the woman knew his name. The voice sounded familiar, but his head was too muzzy to place it. He had to hope it was someone he could trust.

He held tight to Usi as the rescuers towed both of them clear of the tumbled building. Devak staggered to his feet, gulping fresh air into his lungs, the glare of a lorry's headlights blinding him. He squinted to see Junjie carefully laying Usi in a patch of scrap grass, then kneeling beside him.

As Devak's eyes accustomed themselves to the light, he stared at the familiar lorry, then at the women who had pulled him to safety. Risa Mandoza and her wife Kiyomi.

"You're here," Devak said, feeling thick-headed. "You're not in Dika."

Dimly, he heard Risa's rusty laugh. Then the world spun and went black.

Devak woke in the dark with a gasp, banging his elbow on something hard, the stench of melting plasscrete replaced by the faint aroma of drom wool. "Junjie!"

Devak's heart clenched tight at the moments of silence, then Junjie said sleepily, "I'm here."

"Where are we?" Devak asked. He felt the bump and sway, remembered Risa's miraculous rescue, and answered the question himself. "In the lorry. In the bay?"

"Yeah," Junjie said. "We're jammed into a skinny space between the doors and the cargo."

"Smells like drom," Devak said.

"There's rolls of woven drom wool and crates of uttama-silk squares. And a ticked off seycat."

Risa kept a barely tamed seycat—five-legged since it had lost one leg to a bhimkay—in the bay. "Nishi probably doesn't like us invading her territory. Is Usi there with you?" The darkness was so absolute in the closed up bay, Devak couldn't see.

Another pause, then Junjie said, "He's up front in the sleeper bed."

From when Kayla traveled with Risa, Devak knew that there was a tiny sleeproom in the cab, tucked up behind the driver and passenger seats. There was a washroom crammed in there too.

"But he's okay?"

"He's still unconscious," Junjie said. "Not just asleep. But Kiyomi thinks he'll be all right."

"Shouldn't they take Usi to a medic?" Devak asked.

"A regular medic would report Usi to the Brigade for sure."

"What about a Kinship one?" Devak asked.

"We can't even trust the Kinship anymore," Junjie said. "And Kiyomi's not a bad healer. How's your wrist?"

Now Devak felt the wrappings on his arm. He opened and closed his hand, feeling just a twinge of pain. He'd completely forgotten that he'd banged his wrist. "It's better. I must have been out for a long time."

"Yeah, you got a conk on the head as you fell," Junjie said. "You were out all night and all day. It's early evening. I've spent a lot of that time sleeping too."

Devak fought his exhaustion and sat up, slapping away a tickle on his neck. He felt the tug on his right ear and realized he wore a long dangling earring. "Where's my bali?"

"Same place as mine and Usi's," Junjie said. "In a safe in the sleeper."

"What is this thing in my ear?"

A sudden burst of light from Junjie's side of the bay briefly blinded Devak. He covered his eyes with his arm until he could get used to the handheld illuminator Junjie had switched on.

Now he saw the ornate, dangling earring in Junjie's right ear, although it didn't look as long as Devak's felt. His must have been a good fifteen centimeters since it brushed his shoulder.

"They're allabain-style," Junjie said. "First thing Risa did was trade out the balis for them."

"So we're allabain lowborns now? They dress better than this." Devak plucked at his torn and dirty korta. "You don't think I look too high-status, do you?"

Junjie laughed. "Considering what we've been through, that face of yours has been knocked down a few notches. Mine too. Even after Kiyomi cleaned us up."

"True enough. We'd better keep our mouths shut, though. Harder to hide the accent." Devak leaned against the bay wall, and the earring tickled his neck again. "How far is she taking us?"

"Almost to Beck sector. She managed to get a travel plan approved to take us to the border. She and Kiyomi are taking turns driving and resting." Junjie tossed Devak another illuminator. "Risa told me what really happened to Zul when that bomb went off at his house. Turns out he came close to being killed."

Typical of Pitamah to refuse to tell the whole truth, although an enforcer had been hovering over them at the time. "So he *was* home?"

"Not in the house, thank the Infinite, but just outside," Junjie said. "Jemali was there in his WindSpear, about to pick Zul up for a Kinship meeting. Zul had made it to the walkway when the bomb went off. Threw him off his feet."

"But he's all right?"

"A few cuts and scrapes. Jemali helped Zul into the WindSpear, and they got out of there before the Brigade showed up. Zul's staying with Jemali now in Foresthill."

"Why would someone want to kill Pitamah?" Devak asked. "My father might, but he's in prison and all his adhikar has been stripped away. It doesn't make sense for it to be someone in the Kinship—Pitamah's got so little power there anymore. Any other trueborns who don't like him don't worry about him anymore, even if they do know his history with the creation of the GENs. He's a has-been to them."

"You're missing the obvious," Junjie said. "FHE."

"But why?"

"No idea. But they went after you too."

Devak shook his head. "The bomb at the gen-lab had to be a strike against GAMA. FHE must hate them. It's GAMA that creates GENs to become slaves."

"If it was against GAMA," Junjie said, "then why pick one of the smallest labs? Why not go for Plator's, or even Ekat's? Both are much bigger—it'd be much more showy if you destroyed them instead of the Amik lab."

"Why would the FHE think Pitamah or I were important enough to kill? And how did they know we were there?" A sudden thought clutched Devak's belly. "It wasn't Usi, was it?"

"No!" Junjie looked ready to bite Devak's head off.

"He was with FHE until just recently."

"But they abandoned him, remember?" Junjie almost shouted the words, disturbing Nishi into an angry hiss. "And when would Usi have had the chance to get in touch with FHE? We only had the one wristlink, and until Yasi took it, it was either on your wrist or mine. He never asked to borrow it from me."

"Okay, calm down," Devak said. "Usi didn't do it. Then how?"

Junjie took a breath. "Risa and I were talking about that. She thinks they were tracking the wristlink. They knew the ID from when I was in FHE. They knew I was your friend and guessed that I might be with you."

"But after Yasi took it?"

"They were already tracking Zul's wristlink ID. When you called him, they tapped the call."

"How did Risa know to come?"

"After the bomb at his house," Junjie said, "Zul guessed that you might be in danger too, and since he knew we would be at the Amik gen-lab, he sent her."

Suddenly, Devak remembered Fahim. "What happened to the guard?"

Junjie's expression was grim. "Blown apart. Risa said there was nothing she could do."

"Denking hell. If I hadn't been there—"

"It wasn't your fault. Only FHE's."

The lorry bumped and shuddered, then with a jerk came to a stop. The suspension engine sighed as the lorry settled into parking mode. The bay illuminators flickered on.

Levering himself on a stack of crates, Devak got to his feet. He reached for the inner door handles.

"Don't!" Junjie said. "Risa said to let her open it."

When they swung open, Devak saw why. An enforcer stood beside Risa, the red and black bhimkay emblem on his black uniform glittering in the streetlights.

Devak didn't recognize the sector they were in, but it looked like they'd been stopped in the central square of a mixed sector. The enforcer was scrolling through something on a sekai reader.

Risa chomped hard on the devil weed in her cheek, gesturing toward the sekai. "See for yourself, all three allabain legal and signed for."

"What happened to the one up front?" the enforcer asked.

Risa spat out a mouthful of devil weed juice. "Sanaki allabain moved too slow when a crate tower tipped over in Qaf warehouse. Hit his head."

"And you haven't been in Amik?" the enforcer asked.

"Nowhere near." Risa pointed to something on the sekai's screen. "Check the lorry logs."

The enforcer flipped through a few more displays, then tapped something into the sekai and handed it back to Risa. He made a quick scan of the bay, his lip curling when his gaze fell on Junjie and Devak, his eyes going wide when he spotted the hissing seycat perched on top of the drom wool bales.

The enforcer turned away, headed for another lorry stopped behind Risa's. Risa leaned in close enough to whisper, "Heading up the road just a few more kilometers. Get into the open. Then you can use the washroom, change clothes, and eat."

She slammed the doors shut, and the engine rumbled to life again. A half hour or so later, they stopped and Risa opened the doors again. It was darker here, with the lights of the settled areas of the sector out of sight.

As Devak followed Risa toward the front of the lorry, a familiar smell drifted on the breeze. "Is that the Chadi?" He'd grown up in Foresthill sector, just south of the Chadi River.

"It is," Risa said. "We're in Cayit."

Cayit was northeast of Foresthill. He could hear the rush of the Chadi, see its moonlit glitter off in the distance.

He and Junjie took turns in the washroom, changing into spare sets of clothes that Risa had on hand. Devak's chera pants weren't quite long enough, but they were clean and in far better condition than what he'd been wearing, especially considering the last set had gone through a building collapse.

Then they all stood in front of the lorry, sharing some dried rat-snake meat and a pair of juicy redfruit. They were just finishing their evening meal when a groan and a raspy, "Junjie?" sent Devak's friend leaping into the cab.

A few moments later, Junjie poked his head out, grinning. "He's awake!"

Kiyomi went to check on Usi. A short while later, with Kiyomi complaining that it was a bad idea, Junjie emerged with Usi, his arm around him, supporting the injured boy as they headed slowly toward the back of the bay.

Kiyomi scowled. "He'd be better off in that bed."

"I'm thinking he'll be better off with Junjie," Devak said.

As a compromise, Kiyomi sent blankets and her own pillow back with Devak. By the light of a couple of handheld illuminators, Devak helped Junjie move a few crates and get Usi comfortably settled beside him. Then, as the lorry pulled back onto the road, Devak squeezed into his own spot opposite his friends.

Junjie held Usi close. "I've been thinking . . . what if we can't find Kayla in Belk? What if we get there and—"

"—and we find out Kayla was on the other side of Svarga continent all along?" Devak shook his head. "I hate to think this is a wild drom chase."

Junjie wrapped and unwrapped his long earring around his index finger. "Especially dragging Risa and Kiyomi along with us."

"Right," Devak said. "We put them into danger any time the Brigade stops them. But that message Mishalla got, it came through Belk. And that's the only reliable clue we have."

Usi roused, his sleepy eyes focusing on Devak. "I really thought Kayla was in Nafi. Honestly."

"But you got that information from Aideen," Devak said, "who we know *isn't* reliable. Not your fault."

The combination of his full stomach and the swaying of the lorry was mesmerizing. After days of living on the edge, never knowing who to trust, if their dhans would last, if they'd be able to buy another meal, just sitting in the back of a lorry seemed like a blessed luxury. He let himself be lulled back to sleep and dreamed of Kayla.

Two more days passed the same way. There were occasional stops to trade drivers, use the washroom, and eat. In between, Devak, Junjie, and Usi slept or talked or played sarka in their heads, not having a board or playing pieces.

There was another Brigade check in Saya sector that kept them there for the night. The enforcers demanded that every crate and roll be removed from the bay and inspected. Of course, the enforcers wouldn't do the work themselves, leaving it to Devak, Junjie, Risa, and Kiyomi. Kiyomi wouldn't let Usi lift so much as a tuft of drom wool, so he sat in the sleeper with the quixotic Nishi purring in his lap.

They got an early start the next morning, but Devak lost count of the hours after. He was sore from sitting and could scarcely bear his own stink after days since a decent bath. If he found Kayla today, she'd probably run from him in disgust.

The lorry jounced and shuddered, knocking Devak into the door. The sudden stop sent a couple rolls of drom wool tumbling on top of him.

As Devak righted the wool, Junjie gave him a worried look. "They can't be swapping drivers already. It's only been a couple hours since Risa took over."

"Another Brigade checkpoint?" Usi fingered his earring, as if making sure it was properly in place.

Light footsteps approached, then the doors swung open. To Devak's relief, it was only Risa and Kiyomi.

"We're in Pashi sector," Risa said. "Just across the border from Belk. Can't drive you any farther. Lorry isn't licensed in Belk, and Brigade would grab us up quick as a seycat on a rat-snake."

"Just stay together," Kiyomi said, "and you'll be all right with the bhimkay."

Even knowing the truth of that, Devak didn't like the reminder of the big spiders. He rose, stretching his cramped leg muscles and jumping from the lorry. "You did enough. More than enough. Thank you."

Risa handed over a carrysak, then held out her hand, palm up. The three balis gleamed in the moonlight. Devak took them, handing Junjie and Usi theirs.

"Suggest you put them in the hem of your shirt," Risa said.

"Good idea." Devak slipped his small sapphire between the stitches in his hem as Junjie and Usi did the same.

Risa gestured at the carrysak. "Some water in there. A few illuminators. As many dhans as we could spare. And more nutra bars than you'll likely want to eat."

Devak hung the carrysak over his shoulder. Junjie helped Usi out, then Risa latched the doors again. The two lowborn women gave the three of them hugs in turn, Kiyomi's a light embrace, Risa's vigorous enough to push the air from Devak's lungs.

Devak headed off, footsteps crunching in the dirt and gravel alongside the road. Junjie and Usi fell in a few paces behind him, murmuring intimacies to one another. That set off a heavy longing in Devak's heart, and he felt an almost desperate need for Kayla. He couldn't, wouldn't even think about the possibility that this was a dead end.

Behind him, he could hear the lorry's suspension engine starting up, then the scattering of gravel as the lev-truck turned around and pulled back on the roadway. Devak and his friends were on their own again.

At least it was a warm breeze swirling around instead of the chill they'd endured in Cati and Amik sectors. He'd never been this far southeast—in fact he'd never been in Eastern Territory at all.

The lights of Belk's central ward shone faintly in the distance. Devak guessed they had an hour's walk.

Usi moved up beside Devak. "What if these GENs are like the ones in Cati sector?"

"Those GENs hated trueborns," Devak said. "We're not trueborns. We're allabain."

Junjie came up on Devak's other side. "From what I've heard, Belk sector GENs tend to have a different attitude about other ranks. They're treated better—still not quite equal to a trueborn, but their supervisors know they can't be easily replaced, so they get more respect. And besides the special way they're genned, there's the value of plassfiber itself."

Devak's Academy network had had a year-long module that taught all aspects of the plassfiber mining and production cycle. Gasified plassfiber powered electrical plants. Melted, it was used to make plasscine, plasscrete, and plassteel. Even the nomadic allabain lowborns used plass products, in particular sturdy plasscine cloth for their portable tent homes.

Raw plassfiber was so hazardous to handle, the GENs who worked in the mines were specially designed genetically to do the work. Their bodies expelled the fiber when it got in their lungs or skin. They could even digest it if it made its way into their food. Otherwise, they wouldn't last more than five or at most ten years at the work.

There was a time when lowborns were the ones mining plassfiber. They had strong enough backs for the work, but their lungs would fill up with the fibers until they got so inflamed, the miners couldn't breathe. It was a horrible way to die.

Junjie patted Devak's shoulder. "Look."

Devak glimpsed the flash of movement in the direction Junjie had pointed. Devak's heart raced at the sight of black on black, a hint of red caught by the moonlight. A bhimkay out hunting. Even though it was several meters away, and despite Risa's assurance that they wouldn't attack three humans together, Devak was relieved when it disappeared into the darkness again.

Even with the bhimkay out of sight, Devak picked up his pace, Junjie and Usi speeding up with him. He was glad when he could finally see the outskirts of Belk's central ward.

Devak's relief vanished when he spied the line of enforcers ranged across the roadway, all of them with shockguns ready.

25

Just as Devak thought to duck into the concealment of the sticker bushes and junk trees on either side of the road, one of the enforcers shouted. Three of them broke off and approached at a fast trot.

The first to reach them was a captain, the name Reit stitched above the bhimkay emblem on his uniform. He replaced his shockgun into its holster, then pulled out a sekai. He tapped at the sekai's screen, and while one of his troops held an illuminator up to Devak's and the other boys' faces, Reit studied each of them. He must be comparing their faces to whatever images he was scrolling through on the sekai.

Devak gave Usi a sidelong look and could see the boy's barely contained terror. Devak could sense that Usi was on the edge of running. The other two enforcers still had their shockguns out and ready. They'd cut the boy down in an instant.

Junjie moved to step behind Usi, and wrapped his arms around him. He rested his chin on Usi's shoulder, just an ordinary embrace, but Devak saw how Junjie's knuckles were white from his tight grip. It worked, though. Usi stayed put.

But the boy couldn't seem to help but squirm as the captain kept his gaze narrowed on him. The captain checked the sekai again, then Usi's face. Was this the moment he would be discovered? What would they do if the Captain had Usi arrested for being involved in the Nafi bombing?

Devak didn't realize he was holding his breath until the captain put away his sekai. "Names and village," Reit demanded.

For a moment, Devak's mind went blank. Then he kicked his brain back into functioning, calling up what they'd worked out with Kiyomi. She had allabain relatives and had coached them.

"I'm Shandor," Devak said, doing his best at a lowborn accent. He pointed to Junjie, then Usi. "This is Besnik and Pesha. We're all from Aki's village."

Aki was Kiyomi's allabain sister. Aki didn't lead the village, none of the nomadic allabain truly did. But on the off chance this particular Brigade captain tracked down Aki, she would vouch for them.

"Business here?" Reit asked.

This, Risa had suggested. "Loading plassfiber bales," Devak said.

Reit's gaze dropped to Devak's hands. Reflexively he closed them, not wanting the captain to see the lack of fiber scars on his palms.

Junjie spoke up. "We never work without gloves. My da died of the fiber fever. Piece of plass made its way from his hands to his brain."

Devak gave Junjie a nudge before he got even more creative. But it seemed to satisfy Reit. That and a thorough search of Devak's carrysak.

To Devak's surprise, although the captain flipped through

the stack of dhans, he didn't filch any. Maybe Reit was just making sure these three scruffy allabain weren't carrying a suspiciously large amount of money. The captain did take note of the three pairs of work gloves, and asked where Devak had gotten the wristlink that Fahim had given him. *From my ma*, Devak told Reit.

Released by the captain, Devak, Junjie, and Usi continued on. Devak could feel the three enforcers following them, but the line of enforcers up ahead let Devak and his friends pass.

As they wove themselves amongst the GENs crowding the streets, Junjie looked back over his shoulder at the vigilant Brigade. "That captain was almost polite."

"Only because it's Belk," Devak suggested. "Like you said, more respect paid to GENs here, and I guess lowborns too."

Usi lowered his voice. "I thought I was done when that captain was checking our faces. I was sure I'd be on his sekai."

"You might have been," Devak said. "But between the allabain earring and all the grime, you must look different from whatever image they have."

"Speaking of which," Junjie said, "there's a water spigot. We ought to at least wash our faces and hands."

The spigot, set in front of a GEN warehouse, had a line of three GENs waiting to use it. As Devak waited, he kept an eye on the Brigade in the distance. He washed quickly when it was his turn, then stepped aside for Junjie and Usi, still wary of the enforcers.

"So who are the Brigade looking for, do you suppose?" Junjie asked as they edged back into the crowd.

Devak stepped aside out of the path of a GEN, nodding a greeting. "Whoever set those bombs in Ekat and Amik would be my guess."

"Yeah, likely," Junjie said. "And no wonder they're watching everyone coming into Belk. An explosion like that at any of the plassfiber mines would be disastrous. Can you imagine if there wasn't any fuel for the power generators? Nothing to build houses with, or even make something as simple as a sheet of plasscine for an allabain tent?"

Devak scanned the warrens up ahead. "Where do you suppose we'll find a public house?"

"In a GEN sector?" Usi said. "I doubt even Belk has one of those."

"We can't just barge into someone's warren," Devak said.

Usi flushed. "I never would have done that if I'd had any other choices."

Devak shrugged. "You did what you had to. Do we sleep outside, between the buildings in one of the alleyways? That's what real allabain would do. Especially since it's not that cold. We could probably find an out of the way spot."

Although that might be easier said than done, considering the crowd. It being Belk, where the mining operations went on around the clock, the streets were as busy this late in the evening as they would have been in midday. The bustle meant sometimes a GEN would bump into Devak, mutter a quick apology, then hurry on. It was a relief to just be an allabain, to not have GENs cowering from him or lowborns angry and resentful seeing him.

They'd reached the teeming center of the ward, where five-story warrens on either side loomed over the main street, Sischa. Other than the lack of a patch of green scrap grass, you could have mistaken Belk's central ward for the square in a mixed sector.

Booths were set up along the fronts of the warrens, GEN

merchants selling men's kortas and women's skirts, brilliantly colored woven plasscine scarves that looked almost as fine as uttama silk. Every plassfiber-based item you could imagine was arrayed in the booths—serving bowls and utensils, small tables, and jewelry. Miniature carved seycats, droms, and even bhimkay.

A foodstand offered roasted meat, kel-grain rolls, and fruit melds. The line leading up to it snaked across the ward.

"If we're going to start asking about Kayla," Devak said, "this would be the place to do it."

"Except everyone is on their way to somewhere else," Junjie said.

Junjie pulled Usi aside to allow a group of broad-shouldered GENs to pass. The men and women had the signs of having just finished their shift in the mines—their hair was wet from the cleansing shower used to rinse away lingering fibers.

They were close enough to the foodstand that the rich fragrance of meat and fresh-baked rolls beckoned to Devak. He inhaled deeply, eyeing the long line.

"There's one group that's not going anywhere," Devak said, starting toward the end of the line.

Junjie followed, Usi's arm tucked in his. As they took their places, a young GEN woman in a miner's coverall immediately queued up after them. Her short brown curls were still dripping with the cleansing fluid.

Devak wasn't sure what to say. He couldn't just blurt out why they were in Belk, especially to this stranger who looked to be nearly ten years older than him. And having had to leave the holo projector behind in the carrysak, he didn't have Kayla's image to share anymore.

He supposed he could start with small talk. "Is the food worth the wait?"

The GEN woman smiled. "It is. I haven't seen you in Patia's line before. Have you just arrived here?"

"We have," Devak said. "We're hoping for some work toting plassfiber bales. I'm Shandor. These are my village brothers, Pesha and Besnik."

"I'm Qia," the woman said, dipping her head in greeting to Junjie and Usi.

Devak scrambled for a way to continue the conversation. "Have you been in Belk a long time?"

"Twelve years," Qia said. "This was my first Assignment. Only Assignment. You know, designed for Belk."

"You like the work?" Devak asked, then mentally kicked himself. As a GEN designed for the work, she hadn't had any choice but to labor in the plassfiber mines.

But Qia didn't seem to take offense. "It's better than some Assignments a GEN could have."

Then the GEN man behind Qia claimed her attention, and Devak realized he'd have to start over with another GEN. But Junjie nudged Devak aside and stepped up to Qia.

"We were asked to pass on a message to a GEN girl who might be here in Belk," Junjie said. "She's a nurture daughter of Tala."

Qia's eyes went wide. "Tala of Chadi sector?"

A shock ran through Devak. "You know Tala?"

"Tala is Patia's nurture mother," Qia said. "Patia who runs the foodstand. She and her nurture sister, Peria, were both designed for the mines, and were Assigned here together the year before I was. But there was a problem with the way Patia was genned. The fibers made her sick. Her patron found out she could cook and re-Assigned her to the foodstand. Peria still works in the mines."

"It's hard to believe a trueborn would be so compassionate," Devak said. "Give Patia a new Assignment here where she could be close to her sister."

"It's different here," Qia said. "Whoever you're looking for would be Patia's nurture sister. You can ask her when you get up to the front."

Qia again turned to the GEN man behind her, smiling and flirting at him in a way that made it clear they knew each other. A few moments later, Qia and the man left the line and disappeared into the crowd.

The line's forward progress seemed to have slowed to a crawl. Devak leaned around to try to see why, but there were too many people in the way. "Maybe we should forget about the food and just go up front to talk to Patia."

"I say be patient," Junjie said. "I'm hungry enough to eat a drom whole, and anyway, I think Patia would feel better about talking to us if we bought the food she's cooking."

Devak turned to Usi to ask his opinion, then noticed the intent way the boy was staring at the last warren on the same side of Sischa Street as the foodstand. "What is it?" Devak asked.

"A girl just went in that last warren with a carrysak," Usi said.

"What's wrong with that?" Devak asked.

Usi kept his gaze fixed on the warren. "First, from her looks and the way she was dressed—nicer than everything I've seen here yet—she looked like a trueborn, not a lowborn or GEN. Second, even worse . . ."

Just then, a light-skinned girl about Kayla's age emerged from the warren. "She doesn't have the carrysak anymore," Devak said.

"Chutting hell!" Usi spat out. "We have to get the enforcers. Now!"

Trivial thoughts ran through Devak's mind, that they shouldn't leave their place in line, that they had to buy their food. But when Usi took off through the crowd toward the Brigade, Junjie on his heels, Devak was only a half step behind them.

"Let me through!" Usi was shouting, "let me through!"

Devak forced his way ahead of Usi, using his taller, broader body to make a path. Once they were clear of the crowd and into the near-empty buffer zone around the Brigade, Usi surged ahead.

"I think I just saw someone plant a bomb!" Usi yelled. "The last warren on the left."

Reit hurried over, motioning his enforcers to join him. He planted a hand on Usi's back, directing him toward the warren. The crowd parted for the captain and his enforcers, giving ample room for Devak and Junjie on either side of Usi and the captain.

"What did you see?" Reit asked.

"A trueborn girl went in with a heavy carrysak," Usi said, gasping for breath. "She came out without it."

"Then she left it in there?" Reit lowered his voice, so that only he, Usi, Devak, and Junjie could have heard. "Where do you think she might have put it?"

Devak jumped in. "We weren't anywhere near the warren. He has no way of knowing."

"Under the first floor stairs," Usi said. "That way the explosion goes all the way up to the top floor."

Reit didn't even blink. "Will it damage the other warrens?"

"Don't think so," Usi said. "Not with what it looked like she was carrying."

Reit nodded, then spoke into his wristlink. "Eighth warren,

under the first floor stairs." To the squad behind him, he said, "As quietly as you can, clear the ward. Pray to the Lord Creator we can get the shield in place in time. No telling how many first and third shift mine workers are in their flats in the eighth."

An alarm screamed from the other side of the ward. It was all the enforcers could do to keep the crowd organized enough to move away from the eighth warren without trampling anyone.

Once most of the crowd was behind him, Devak could see the big Brigade lorry, its black sides emblazoned with the bhimkay emblem, backing up to the eighth warren. Several enforcers dressed in helmets and body armor poured out the back.

Two enforcers ran into the warren. The rest wrestled with something heavy in the lorry's bay. When it cleared the back doors, Devak could make out what looked like a heavy plassteel dome. It took six men to carry it to the middle of the now-empty ward.

Devak's heart pounded so loud the noise of the crowd blurred. There was no way to know when that bomb might get set off. Would the enforcers get the shield in place in time? Would it even have enough strength to contain the explosion?

The two enforcers emerged from the building, walking close together with the carrysak between them. Their body armor would mute the destructive power of the explosion, although they'd die themselves. Was their motive for saving those inside only because of the GENs' value as plass miners? Or did they simply want to protect lives? Either way, it was an incredibly brave act.

They set the carrysak down beside the shield, and the other team of enforcers shifted the plassteel dome on top of it. Could the trueborn girl see what had happened? Where had she gone?

Did she have a detonator, or was the bomb on a timer?

Even expecting it, the thunder of the detonation caught Devak off guard. He hunched in reaction, fearing flying debris. But the shield did its job, containing the explosion.

Reit turned to Usi, his sekai in his hand. "This *is* you."

Devak got a glimpse of the image. Usi was likely a year or two younger in the picture, maybe his last Academy identity capture, before he joined FHE. Devak could see why the captain wasn't sure. Usi had changed a lot over the intervening time, his hair longer, his cheekbones more prominent and his chin narrower because he'd lost so much weight.

"I didn't know what was in the carrysak at Nafi," Usi said. "That girl might not have known, either."

Reit gestured with the sekai. "Even so, I have to arrest you."

"No," Junjie moaned.

Usi got a wild look in his eyes, not so much fear as defiance. He turned and pelted across the ward, dodging enforcers and GENs who had filtered back.

Reit pulled his shockgun. Junjie, roaring, body-blocked the captain hard, sending Reit to the pavement. Scrambling back onto his feet, Junjie took off after Usi, Devak right behind him.

Dimly, Devak heard shouting, orders from Reit. *Catch them!* Devak spied Usi ducking down the alley between the eighth warren and the seventh next to it. Junjie had nearly caught up with him. By the time Devak reached the alley, he could see Usi and Junjie running together and could hear the thunder of bootsteps behind him.

When Devak turned at the far end of the alley, Usi and Junjie were nowhere in sight. As Devak looked desperately to the left and right, someone grabbed the back of his shirt and yanked him to the left.

338

"Enforcers will be here any second," a woman's voice whispered.

Devak let himself be pulled into the dark ground floor flat at the back of the seventh warren. The door latched shut behind them.

"Your friends are here," the woman said, and now Devak recognized her as Qia, who had stood behind them in line.

She didn't turn on a light, just kept pulling Devak along. He tried to picture the flat, based on his guess that it looked like the one the GEN enforcer, Waji, had in Cati sector. They must be in the sleeproom. He heard a door slide open. The closet?

Qia tugged him inside, and hanging clothes slapped him in the face. "Slide the door shut behind you," she whispered.

Just as he did, he heard a banging on the door. Qia muttered under her breath, "Denk it. They're here already." A crash signaled that the enforcers were trying to break the door down.

Devak heard a scraping sound, then felt a roil of cool air from the back of the closet. Qia grabbed his arm and pulled him through the hanging clothes, closer to the chill. Stretching out his arm, she placed his hand on what felt like a plasscrete rung that protruded from the wall of whatever space lay in the darkness. To hold on, he had to lean into the unseen.

"I don't dare turn on an illuminator," Qia whispered. "They might see it through the closet door. That's a ladder rung. You're going to have to feel with your foot to climb down. Your friends are below."

"Aren't you coming?" Devak asked.

"This is my flat," Qia said. "If I don't answer soon, those enforcers will make a mess of my door. Patia is down there to help you. Stay clear of the walls."

When Devak hesitated, Qia all but shoved him into the blackness so that he had to grope with his other hand for the rung. He swung out into the access, feet dangling until he managed to get a toehold. He heard the secret door slide shut, giving him no choice but to descend.

The ladder seemed to go forever, nothing like the Kinship safe house access tunnels that tended to go six or so meters belowground. It got colder the lower he got until he started to shiver. The korta Risa had given him was more suited to Belk's balmy climate, not this growing iciness. His legs and arms trembled from the exertion as well.

Finally he heard voices, faint but audible. He couldn't make out words, but he recognized Junjie's light tenor. And Usi answering, interwoven with a woman's voice. Relieved that there was an end to his descent, Devak pushed himself to keep going.

"Devak?" Junjie called up, not so far away now. "I'm going to turn on the illuminator."

Devak was glad for the warning because the light pierced his eyes. He stopped long enough to let himself adjust to the glow.

So tired. He sagged a little, just about to lean against the wall for a rest.

"Don't touch the walls!" the woman shouted up at him, her voice harsh and raspy, far worse than Risa's.

"This is all part of the plass mines," Junjie called out. "Not as much of the fiber here, but you want to avoid contact."

Now that the illuminator was on, Devak became aware of just how tight the space was that he was in. Had he rubbed against that rough yellowish surface? He couldn't feel the prick of the dangerous raw fibers.

Now his muscles trembled even more as he continued on. As

he got close to the bottom, he felt hands steadying him. When he stepped off the last rung of the ladder, he was so relieved to see Junjie and Usi safe, he threw his arms around them both.

Patia, the woman from the food stall, stood just beyond Junjie and Usi in the tunnel. She eyed Devak as if she wasn't sure she liked him. She was well-muscled but compact, likely genned to work in some of the smaller spaces in the mine before her fiber-sickness lost her that Assignment. Her skin was a red-brown, her long hair thick and dark. If she'd been Assigned in Belk thirteen years ago as a fifteenth-year, she would have left Tala's home before Kayla arrived.

Devak could see questions in the GEN woman's eyes, but she just motioned them along. "Let's get a little farther on where it's wider." Just a few feet on, Patia coughed, hacking so hard she had to stop and lean her hands on her knees. "Denking plassfiber."

They walked single file for several minutes after Patia got her breath back. She led the way with one illuminator, and Junjie and Usi each had one of their own. Devak could have pulled one from his carrysak, but he was worried he'd knock an elbow into the wall in the process.

They reached a T where there was more space, and Patia stopped to face Devak. "You say you know Tala."

"I've never met Tala," Devak admitted. "I know her nurture daughter, Kayla."

"Everyone knows Kayla," Patia rasped. "Knows how she saved those lowborn children in Sheysa sector."

"I'm Devak, one of the trueborns who helped her."

Patia's dark gaze continued to flay him for several moments more. "Where's your bali?"

Devak took the long allabain earring from his ear and

stuffed it into the carrysak. He pinched the sapphire from the hem of his shirt and replaced it in his right ear.

"And everyone knows," Patia went on, "that Kayla was killed by a bomb."

"Not killed," Devak said. "I had an image of her from after the bomb. FHE took her and somehow saved her."

Now Patia's eyes flickered a little wider. "They took her . . ."

"Do you know something?" Devak asked.

"Maybe. Qia's the one in charge of these tunnels," Patia said. "These aren't part of the company excavation. Over the years, GENs have dug tunnels on their own, on the sly. Kept rich veins hidden, sold the plass on the black market. Then a couple years ago, a GEN named Ohin approached Qia, told her if she dug some tunnels for him in certain places, he'd pay enough to make it worth her while."

Devak turned to Junjie and Usi. "Any idea who Ohin is?" They both shook their heads.

"Qia couldn't do it herself, and I'm less than useless with my fiber-sickness," Patia said. "My nurture sister, Pelia, helped, and a select few of the other miners, the ones we could trust not to go squawking to the Brigade. And we all share the dhans when they're paid out."

"Is it this Ohin who pays?" Devak asked.

Patia shook her head. "Not since the first visit. They change who pays nearly every time. And Qia's picked up hints that these tunnels that we built aren't all of them."

"But do you know something about Kayla?" Devak asked again.

"Months ago," Patia said, "right around when that explosion happened in Two Rivers, two trueborns came through Belk. They found Qia and paid the fee to use the passageway."

Devak was beginning to lose patience with Patia's roundabout way of telling her story. "How does that connect to Kayla?" he asked.

"Qia said when the trueborns came through her flat, they had a portable gen-tank with them. Ever seen one? Like a plasscine bag, with a board inside to keep the GEN stable. The girl in the tank was a little thing, but they still had a denking hard time getting the tank through. Had to lower it with ropes. That was Kayla?"

"Must have been." Stunned by what Patia had told him, it took Devak a moment to pull his thoughts together. "Where did they go?"

Patia shrugged. "Other than back into the mine"—she gestured down the T—"there's only one other place this tunnel goes. To the western edge of the Badlands."

Kayla and Shakki traveled all night, by moonlight while the trinity moons were in the sky, then by starlight after the moons set. Kayla clung to Tak's hair barbs, eyes straining to see in the darkness, praying to the Infinite that the bhimkay's vision was better than hers. And that she was reading her inner map correctly, and they were heading due west toward the settled sectors.

The big spiders kept up their swift pace, springing from boulder to boulder, jumping across the gaps between them as if they were only centimeters wide instead of meters.

Finally the sky lightened to pale green, Iyenku rising in the east, its white light brilliant as the first of the brother suns lifted above the horizon of boulders. Now Kayla could see the stunted junk trees and sticker bushes trying to grow from the crevasses in the more western edge of the Badlands, the occasional naga squirming into a crack in fear as the bhimkay passed. A cluster of wild spiders, luckily far off in the distance, leapt and galloped almost in sync with Tak and Pev.

When their bhimkay began to hesitate, Kayla started

watching for a crevasse shallow enough to climb in and out of, but narrow enough that a wild bhimkay couldn't reach them. She halted Tak. Shakki jumped Pev over to the same boulder. "They're tiring," Kayla said. "We've got to stop."

They both dismounted and threw their carrysaks down into the crevasse. Kayla lowered Shakki inside, then slipped in herself. After scrambling along the crevasse in opposite directions, they relieved themselves, then returned to wolf down a nutra and a strip of rat-snake meat. After a few swallows of water, they lay down and fell immediately to sleep.

Three hours later, Kayla jolted awake, flooded by the urgency to get moving. She woke Shakki and climbed from the crevasse, three of the five carrysaks on her shoulders. Then she pulled Shakki up with the last two carrysaks. The bhimkay were finishing off a naga they'd found. Kayla and Shakki mounted and once the spiders finished, they were off again.

Thick black clouds coiled off to the east, although at the moment, they stayed there. The refreshed spiders leapt and galloped across the crevasse-split boulders as the brother suns rose high in the sky. Their light shed no warmth, the air remaining cold as they traveled.

When it grew dark, they stopped again. Lowering Shakki down was harder for Kayla this time, her muscles fatigued by the long hours riding. The bhimkay seemed disinclined to hunt as well. The spiders each took a few moments to straddle a crevasse several meters from the one Shakki was in and drop scat, then crouched to rest.

Kayla lowered herself into the shallow crevasse and stumbled along to find her own spot to relieve herself. When she returned, Shakki was already asleep. There was space, so Kayla squeezed in beside the smaller girl.

As she lay there too exhausted to sleep, the drumbeat to find Devak thrummed inside her. But it would do none of them any good to exhaust themselves into injury or worse.

Shakki was shivering, maybe too deeply asleep to engage her warming circuitry. Kayla got up and fumbled for Jadi's larger carrysak until she put her hands on one of the illuminators. Making sure to keep the light away from Shakki's face, she found two of Jadi's shirts.

She spread one of them over Shakki, then pulled the other one on herself. She would burn less energy wearing the extra shirt than by using her circuitry. She had to roll up the long sleeves to keep her hands free, but it was nice how it dropped to her knees.

Kayla's heart ached at this last gift from Jadi. If he now lay peacefully in the Infinite's mighty hands, could the boy see how he was keeping her and Shakki warm?

She was so edgy anyway, she decided she might as well take a closer look at the contents of Jadi's carrysak. *There's something inside*, he'd said. *You'll know when you see it.*

The illuminator clenched in her teeth, she pulled everything from the carrysak. She found his leggings, which she shook out before folding them again. Some dried naga meat—that would be tastier than the rat-snake—and plenty of water. Some handheld illuminators. His prayer mirror, made of a thin sheet of precious shiny metal, worn from much use.

Whatever he'd meant by his dying words, she hadn't found it yet. She examined the clear plasscine sheet that Jadi had wrapped the dried meat in, and opened each of the half dozen water bottles to peer inside. She found nothing.

He'd brought a sekai, which excited her at first until she realized it had no networking function installed. It was only a reader, filled with the kind of bloody stories boys seemed to like.

She checked the empty carrysak, running the illuminator over its insides. Back when she'd first been Assigned, the carrysak she'd been given had had a false bottom attached with mag-connectors. There had been a packet of DNA underneath, which she'd been asked to transport for what she later learned was the Kinship.

But the bottom of Jadi's carrysak was the same rugged woven plasscine on the inside as it was on the outside. Had Jadi's terror in his last moments given more weight to his words? Had he only meant they'd need the extra provisions?

That made no sense. There had to be something more in the carrysak. Unless, sweet Infinite, they'd lost it in their mad rush during the night.

Kayla hoped that wasn't the case. The way Jadi had died had been so horrible. And to have to leave him there—Kayla's heart was still heavy at the thought.

Taking up Jadi's prayer mirror, she sent a silent prayer up to the Infinite. Surely Jadi was there in His hands.

She carefully wrapped the prayer mirror in a pair of Jadi's leggings, then returned everything to the carrysak. When they got to the settled sectors, she'd be able to search it more thoroughly. She could be missing something in the poor light.

One of the bhimkay stirred on the boulder above her, and her stomach lurched. Could Ohin and the Bhimkay Boys be pursuing them on their own spiders?

But Ohin's other bhimkay had scattered, and the babies had to be crawling around everywhere. That had to slow Ohin and the boys down. And they wouldn't be able to make it through the terrain she and Shakki had just crossed on anything but a bhimkay.

But then there were Ohin's secret passageways. There

was no way of knowing where those let out.

That sent a new kind of chill up Kayla's back. Images flashed through her mind of Ohin suddenly appearing out of nowhere into the crevasse, the Bhimkay Boys right behind him.

Kayla forced the nightmare thoughts from her mind and lay beside Shakki. She had to rest, or she'd be no good to anyone.

An eerie howling woke Kayla from a deep sleep, chill wind reaching into the crevasse almost like a live thing. Dim light seeped into the crevasse, looking more like dusk despite her inner clock telling her it was morning.

Kayla nudged Shakki, then climbed the steep wall of the crevasse. When she got high enough to see out, it was a fight to hold on with the growing gale. Both spiders were hunkered down as low as they could go. The thick black clouds she'd seen off in the distance yesterday now boiled toward them with the wind.

Kayla carefully descended again. "Storm coming," she told Shakki. "Bad one."

"Even if this crevasse was enough to protect us," Shakki said, "the bhimkay might get hurt. They're too exposed."

"Then we'll need to find a place for all of us to hole up."

They quickly cleared out of the crevasse, Kayla grabbing carrysaks, then helping Shakki out. Once they'd mounted, the bhimkay seemed eager to go. Tak quickly headed off on an angle to their previous route, more southwest than west. But as Pev kept pace beside the female, Kayla was inclined to let the bhimkay's instincts guide them.

The storm was like a monster stalking them, like some horror out of a bedtime tale. At one point, a gust struck Tak in mid-leap and nearly cast both bhimkay and rider into a wide crevasse. Pev stumbled on a landing, and Shakki shrieked. Kayla spared a quick glance back to see the girl hanging off Pev's side, scrambling up on his back.

The gale gained even more power, strong enough that one of the carrysaks threatened to fly off Kayla's shoulder. She scanned their surroundings, praying the bhimkay were taking them somewhere safe. Then she spotted a bit of darkness centered in the boulders up ahead.

"Could that be a cave?" Kayla asked.

"Can't see it," Shakki said. "But if you think we should try . . ."

Even with Tak's and Pev's willingness, it was a struggle to get across the rocky, crevasse-sliced terrain with the ever increasing wind slamming into them. Tak kept choosing an indirect route to that shadow in the rocks, avoiding spans that were too wide. The longer the bhimkay were jumping through the air, the farther they could be blown off course or into disaster.

Infinite, let that be a shelter, Kayla silently prayed. It was getting dimmer still as the clouds closed in, and she wasn't sure anymore of what she'd seen at a distance.

But bit by bit, Tak and Pev directed their jumps toward that spot of black. And as they got nearer, Kayla could see the pile of boulders and the protected gap within it.

And it was bhimkay-sized, she realized with relief. She and Shakki had to dismount, and the spiders had to crouch at the entrance, but once inside, they could stand full height. There was enough space for them all to get fully out of the storm's force. Tak and Pev settled in a dark alcove in the back, the bhimkay's legs entangling as they tucked them under.

"What's that?" Shakki asked, peering into a shadowy corner. "Looks like a stack of crates."

Kayla surveyed the three crates locked together like the ones in Godama 2. "Then someone's been here before us."

Shakki opened the top one. "Medical supplies. Some of the packages have been opened, vac-seals removed."

"I suppose it makes sense that they've staged supplies here."

"Except . . ." Shakki unlocked the top crate from the next one down. "It's all the sort of material you'd use in a gen-tank. There's gen-fluid. Some pretty powerful healing drugs. Pratija, like what Palla used on me when I got cut up by Pev. And even some crysophora. We should probably take some of this with us."

Shakki set aside the second crate to reach the one on the bottom. There was only one item inside, and it was sani-sealed. "Huh. I've never seen one of these before."

"What is it?" Kayla asked, coming over. For some reason, the greenish, plasscine-looking thing gave her a chill.

"A portable gen-tank," Shakki said. "Not really a tank. More like a bag that you'd use in an emergency if someone was badly ill or injured. There'd be a board to keep the person stable and—"

Suddenly, Kayla swayed and grabbed the rock wall. "Ohin said they brought me to Antara in a portable tank. Could that be it?"

Shakki looked down at it. "Maybe. They could have kept you here until you were stable enough to take the rest of the way on spider-back."

"But I don't remember any of that," Kayla said.

"They've manipulated your memories before," Shakki pointed out.

"Maybe that's how Tak and Pev made their way to this cave," Kayla guessed. "They've been here before and they knew they'd find shelter."

"Spider-back would have been the quickest way to get you to Antara," Shakki said. "Way quicker than the passageways.

But it would have been too awkward to try to carry you in the portable tank on top of a bhimkay."

"So they had me astride a spider," Kayla said, "maybe strapped to one of them while I was unconscious. Then they put me into the regular tank once they got me to Antara. I *do* have some very vague memories of being in the tank. Dreams, sort of. And that's where I was when I woke up."

While Shakki replaced the contents of the crates and restacked them, Kayla wandered over to the other side of the small cavern, opposite the alcove where the spiders were. "There's an opening over here that goes in deeper. Like a passageway. Do you think this is where they brought me through the Wall?"

"Maybe. If that *is* the portable tank you were in. I never knew about a passageway this far out though."

"Do you think it connects with any others?" Kayla asked.

"No idea," Shakki said. "But it doesn't make sense to dig a passageway to here when you can just ride the spiders."

"We'd better stay out of it. I don't want to be anywhere the bhimkay can't reach us."

Worry gnawed at Kayla. What if this passageway *was* connected to the others? What if Ohin could find them here that way? Despairing, Kayla looked out the cave entrance at the dark power of the storm. "How long will this last? How long before we can travel again?"

Shakki came over and gave her a hug. "We'll get to your trueborn in time. I'm sure of it."

Kayla wanted to believe her, but it had been two days already. Even so, there was nothing they could do but wait the storm out.

Kayla and Shakki each used a palmful of their precious

water to wash their hands and faces. Kayla doled out some of the naga meat and divided a redfruit between them. She wasn't the least bit hungry, but she knew her body needed fuel, so she forced herself to eat.

The bhimkay got a meal as well when a naga blundered through a crack in the cavern just above the spiders. Kayla had never seen Tak move so fast. The bhimkay had the snake-like creature bitten and half-paralyzed in seconds. Tak fed on one end and deigned to let Pev enjoy the other.

Kayla thought she wouldn't be able to drop off, especially since she'd slept so hard the night before. But her body had other ideas. Snuggled up to Shakki for shared warmth, dressed in Jadi's shirt, sleep quickly pulled her under.

Tak's hiss woke her to a drowsy awareness. Then footsteps—human footsteps—jolted her completely awake.

She sat up, Shakki rousing beside her. *Someone's coming,* Kayla said.

Shakki glanced out the opening where the wind still howled. *Not from outside. From that passageway you found.* Shakki's eyes went wide. *What do we do? What if it's Ohin?*

They had no weapons but themselves . . . and the bhimkay. Motioning to Shakki, Kayla grabbed her three carrysaks. Shakki hooked her two and they retreated to where the two spiders now stood at full alert.

The footsteps grew louder. She heard a murmur of voices, could see glimmers of light.

She fumbled in Jadi's carrysak and found an illuminator and shined it in the direction of the passageway.

Someone emerged, tall and broad-shouldered. Kayla tipped her illuminator up to the figure's face.

It was Devak.

27

Kayla?"

He said her name so softly, Kayla thought for sure it was an illusion, a hallucination created by her aching heart after so many hopeless days and nights of longing for him. Then she dropped the carrysaks and ran across the cavern toward him. She flung herself into his arms.

She didn't care if she'd gone crazy and was imagining him. She only cared that he felt warm and alive and was *here*, miraculously restored to her.

"Kayla," he whispered, holding her close, as if he wanted to draw her inside him. "Thank the Lord Creator I found you."

Her heart shouted, *I love you, Devak!* but she feared saying the words out loud, afraid it would cause him and the dream to vanish. "How did you get here? We were on our way to you!"

"We followed your trail," Devak said. "Mishalla passed on the message you sent. That got us to Belk. Then in Belk we found one of Tala's nurture daughters, and she remembered your portable gen-tank coming through the passageway. But to find you here, where the passageway ends . . . that has to be the Lord Creator's blessing."

"And the Infinite's."

A hiss from the opposite side of the cavern where Tak crouched with Pev drew Kayla's attention briefly from Devak. Devak didn't seem to notice, his gaze only on her.

Kayla put out a hand in a calming gesture, hoping Tak would obey. "Who came with you?" she asked Devak.

More footsteps sounded from the passageway and Junjie emerged, supporting another boy a head shorter than him. The other boy seemed dazed and in pain.

"Shakki!" Kayla called when she saw the boy.

Shakki had stayed back while Kayla greeted Devak, but now the younger girl hurried to assist Junjie. "This is Usi," Junjie said, his voice trembling. "You have to help him."

Shakki directed Junjie back toward the mouth of the cave where the crates were. "I've got some med training. And we have plenty of supplies, thank the Infinite."

Another hiss from Tak, and now Pev joined in. The bhimkay had had enough of the intruders. They lunged out of their hiding place toward Devak.

Devak put an arm out to push Kayla behind him, but that only agitated Tak more. "If we can get everyone to the tunnel," Devak said, "I don't think they can follow. The entry is too narrow."

Kayla got in front of Devak. "You're safe if you just stay back a moment, until I reassure them. Better yet, go over there by Shakki."

"Where did they come from?" Devak asked.

Kayla made the calming gesture to Pev and Tak in turn. "We rode them here." She glanced over her shoulder to see

Devak was still right behind her. "Please. *I'm* fine, but you're not. You've got to go over where Shakki is."

Devak finally retreated. It took a little longer than usual for Kayla to persuade Pev to relax into his familiar indolent crouch, but he did finally. That seemed to ease Tak's anxiety, because she quieted too, curling her legs beside Pev.

Once the bhimkay were calmed, Kayla felt she could focus on helping Shakki with Usi. Shakki had shucked the extra shirt of Jadi's that she'd been wearing. Kayla did the same, and they made a bed for the boy, using a rolled-up pair of Jadi's leggings for a pillow. Junjie helped Usi lie down, especially careful of his head.

Shakki shone an illuminator into the boy's eyes, one at a time. "How do you feel?"

"Sleepy. Sick to my stomach," Usi said. "Everything's blurry."

Junjie sat cross-legged opposite Shakki and took the boy's hand. "There was an explosion at the Amik GAMA lab where we were hiding and Usi was badly hurt. Risa and Kiyomi picked us up and Usi had some time to recover, but he overdid it in Belk running from the Brigade. Then a few hours ago he stumbled in the tunnel and bumped his head again."

"I overheard Ohin order someone to kill you and Zul," Kayla said to Devak. "Was that the GAMA lab explosion? Were you hurt? Is Zul okay?"

Devak grimaced. "As far as I know, Pitamah is fine. I spoke to him a few days ago. I did get a conk on the head too, but milder, and sprained my wrist." Devak held up his arm, where Kayla could see the snug bandage in the faint illuminator light. "Junjie and I both got some bruises, but Usi's the one who got the worst of it."

Shakki wielded a vac-seal filled with pratija. "It looks like he's having a reaction to the plassfiber in the passageway. This pink stuff is good for that. It should work on a trueborn as well as a GEN." She applied it liberally to Usi's hands and face.

Devak eyed Tak and Pev warily. "Why are the bhimkay so big?"

"Everything is in the Badlands. Bhimkay, rat-snakes. The naga are huge." Kayla pointed to the husk that Tak and Pev had left.

Shakki continued her ministrations to Usi, using the ample supplies from the crates, and it was obvious Kayla would only get in the way. So she took Devak's hand and walked him to another fold in the cavern wall, an alcove just the right size for the two of them.

Kayla pulled him inside and wrapped her arms around him. "I was so sure when I got to the settled sectors that I'd find out you were already dead."

"I nearly was." As he spoke, his breath warmed her ear.

"Your earring—it's sapphire." She stroked his right earlobe, liking the way he shivered in response.

He laughed softly. "Pitamah and I are minor-status now. I thought it would matter more to me, but it doesn't anymore."

Her fingers left his ear to trail along his cheek, and she felt a new roughness there. She looked closer and saw the scarring. "How did you get that?"

"The bomb blast in Two Rivers," Devak said. "The one that you—"

"It almost looks like—"

"A GEN tattoo. Pitamah said the gen-techs might still be able to fix it, but I wanted to keep it. Because it reminded me of you."

"Everything reminded me of you," Kayla said. "Thank the Infinite you found me."

Then he bent to kiss her and everything else melted away—the storm outside, her captivity with FHE, his near-death, the chasm between them as GEN and trueborn.

Devak kissed her again and again. Kayla never wanted to leave the relative privacy of the alcove. He whispered to her, "Whatever happens in the outside world, I want you with me, forever."

"Yes," she said.

More kisses, then dimly she heard Shakki call her name.

Kayla and Devak stepped back into the main cavern. "Is Usi okay?" Devak asked.

"Fine," Shakki said, "or he will be, with rest. But Junjie might have found something in Jadi's carrysak."

As Devak and Kayla walked over to the others, she explained to Devak, "Jadi was a friend who was killed during our escape."

Junjie held out the carrysak. "I was digging out some water to clean another head wound Shakki found on Usi, and I felt a lump in the side of the carrysak."

Kayla took it from Junjie. "I searched it. I never felt that." But now she could see the slight lump.

"Probably a secret pocket," Devak said. "I had one in my old carrysak. You need a thumbprint to open it. Ours was programmed for just me and Junjie."

Kayla went to the cavern entrance, hoping for a little more light. Outside, the wind roared explosively, driving dust and broken junk trees and sticker bushes sideways. Although her internal clock told her it was mid-afternoon, it looked like dusk.

But she could see the small bulge, and a faint mark inside the carrysak where a thumb should press. She tried putting her own thumb there, but the barely visible seam didn't open.

"It's set to Jadi's, not mine."

"But you're strong enough to rip it open," Devak said. "The thumb lock is only meant to slow a thief down, not stop him."

True enough. She pushed two fingers into the seam. When she felt she had a good enough grip, she ripped the inner pocket from the carrysak.

There was a clatter as whatever had been inside flew out and struck the floor. A datapod sat a meter from her foot.

She scooped up the thumb-sized device. "It's just as well I found this here. I could have lost it in one of the crevasses."

She lifted the datapod to her tattooed cheek. Devak grabbed her wrist to stop her. "What if it resets you?"

"I can block a reset. And it must be very important if Jadi locked it in his carrysak."

With the datapod lined up to the electronics embedded in her face, she pressed the activate button. The extendibles bit her skin, the pricks of pain so familiar she barely winced. She acknowledged and accepted the contents of the datapod.

First a stream of data flooded in. It seemed to be dates and locations, although she let it pass without too much analysis. Hopefully there would be something that followed it that would explain.

Then she heard Aideen's voice, as if she were speaking through a circuit-comm. Kayla jolted and nearly pulled the datapod free before it finished. She had to stop the message and request that it restart.

I couldn't take the chance, Aideen said, *that something would happen to Jadi and he couldn't pass this information on. So I downloaded the data in his annexed brain and used his circuit-comm to record the data and this message onto the datapod.*

What you have to know is this—Ohin is truly starting a war. This isn't something he's playing at. He's used lies to stir up his followers, pretending to have made inroads into trueborn defenses. But he's actually gone much further than any of them know.

That bomb that nearly killed you in Two Rivers? That was just a test, to see if FHE could do in trueborn and mixed sectors what they did in GEN warrens and warehouses.

The offensive begins tonight in Belk sector, both as a way to damage the plassfiber mining industry, and as a signal. Operatives he's placed throughout Svarga know to time their bombs in waves after they've gotten word that Belk has exploded.

By now, Ohin has discovered you're gone. He's sent the remaining Bhimkay Boys overland on spider-back to Pashi sector and other surrounding trueborn and mixed sectors to assist in the coming battles. He himself is leading an army of himayati GENs and trueborns through the passageways that lead from here to Belk.

All the trueborns with him will be glad to die, eager to. But what the himayati trueborns don't know is that he intends to kill them as well as outsiders. He intends that GENs alone will rule.

I doubt that I will be an exception, Aideen said. *He hates me as much as any trueborn, although he hides it well. By the time you hear this, I'll be in hiding, but I expect to be found. If I'm lucky, I'll only be imprisoned in a gen-tank.*

One last thing. After Ohin and FHE have defeated the trueborns, he has an even worse attack planned—the release of a fungus he had his techs gen that will destroy the kel-grain and soy fields on trueborn adhikar. He has immune varieties in reserve, but those will only be for GENs' benefit.

The data you've uploaded from the datapod are the locations and times of the planned bombings. I'd been waiting for a chance to download it from one of the Bhimkay Boys and Jadi provided the perfect opportunity. That's why I didn't stop him from going to you. You have to get the information to someone who can help.

Aideen's message ended. Kayla replayed it to make sure she'd not missed anything. Then she deactivated the datapod and took it from her cheek.

"What is it?" Devak said.

Groping for his hand, she walked over to the others. They all must have seen her horror. The fear in their faces echoed her own. Her mouth dried as she tried to find a way to explain what she'd just heard.

"Ohin is starting a war," she said when she could get the words out.

28

She related Aideen's long, urgent message to them, word for word from her annexed brain.

"They didn't succeed in Belk," Devak said. "Thanks to Usi. So the rest of them haven't gotten the signal yet."

"How long ago was that? Two days?" Kayla asked.

"A day and a half," Devak said. "If Usi hadn't been injured, we might have made it here sooner."

"In any case," Kayla said, "I don't think they'll wait forever." An even worse thought struck her. "Ohin told me he was bringing Tala and Jal to FHE. I think he was lying. Sweet Infinite, I hope he was."

"When and where was the next bomb supposed to be set?" Devak asked.

Kayla tapped the data in her annexed brain. "Sheysa, then Leisa. Moving around the continent from Southwest Territory to Central Western. Then they go north and east." Kayla finally noticed the wristlink on Devak's arm. "Does it work here?"

He shook his head. "I haven't been able to get a signal since we first entered the tunnel."

"We need to get a message out," Kayla said. "That passageway goes back to Belk?"

"That's how we got here," Devak said.

Kayla considered the risks. "Devak, I'm not putting you on a spider. We saw what happened to Jadi and you're even less experienced. It's possible one of Ohin's passageways connects with this one back to Belk, but since it's our only choice, we have to hope not, that the only way to get to us is via spiderback. And he sent the Bhimkay Boys off with all the spiders."

Shakki said, "My guess is Ohin would take a passageway that leads directly from Antara to Belk, the one they used to take me to Antara. You just have to hope that there is no connection between them."

"It took you a day and a half to get here," Kayla said to Devak. "I'm worried that will be too late. Shakki said the direct Belk to Antara route took three days, and we've already been gone two ourselves. If he left right after us, he's likely only a day away from Belk."

"It took us longer because it was uphill coming this way, mostly," Devak said. "Usi getting hurt again slowed us down. If it's just you and me, it will be much quicker."

Shakki didn't look happy staying behind, but she understood that her med skills meant she had to tend to Usi. Junjie wasn't about to leave Usi's side.

Kayla and Devak each took one carrysak with enough food and water for a day if they ate sparingly. They divided the illuminators. Although Kayla had uploaded the war plans in her annexed brain and had Shakki do the same, they took the datapod with them, Devak tucking it into the hem of his shirt.

Outside, the storm still raged. "If the bhimkay will carry you all safely," Kayla said, "ride them to Belk after the storm passes. Otherwise, you'll have to leave Pev and Tak behind and use the passageway."

Kayla went to stand with Tak, rubbing the bhimkay's pedipalps. Kayla's throat tightened at Tak's growl of pleasure, knowing she might not see the spider again.

Kayla hugged Shakki goodbye. "I'll see you soon."

Devak gripped Junjie's and Usi's hands. "Take care of yourselves."

Carrysaks over their shoulders, Devak and Kayla headed for the tunnel. Devak led the way inside. "Don't touch the walls."

"I've lived with plassfiber all my life," Kayla said. "The warrens are full of it with the cheap plasscrete they use. And I toted enough sacks of it when I worked for Risa."

"That stuff is processed enough to break down the fibers, wash away most of the toxicity. Your GEN healing can handle that. But this stuff would make even you sick."

They walked on as quickly as they dared down the steep slope. Kayla had to resist the temptation to touch the walls on either side for balance.

For a short way, the tunnel widened enough that she could walk beside Devak, his arm around her holding her close. He pressed a kiss to her temple. "When Pitamah told me you were dead, it was the worst moment of my life. I thought it would kill me."

"They told me the same about you. Some days it was all I could do to keep from dying of grief." Kayla buried her face in his shirt, just to prove to herself that he was real. "Thank the Infinite it was all lies."

The way narrowed again, and she had to follow. Devak reached behind himself and took her hand. Their fingers stayed linked until the steeper going made it too hard to keep their balance.

"As soon as we can get a signal with the wristlink," Devak said, "we'll call Pitamah."

"It might be better just to go directly to the Brigade and hand them the datapod."

"As long as you're well clear of them," Devak said. "I don't want to risk an enforcer resetting you."

"I can't be reset. They can only kill me and break me down to DNA."

He glanced over his shoulder at her. "I would never let that happen. I'd die myself first."

They reached a T, and Kayla started to go straight through. Devak stopped her and redirected her to the right. "That's one of the places we got lost. Qia told us to keep to the main passageway, but I think it might have changed after the GENs excavated."

"Sounds like something Ohin would do. Send a crew back to change the route."

They continued on as the tunnel gently curved left again. Devak told Kayla about how he and Pitamah had lost nearly all their adhikar and became minor-status. She shared what her life had been like in the months since he'd seen her last. Trapped in Antara, scheming to get out. How those who questioned FHE or Ohin ended up in the gen-tank and reset.

He told her that as soon as he knew the truth, that she was alive, he went looking for her. He told her about finding Usi, about the tragedy and treachery of the vidrohi GENs.

Then they just fell silent, walking on and on, occasionally linked by a brush of his hand on hers. They would stop to rest at T's in the tunnel and Devak would pull her into his arms, kissing her. Kayla reveled in the pressure of his mouth, and she kissed him back, loving the feel of his body against hers. They would only give themselves a few minutes before they'd start walking again, always descending.

"How long has it been?" Kayla murmured after a long quiet time.

He checked his wristlink and sighed. "A little over ten hours. But I think we're farther along than on the trip up."

They continued on, Kayla behind Devak, her legs wobbly from the constant downhill. After an endless time, the slope decreased. Still not level, but not as treacherously steep either.

"I think we're getting close," Devak said. "I remember that last turn, how sharp it was."

"How much farther?" Kayla asked.

"Two or three kilometers?"

Suddenly, the ground beneath them trembled, a slight, brief shake. "What was that?" Kayla asked.

"Earthquake?" Devak said, although Kayla heard the doubt in his voice.

"Manmade, maybe. Can you walk faster?"

They hurried on in silence, as quickly as they could. A second time Kayla felt the earth shake, this one stronger than the one before it. Devak pitched forward and she had to grab the back of his shirt to keep him on his feet.

Not long after the second quake, he said, "We're nearly to the end. You can't see the ladder quite yet, but—"

Now the ground shuddered hard under them, knocking Kayla off her feet. Devak pulled her back up and held her close a moment as her heart thundered in her ears.

"Three bombs," Devak said, hunching against a fall of dust. "They want to make sure the others hear the signal."

"We have to get out of here." Kayla edged past him and took off at a run.

The tunnel path had leveled considerably, but it was still

awkward to take at such a fast pace. Luckily, Devak kept up with her, grabbing her arm or the back of her shirt to steady her as she stumbled again and again.

Another explosion took them both to their knees. Devak pulled Kayla back to her feet as rubble tumbled down on them. They ran as the tunnel behind them filled with plassfiber-filled crushed rock.

"If they take down Qia's warren, we're trapped," Devak shouted over the noise. "I don't know another way out." Devak squinted through the dust. "There's the ladder!"

They struggled toward it as the ground shuddered under their feet. Another explosion dropped more rubble, half filling the transition from the tunnel to the ladder.

"You go first," Devak said.

She wanted to argue, but there wasn't time. She climbed the pile of crushed and broken rock, her bare hands vulnerable to the splinters of the dangerous fiber.

The space between the rock pile and the ceiling was narrow, not much bigger than her. She squeezed through, then felt a ladder rung. She called out, "I found it."

As he scaled the pile after her, she held her illuminator in her teeth and cleared away rocks to make room for him. Blood dripped from her fingers from the plassfiber, but she ignored it. She had to make sure Devak made it through. As he climbed up, she could see he was bleeding too.

The opening through the rubble was still barely wide enough. He reached through with his arms first, but his shoulders got stuck. Kayla hooked an arm through a ladder rung and grabbed one of his hands. She pulled until she'd dragged him through.

He cried out at the pain of the rock scraping him. The moment she saw he could push to his feet, Kayla started climbing, looking back only once to make sure he was following.

The ladder seemed to go on forever. Kayla couldn't let herself think about what she was doing, just put one hand higher, then the other, one foot following, then the other. Below her, Devak gasped for breath. He likely felt the same stabbing pain in his lungs as she did—whether from the exertion or the inhaled fiber she didn't know.

Finally Kayla reached the top. She hooked an arm around a rung. "What . . . now?"

"That . . . plasscine panel . . . at the top . . . should slide away."

As she laid her hand on it and pushed, Kayla's heart lodged in her throat. What if the GEN woman's warren *had* come down? Would they find nothing but rubble on the other side, a barricade they couldn't get through?

"Doesn't want to move," Kayla said.

Sweet Infinite, she didn't want to die here. Even worse, she couldn't bear the thought of Devak breathing his last with her helpless to do anything.

Then the panel scraped opened a few centimeters. "Can you see what's inside?" Devak asked. "Is it blocked?"

Kayla wrapped her fingers around the open edge. "I think just warped. Does it lead to a closet?"

"Yes!"

"Going to pull it out. Watch it."

She wrenched the plasscine panel and it broke, cracking at a diagonal. Devak plastered himself as close to the ladder as he could and Kayla let go of the panel piece. It fell safely past him.

Kayla wedged her smaller body through the opening, then as Devak climbed the last few rungs, she broke the other half of the panel from its channel. There was now plenty of space for him to step to safety.

They emerged from the closet and made their way through the sleeproom. Besides dust, the GEN woman's flat looked to be intact. Her building must not have been a target. They unlatched the front door and stepped outside into the dim pre-dawn light.

Of the four warrens in the row with Qia's, only hers was still standing. Nothing but crushed and blackened walls were left behind of the three destroyed.

"Oh, sweet Infinite," Kayla murmured. "Were there people inside?"

"I don't know," Devak said. "Maybe the enforcers were able to evacuate."

If the Brigade even knew what was coming. Kayla found a path through the destruction and they made their way to the central ward. Debris and dust had blanketed the open space, so at first Kayla wasn't sure what she was seeing. Then she registered what those sprawled forms were and she couldn't hold back a sound of distress.

Bodies lay everywhere across the plasscrete strewn ward. Most lay silent, some moaned in pain. On the other side of the ward, two of the four warrens lay in rubble. A crowd of armed GENs—himayati, Kayla guessed—were gathered in front of one of the intact warrens. None of them moved forward to help the injured.

"Are all these dead and injured from the warrens?" Kayla asked. "Could they have already been pulled from the wreckage? But why are none of the GENs helping? And where is the Brigade? Where are the medics?"

"There are enforcers among the dead," Devak said, pointing to one of the nearest bodies. "That's Reit, the captain I spoke to when we were here before."

They moved closer and Kayla saw the blackened burns on

the dead. "That's from shockgun fire. None of them are bleeding the way they should be if they'd been hit by debris."

Devak squeezed Kayla's shoulder. "It looks like these are nearly all trueborns. Only a few with GEN tattoos."

Now they stood at the edge of the sea of bodies. Kayla forced herself to scan the faces.

"Sweet Infinite," she whispered as she fixed on a stout trueborn woman. "That's Charf." Her gaze fell on a tall trueborn man. "Aasif. He operated the lift." Her knees nearly buckled when she saw a golden-haired GEN, and she barely could whisper the name. "Lovise."

She turned to Devak and buried her face in his chest. "He's killed his own trueborn followers. His own himayati GENs. Dear Infinite—Aideen might be here." Despite the hatred she'd once felt for her birth mother, she couldn't bear the thought of her lying dead here.

Devak's grip on her tightened. "Someone's coming."

Kayla looked up. A GEN man dressed in white had pulled away from the other GENs and started across the ward. It took Kayla only a moment to recognize him.

"Who is that?" Devak asked.

He carried a device like a presaka in his hand. He stepped around the broken bodies as if they were nothing.

He stopped fifteen meters away. "I waited to finish it so you could see, Kayla. The destruction of the mine. One glorious explosion and *we* will rule the trueborns."

"No!" Kayla shouted.

"Who is that, Kayla?" Devak asked.

"It's Ohin," she answered, despair washing over her. "My father."

29

I thought you didn't have a nurture father," Devak said. "I thought he died."

"Not nurture," she said. "Genetic. He and Aideen . . ."

"Oh." Devak reached for her, his touch anchoring her. "I'd heard that GEN men could sometimes . . . I guess it's true. But with a trueborn woman . . ."

To Kayla's relief, she didn't hear revulsion in his voice. "I have to stop him before he sets off any more bombs."

She pulled away from Devak and toward Ohin, judging the distance between them. Could she get to him, disable him before he set off another explosion with that presaka in his hand? He had a shockgun at his hip as well. How many of these dead had he killed himself? Was Aideen one of them?

She heard footsteps behind her. "Stay back," she tossed over her shoulder at Devak.

"Kayla—"

"Stay back," she repeated, then she turned to meet Devak's eyes. "Please. It's better if I talk to him."

As she took a few steps toward Ohin, a half dozen or so of the himayati GENs behind him started to surge forward. Ohin must have heard their footsteps because he waved them back.

He turned to Kayla and raised the presaka. "I've packed the rest of the warrens with explosives. This time, I did the work myself. It will only take the touch of a button."

"All these trueborns, Aasif, Charf," Kayla said. "They were faithful to you. They were himayati. How could you have killed them?"

"You can never truly trust a trueborn," Ohin said. "No matter how many oaths they speak. Once they started seeing their own kind killed, their true allegiance would have emerged."

"But there are GENs out here too." Kayla's hand swept the ward filled with the dead, her heart stuttering as she glimpsed Lovise again. "You've killed your own people."

"They chose to defend the trueborns," Ohin said. "They weren't true himayati after all."

"What about the Belk GENs? The ones in the warrens you bombed?" Kayla asked.

"Evacuated and safe," Ohin said. "No GENs in the mines, either. The last of the trueborns from Antara, and the trueborns from Belk that I could find, are all locked inside that second warren. They thought they would be guarding GENs inside. I'm sure they've found out by now they're the only ones in there."

His treachery stunned her. He'd herded the trueborns in there with a lie, then let them see their fellow himayati mowed down by shockgun fire. They had to know something worse was coming for them.

"Is that where Aideen is, inside the warren?" Kayla asked, praying he'd say no.

Ohin's expression darkened. "She should never have betrayed me. Helped you escape. At least the other trueborns came here ready to fight alongside me."

Did that mean she was dead here on the central ward? Or about to die in the warren?

"It should have been enough just to follow me. To be one with me." He shook his head. "The only sure way is to wipe the trueborns out, sector by sector."

"You can't possibly," Kayla said, moving toward him, a few more steps. "There are more of them than there are of us."

"But GENs have abilities and talents that trueborns lack. They built us that way—with physical strength like yours, mental capacity like mine. Trueborns have gotten lazy in their reliance on GENs."

Kayla edged ever closer, glancing down as her foot brushed against something. She'd nearly trod on the hand of a trueborn woman with red-brown skin and long, thick black hair. Her brown eyes were open and unseeing. Kayla's heart fell as she recognized the woman as one of the cooks from Mahala. She said a brief, silent prayer as she stepped around the woman.

"Far enough." Ohin pressed a control on the presaka, and behind him the first warren—the empty one—exploded, plasscrete flying as the dust enveloped the building.

Small bits of debris pelted Kayla and she turned away, covering her face. When she dropped her hands, she could see Devak dodging in and out of the dust cloud, taking advantage of its cover to cross the central ward.

Was he thinking he could get to the last intact warren and free the trueborns inside? All that way with no cover? She wanted to shout at him to stay away, but if she did, she'd call Ohin's attention to him.

"Their mining operations are next," Ohin said. "Trueborns can't survive long without plassfiber, with nothing to power their world. They'll fall into chaos."

"And we will too. You'd send us all into the dark just to spite the trueborns?" Kayla asked.

"I'll send all of us into the dark for our freedom," Ohin declared.

Where was Devak? The dust had started to disperse. It certainly wasn't thick enough for him to hide.

"I'm only destroying the trueborn operations. We have a half dozen access tunnels to the main fiber veins that lead all the way to Antara. Himayati GENs will be working the mines. We'll be the ones running the power plants, the extrusion factories."

She caught movement behind Ohin to his right and thought at first it was one of the victims that was still alive. But she realized it was Devak, flat on the ground, creeping toward the second warren.

She had to keep Ohin distracted, to keep him from noticing Devak. "I know about your DNA, the DNA you put inside me." Kayla took a few more steps, picking her way through the dead that littered the ward. "Do you know it lets me hear you? Everything you say on your circuit-comm, I can hear."

His body visibly shook. So he hadn't known. But he recovered quickly. "Then I've given you something valuable. A true connection to your genetic father."

"I would just as soon be sucked dry by a bhimkay," Kayla spat out. "Then at least your parasite DNA would be gone from my body."

Ohin's hand slapped his shockgun, and for a moment, Kayla wondered if he would shoot her dead like all the rest. But then his hand dropped, and she could breathe again.

She still wasn't anywhere near enough to take that presaka away. Devak, trying to stay concealed amongst the bodies, was making slow progress toward the warren where the trueborns were trapped.

Then he rose cautiously to his knees, and she made the mistake of glancing his way. Ohin noticed her distraction. As quick as a bhimkay strike, Ohin whirled and whipped out his shockgun. The blast hit Devak square in the back.

Kayla cried out as Devak spasmed and went still. Uncaring of what Ohin might do, Kayla ran past him across the ward, jumping over the dead and dying, to Devak's side.

A fist-sized black mark charred the middle back of Devak's gray-dusted shirt, just above his waist. Fingers trembling, she felt at his throat for a pulse. It was there, but weak.

"He needs a medic!" Kayla screamed, anger and tears shredding her words.

"Carry him to the second warren," Ohin said, slipping his shockgun back in its holster. "His death will be quicker."

"You can't do this! It's evil! The Infinite will strike you from his hands."

"The Infinite is a myth," Ohin said, "created by trueborns to control us. There is no deity. I choose my own fate."

He lifted the presaka, pressed it. The warren filled with trueborns exploded. Kayla leaned over Devak to protect him from the fall of plasscrete chunks, wincing as a large piece struck her shoulder.

Her eyes burned as she tried to see through the roil of dust. Added to the particles already suspended in the air, the new cloud settled more slowly, first revealing the closest bodies, then Ohin still meters away from her with the presaka. Behind him more bodies sprawled in front of the last destroyed warren. GEN bodies, his own himayati who had been standing guard, hurt and possibly dead from the shrapnel thrown by the last explosion.

"You've killed them all," Kayla said, sick at heart.

Ohin turned, swaying as he saw the bodies. "I packed those explosives myself. The debris should never have gone so far."

He whipped back around toward Kayla, rage twisting his face. He raised his shockgun, aiming for her.

Then from a roiling cloud of dust, a tall, hair-barbed black spider leg moved into view. A hiss echoed across the ward.

Ohin whirled to look behind him. He tried to aim his shockgun, but he wasn't nearly quick enough. The bhimkay sank her mandible into Ohin's back and the GEN dropped like a rock.

Kayla jumped up and ran across the ward to Ohin. She wrenched the presaka and shockgun from his paralyzed hands. Tak towered above Kayla, dancing in the debris in agitation. On her back, Shakki ordered the bhimkay to step back and stand still. A wide-eyed Usi rode Tak behind Shakki, with Jadi's shirt tied around them both to keep him on.

Pev thundered up from around the wrecked fourth warren, Junjie looking exhilarated, holding on for dear life. "Pev just couldn't keep up with Tak!" he called out.

"Shakki!" Kayla called. "I need you down here. Devak's taken a shockgun hit. Junjie, take his wristlink and call for help. Usi, tie up that evil son of a rat-snake."

While Shakki dismounted and helped Usi down, Kayla stumbled back to Devak's side. He lay so still.

Kayla leaned close. "You can't die, Devak. I won't let you." Choking through the dust that lingered in the air, Kayla's voice cracked. "I love you. I love you."

As her tears wet his cheeks and washed away the dust, she prayed that her declaration of love hadn't come too late.

30

With Ohin injured and captured, Kayla sent Junjie and Usi in search of help. They found the Belk GENs sequestered in a warehouse with the last remaining himayati. The GENs had managed to provide sanctuary for a few dozen local trueborns, secluding them behind stacks of crates.

Word of the FHE leader's betrayal of his own followers filtered down, convincing GENs and even trueborns to follow Kayla's lead. The former himayati came to their senses once they learned the full magnitude of Ohin's terrifying schemes.

Shakki set those with healing skills to triaging the injured with the medical supplies she'd brought from the cave—pratija, bandages, and sani-wipes were all put to use. And a healer amongst the local GENs, a man named Ili, knew of a gen-tank, supply of gen-fluid, and power generator that the trueborn sector medic—now dead—had stored in the supply warehouse. Thank the Infinite that Belk plass miners were considered valuable enough to keep a gen-tank handy, and that between Junjie's knowledge of the process and Ili's experience, they could get Devak into it quickly.

Kayla emptied a small storeroom within the warehouse where Ili and Junjie got Devak installed in the tank, the generator chugging along beside him. Junjie was worried about how old the gen-fluid was; Ili fretted over the programming since they weren't sure what Devak's exact injuries were. There was also the matter of fuel for the generator, and whether there was enough of it to keep the gen-tank running long enough. The wristlink proved to be useless—the communications network was down, at least in Belk. It was impossible to ask for help.

Finally, Junjie stepped back from the tank. "I can't do anything more now. Ili will stay. I should go help Usi with the communications. See if we can get it working."

"Go ahead," Kayla said. "That's important too."

The GEN healer sat in a corner of the bare, white-walled room, eyes on the monitor connected to the tank. Kayla pulled over a chair. While the monitor beeped in the corner, Ili sighed and shifted in his own chair. Kayla slumped against Devak's tank, willing him to heal, to live.

Shakki came in, looking as exhausted and grief-stricken as Kayla felt. "Thank the Infinite I brought as much of the medical supplies with me as I could."

"Have you been able to find Aideen?" Kayla asked.

"Not on the ward. If she was in the warren . . ." Shakki shook her head, then called to Ili, "Could you look at Ohin? I had a couple of GENs carry him into the warehouse."

Kayla wanted to tell Shakki to feed her birth father to Tak and Pev, but she kept that suggestion to herself. But when Ili went out, Kayla only went as far as the storeroom door.

They'd laid him out on a plasscine blanket next to several tall towers of kel-grain crates. Ohin's chest still rose and fell, although with difficulty. His light brown skin had a bluish tinge.

Ili bent over Ohin, listening to his heart, then pulled aside his shirt. It looked like the mandible had come straight through from the back and pierced Ohin's chest. Kayla could see blood pulsing out, a little ooze every second or so.

Ili rose. "My guess is the bhimkay nicked his heart. He needs a gen-tank."

Kayla glanced back at Devak, floating in green gen-fluid. "But there isn't another, is there?"

"Just the one tank," Ili said.

Ohin's eyes fluttered open. His gaze found Kayla, standing in the doorway of the storeroom. He tried to say something, his lips moving soundlessly. To ask for mercy? To curse her for refusing to come to his side?

Kayla stared back at him, her voice hard as she spoke. "He's in the Infinite's hands, then."

She returned to Devak's side, closing her mind to the man dying in the warehouse. Sagging against the cool glass of the tank, she sent up prayer after prayer to the Infinite for Devak.

The hours blurred into one another. At some point, Shakki came in to tell her Ohin had breathed his last. Shakki still hadn't found Aideen, although of the trueborns who'd been in the warren, few could be identified.

Shakki left and Kayla dozed off. When she jarred awake, it was hours later according to her internal clock. She looked first at Devak, seemingly unchanged, then at Ili, alert but unconcerned at his monitor.

As she tried to figure out what had woken her, she heard the voice again. *Kayla?*

The breath left her lungs. It wasn't—it couldn't be— *Aideen? Where are you?*

Still in Antara. I told you, I hid. With Palla.

I thought you were here. I thought you were dead. He killed almost everyone else.

Is he dead? Even with the flat tone of the circuit-comm, Kayla could hear Aideen's fervent wish that he was.

Yes.

Aideen was silent for a long time, then she said, *Reports have come in via circuit-comm. Several bombs went off in other sectors. But there weren't enough himayati anywhere to follow through. The local Brigade got most of them under control. Ohin thought the GEN enforcers would join with FHE's cause, but he was wrong about that. Most of them are too angry about the bombings of warehouses and GENs going hungry.*

That's good. Kayla stroked the side of Devak's gen-tank. So Ohin's plans had only partly succeeded. The Brigade was too busy dealing with the chaos elsewhere to clamp down on what was left of Belk, but Kayla wondered when they'd arrive and what she and her compatriots would have to do when they did.

Ohin made another attack not even the Bhimkay Boys knew anything about. He sent a rogue computer program ripping through the Grid Monitoring system. It's damaged beyond repair. The databases filled with GEN IDs were erased. Another virus initiated a cascade of database backups, so the corrupt data is stored over the good. All the stored GEN IDs are lost. Even if the Grid wasn't ruined, there are no GEN IDs to track. The trueborns are frantic.

Then she was truly free. All the GENs were. If she couldn't be tracked, couldn't be uploaded or downloaded or reset—what could the trueborns do to her? As long as she wasn't caught by an enforcer with a shockgun, nothing. And the Brigade wouldn't make it to Belk until they figured out how to restore communications.

What's wrong with communications? Kayla asked. *We couldn't use a wristlink.*

Something the Bhimkay Boys did, Aideen said. *Uploaded malware into the power-generating network. So there are intermittent outages, which keeps taking down the communications network. Right now the only way to communicate is via circuit-comms.*

What about that fungus? Kayla asked. *Did he release it?* If the trueborn kel-grain fields and soy were dying, thousands of people would starve, trueborn and GEN alike.

No, thank the Infinite, Aideen said. *Palla helped me destroy all of it.* Aideen paused, then asked, *How is that trueborn boy of yours?*

I don't know yet, Kayla said, close to tears. *If I could just get hold of Jemali.*

Who is he?

Kayla explained that Jemali was a friend of Zul, and the most skilled medic and gen-tech she knew.

I'll find him, Aideen said, then she signed off.

Kayla didn't want to hope. Junjie, with all his technical skill, still couldn't get any message out of Belk. Before Kayla had dozed off, some of the surviving Belk trueborns had taken cargo lorries and Brigade lev-cars to Pashi and other surrounding sectors, but they found the same chaos there. The best they'd been able to do was scrounge a little more fuel for the generator, although that had been hard to come by with everyone hoarding supplies.

Every time Junjie or Ili checked on Devak, they looked so grim, it terrified Kayla. Junjie finally told her that if not for the tank's life-support, Devak would be dead. And even with the extra fuel the Belk trueborns had found, Junjie wasn't sure that it would give them enough time to track down Jemali and get the old medic to Belk.

Two more days drifted by. Kayla heard from Aideen several times. Her birth mother told her that thankfully Ohin had been lying about bringing Tala and Jal to Antara. They were both found safe in Chadi. The vid Ohin had shown Kayla had been faked, Tala's face and voice simulated.

Aideen had sent a trustworthy FHE operative to Tala. With Tala's permission, the operative installed the circuit-comm programming into both her and Jal.

When Kayla first heard her nurture mother's voice on her circuit-comm, she started crying and didn't stop the whole time. She lost count of the number of times she'd said, *I love you.*

Then Jal got on the circuit-comm. *I'm part of a team,* he said. *We're going to fix the power system. A bunch of us are working together—minor-status trueborns, lowborns, GENs like me. We've hacked into Ohin's malware.*

Excitement filled Kayla. If they could get the power system going, they wouldn't have to worry about the dwindling fuel for the generator. *So you'll be able to fix it soon?*

Not really, Jal said. *It's pretty bad. But we'll figure it out eventually.*

Eventually. Kayla signed off with Jal and sank back in her chair. Eventually might not be good enough for Devak. What would she do if he died? She couldn't even bear thinking about it.

Heartsick, she tore herself away from Devak long enough to go to the washroom at the other end of the warehouse. As she returned, she heard voices from the storeroom. Junjie, Ili, and two others that were very familiar, that she hadn't heard in quite some time.

She took off at a run. When she swung into the small storeroom, there was Zul. And Jemali was with him. She broke down and sobbed.

Hours later, Jemali had finished his evaluation of Devak. He took Kayla aside.

"Did you know Devak already had a spinal injury?" Jemali asked her. "From the explosion in Two Rivers?"

"I knew he was injured and in the tank before," Kayla said.

"Well, that shockgun strike injured him again," Jemali said. "In fact, it had never really had a chance to heal properly in the first place. I've reprogrammed the gen-fluid to better heal Devak's spinal trauma. But I'm thinking the best solution would be to install some GEN circuitry in his body."

"No." Kayla shook her head. "Devak's too old. It would kill him."

"Not necessarily," Jemali said. "There's a new technique I've actually used on Zul. Not as extensive as what's needed for Devak, but it's very focused, just along his spine, and partly into his brain. Just enough to install part of the GEN healing program that can do the job the gen-tank can't."

Jemali took her hand. "Zul has given me his permission to do the procedure on Devak, but I wanted to ask you. I think you're the one Devak would want making the decision, more than his great-grandfather. The thing is, it's risky. And once it's installed, there's no removing it."

"Is there an alternative?" Kayla asked.

"Yes," Jemali said. "He stays in the gen-tank. Forever."

Or until the generator fuel ran out. Even if the power came back on, would Devak want to be forever trapped in a gen-tank?

He would want to take the risk. "Do the procedure," Kayla said. "I think it's what he would want."

She went back in the storeroom, to Devak. "I love you," she whispered. Then she walked away, praying to the Infinite it wouldn't be the last time she saw him alive.

EPILOGUE

two and a half years later

Arms full of fat patagobi root, Kayla elbowed her way inside the back door of the Plator sector cottage she shared with her forever friend, Mishalla, and Mishalla's husband, Eoghan. She dodged as Nishi, Risa Mandoza's five-legged seycat, burst out the door.

Nishi had been temporarily banned from the lorry while Risa transported a herd of droms to richer grazing. The high-bred droms didn't like lorry travel in the first place, despite the sliding windows Risa had installed for air. They might work off a hundred pounds of valuable weight if they had to share the lorry bay with a predator, no matter that the seycat didn't even reach their knees.

Kayla added the load of patagobi to the harvest of patagobi leaves in the sink as Mishalla entered the tiny kitchen. "Is that the last of it?" Mishalla asked.

"Best I can tell." Kayla started in on knocking the dirt off the roots with a brush. "Should just about last us through winter if we pickle some of it."

"And if we're not shorted on our drom share."

Kayla nodded in acknowledgement of that possibility. "If we can talk Risa into leaving Nishi with us through the winter, she can supplement with rat-snakes. That and any naga meat Risa can smuggle in might be enough."

Besides smuggling naga meat out of the Badlands via Ohin's passageways, Risa would transport GENs in the other direction for the FHE reprogramming that defied trueborn datapod uploads and downloads. With the Grid destroyed and more and more GENs reprogrammed, Loka was shifting, drip by drip, toward a more just society.

With the power system still only working sporadically, and so many trueborn machines no longer able to function, lowborn and GEN labor was more in demand. Minor-status trueborns might be willing to do physical work once restricted to GENs and lowborns, but not the high and demi-status who still saw themselves above that kind of labor. They hired out GENs and lowborns, who insisted they be paid well for it.

And with the Brigade decimated by the fighting, the trueborns found they had no choice but to pay. Ohin's techs had restructured the circuitry of his himayati soldiers to absorb the energy from a shockgun hit, to step it down to a safe level and dissipate what the body couldn't use. The himayati GENs could still be killed with a maximum hit, but hundreds of enforcers were killed or incapacitated before they figured that out.

Even where Ohin's war hadn't spread, Brigade members saw the way the world was changing. Most of the GENs that had been conscripted into the Brigade quit. Many of the minor-status that had been forced into that employment by their low rank deserted to find another way to earn their dhans. There was a small force left, minor-status and GENs working together, but their focus was on public safety.

Of the remaining five Bhimkay Boys, two died in the fighting, and the other three vanished when the Grid went down. One of the boys' bhimkay fell to a Brigade shockgun, and the four others dodged the enforcers for weeks before they could be rounded up by presaka commands. Unfit to return to the wild, they were trained to tolerate a new set of riders and were used to ferry messages in the settled sectors in lieu of wristlinks. Tak and Pev stayed in the Badlands.

Wanting to make sure her family was protected from trueborn interference, Kayla had personally escorted Tala and her nurture brother, Jal, to Antara for their reprogramming. Rather, she'd escorted Tala. Her nurture brother, given the choice between walking the passageways or riding Tak with Shakki across the surface, chose the bhimkay.

At Antara, Tala had met Aideen, who ran the cavern now with Shakki. Some GENs who had come for reprogramming remained there, along with a number of lowborns and even some minor-status trueborns. Under Aideen and Shakki, Antara had become the model for what the rest of Loka—at least those who looked to the future instead of the past—was fighting so hard to become. Equal treatment, an open society. Marriages and joinings across classes were sanctified there, blessed by the Infinite, or the Lord Creator, or Iyenkas, or even all three.

Kayla returned her focus to scrubbing patagobi roots as Mishalla brought up an empty crate from the cold room under the cottage. Kayla and Mishalla filled the crate with the cleaned roots, setting aside a few with the washed greens for trading.

Kayla carried the crate down to the cold store, careful on the uneven stone steps. When she returned, Mishalla handed her a sani-wipe.

"I just checked," Mishalla said. "He's not awake yet."

"Lazy boy." Kayla smiled, although her heart ached a little.

Done with the sani-wipe, Kayla dropped it into a bucket beside the food prep counter. Mishalla would re-sanitize the sturdy cloth along with the others they used during the day. Using a sani-wipe only once was a luxury no one could afford anymore, not when the iffy power system made manufacturing more difficult.

Mishalla loaded the greens and patagobi roots into a carrysak. "I'm going down to the central square for synth-protein."

Kayla headed down the hall to her own sleeproom, the smaller one in the back. Then she stretched out on the bed and watched Devak sleep.

He was sprawled on the bed, his left side facing her, strands of his nearly chin-length black hair spread across his cheek. She brushed his hair back, then fingered the pale lines of scarring between right cheekbone and chin.

It wouldn't wake him. There were only two ways to do that now. Wait for his body's circuitry to signal the end of its sleep cycle, or for her to send a message to his circuit-comm. Which she didn't like to do since that meant she was disturbing the rest his body needed.

He sighed and Kayla's heart soared. He was waking.

His eyes drifted open, and a sweet smile lit his face as he saw her. He leaned in close and kissed her, his mouth lingering on hers a long time.

"Mid-morning?" he asked.

He was still getting used to accessing the time from the GEN-style inner clock. Its alerts made it easier for him to track when his next scheduled rest cycle was due.

"Just past," Kayla said.

"Are Mishalla and Eoghan here?"

"Mishalla went to the central square. Eoghan is helping repair equipment at the plass extrusion factory."

With a smile, Devak leaned in to kiss her again. His touch stole her breath.

He sighed. "I suppose Pitamah and Jemali will be here soon."

She traced his scar again, so like a GEN tattoo. "In another hour or so. Junjie and Usi are walking over for midday meal too."

Junjie and Usi were sharing a flat in a mixed trueborn/lowborn housing unit. Junjie was back at work at the Plator GAMA lab where he used to work, although his research on GEN reproduction was limited by power outages. Usi was helping to rebuild some of the bombed GEN warehouses and warrens in surrounding sectors.

It was Junjie and Usi who took the time to track down the vidrohi, the GENs who had damaged their nervous systems trying to burn out their circuitry. Most of the ones Devak had met were dead, but a few had survived. Junjie and Usi had brought medics in to do what they could to treat the survivors.

Zul and Jemali were sharing a small house in Leisa, a trueborn sector east of Plator. It was a sensible choice because the two were long-time friends, but also because medic Jemali could help care for Zul and monitor the old man's health.

Devak's great-grandfather, in ill health for decades, had been made even frailer by the circuitry treatments Jemali had done to try to prolong the old man's life. Zul had survived these last two and a half years by sheer grit, but Jemali had told Devak and Kayla privately that Zul likely had only months left.

Devak gave Kayla a last kiss, then laboriously pushed

himself up to sit and swing his legs over the side of the bed. "Washroom first."

He got to his feet on his own. He picked out a fresh korta, chera pants, and skivs himself, but he let Kayla carry them. Although he could pretty much walk without help, it was always better to have his hands free. Sometimes he'd have to grab her when his strength suddenly gave out.

He was better now than at first, when he was fresh out of the tank. His body's circuitry would sense that the preset limits for exertion had been exceeded. It would abruptly shut itself off to rest, and either someone was there to catch him, or he'd hit the floor.

Now Devak would feel the rest cycle coming on as ordinary sleepiness. Kayla didn't have to send circuit-comm messages to wake him anymore to eat or use the washroom. He would wake on his own.

He left her waiting for him at the washroom door, then emerged clean and dressed. They walked together to the kitchen where Kayla served him up sweetened wild kel-grain re-heated in the flash oven, one of the devices Junjie had connected to the generator.

When Devak had finished the bowl and set it aside, he laid his hand on hers to stop her from clearing the table. "It's time for you to say yes."

A nervous excitement tightened her stomach. "Is it?"

"Before you list all the excuses," Devak said, "I'll name them. One." His index finger went up. "You're a GEN and I'm not. Except, I'm at least a quarter-GEN now. And lately I've been feeling a lot more like a lowborn than a trueborn."

"A quarter-GEN?" She couldn't stop her mouth curving into a smile.

"Maybe a third. Two." A second finger. "I need to get stronger." He wiped that away. "Jemali will drive me to Belk. I can ride in Pitamah's old lev-chair through the tunnels."

"Those tunnels are pretty steep for a lev-chair."

"Then you'll carry me," Devak said. "Three, I'm a follower of the Lord Creator, and you worship the Infinite. Even if we put aside the fact that they're probably the same deity, we'll include them both. Four, we're too young. But you're nearly a nineteenth-year now and I'm a twentieth-year. Five—"

"Yes," Kayla said.

"What?"

"Yes, let's join. Marry. However you want to call it."

His face lit and he pushed to his feet to throw his arms around her. "I love you, Kayla."

She drew back, stroked his face. "There will always be reasons to say no. But none of them matter as much as the reason to say yes. I love you."

He held her so close, she thought her heart would burst with joy. Thank the Infinite, thank the Lord Creator, for the beautiful new world opening up for them.

adhikar: Tracts of land that only trueborns possess. The more adhikar a trueborn owns, the higher the trueborn's status. Only trueborns are allowed to own adhikar.

allabain: A nomadic subset of lowborns. They use temporary tent-like homes called bhaile that they carry from place to place.

annexed brain: A partitioned section of a GEN's brain that the GEN circuitry accesses and utilizes as storage and computational space using datapod uploads. When GENs are created in the tank, their brains are partitioned to create the annexed brain and bare brain sections.

Assignment: The "job" to which a GEN is Assigned. According to the Humane Edicts, GENs are to be Assigned to a job to which they are suited, i.e., one that utilizes their genetically designed skill set.

Assignment specialist: A trueborn responsible for uploading the appropriate information for GENs, both for their first Assignment and for subsequent Assignments if their situation changes.

Badlands: A barren wasteland that comprises the most eastern one-third of the continent of Svarga on the planet Loka.

bali: The earring worn by trueborns in their right earlobe that identifies their status. High-status wear diamonds, demi-status wear emeralds, and minor-status wear sapphires. A genuine bali can detect the DNA of the wearer and will be rejected by the body of someone who is wearing it illegally.

bare brain: The section of a GEN's brain where ordinary memories of experiences and study are stored. It's effortless for a GEN to retrieve memories from this section. They must learn to access their annexed brain to retrieve data and programming from it.

bhaile: A portable tent-like home used by the nomadic allabain lowborns. Originally made with the woven fiber of pulped sticker bush roots, the walls are now made from plasscine. The ribs of the tent are sticker bush branches.

bhimkay: The meter-high spider that is at the top of the arachnid food chain on Loka. A bhimkay can easily bring down even an adult-sized drom. Trueborns use electrified fencing to protect their drom herds from the bhimkay.

Brigade: Loka's police force. At least one Brigade is assigned to each sector within Svarga.

chera pants: Derived from churidar pants, tightly fitting pants worn by men and women in South & Central Asia.

crèche: A daycare center for lowborn children. The cost of the care in the crèche would be deducted from the pay of the lowborns.

datapod: A thumb-sized device used to upload and download information into GENs. It is also used to interface with hardware such as computers.

demi-status: A class of trueborn lower than high-status and higher than minor-status. They're affluent, but not as wealthy as a high-status. Demi-status trueborns hold thirty-two of the 160 seats of the Lokan parliament.

dhan: The currency on Loka.

DNA Mark: The official name for the GEN tattoo. Each tattoo is unique for a given GEN.

drom: A shaggy camel-like six-legged mammal that roams the open scrap grass plains. The native droms are about the size of a pony, and therefore more vulnerable to bhimkay. The genetically engineered version of droms are the size of a dromedary camel.

enforcer: A member of the Brigade. Largely comprised of minor-status trueborns who have lost their adhikar and would be demoted from trueborn status to lowborn if not for their service as a Brigade enforcer. Each Brigade includes one or two GEN enforcers for duties such as physically handling GENs and delivery of GEN tack (clothes and equipment) for GEN Assignments.

extendibles: Metal pins that extend from a datapod when it is activated. When the datapod is applied to a GEN's facial tattoo, the extendibles pierce the skin and link with the GEN's internal circuitry.

FHE: An underground organization consisting of GEN and trueborn members. FHE stands for Freedom, Humanity, Equality.

gajara: A small, spicy root vegetable native to Loka.

GAMA: The Genetic Augmentation and Manipulation Agency. GAMA is responsible for creating GENs and all other genetic alterations that take place in gen-tanks.

GEN: A Genetically Engineered Non-Human. Using mostly human DNA and some animal DNA, each GEN is created with a specific physical or mental ability. They are gestated in a tank.

gen-fluid: A thick green fluid that's used in a gen-tank. Gen-fluid must be programmed for the specific genetic makeup of the occupant of the tank.

gen-lab: A genetics lab where GENs are created or reset (or wealthy trueborns are healed) in gen-tanks.

gen-tank: A large fish tank-like vessel filled with gen-fluid that's used for both the gestation/alteration of GENs and for healing certain trueborn injuries and diseases.

gene-splicer: A trueborn genetic engineer (likely minor-status) who designs and creates GENs. Gene-splicers also use the tank to correct trueborn abnormalities, but a gene-splicer with that position would likely be a demi-status trueborn.

Grid: The Monitoring Grid that tracks every GEN on Svarga. It has two modes—active tracking where the software searches for particular GENs to check that they are where they belong, and passive mode, where the GENs' locations are read and stored in a database for possible later use.

healer: An uneducated GEN medic of sorts. They use mostly folklore and dubious, untested methods to treat their GEN patients.

high-status: The highest level of trueborn. They are lavishly wealthy and hold 120 of the 160 seats of the Lokan parliament.

himayati: A zealot who follows the FHE leader, Ohin.

holo-projector: A device that projects three-dimensional video or still images for viewing.

Humane Treatment Edicts: An agreement reached two decades before the start of Tankborn. The Edicts specify how many hours GENs are to work in a day, give them one rest day off a week, forbid physical abuse, and require a safe and sanitary living space. Trueborns tend to follow the Edicts as it suits them, many ignoring them entirely.

Jahaja: A multi-lev used exclusively by the Brigade. From the Hindi word for transport.

jik: An extremely derogatory term for a GEN. Used largely by trueborns.

Judicial Council: The judiciary on Loka. The JC adjudicates laws passed by the parliament. This includes passing judgment on GENs who break trueborn laws (such as straying outside their radius or disrespecting trueborns). In these cases, they decide if a GEN should be realigned and reset as punishment (if a Brigade enforcer hasn't already done so). Trueborns have many ways to both avoid judgment by the JC and avoid any punishment if they're found guilty.

junk tree: A leafless tree that uses a symbiotic relationship with a fungus (and the jot spider) to survive.

kelfa: A hot GEN drink made from roasted kel-grain (also consumed in some mixed lowborn/trueborn sectors). GENs often compare the skin color of high-status trueborns to the color of kelfa.

Kinship: A secret group of trueborns, lowborns, and GENs whose goal is to secure fair treatment for lowborns and equal rights for GENs.

kit: Derogatory term for a young GEN.

korta: Derived from kurta, a tunic-style Indian shirt.

lev-car: A form of transportation that uses a suspension engine. Like a sedan. They are electrically charged. There are also micro-levs (like a sports car), multi-levs (like a small bus), and pub-trans (like a large bus).

Loka: The barely habitable planet where the refugees from Earth settled. Loka has four continents, but only Svarga is suitable for humans. The others are polar Virynand, earthquake-ridden Utul, and volcanic Peralor.

lowborn: A class of humans who are born of a mother but do not own adhikar. The poorest among them are somewhat nomadic and live on the outskirts of trueborn-only sectors, often where the sector borders GEN-only sectors. The more prosperous lowborns are merchants or factory supervisors who live in mixed sectors with minor-status trueborns.

Mar: An honorific title similar to "sir" or "lord."

medic: A trueborn physician. A high-status medic would treat high or demi-status trueborns. Lower status medics would treat minor-status trueborns or possibly lowborns if they had the funds to pay. A demi-status medic might also be required to work in a GEN sector.

mini-cin: A small, indoor incinerator for burning trash.

multi-lev: Any lev-type vehicle with a higher capacity than a passenger vehicle. Most multi-levs are used for public transit (pub-trans), but the Brigade also uses a multi-lev called a Jahaja for rounding up and transporting large groups of GENs.

minor-status: The lowest class of trueborns. If they're smart, they become technology specialists in some computerized area (such as the Grid) or teachers. If they're not deep thinkers, they work in bureaucratic jobs or serve in the Brigade. Minor-status trueborns hold eight of the 160 seats of the Lokan parliament.

nagas: Purple snakelike creatures that reside in the Badlands.

nasaka: A toxic waste byproduct of the process that converts plassfiber into its various useful products (plasscine, plasscrete, etc).

nurture mother: A nurture mother is a GEN female who has been genetically engineered to nurture young children. They might be Assigned to nurture GENs in their home sector or another, or possibly to nuture lowborns. Trueborns would be cared for by lowborns. A nurturer could be male (nurture father). GEN siblings within the same home are nurture brothers or nurture sisters.

patagobi: A mild, turnip-like root vegetable native to Loka.

pishacha: A ghoul, someone who steals body parts from GENs. From the Hindi.

plasscine: A processed form of plassfiber that is used to make cheap furniture and other home items, clothing, jewelry, etc.

plasscrete: A processed form of plassfiber that is mixed with a cement-like mineral native to Loka to create a very strong material used for construction.

plassfiber: A naturally occuring mineral on Loka that is mined from the western side of a mountain range called The Wall. Plass is analogous to a solid form of petroleum and can be processed similarly to provide an energy source. It fuels the electrical grid on Svarga. As plasscine, it can be molded into furniture and even fabric for clothing. Plasscrete and steelcrete are used in construction.

plassteel: A processed form of plassfiber that incorporates some of Loka's scarce metal to achieve a stronger final product. Where steelcrete would be used in construction, plassteel would be used in smaller quantities.

pratija: An antibiotic. From the Hindi word pratijaivika.

presaka: A remote control transmitter. From the Hindi word prēṣaka.

rat-snake: A spider creature with a rat-like head and a long, flexible thorax like a snake's.

realignment: The first step before resetting a GEN. Realignment erases the GEN's current identity by both wiping the annexed brain and disrupting neural pathways in the bare brain. The bare brain isn't damaged by realignment, but all memories are essentially destroyed.

reset: The process of creating a new identity in a GEN after the previous identity has been wiped away with a realignment.

sarka: A strategy-type game like chess.

scrap grass: A grass native to Loka that is fodder for both native and genetically engineered droms.

sector: A portion of a territory. Of the 106 sectors in Svarga, sixty-three sectors are defined as trueborn only (restricted to high-status and demi-status trueborns), twenty-eight are mixed (minor-status trueborns and lowborns allowed), and fifteen are GEN (GENs only).

sekai: A hand-held reader and networking device.

sewer toad: A small toad-like arachnid about the size of a large grapefruit that prefers wet, dank places. It loves polluted rivers.

seycat: A six-legged feline, about twelve inches tall at the shoulder, with a striped pelt and large tufted ears. Rat-snakes and sewer toads are seycats' favorite prey. Seycats are very fierce, and although they are sometimes kept as pets, they can never truly be domesticated.

shockgun: A weapon carried by non-GEN Brigade members. It disrupts the central nervous system. Depending on the setting, it can simply incapacitate an individual or kill them.

sket: Slang for skill set.

skill set: A GEN's special skill or ability. Using human and animal DNA, the skill set is genetically programmed into a GEN in the tank early in the gestation process.

Social Benevolence: Social Benevolence, or SB, is responsible mainly for lowborn welfare. As a consequence of the lowborn insurrection in 359 (thirteen years prior to the start of Tankborn) the parliament passed laws creating Social Benevolence to placate lowborns.

steelcrete: A processed form of plassfiber that is mixed with iron and other minerals to create an extra-sturdy material used in larger, taller structures and for especially secure places (e.g., prisons).

Svarga: The single habitable continent on the planet Loka. Svarga is divided into five territories and each territory into sectors.

synth-protein: Vegetable-based protein made from a soy-like legume.

tank: The gestation tank that is used to gestate GENs in lieu of a woman's womb. The tank is also sometimes used to correct trueborn abnormalities or injuries.

tankborn: A derogatory term used for GENs. GENs do use this term amongst themselves.

thinsteel: A steel-plass amalgam that can be extruded as thinly as paper yet is as strong as centimeter-thick steel.

trueborn: The ruling class on Loka. They are born of a mother and posses varying amounts of adhikar to establish their status. The three status levels are high, demi, and minor.

vidrohi: A splinter group of self-liberated GENs who live in isolation.

warren: The large apartment complexes in which GENs are housed.

wristlink: A communication/networking device worn on the wrist. Mainly used by trueborns (since only they can afford them), but sometimes handed down in families of lowborns.

AUTHOR'S NOTE

It seems strange to say goodbye to this story and these characters that have encompassed so much of my life for so many years. Truly, they've been with me for decades if you consider the original source—a script from the mid-eighties that never made it to the movie screen. Maybe that's just as well since it led to the opportunity to write about Kayla and Devak in these books for teens.

And now with *Rebellion*, the story ends. I'm happy with where I brought Kayla and Devak, Mishalla and Eoghan, Junjie and Usi. The loose ends are tied up—not always in the prettiest of ways, but satisfactorily, I hope. And yes, some of the open questions are still open. Life is like that here in the real world, and I thought it should be that way in the fictional world of Loka.

But even if *Rebellion* is the last book of the series, I know its world and characters will still be floating around in my mind for some time to come. They've become real to me as I've told their stories. And I'll always be glad to have had them part of my life.

ACKNOWLEDGMENTS

A special thank you to the fans and supporters of the Tankborn series: Those of you who have written to me to let me know how much you've enjoyed the books; the bloggers who have posted wonderful interviews and reviews about the trilogy; the librarians who have made it part of their collections; and the teachers who have included it in their curriculum. You are all the best.